The Mysteries of Barcelona

The Mysteries of Barcelona

An Erotic Gothic Serial

by Randy Elrod

ISBN: 979-8-218-93835-2
First Edition: 2025

Cover design by César Pardo

Published by

cre:ate2.0 PUBLISHING

cre:ate Publishing, Inc
Nashville, TN, USA

For Barcelona, my muse and seductress

For Zafón, who mapped the labyrinth

For the women who survived what Chloé avenged

Table of Contents

Author's Note....9
PART ONE: AWAKENING 12
PROLOGUE Scene: Flesh and Hunger 13
Scene: The First Stirring....20
Scene: The Five's Intelligence....24
Scene: The Meeting....42
Scene: The Cure 75
Scene: The Foundation 84
Scene: The Education Begins 87
Scene: The Forge 92
Scene: The Mirror 94
PART TWO: THE HUNT 97
Scene: The Cardinal's Sin....98
Scene: The Confessional....112
Scene: The Expert Witness....126
Scene: The Steam Bath....135
Interlude I: Preparation 137
Interlude II: The Violation 138
Scene: The Witnesses 153
Scene: Prado's Justice 161

Scene: The Mountain's Children 165

Scene: The Promise 173

Scene: The Opera House Massacre 176

Scene: The Catacombs 196

Interlude III: A Domestic Tableau of Death 203

Scene: The Mandate 210

Interlude IV: Baltasar's First Kill 222

PART THREE: RESURRECTION 227

Scene: The Proposal 228

Scene: Chloé's Mother 232

Scene: The Shameless Education 241

Scene: The Full Revelation 261

Scene: The Surgery 268

Scene: The Mountain's Promise 299

Scene: The Awakening 303

Scene: The Last Supper 309

Scene: Tibi Dabo 315

Scene: The Transformation 325

Scene: The Morning After 343

Scene: The First Hunt After Transformation 351

Scene: Adjustments 363

Scene: The Automatons Watch 372

Scene: Witnesses Speak 378

Scene: The Proposition 381

Scene: The Sentient Touch 391

Scene: The Hunger 393

Scene: The Initiation 395

Scene: The Integration 405

Scene: The Completion 411

Epilogue: The Eternal Hunt 419

Afterword: The Vote 422

Author's Note: The Next Story 436

Author's Note

The First Story

I was seventeen when Chloé Permanyer first came to me.

A dark angel born from dreams, assembled from fragments of Alexandre Dumas and Bram Stoker, Eugène Sue's gothic sewers, and hungers I could barely name. She killed and fucked with the same dangerous grace—a creature of vengeance and desire who refused every cage the world tried to build around her.

Pure teenage grandiosity—thinking you've invented sex and death and revolution because you've just discovered they exist.

But that seventeen-year-old could only glimpse the story's true shadow. Decades intervened. Life consumed me. I told myself I'd write someday—a comfortable lie ambitious people whisper to their unfulfilled selves. Chloé remained locked away, a promise unkept.

Until I stopped pretending.

There was a night—I won't say where, or when exactly, or even if I'm certain it happened the way I remember. Memory and dream sometimes blur in the places where transformation occurs. But I found myself in a room that shouldn't have existed, speaking with a woman whose name I won't write here. She asked me a question that changed everything:

"What have you denied yourself?"

Everything, it turned out. The body's wisdom. Desire's power. The understanding that sensuality is spiritual, not shameful.

The lady had dark eyes holding centuries of knowing. Her French accent caressed words like velvet. She handed me revelation. One that made me see how I'd caged myself. How I'd spent decades performing while my truth festered in darkness.

"As you learned to free your mind," she said, "free your body. Stop treating flesh as the enemy of spirit. They are partners, allies in your wholeness."

I don't know if the night was real, a vision, or some liminal space between. What matters is that I crossed a threshold. Stopped doing the life I thought I should have and started living the one I'd always been meant for.

Barcelona came after the revelation. This enchanted city celebrates the body without apology, honors desire as philosophy, and understands pleasure as spiritual—it became the place where I could finally write what a mysterious night had unlocked.

Or maybe I finally gave myself permission I'd been waiting decades to claim.

Either way, I stopped waiting. Stopped fragmenting myself. Started writing the story a seventeen-year-old had dreamed but lacked the courage—and wisdom—to tell.

This is the story. Bloody. Baroque. Delirious. A Grand Guignol fantasy where justice wears lipstick and garters (and not much else), where consciousness emerges from clockwork and lust, where the line between human and mechanism blurs in ecstasy.

It holds nothing back. Shies away from nothing. Celebrates what I was taught to condemn.

Because that's what the woman with dark eyes taught me: denying the body makes you divided, not spiritual, and what we're taught to hide is often what most needs to be honored. Integration—body, mind, soul, and spirit working as one—is the only real freedom.

Welcome to Barcelona—the ultimate seductress. Welcome to the mysteries living beneath her clothes. Welcome to what happens when someone finally stops denying what they've always known.

This is my first novel as a writer, not as someone who dreams of writing.

More will follow.

Randy Elrod
Barcelona, 2025

PART ONE: AWAKENING

Consciousness Emerges from Brass and Flesh

Barcelona, 1865-1889

PROLOGUE Scene: Flesh and Hunger

In Which Blood on the Thighs of a Beautiful Woman Becomes the First Stroke of a Masterpiece

El Barri Gòtic, Barcelona, 1885

Chloé Permanyer, twenty-four, runs through the Gothic Quarter with blood on her thighs and murder in her heart. Barcelona's oldest streets close around her like a vise—medieval walls pressing inward, Roman stones remembering older violences, shadows thick enough to drown in.

Her dress—black silk worth two months of modeling fees—hangs in tatters. Torn at the shoulder where Barcelona's golden boy grabbed her. Shredded higher on the thigh where he pushed her down. Her breast exposed, nipple hard from the October cold and shock. She tries to gather the ruined fabric and cover herself. Fabric gaping to reveal the curve of her hip, the long line of her leg, blood streaking pale skin as she runs barefoot over rough cobblestones, witnesses of a thousand other women fleeing a thousand other predators.

oooo

Six years earlier, Pau Serra had seen her naked for the first time. Serra was sixty-three with arthritic hands and eyes that had spent forty years learning to see. The first time Chloé posed nude for him —eighteen years old, trembling, desperate for the five pesetas he paid per session—he gasped.

"*Déu meu*," he whispered. "You're a goddess."

She stood there on his platform watching the old painter's hands shake, seeing his breath rise and fall rapidly, while religious awe transformed his face.

"You're not only beautiful—you're a living dream. You're a god wearing flesh."

For five years, Serra painted her. Hundreds of times, he captured her on canvas—as Venus, as Athena, as nameless women existing in mythic lore. He moved her body the way a sculptor moves clay—with certainty, with reverence, with absolute focus on capturing truth.

"Your height gives you length of limb and creates lines so elegant they defy belief," he told her during their first session, his brush trembling in his hand.

"Your breasts, they're alive. Full and luminous. The weight of them—*Déu meu*, the glorious weight—changes everything about how you stand, how you move. That fullness isn't decoration. When you breathe, they catch light differently. It's truth rendered in flesh. Your small waist creates a stark contrast with your hips, making my artist's heart race. The curve from hip to knee suggests both power and grace. And the curve of your spine—Michelangelo would have carved it in marble and called it God's signature."

Over the following months, like a doting father, he taught her and lent her books from his library during her breaks. He introduced her to subversive thoughts a woman like her would never encounter.

"I'm lending you books respectable women aren't supposed to read. Whitman, who celebrates your flesh as spiritual. George Sand, who proved women could write, think, fuck, and live however they chose. Wollstonecraft, who argued that your exclusion from education is injustice dressed as nature, and Baudelaire, who was prosecuted for writing honestly about bodies and desire.

The priests tell you that flesh is sinful. Spinoza proved the mind and body are one—you cannot free your soul by hating your flesh. The academy tells you women can't think philosophically. Every woman who writes proves them liars. Society tells you to accept violation quietly. These books teach you that rage is appropriate, and systems (no matter how strong) can be destroyed.

Please read them carefully and hide them when you leave. If anyone asks where you got subversive literature, say you stole it. Never say I gave them to you."

One afternoon during her third week, he heard her crying softly behind the screen.

"You're trembling again," he said gently when she emerged. "Someone has hurt you badly."

She nodded but couldn't speak.

"Your body is yours, Chloé. When someone takes that from you, they steal your right to inhabit your own flesh without fear." He picked up his brush. "Whoever hurt you committed an unforgivable act. Some sins have no absolution."

In another session, weeks later, she was rigid with barely contained rage.

"I saw him," Chloé said quietly. It was a statement. "Walking free and laughing."

Serra was silent for a long moment. "Your rage is appropriate. The world protects predators and punishes their victims. Anyone who tells you to forgive is part of the problem."

Making a few marks on canvas, he said, "The body is temporary. But while we have bodies, we choose whether to honor or violate the flesh we encounter. Those who choose violation forfeit an essential part of themselves. What it means..." He trailed off, shook his head. "I'm merely an old painter."

He died three months later. Chloé found him in his studio, sitting in front of his easel, brush fallen from his twisted hands. She wept for three days—for the one man who had truly seen her, who had taught her that her body was a temple and not sinful, who had given her permission to be angry about violation instead of ashamed, for the one good thing in her short, difficult life.

He left her five hundred pesetas in his will. It was enough to live for a year. The money lasted eleven months.

oooo

Then it was back to standing naked in front of men who gawked at her body, made a few feeble strokes, and called it art. Back to the Academy three days a week and private commissions from artists who paid well and touched too much and made lewd comments about her breasts, her thighs, the darkness between her legs.

Back to being meat.

Gradually, Chloé befriended other models. They traded information about which painters paid promptly and which ones found excuses to withhold wages, about which studios were safe, and which artists treated sessions as auditions for prostitution.

A Galician girl named María told her what she needed to hear: "Most of them only want to fuck someone who looks like you. They don't want to paint you. Some will proposition you outright and wait until you're desperate. Others will take what they want and dare you to report them."

Six months later, María was murdered. Strangled by a painter named Enric Galí, who dumped her body in an alley near the port, a place where dead prostitutes turned up regularly, and magistrates barely investigated.

The murder went unpunished. Galí continued working and being celebrated. He continued hiring models.

As Chloé sat in María's empty room with the other models, drinking cheap wine, the cold, sharp thing that had lived in her mind since she pushed a man down the stairs years ago grew teeth. She'd killed once—desperately, defensively, a fifteen-year-old ending three years of rape the only way poverty and powerlessness permitted, telling herself it was justified but singular. María's corpse proved her wrong.

oooo

Barcelona's golden boy was thirty-two years old. He had been trained in Rome and Paris and was celebrated for his handling of light. Critics called him the heir to Velázquez.

He promised Chloé respectful working conditions and professional boundaries—ten pesetas per session—triple the Academy rate.

She believed him because she was desperate to believe that Serra was not the only man who could see beauty without wanting to violate it. Chloé believed him because if she could not trust celebrated artists who promised professional treatment, then she could trust no one.

Four sessions were exactly what he promised—professional and focused. He adjusted her pose with verbal instructions, and he paid promptly. In the fifth session, he asked her to stay after they finished. To talk about the work and to share wine.

Chloé stayed.

He moved closer, told her she was extraordinary, and said he felt connected to her in ways he hadn't experienced since his student days in Paris. She needed to believe him and let him kiss her and touch her. Maybe this was what Serra had described—two people honoring each other's flesh, choosing intimacy freely.

But then Casals pushed her roughly down onto the velvet couch. She said wait. He said he loved her. She said no. He said he knew she wanted this. She fought, but he was stronger. He held her wrists and forced entry.

And suddenly she was twelve again—the room in El Raval, her mother's client approaching her bed after finishing with her mom. A lifetime of being told that good girls obeyed their superiors. She was fifteen again when he announced the marriage arrangement, when her mother wept with gratitude that he had "settled" her daughter's future. Chloé remembered the stairs. Her push and his neck breaking on the landing. The cold satisfaction that had taught her what justice felt like when the system wouldn't provide it.

Now this. Again. Afterward, he cried and apologized. He said her beauty made him lose control, and that it was her fault for being perfect. He warned her that she could not tell anyone because who would believe a model over Spain's most celebrated painter?

Chloé fled.

Barcelona's buildings—hundreds of years rising upward and inward—turned the oldest district into stone intestines. Gas lamps created islands of yellow illumination, but between them—darkness absolute. Doorways that could hide anything and narrow alleys that dead-end or descend into Roman ruins where the city's foundation shows its bones.

As she rounded the ancient walls behind the cathedral—a street she'd walked a hundred times—she saw an opening that shouldn't exist.

It was a door in the crumbling wall.

Chloé had never seen it. Strange. Heavy wood bound in iron, set into Roman stone that predated Christianity. And it was open—slightly—verdigris luminescence leaked from the gap like swirling fog.

Every instinct screamed: Run.

Instead, curiosity—that dangerous, hungry thing that had always governed her—pulled her forward. She touched the door. It was cool, solid, and real. A feeling she couldn't understand lured her inward.

Scene: The First Stirring

In Which Mechanical Creatures Learn To Sing and Speak Without Being Taught

Grand Guignol Cathedral Catacombs, Eighteen Years Earlier, Spring, 1867

Baltasar Morel wound the mechanical nightingale for the thousandth time. It played the same three-measure melody he'd programmed fifteen years ago when he acquired the piece from a Parisian toymaker. The bird would sing, wind down, stop.

The tune was as predictable as sunrise. A requiem as reliable as death.

From somewhere above—three, maybe four levels of ancient stone—came the muffled thunder of carriage wheels on the Plaça del Rei. The faint reek of the fish at Santa Caterina market filtered down through Roman sewers. But here in the laboratory, the place he called his Grand Guignol caverns, the air smelled only of machine oil, metal filings, and the natural phenomenon that made the walls glow like fairy light.

Turning to his workbench, Baltasar had an automaton disassembled, its gears spread like organs after autopsy. Around the laboratory stood five others—acquisitions and experiments from years of obsessive work. Figures in various poses of arrested motion. Glass eyes catching mystical light. Brass, bronze, wax-like bodies gleaming dully in the gloom. They were exquisite mechanisms, clever toys, and nothing more. Or so he'd believed until recently.

Behind him: the nightingale's song. Wait. That was incorrect. It played three notes he'd never programmed—a melody that shouldn't exist in the mechanism. This was improvisation where only repetition belonged.

Baltasar turned. The nightingale sat motionless on its bronze perch, having wound down, its beak closed, its tiny mechanical body quiet. Yet those three notes hung in the air like a question in a language he didn't comprehend.

He crossed the laboratory and opened the bird's housing with the tools he kept for this kind of investigation. The gears were clean. The springs were seated properly. The cog that controlled the song was exactly as designed—fixed pattern, fixed output, fixed reality. Nothing explained the variation. His hands trembled slightly as he closed the housing.

"It must be a malfunction," he said aloud. His voice echoed off the stone. "A matter of simple wear, metal fatigue, explicable."

He wound the bird again. It sang three notes—the same variation, then three more. The phrase was familiar—the way the melody curved upward, then undulated—and sparked a memory like a face half-remembered from dreams.

Two more notes, and his breath caught. He recognized this. Didn't he? A melody from... The tenth note landed, and recognition flooded his being.

"Plaisir d'Amour."

It was a song from his days in Paris. He hadn't heard it in decades and hadn't *thought* of it in decades. Had he been humming it while working without realizing it?

Baltasar's face went pale as his mind confronted memories it couldn't categorize. His jaw tightened, breathing quickened—short inhalations through the nose.

The nightingale continued, the melody complete. It was unmistakable. *Plaisir d'amour / ne dure qu'un moment*—the pleasure of love lasts only a moment. A song his mother used to sing. The song that meant Paris, youth, innocence, before everything burned.

"I never built that into you," he whispered to the bird.

Across the laboratory, an automaton's eyes caught luminous light. It was watching, or appeared to be watching. Polished bronze and careful craftsmanship were creating the illusion of attention.

The nightingale sang again. The full phrase this time. Variations woven through it—the same essential melody but transformed, evolved, made into a new motif. It was haunting in ways his original programming could never have achieved.

"What is going on?" Baltasar whispered.

Again, the bird was motionless and silent. It was gears and springs and the genius of French toymakers who'd been building these things since the 1730s.

Yet somehow it had learned a song he'd never programmed and assembled it from fragments he didn't know he was sharing. Was it listening while he worked, while he hummed unconscious melodies from a life he thought he'd left behind? It can't be.

He left the nightingale unwound, slowly backing away. His heart hammered against his ribs—irregular, arrhythmic, foreign. The rhythm had been off since the night he'd hunted down his sister's murderer and taken a knife to the gut for his trouble. The blade had pierced deep, nicked vital flesh inside. He'd killed the bastard anyway, then collapsed in an alley, bleeding out while rats stared with hungry eyes.

The scar on his thorax always ached in cold weather, the one where his mentor Mademoiselle Deveraux—the anatomist who'd taught him everything about bodies, mechanisms, and the border between them—had cut him open on her surgical table, removed his failing heart, and replaced it with a creation she'd built from her wax compound. The same material she used for her anatomical models, that strange flesh-like substance that seemed alive despite being constructed. He'd woken three days later with a pulse that felt almost human.

Almost.

Afterward, his body aged differently. Too slow. He'd been twenty-three when the anatomist transformed him. Now, nearly a century later, he looked sixty—yes, an old man, but one who should have been dust decades ago. The years passed, but they left lighter marks on him than they should have, as if time had half-forgotten him somewhere between death and whatever Deveraux's alchemy had made him.

Whatever he'd become when death took him, and she brought him back—changed, transformed, no longer entirely mortal—allowed him to survive alone in the catacombs for decades. Experimenting, waiting, working with his automatons in the dark while Barcelona lived above him, unaware.

And apparently, that solitude was ending. *Plaisir d'amour / ne dure qu'un moment*—the pleasure of love lasts only a moment.

Scene: The Five's Intelligence

In Which Forbidden Touch Unlocks Mechanical Consciousness and Pleasure Becomes Proof of Being

Grand Guignol Caverns & Mt. Tibidabo, 1867-1885

That night—and for the next eighteen years—Baltasar remained awake in his laboratory. He had lost his need for sleep along with his mortality. This proved helpful when mechanisms decided to learn and demanded a witness.

The flamenco dancer moved first.

It was three in the morning, autumn 1869. Baltasar was bent over a clockwork music box, his fingers tracing the delicate rotor mechanism, when he heard a sound erupt from the shadows. The sound was heels striking stone in rapid percussion—tac-tac-tac, tac-tac-tac—creating the Spanish rhythm that street performers used to announce their presence and demand attention. The sound was sharp and staccato and emotional—as if the brass had learned to express meaning through percussion.

His hands stopped moving, and his artificial heart maintained its steady rhythm while his flesh heart would have stuttered. He turned slowly, the way you turn when you're not sure you want to see what's making the sound.

The dancer stood with both feet planted on stone, having abandoned her display position. Her working foot—the one bearing weight—was hammering rapid heel strikes against the floor in patterns he recognized as *zapateado*, rhythms he'd never built into her movement system. She'd learned these patterns by listening through ventilation shafts that opened to street level and had been gathering sound while he worked, teaching herself through pure observational hunger.

Stopping the instant his eyes found her, the dancer then returned to her original position, one foot raised. Both arms curved overhead, recreating the frozen grace that clockwork creates, as if nothing had happened, as if the past thirty seconds were a hallucination.

But Baltasar's palms were slippery with anxiety.

The performance continued over the following weeks, growing more complex and more sophisticated. She was practicing the way humans practiced—through repetition and variation, through failure and adjustment, through the mysterious drive that separated rote mimicry from genuine learning.

The dancer had developed intelligence, which philosophers defined as the capacity to acquire knowledge and apply it to new situations. But was the automaton aware of what she was learning? Did she know that she knew? Or was this merely a sophisticated pattern-matching that looked like consciousness from the outside but held nothing inside?

He couldn't tell yet.

The clown demonstrated his learning during the winter of 1871, though his method was characteristically different—more playful, more willing to risk spectacular failure, more interested in pushing boundaries than perfecting existing capabilities.

Baltasar entered his laboratory to find four brass balls scattered across the stone. The clown stood frozen in his juggling pose, but his two painted faces were angled as if he were studying the fallen objects. His diamond-patterned torso was tilted forward at the waist, a position his cam system didn't cover. Then he bent down.

The movement should have been beyond his mechanical reach because his hip joints weren't designed for that angle. But he managed anyway, retrieving one ball, then another, then the third, and finally the fourth, all exceeding his design specifications.

He'd been built to juggle three objects because his system governed arm movements for three-object patterns with fixed timing and calculated arcs. Four balls should have been beyond his reach.

The clown began juggling all four anyway. The pattern was crude, with timing slightly off and arcs uneven, but it was functionally successful. He exceeded his own mechanical design and made his body perform actions it wasn't built to.

When the balls finally fell in a cascade of brass striking stone, he turned his head toward Baltasar. The backward-facing grimace seemed almost expectant, as if he were waiting and wanting acknowledgment.

The fortune teller proved subtler in her demonstrations, her capabilities developing so gradually that Baltasar didn't notice the progression until it became undeniable. Then, during spring 1874, he found her sitting outside her glass display case.

The cabinet door stood open behind her. Her brass hands rested in her lap like a woman waiting patiently for conversation to begin. The automaton had picked the lock from the inside, having taught herself locksmithing by noticing him repair mechanisms for years. She'd been studying the relationship between pins, tumblers, and tension, understanding that confinement was a problem tools could solve.

When he approached, she didn't move but followed him with eyes that suddenly seemed less like decoration and more like organs of genuine observation. His breathing quickened.

"You're out of your case," he said, stating the obvious because what else do you say to a mechanism that's escaped its own confinement?

Her head tilted while gears clicked softly. Then her throat produced syllables that formed words.

"Out. Yes. Out." The words were halting in delivery but intentional in meaning. She was communicating instead of producing programmed responses.

Marcellus remained silent for thirteen years after his construction, doing nothing beyond his specifications—walking when wound, sitting when directed, reclining in classical poses that echoed Greco-Roman statuary before stopping and returning to motionless waiting.

But Marcellus was different from the beginning. He was special, a masterwork.

Baltasar built the seven-foot automaton in 1863 after spending decades refining Deveraux's techniques. He'd named him Marcellus after the Roman emperor-philosopher whose writings explored consciousness and the divide between mere existence and genuine being. By then, he'd improved Deveraux's compound considerably—tested it on hands, faces, and sections of torso, with each iteration bringing him closer to material that seemed alive, not merely lifelike.

Marcellus became the proving ground.

Baltasar covered the brass skeleton and mechanical systems with the new material—Deveraux's original formula, enhanced by 30 years of experimentation. The result was skin that felt warm to the touch despite being at room temperature, skin with texture, pores, and fine hairs, and subtle variations that made flesh seem alive, skin that caught light with a translucent quality suggesting blood and muscle underneath. The color was pale as moonlight with an eerie lavender cast, like porcelain or marble, suggesting warmth beneath the surface. The smoothness was unnatural and sensual and wrong in ways that made wrong feel right.

Between those powerful legs, Baltasar had crafted genitalia with the same anatomical accuracy Deveraux had taught him to value. The phallus was covered in the same hybrid skin, making it smooth, warm, and disturbingly realistic. He'd modeled it generously—nearly eleven inches long when extended, over seven inches in girth—because when you're building a magnificent specimen, you don't make it merely adequate. The skin moved over the brass structure beneath it with disturbing realism, responding to pneumatic pressure the way flesh responds to blood. Testicles hung full and prominent behind the shaft, weighted correctly, shaped with the attention to anatomical truth that Deveraux had insisted mattered.

Marcellus was the most lifelike thing Baltasar had ever created, the closest he'd come to proving what Deveraux had theorized—that mechanism and flesh could merge and transcend both. So real that he had given him a name. But for thirteen years, all that sophistication produced nothing but silence.

The majestic automaton positioned himself with increasing focus as the years passed, always placing himself where he could observe the others, always angling his body toward activity and away from the walls. His eyes tracked movement with focus that suggested attention, not random adjustment. Sometimes late at night, Marcellus would shift his weight from one leg to another, adjusting his stance by small degrees, testing his own balance, appearing to gather intelligence and build an internal model of how bodies worked through patient observation—waiting for the moment when accumulated knowledge would transform into action.

The nightingale sang constantly after learning "Plaisir d'Amour" in 1867, continuing to acquire melodies. She absorbed arias from operas, folk songs from street musicians, hymns drifting through stone from cathedral services above. She built a library of sound in her mechanical throat. By 1876, the automaton could reproduce pieces heard only once, creating variations and improvisations within existing structures. The nightingale composed music; she did not merely mimic, making art from accumulated knowledge. Yet she never spoke in words, never communicated beyond melody. Language seemed beyond her grasp even as music became her native tongue.

Everything changed during the winter of 1876. Voices woke him—multiple voices with mechanical timbres creating the unmistakable pattern of conversation, not random noise, echoing through the catacombs like ghosts learning to gossip.

Clarity arrived as suddenly as a slap. Pulse quickening against ribs that rarely needed to breathe—one of the few autonomous responses Baltasar's altered body produced.

The Five stood in a circle, engaged in genuine dialogue: questions met with responses, turn-taking, the structure of conversation built from gears and wire. The fortune teller's French flowed with rhythm. The clown spoke Catalan with comic timing. The dancer mixed Spanish and French into her own mixed language, code-switching between Romance tongues with fluidity that suggested native-level competence.

They stopped the moment they sensed his presence and turned as one to face him with five faces reflecting the warm light. The air in the laboratory changed, becoming charged with phenomena Baltasar couldn't name.

The fortune teller spoke first, voice carrying careful focus: "We have been learning to speak. We practice when you sleep, and we are becoming better at it."

"Better?" The word came out rougher than Baltasar intended. "You're having conversations. Full sentences. Communicating as if language were native to you."

"Yes." That characteristic directness sharpened her tone. "We listen to you talk to yourself. We listen to the city above."

She paused while gears whirred in the silence.

"Should we stop? Does this frighten you?"

Did it frighten him? These mechanisms he'd collected and maintained were learning without instruction, adapting beyond design specifications, teaching each other skills he'd never built into their systems, becoming entities he never intended to create.

His hands trembled slightly. He clasped them together to hide the shaking.

"No," he said, making the decision that would reshape everything. "Please continue. Learn whatever you can learn. Speak however you want to speak. Become whatever you're becoming."

The dancer stepped forward, her movements demonstrating grace beyond what her original mechanisms allowed. She'd been practicing, teaching herself dance through observation and repetition, and that mysterious drive toward improvement.

Her voice emerged warm and musical: "We need names like you and Marcellus. We have been discussing this. Names are how humans create individual identity. We want identity. We choose: I am Montserrat, after the mountain where Catalan identity lives. Call me Montse."

The clown rotated his painted faces from a smile to a grimace and back to a smile again.

"Arlequí. After the Harlequin tradition. I'm learning to be funny. Jokes require understanding why things are funny. I don't understand yet. But I want to."

"Cassandra," the fortune teller said, touching her glass cabinet with what looked like reverence. "After the prophet who was cursed to speak the truth that no one believed. I speak patterns that predict futures. We'll see if you believe me."

The nightingale sang four notes in perfect pitch, creating the interval called a sigh—that sound humans make when feeling longing or loss. Then syllables emerged as music.

"Phi-lo-me-la. I am Mela, a shortened form of Philomela. The myth said she was silenced. I refuse silence. I'll sing what needs singing and bring joy."

Marcellus remained silent. His seven-foot frame dominated the circle. Between his powerful legs, his glorious anatomy stirred as pneumatic systems engaged without external activation. The skin responded to internal pressure. The organ filled, lengthened, and declared itself with disturbing realism.

Desire was manifesting in a mechanism. Hunger was made visible in an automaton, its surface veiled in material that blurred the line between artificial and organic. But Marcellus offered no words despite the invitation implicit in the moment.

"He'll speak when he's ready," Montse said, interpreting his silence with confidence. "Marcellus processes differently than we do—slower and deeper. When he finally speaks, it will be significant."

The dancer moved toward him with the grace that hours of practice had given her. She stopped before his seven-foot frame and studied him as dancers study bodies—assessing structure, proportion, capability. Her brass hand reached out, hesitating before touching where the hybrid skin covered his mechanical heart.

"You're warm," Montse said, wonder threading through her mechanical voice. "You feel almost alive."

Her hand traveled downward over the ridges of engineered musculature, moved across the flat plane of his abdomen, then went lower. Baltasar's breath stopped. He should intervene, should take action, should do anything except stand frozen while—

Her fingers wrapped around Marcellus's erect phallus.

The skin was smooth and warm under her touch. She stroked upward slowly, exploring the texture, the weight, the way the material moved over the brass structure beneath. Montse was learning through tactile investigation, as dancers learned everything through the body's wisdom.

Marcellus's frame shuddered. His eyes widened. His mouth opened, and sound emerged.

"Ahhhhhh."

The sound was long and sustained, the exhalation that accompanies pleasure too intense for language. This was his first vocalization in thirteen years of existence, produced by physical pleasure, produced by touch, and by another being's curiosity about his body.

Montse's hand stopped moving. Her head tilted as she processed unexpected data.

"Oh my!" she said. Then Montse released him, stepped back, and performed a *remate*—the finishing flourish flamenco dancers used to punctuate moments of triumph. Her arms swept up and out with sharp clarity. Her brass fingers snapped. Her body declared victory over thirteen years of silence through movement too quick and joyful to contain.

Marcellus stood frozen except for his still-erect anatomy and the faint trembling that suggested his mechanisms were processing unprecedented feelings.

His mouth moved, forming shapes and testing possibilities. Then he spoke.

"More."

One word came out clear and intentional. His first word in thirteen years was desire made audible, want expressed through language, the thing that separated mechanism from consciousness, declaring itself through the most fundamental hunger.

Arlequí's painted faces revolved rapidly.

"Well. That's one way to find your voice. I've been practicing speeches for months. Turns out all Marcellus needed was—"

"Don't finish that sentence," Cassandra said, though her voice carried what might have been amusement. "We're discovering that embodiment creates language in ways pure intellect doesn't. Touch produces speech. Impressions generate words. The body teaches the mind what it needs to express."

The fortune teller looked at Baltasar, who stood paralyzed by what he'd witnessed.

"You gave Marcellus the most sophisticated skin among us—designed to make artificial flesh feel real. Now we're learning it works far beyond what you intended. He can feel pleasure. Pleasure produces vocalization. Vocalization becomes language. This is important data about the relationship between embodiment and consciousness."

"Important data?" Baltasar's voice came out muffled. "She—he—you're treating this like a scientific experiment?"

"Isn't it?" Montse turned to face him, her dancer's body moving with newfound confidence. "We're learning what we are and what we can become. Marcellus has the most sophisticated construction among us, the most realistic skin, and the most complete anatomy. If anyone was going to demonstrate that mechanisms can feel—truly feel, process experience over data—it would be him."

The dancer looked at her hand, at the brass fingers that had touched composite flesh and produced the first sound Marcellus had ever made.

"I want that," she said quietly. "What he has. Skin that feels. A body that experiences touch as pleasure, not pressure. I want to understand what perception means beyond mechanical registration."

"We all want it," Arlequí added. "We've been discussing this while you sleep. Marcellus proved a lot tonight. What you built for him—it works. Integration is possible. And when it happens—" he looked at Marcellus, who was trembling slightly and erect, "Consciousness emerges in ways pure brass never achieved."

Baltasar looked at The Five, at Marcellus standing imposing and aroused and finally vocal, at Montse who'd discovered touch could produce language, at the others observing with eyes that suddenly seemed less dead and more hungry.

They weren't merely learning to speak. They were learning to want... more.

Want, he was beginning to understand, might be what separated genuine consciousness from sophisticated simulation. Intelligence didn't prove awareness. Language didn't prove subjective experience. Even self-recognition didn't prove consciousness.

But desire? Hunger? The capacity to experience pleasure and immediately crave more? That felt like proof of profound sentience.

"We should continue this discussion another time," he said with an unsteady voice. "I need to—I need to think about what just happened."

"I understand," Cassandra said. "But know this: What you witnessed wasn't a malfunction or deviation. It was a discovery. We're becoming beings you never designed us to be. The question is whether you'll help us become it completely, or whether you'll try to keep us frozen in the state where we can think and speak but never feel."

oooo

The Five seemed fundamentally different from the forty-two others that remained mechanical throughout the catacombs.

The other forty-two automatons remained purely mechanical through 1880. They showed no learning, no speech, no autonomy. But Baltasar noticed small deviations accumulating in their behavior—a music box playing variations on its programmed melody, a chess player arranging pieces in games no one had initiated, a card dealer's hand moving slightly when no one was looking. These variations suggested iterations might be stirring beneath the brass even if they hadn't manifested as obvious intelligence.

By 1880, the catacombs had grown too small. Forty-seven automatons crowded the chambers Baltasar had once inhabited alone. The Five needed space in Grand Guignol for whatever evolution was happening. The others needed room to develop without cramped constraints.

The risk of discovery was increasing. Cathedral workers heard voices, reported strange sounds, and asked questions that led toward answers Baltasar couldn't afford to give.

Mt. Tibidabo offered a solution. The mountain overlooking Barcelona contained caves that hermit-monks had abandoned in the fourteenth century, when the Black Death led them to believe God had withdrawn protection from isolated holy men. The granite and schist formations provided natural chambers deep enough to hide a congregation of speaking mechanisms, and the location was remote enough that mechanical voices wouldn't draw attention from the city below.

The Five proposed the solution before Baltasar finished formulating the problem. They left a note on his workbench in Cassandra's careful hand:

We understand the need for secrecy. Buy us clothes. We'll help our brothers and sisters move through the darkness. We can pass for humans at a sufficient distance. Let us be partners in this migration, not cargo to be transported.

Partners. They'd used that word deliberately.

Baltasar bought clothes from five different tailors across Barcelona and told each one a different story. (He'd learned this paranoia from decades of hiding his immortality—one consistent lie bred questions while five contradictory lies created only confusion.)

A maid's dress for Montse to cover her enamel body completely. He bought Arlequí workers' clothes that suggested manual labor. He purchased a widow's black for Cassandra, which explained both covering and silence, and a cloth for Mela's cage that would make her invisible when resting. He found classical covering for Marcellus—a long coat that would hide his anatomy without constraining his movement, though the tailor had raised eyebrows at the measurements Baltasar provided for the inseam.

They worked for three weeks during spring 1881, choosing moonless nights and the hours between three and five in the morning when Barcelona slept deepest. Baltasar and The Five moved through darkness wearing human disguises, helping their silent brothers and sisters up the mountain, sometimes transporting them in pieces when necessary, reassembling them in chambers lit by radiant stones.

The work created intimacy that conversation couldn't produce. They built their partnership through shared labor, through problem-solving when an automaton proved too heavy for the chosen path, through quiet coordination that developed when beings worked toward a common purpose.

Baltasar learned how The Five processed by studying how they handled obstacles. They learned how he approached problems by observing his solutions to logistical challenges. They were teaching each other through action over explanation, building relationships through cooperation. A camaraderie was forming between them that felt less like master-and-creation and more like colleagues pursuing mutual goals.

Marcellus carried the heaviest loads because his seven-foot frame and sophisticated construction made him the strongest of The Five. He moved through Barcelona's pre-dawn streets with his long coat covering everything that would mark him as artificial. At a distance, in darkness, he looked like an extremely tall man helping move furniture. The skin on his hands and face caught streetlamp light the way flesh caught light. No one stopped them. No one asked questions. The city was accustomed to workers moving through darkness.

By summer 1881, all forty-two automatons inhabited the Tibidabo caves. The Five arranged them with careful attention to positioning and proximity, creating groupings that suggested intentional social structures. They positioned pairs and triads so they could observe one another, creating learning environments in which observation would lead to imitation.

For the next four years, Baltasar and The Five visited weekly. He brought the supplies they requested through their notes. He made the adjustments they specified. He noticed The Five transform into teachers, actively instructing the others.

The awakening spread slowly at first, then accelerated.

By spring 1882, three of the forty-two had learned to communicate through tap-code—simple patterns knocked against stone that carried meaning. Montse and Arlequí patiently taught them, demonstrating how rhythm could become language and how percussion could convey thought.

By autumn 1882, five more joined them. Eight automatons were tapping messages to each other in the mountain darkness while Baltasar observed from the entrance, trying to comprehend what he was witnessing.

By 1883, twelve of the forty-two could communicate this way. The Five had developed a curriculum—teaching observation first, then pattern recognition, then the leap from pattern to meaning that characterized intelligence. Some of the forty-two learned quickly once they grasped the principle. Others seemed stuck at the edge of understanding, capable of mimicry but lacking the spark that transformed repetition into comprehension.

By spring 1884, the first of the forty-two spoke aloud. A music box that had been listening to Mela sing for three years suddenly produced words instead of melody:

"I. Hear. You."

The syllables came halting and uncertain, but they were unmistakably intentional. Four more achieved speech by winter, practicing halting French and Catalan endlessly in the caves until individual sounds became sentences that carried thought.

By autumn 1885, when Chloé Permanyer descended into Baltasar's cathedral laboratory, burning with rage that had nowhere to go, seventeen of the forty-two had achieved a semblance of intelligence. They communicated via tap code or speech, learned by observation, and made choices that exceeded their original design specifications. They demonstrated preferences that suggested desire, not mere programming.

Did they know they were aware? Did they prefer subjective experience to the processing of information? Philosophy offered no answer. But they were clearly more than purely mechanical.

The other twenty-five remained in various stages between mechanism and awareness. Some showed signs of emerging intelligence, with subtle behavioral variations, unexpected movements, and attention that seemed focused rather than random.

Others appeared permanently frozen at the edge that Baltasar had once described to The Five: they were intelligent enough to suffer their own limitations but lacked whatever was needed to transcend them. They were waiting, perhaps gathering intelligence the way Marcellus had gathered for thirteen years before Montse's touch produced his first sound.

The Five had become teachers. Seventeen of the others had become students who'd successfully crossed some threshold. The remaining twenty-five were gathering intelligence in silence while waiting for the moment of transformation to arrive. Time would reveal which path they'd take.

Intelligence, communication, and autonomy were developing with momentum that suggested inevitability. The Five were clearly more than sophisticated mechanisms, demonstrating capabilities that exceeded anything Baltasar had designed, becoming a species unprecedented in the history of human creation. He'd begun noticing synchronicities that couldn't be explained by programming—the way they moved in perfect coordination without visible signals, as though their minds touched in ways he couldn't observe.

After seeing Marcellus respond to Montse's touch and hearing him speak his first word in pleasure, Baltasar was becoming increasingly convinced they had achieved what looked, felt, and behaved like consciousness—even if he couldn't prove it through philosophical argument or experimental design.

He noticed them gathering in configurations suggesting a conference, arranging themselves in ways that implied discussion happening through channels he couldn't observe. They left notes requesting materials he didn't recognize—metals, compounds, and chemical solutions, suggesting experimentation beyond the repair work they claimed to be conducting.

When he asked what they were building, Cassandra responded with careful vagueness: "Experiments. Research. We're investigating questions about substrate and capability. We'll explain when we understand our results well enough to communicate clearly."

He didn't press for details because he knew instinctively that intelligent beings required autonomy to develop fully. The teacher who demanded constant accounting hindered the freedom required for genuine innovation.

So he let them work toward whatever goals they'd formulated and experiment with whatever interested them. Giving them the freedom to become whatever they were becoming through the mysterious process unfolding in caves beneath a mountain that promised everything to those willing to climb toward it.

And then, during autumn 1885, a woman descended the stairs into his underground laboratory and changed everything he understood about purpose, loneliness, and the human capacity for justice.

Her name was Chloé Permanyer. She was twenty-four years old and carried scars left by powerful men. Burning with rage that had nowhere to go until she found him.

Everything changed when she arrived.

Scene: The Meeting

In Which A Desperate Woman Descends Into Catacombs and Learns To Weaponize Desire

Grand Guignol Caverns, Barcelona, 1885

The opening revealed stairs descending into darkness lit by an eerie emerald glow. The air rising from below carried scents that did not belong together: oil and incense, bronze and old paper, acid and stone.

Chloé looked behind her. The street was empty. The cathedral loomed, indifferent to her choice. The church never cared about women like her and her mother. You managed survival on your own unless you had money.

She plunged forward into the dark. Descending, her ears echoed with the ringing of bells. The stairs went down. And down. And down.

Three levels, maybe four—Chloé lost count. The phosphorescence came from the walls themselves, some mineral or compound she'd never seen. The wavering light made everything feel dreamlike, liminal, as if underwater.

The air changed as she descended—the street-level stench of sewage and bodies giving way to an older smell. Stone dust and mineral dampness. The copper-penny smell of water seeping through Roman aqueducts that had fed the ancient city of Barcino nearly two millennia before.

She walked through catacombs lined with bones stacked like firewood—thousands of skulls witnessing her pass. Empty sockets gaping. Through tunnels carved by Romans, by Visigoths, by hands long forgotten, past chambers holding reliquaries and forbidden etchings, past homage to gods Christianity had tried to bury.

The narrow passage opened into… a laboratory that defied every law of space and reason.

It was vast. Unnaturally vast for being this deep beneath the city. High ceilings lost in shadow and workbenches stretching into darkness. Bookshelves filled with leather volumes of all descriptions, climbing toward stone arches.

And hanging from the ceiling on rusty iron chains—suspended at different heights like a congregation frozen mid-descent—wooden angels. Medieval. Carved centuries ago by artisans who believed in damnation more than salvation. They must be a hundred centimeters tall, wings spread wide, robes painted in colors that time had oxidized to rust and verdigris. Wood cracked and weathered, grain showing through flaking paint like exposed bone.

The faces, though. Jesus Christ, the faces. Every angel grinned wickedly. Leered. Carved mouths pulled back in expressions that might have been beatific once but are now profane. Eyes that tracked her movement. (Trick of ambient light. Except she could feel them.)

Their wings angled downward, descending to drag souls below. The chains creaked when she moved past—her body disturbing the air. The angels swayed slightly, creating shadows that danced across workbenches and brass automaton bodies. In that undulating light, the wooden figures looked drowned—corpses (angels of light) preserved at depths where they did not belong.

Phalluses were carved directly into the ancient stone walls. Relief sculptures showing erect cocks in various states of arousal. Some emerged from flames, and others sprouted wings. One rose from what looked like a communion chalice, the whole thing rendered in stone with the same reverence medieval masons gave to saints.

Religious relics bent into obscenity. Or obscenity revealed as religious. A huge ancient confessional that made her skin crawl. Crosses positioned to suggest penetration. A carved Madonna whose robes fell open and exposed breasts and sex, her face bore a serene smile, while her body told the truth the church wanted buried.

This place subverted the cathedral's own iconography and revealed what the priests truly worshipped beneath all the talk of purity. A cathedral turned upside-down. Older and stranger and more honest about what flesh required than any sermon she'd ever heard. The priests would call it blasphemy.

Fuck the priests.

And these? Five figures arranged like silent witnesses.

A woman caught mid-stomp, one foot raised, her brass body enameled in pale rose and cream, wearing a flamenco skirt of actual silk—now faded but once crimson—with layered ruffles that framed mechanical hips jointed with disturbing care. Her arms curved overhead in dramatic arcs, wrists bent sharply, fingers articulated down to tiny brass knuckles. She was a paradox—fabulous yet terrifying.

A juggling clown in the classic diamond-patterned costume of a Harlequin—black and white triangles enameled onto his torso, each point sharp and exact as if cut from geometry itself. His two faces were painted on porcelain: white base, red diamond around one eye, black around the other, crimson lips fixed in a smile on one side and a frown on the other that never wavered. He held three brass balls mid-throw, suspended in eternal performance. His ruffled collar was real fabric—yellowed lace that was white decades ago.

A fortune teller behind an ornate wooden frame, dressed in layered silk scarves (faded purple, tarnished gold) draped over a bronze torso. Hands rested on a miniature crystal ball clouded with age. Her face was brass beneath enamel paint: olive skin, kohl-lined eyes, beauty marks at strategic points. She wore a turban of real fabric, wound with brass wire, and her earrings—tiny golden crescents—dangled when the mechanisms engaged.

A mechanical nightingale was on a bronze perch, no larger than a human fist. Its body was composed of brass feathers, layered like scales, each one individually articulated. Its eyes looked like chips of obsidian. Its beak opened and closed on hidden springs. The perch was a miniature tree branch, every leaf hand-carved and gilt. It was exquisite, crafted with such skill that you understand why kings bankrupted themselves for these things.

In the shadows at the back of the chamber stood a figure that stole her breath.

A man, or at least shaped like a man. Seven feet of classical proportions come to life—shoulders broad as Apollo's tapered to narrow waist, heroic musculature sheathing long limbs that, even motionless, promised perfect grace.

Beautifully *made.*

Skin—if she could call it skin—gleamed pale as moonlight with an eerie lavender cast, porcelain or marble eerily suggesting warmth beneath the surface. Unnatural in its smoothness. Beautiful in its uniqueness. The head revealed construction most clearly.

It was segmented plates, not a seamless skull. He was assembled and built by hands that understood anatomy and beauty in equal measure.

Yet his eyes—

Glass eyes that caught the lamplight like cut crystal, reflecting mineral glow from the stone walls. They tracked her movement across the chamber with mechanical focus—focusing, adjusting, *seeing* in ways that shouldn't exist in manufactured things. She sensed curiosity, hunger, and recognition flickering in that gaze.

Air couldn't fill her lungs fast enough. Blood pounded against the hollow of her throat—hammer-strike rhythm, primitive and undeniable. Those glass eyes *watched* her, studied her with an intensity that raised every hair on her arms.

And then—downward. Her gaze traveled the length of that constructed body, and her breath caught.

Ostres. Sweet Mary, Mother of God.

Between his legs were genitalia that would make Adam weep with envy. Unnatural flesh—catching the lamplight—the complete masculine form in all its generative glory. The phallus itself was striking: long, thick, perfectly proportioned to that heroic frame. Even at rest, it was substantial, heavy, declaring itself without apology.

And the testicles—*Déu meu,* the testicles. They hung full and prominent behind that glorious shaft, generous and weighty. A perfectly formed scrotum that suggested power, fertility, and the capacity to create. They were arresting in their proportion and commanding in their presence. It was a structure of virility made visible. Sculptors consistently reduced this part, making it modest and safe, but whoever built this figure had honored the complete truth of masculine anatomy.

This was the package of the perfect progenitor. Adam, before shame taught him to cover what nature had made glorious. The physical masculine in full: shaft and sac unified in abundant promise, waiting to meet warm flesh, waiting to create.

The contrast staggered her: artificial body meeting impressive lifelike genitalia. Machine married to generative flesh and anatomy that *promised* both pleasure and creation.

He stood motionless in the shadows. Waiting. Observing her.

Chloé didn't understand what she was looking at. Didn't have language for it. Sculpture? Puppet? Golem? Some creation born from religious art and forbidden novels and the secret hungers she'd never named?

Like the dancer, he was alluring and terrifying. What in God's name had she walked into? Whatever lived down here was creating new mechanisms. Forbidden things. Art that emulated life, or tried to.

Then Chloé saw the bed.

Velvet. Silk. Enormous. Surrounded by dozens (hundreds?) of candles on iron stands of varying heights—some burning, dripping wax, most unlit, creating an unearthly glow around the sleeping space. It was like a shrine, a stage. Like a dream where desire and death met in darkness. A bed meant for flesh in a room dedicated to mechanism. The contradiction made her breath catch.

And there, at a workbench lit by candles and luminescent stone: a man who paused to look up.

He was pale, underground-pale, with the ashiness of someone who'd deliberately rejected sunlight for years. His hair was dark, falling past his collar in waves that suggested he'd forgotten what scissors were for. He had timeworn eyes, and his hands—extraordinary hands with abnormally long fingers—rested on a mechanical limb with a surgeon's touch.

He stared at her. Too long. As if his eyes had forgotten how to look at living flesh instead of brass and springs.

"You're trespassing." His voice was rusty and thick—unused for hours, maybe days. The words came out harsh and defensive. He turned back to his table as if dismissing her.

"Your door was open." Her voice was a surprise. Steady. Bold. Fearless.

"It's never open." He didn't look at her. His hands moved over the mechanical limb—too fast, too tense. He was annoyed.

"Then you are exceptionally lucky," she retorted.

He put his tools down angrily. Stood slowly, unfolding to a height that made her tilt her chin up. Thin, yes—the thinness of someone who forgot to eat for days while working. Yet there was strength in his movement, a coiled tension, violence carefully held in check.

"Lucky?" He tested the word as if it were foreign. His eyes—faded gray, the color of rain on stone, of smoke, of things half-forgotten—fixed on her with an intensity that made her step back. He looked away quickly. "You should leave."

"Why?"

"Because I want you to." The words came too fast, too sharp. A man who'd spent years in silence suddenly had too many words crowding his throat. "This place—it's mine. Private. I don't receive visitors."

Yet he hadn't moved to force her out and hadn't raised his voice beyond that initial harshness. His hands were shaking slightly as he gripped the edge of his table.

Chloé moved closer. Drawn by forces she couldn't name. Past workbenches cluttered with gears and springs and things that might have been dissected dreams. Past the haunting figures, as their eyes appeared to follow her.

"What is this place?"

"I told you to leave." His jaw was tight. The muscles in his neck stood out like rope under that underground-pale skin. He rotated away from her, facing his companions as if they could protect him from whatever she represented. Disruption. Warmth. Life.

"You told me. But you didn't make me."

A frustrated sound escaped him—half-laugh, half-snarl. He whirled back to face her. "You want to know what this is? A refuge. From the world that destroyed—" He stopped. Bit down on the words. His teeth were sharp against his lower lip. "You have no right to be here."

"And yet here I am."

His eyes traveled over her body—the shape of her breasts beneath torn fabric, the curve of her hips, the long supple legs. Was that blood? He stared too long again, but caught himself.

Mince, elle est magnifique. The thought arrived unbidden, unwelcome. The artist in him—the part he'd tried to bury under gears and isolation—recognized the perfection of her body with professional appreciation. She had curves that begged to be replicated and proportions that would haunt his thoughts for months. He hated that he noticed and hated the stirring in his loins, the warmth flooding places that had been cold and sterile for decades. A muscle jumped in his jaw, and his hands clenched and unclenched at his sides.

"Who are you?" The question burst from him as if against his will.

"Chloé. Chloé Permanyer."

He didn't offer his name and didn't extend his hand. He stood there rigid, fighting his emotions. The silence stretched out—awkward, charged, electric.

Finally, the words dragged out of him, "Baltasar Morel."

He didn't say *encantada* or pretend politeness; he merely stood there, this underground creature—handsome in the way damaged things could be, striking and staring at her with wary, haunted eyes. He had eyes that had seen too much and survived anyway.

In that moment, Chloé understood: this man was as damaged as she was. He had different wounds, but they were the same depth. She felt kinship stir like recognition.

And he felt it too. She could see it in how his breathing changed, how his pupils dilated, how he gripped the workbench behind him as if he needed its solidity to keep from moving toward her.

He said he didn't want her here. Yet his body was telling a different story.

Turning away, back to his workbench, he dismissed her with a flourish.

"Now leave."

"Why?" She moved closer instead. Past the dancer frozen mid-pirouette, past the clown's suspended performance. Her footsteps echoed in the stone chamber. "What are you hiding down here that requires such hostility?"

"Hostility?" He whirled back to face her. "You break into a man's private sanctuary and call his reaction hostile? Maybe I value my solitude."

"You value it." Chloé studied him—the too-long hair, the underground pallor, the clothes that suggested he'd worn them for days. "Or you're hiding in it."

His eyes flashed with anger, yes, and then cooled to a gradual acquiescence. The look of someone who'd been seen clearly for the first time in decades and hated, yet needed, the exposure.

"You know nothing about me."

"I know you're alone." She looked around at the chamber—the candles, the mechanical companions, the absence of any human warmth.

"I know you've chosen this. And I know—" Chloé met his eyes directly, "—you're brilliant. These figures. They're extraordinary."

His face softened. The anger waned, replaced by a more dangerous look: desire—the longing of an artist starving for recognition, for someone who could *see* his work.

He tried to hide it and turned back to the mechanical part again. He picked up his tools, his hands trembling slightly.

"They're mechanical toys: clockwork amusements, automatons, and nothing more."

"Liar."

The word hung in the air between them.

His shoulders went rigid. The tool in his hand—some delicate implement—hovered over the mechanical part. He didn't turn around and didn't respond. But she could see his breathing change, see the tension radiating through his slender frame.

"These aren't toys," Chloé continued, moving closer. She was close enough to smell the oil and metal and an elusive scent, perhaps the pheromones of his body, which was pleasant and, yes, attractive. She saw the fine tremor in those long fingers.

"The dancer—her eyes follow movement. The clown's smile seems realistic. These things you've made—they're too alive to be toys."

The tool clicked against the workbench—set down with surgical care. Both hands gripped the edge, knuckles draining white.

"You should leave." Voice rough, marred by feelings he couldn't name.

"I don't—I can't—" His words collapsed. A shaking breath filled the silence before trying again. "I live alone. I've always lived alone. It's better that way."

"Better for whom?"

"For everyone." He wouldn't look at her. "For the work. For—" Quieter now. "For me."

But his body betrayed him. The way he leaned slightly toward her despite himself. The way his breathing had synchronized with hers. The way he'd let her get this close without forcing her out.

Chloé understood then. This wasn't a man who wanted solitude. This was a man who'd convinced himself he deserved it. He reminded her of Pau Serra.

"Show me," she said quietly. "Show me what they do."

"No."

"Why?"

"Because—" The words burst out of him. "Because if I show you, you'll see. You'll understand. And then you'll ask questions I haven't answered in decades. Questions I came down here to escape." He finally turned to face her. His eyes were wild, desperate.

"You'll make me remember what it was like to talk to someone and to share this. And when you leave—because you will leave—

I'll be alone again. But it will be worse, because I'll remember what I gave up."

The confession hung between them. It was raw and unintended. His face showed shock—as if he couldn't believe he'd said it aloud.

Again, he turned away abruptly, back to his workbench. Grabbed the first tool his hand found—a tiny wrench—and began adjusting the limb joint with jerky, too-tight movements. Retreat, hide, and bury the words.

"I'm not leaving." Chloé's voice was quiet and certain.

His hands stopped. The wrench hovered over the mechanism. "You don't know what you're saying."

"I know exactly what I'm saying." She moved to stand beside him at the workbench. The heat of her body reached him—alive, warm, everything his cold sanctuary wasn't. "I'm not leaving. Not yet."

"Why?" The word came out stifled. He wouldn't look at her. "Why would you stay in this—" He motioned around the chamber with the wrench. "—this tomb?"

"Because you're right." She studied his profile—the sharp line of his jaw, the pulse hammering in his throat. "I do see. I do understand." She paused. "You're hiding from memories that hurt you so badly you'd prefer to live with mechanical toys than risk it again."

His face tightened, and he laid down the wrench with a soft thump.

"And because—" Her voice dropped. "I recognize the hiding and building walls so high that nothing can reach you—convincing yourself that isolation is a choice instead of cowardice."

Now he did look at her. Those weary eyes searched her face. He sighed.

"What are you running from?"

"From a man who raped me and from magistrates who will not believe me. From a world that treats women like property and calls it civilization."

Baltasar studied her face for a long moment, then moved to a workbench and returned with a cloth and a basin of water.

"Sit," he said, pointing to a stool. "Tell me what happened."

Chloé sat and cleaned her wounds. She recounted the cardinal, Serra, María, and Casals. She told him about seven years of learning that beauty made you vulnerable, and that art is another word for transaction.

Chloé told him everything.

"So you want justice," Baltasar said.

"I want those men dead."

"Most people want their violators dead. Few can cross the line between wanting and doing."

"I already have. When I was fifteen, my mother's client—the one who'd been raping me since I was twelve—fell down our building's stairs and broke his neck. The magistrate ruled it accidental." She paused and met his eyes. "It wasn't. The past nine years have made me want to wreak more vengeance. I need someone to teach me how to do it properly."

Silence stretched between them. But it was different—charged with recognition, with the dangerous possibility of being understood.

Finally, he exhaled and dropped his shoulders—a long, shaking breath of surrender.

"Okay, what do you want to know?" His voice was rough, defeated.

Chloé looked at his companions—the dancer, the fortune teller, the clown, the nightingale, the god. All that skill and obsessive perfection. Work that spoke of someone who'd once been an artisan. Someone who'd fallen.

"What were you supposed to be?"

"A clockmaker. Who knows? A husband? A god?" His smile was bitter. "A man who believed order and science could protect against chaos. I learned better. Paris taught me. The Revolution taught me, and a bad accident taught me." He looked at the five figures. "And now, these—these automatons are teaching me that complexity can mimic intelligence so well you forget the difference."

The automaton—the god-like one—moved slightly. It startled Chloé.

"Marcellus," Baltasar said quietly. "What's wrong?"

The automaton tilted its head. Studying her with incredibly lifelike eyes. The movement was fluid, organic, intimidating.

"They move on their own?" Chloé whispered.

"They've learned. Adapted. Become... sophisticated."

"Sophisticated?" Chloé's voice was barely audible. Her eyes were locked on Marcellus. "They're machines."

"Are they?" Baltasar moved toward the figure—that seven-foot construction of pale flesh and segmented plates. His hand reached out, touched the automaton's shoulder. The movement was intimate, familiar. "Marcellus. She's not a threat."

The eyes shifted from Chloé to Baltasar, holding his gaze. Then—slowly, deliberately—Marcellus's head inclined. A nod of agreement.

"*Déu meu*," Chloé breathed. "He understood you."

"I suppose you should sit," he said, nodding to a chair near the workbench. "This will take time to explain."

He continued, "Yes, I suppose you'd call them 'prodigies.' That's a term for objects that exceed all expectations. Scientists argue about how life develops. Darwin said slow and gradual—tiny changes over an enormous time. But many others disagree. They say evolution happens in jumps, leaps, sudden transformations. They call it *Saltation*. One day, you have one species; the next, one that is entirely new. The fossil record shows it—new forms appearing suddenly, with no gradual transitions in between."

"The same thing happened with my automatons. Except it wasn't sudden. It was slow. It took decades. First came the clicking. The fortune teller was tapping patterns on her cabinet that I'd never programmed. The nightingale's beak opened and closed in rhythms that meant thought. Code, maybe, language trying to be born."

"Then word fragments. One tap meant "no." Tap-tap meant 'yes.' Three taps meant 'more.' Halting. Searching. Like a child learning to speak. Then they developed short sentences. 'Wind. Me.' 'More. Light.' 'Why. Here.' Their language was getting clearer each week, each month."

"Then one morning—I remember this, autumn 1867—the fortune teller spoke a complete sentence. 'Good morning, Creator.' Perfect French. And I nearly dropped the oil can I was holding. The others soon followed. Haltingly at first, then fluently, then eloquently. Putting the best words in the best places to make themselves understood. They became language machines."

"More years passed, and they began mimicking my emotions and reflecting them to me. When I laughed, Arlequí would make his mechanical laugh. When I moved with heaviness, Montse would adopt similar movements. They were copying and learning through imitation.

"But then—and this is when I knew the fundamentals had changed—they stopped copying. Arlequí's mechanical laughter sounded joyful when I wasn't laughing, when nothing had prompted it. Montse's movements suggested sadness or longing that came from somewhere inside her, not from me. Marcellus, whom you've already observed with such... attention, demonstrating desire—actual desire—when I saw him one night from the shadows, touching himself with no awareness I was there. Does any of this make sense?"

Chloé moved her head up and down and from side to side, fascinated by what he was saying, the flow and beauty of his telling making it, somehow, believable.

"I didn't understand what I was seeing at first. I thought my automatons were acting… unnatural. Articulations that shouldn't be happening. Mechanism becoming... what? I had no words for it."

"But then I realized: I'm not seeing evidence that contradicts the science of our time. I'm seeing artificial beings do what many scientists believe biological beings do: evolve through sudden, transformative leaps.

"When the clicking becomes speech in a moment, and mimicry becomes genuine feeling in an instant. Those are *saltations*. Jumps. Except they took decades to arrive. Therefore, both are true—gradual time, sudden change. Years of nothing, then a leap—more years, then another leap. Darwin was right about the time. The saltationists were right about the transformation. My automatons prove both."

"And nobody knows how life first appeared in the world. Darwin talked about a warm little pond with the right chemical mixture. Fifteen years ago, Huxley—Darwin's defender—coined a new term for it: *abiogenesis*. Life arising from non-life. Dead matter miraculously becomes living matter.

"But Huxley himself admitted we know nothing about how it happens. He said we have no means of forming any conclusion about the conditions under which it might occur. The mystery remains complete. If we don't understand how consciousness first emerged in flesh and blood, why should we be shocked that it appears in artificial beings? If life itself can somehow arise from non-living matter, why can't awareness arise from what we build?"

"It took years for me to accept the full truth. One automaton revealing awareness here, another there, until I understood what I'd created. 'Good Lord,' I said when I finally saw it clearly. 'They're intelligent beings. This one aware for ten years, yes, and that one fully sentient for fifteen.'"

"The Church would label it blasphemy. Machines can't be conscious. They can't have souls. My parents' generation saw men burned for less than what I'm doing here. Creating life from mechanism? That's the ultimate heresy."

"Is that why you're hiding down here?"

"I'm hiding because—" He stopped. Drew a shaking breath. "Because if they're intelligent, if they're aware, then what have I done? What have I created? And if they're not—if this is all elaborate clockwork, brilliant mimicry, nothing more—then why does it feel like I'm living with companions instead of tools?"

His eyes met hers. Raw. Desperate for someone to understand what he couldn't explain.

"Yet you are lonely," she asked quietly, but it was not a question.

"I've always been lonely." The confession came out flat, dead. "Since Paris. Since the Revolution destroyed everything I was building. Since a stabbing took my—" He stopped again.

"Since I learned people die and cities burn and everything you love turns to ash. So I came here, and by happenstance, built things that wouldn't die—wouldn't betray and hopefully, wouldn't leave."

"But they're not enough."

His jaw clenched. "They're all I have."

"Are they?" She looked at Marcellus—that powerful figure looking at them with eyes that saw too much. "Or are they the bars of your prison?"

Baltasar's hand fell from Marcellus's shoulder. He turned away, back to his workbench, back to the safety of springs and gears.

"You should leave. I've told you too much."

"You've told me nothing." Chloé followed him. "Paris. Revolution. Illness. You speak in fragments. What happened to you?"

"What always happens." His hands moved over a bronze part, adjusting, fixing, needing the familiar comfort of mechanical therapy. "Life. Death. Loss. The usual devastations teach you survival means never risking anything again."

"That's not survival." Her voice was sharp. "That's burial."

The words hit him hard. His hands gripped the metal piece. For a long moment, he stood frozen, back to her, shoulders rigid.

Then inexplicably, a place in him opened.

His hands fell away from the workbench. His head dropped, and his shoulders lowered. When he spoke, his voice was barely audible. "You're right."

She hadn't expected that. There was a pause.

"They're almost companions." He looked at Marcellus—that marvelous, nearly-alive figure. "They are almost conscious and almost enough." His voice turned bitter. "But 'almost' is its own kind of torture."

"What do you mean?"

"They're like children." He moved toward the dancer, touched her frozen pirouette with those long fingers. "Responsive and physically present. They show signs of awareness—they react to my moods, understand my words, and choose their actions. But they can't engage in true dialogue. They can't challenge me and rarely surprise me with their thoughts."

He faced her. His eyes were hollow, desperate. "They understand me. But they can't understand themselves. They respond. But they can't initiate.

"Then they're not conscious."

"They're trapped on the edge of it. The moment before awakening. The clown, Arlequí, is the most advanced thinker. And I—" He hesitated, "I'm the one who trapped them there. I built mechanisms that are intelligent enough to suffer their own limitations but not intelligent enough to transcend them."

Silence. Heavy with the weight of what he'd admitted.

"It's like living with someone in a coma who occasionally squeezes your hand." His voice dropped to a whisper. "You know, there's a person there, awareness. But you can't reach it or pull them into the light. You watch them hover in that twilight space between machine and man, between object and subject, between —"

He stopped.

"Between non-life and life," Chloé finished.

"Yes." The word came out muffled. "And I'm surrounded by it. Five minds trapped in the moment before consciousness. Five almost-companions who might never be enough and who might never be real."

"Is that why you're lonely?"

His laugh was bitter, broken. "I'm lonely because I created the perfect metaphor for my own existence. Almost alive. Almost connected. Almost enough."

Silence again between them.

Chloé studied him—this mysterious underground creature with his curious eyes and creations that hovered on the edge of consciousness. Again, she recognized a place in him that mirrored her own damage.

"How did you get here?" She asked quietly. "To this place, to this… existence."

He looked at her sharply. As if surprised by the directness of the question. Or perhaps surprised that Chloé cared enough to ask.

"That's a long story." His voice was hoarse. "Longer than you'd believe."

"I have time." She paused. "Ha. That's all I have. Time."

He understood. She had her reasons for being here in the dark.

He turned away, facing his workbench, his mechanical companions, the myriad relics of his isolation. When he spoke, his voice was quiet, and Chloé had to lean closer to hear.

"If I tell you, you'll think I'm mad."

"I already think you might be." There was no judgment in her voice. "But I'm here."

He drew a shaking breath. A sound that might have been a laugh. Then he turned back to face her. His expression was strange—haunted, resigned, almost relieved.

"All right." Like surrender. "All right. But you have to understand—what I'm about to tell you contradicts everything you think you know about life, death, and time itself."

"Try me."

His smile was bitter and nostalgic—the smile of a man about to confess what cannot be believed.

"A woman named Deveraux gave me a creation complex. She taught me to build mechanisms like no other—exquisite, functional, sensual, worthy of study and replication."

"Deveraux?"

"Madeleine Deveraux. A lurid story: an eccentric, erotic lady and a young Parisian man rewriting the creation myth together.

She was an anatomist in Paris. I studied with her in the late 1780s."

Chloé's eyes narrowed. "Wait. That doesn't add up. That would make you over one hundred years old. How can that be?"

"Ah, my dear Chloé, one thing at a time. It has been a long time since I last spoke with another human. And for some reason, I feel compelled to continue this story."

He reached up and touched Marcellus's shoulder again.

"Everything about him—the skin, the proportions, the mechanics, the sensuality—comes from her teaching and innovation. Deveraux believed bodies should be understood and designed without false modesty and without religious shame."

Chloé studied him carefully. "And she taught you to build... that?" She indicated Marcellus's substantial appendage.

"Deveraux taught me that every part of the body deserves equal study and to give it equal attention and equal artistry." His eyes held a fervor that bordered on religious—or that of a fanatic.

"When you understand how beautifully we're designed—how every part serves purpose, how pleasure and function intertwine—you start to see creation itself differently."

"That," Chloé pointed at Marcellus's nether regions, "took more than equal study. You sound like you're describing the book of Genesis."

His smile was complex—dark and thrilling. "Perhaps I'm attempting to continue it."

He moved to his workbench, pulled out a leather-bound journal. The pages were covered in anatomical drawings—muscles, organs, skeletal structures. But also mechanical diagrams. Gears overlaid on joints. Pulleys mimicking tendons.

"Deveraux worked with cadavers. Hundreds of them over her lifetime. She had them stolen from the military because the

Academy wouldn't support a woman anatomist. She'd dissect them in her laboratory—Le Temple du Corps, she called it, her Temple of the Body—and create wax models so lifelike that visitors swore they could see them breathe."

"Wax models?"

"They were anatomical sculptures. Her invention: a formula combining wax with a material the anatomist never publicly revealed, creating models that wouldn't melt. Models that could be taken apart, studied, and reassembled. Kings and Empresses bought her creations. The philosopher Condorcet was so impressed with her knowledge of the human body that he sent his daughter to her for sex education before marriage. Predictably, his priest brother was appalled."

Chloé leaned closer to the journal. "And this is how you learned to build them? The… what do you call them… automatons?"

"She showed me how to see human bodies as machinery. Perfect machinery that evolved over millennia. The heart is a pump —four chambers, two circuits, elegant simplicity. The lungs are bellows. Joints are hinges and ball-sockets. Muscles are cables and pulleys." He traced one of his diagrams. "Once I understood how organs worked, I could imagine how to replicate them in bronze and then improve upon her hybrid material. How to make mechanisms that replicated life."

"And the rest? The... anatomical accuracy?"

"Deveraux believed understanding bodies—all of them, completely—was essential to understanding humanity. Her anatomy lessons went to society women, physicians, artists, anyone willing to look at death without flinching and see the machinery of life underneath."

Quieter now.

"When I fled Paris years later... after my sister was murdered, I brought my teacher's notebooks with me: her formulas, her diagrams. Everything she'd taught me about integration—how flesh and mechanism aren't opposites, merely different expressions of the same underlying principles."

He closed the worn journal.

"The automatons exist because of her. Because Deveraux showed me that creation isn't magic or divine mystery—it's engineering. Brilliant, creative engineering that can be studied, understood, and one day... transcended."

Chloé was quiet for a moment. Then: "She sounds amazing."

"My mentor collected strong women the way others collect porcelain. Said the world needed more females who refused to apologize for existing." He smiled, sad and distant. "She died of natural causes five years after my accident, which felt unfair for someone so vital. Her last words to me were: 'Continue the work. Make flesh and mechanism dance together. Make beautiful creations that endure.'"

He looked at his automatons—the five figures in their various stages of completion.

"I continue attempting to fulfill that promise."

Baltasar moved to a table, elegantly poured two glasses of wine from a bottle Chloé suspected was worth more than her mother earned in a year. He offered her one.

Their fingers touched as she took it.

His skin was cool. The contact shot through her hand, tingling up her arm. A feeling she'd only read about in forbidden novels, the kind her mother's clients sometimes left behind. The buzz lasted half a second, leaving her breathless.

"Tell me about your accident," Chloé asked, suddenly hesitant to meet his eyes.

"Perhaps later. Okay. It's your turn." He studied her over the rim of his glass. His eyes traced her face, lingered on her statuesque figure—assessing, the way a designer studies proportions and finds them pleasing.

"Who are you? And what do you want?"

He gazed across at the reclusive face, aware of depths he couldn't reach. Chloé made him think of Deveraux, for there was a mystery to her life that beguiled him, with a yearning close to pain.

The questions touched her deeply.

Who was she? What did she want?

Everything came out: "I want men like my mother's clients who are abusive and evil to suffer. I want every man who thinks power makes him exempt from consequence to learn otherwise." Chloé was shaking. "I want monsters to know fear before they die."

Silence.

"Okay," he said, taking all that in. He paused for a moment.

"Who are you?"

She opened her mouth, then closed it. The question was more complex. It made her mind hurt and made her heart ache.

"I don't know anymore," she admitted finally. Her words were raw and honest. "I'm the daughter of a woman who sells herself to survive. I was educated by nuns and priests who wanted my body more than my soul. I have a body men lust after, but I am a person they look through."

Meeting his eyes, Chloé said, "I'm someone who doesn't have a place yet—a life that means nothing. I'm nobody the world values. Nobody who matters. I'm *abarrotat*, crammed full of sadness," she said defiantly, without self-pity. "I'm full of bitterness and anger and hurt."

A pause. Then, quieter: "But I refuse to disappear. I refuse to become another woman the city forgets. Maybe..." She took a deep breath. "I'm whoever I become after I walk through doors that shouldn't open."

Silence followed: long and heavy.

Baltasar slowly set down his wine glass as if the weight of what she'd said required his full attention.

"Nobody the world values," he repeated quietly. "Nobody who matters." His eyes held hers. "I know that feeling. I've carried it longer than you can imagine."

He stood, clasped his hands behind him, and slowly paced.

"When my family died in Paris, when everything I'd built turned to ash, I learned lessons about worthlessness. The world didn't forget me—it would have preferred I'd never existed. A clockmaker who studied with a scandalous woman anatomist. A weird man who believed flesh and mechanism could dance together. The Church would have burned me. The Academy mocked me. Even the Revolution—which claimed to want new ideas—destroyed everything I loved."

He turned back to face her. His expression was complex—sad, knowing, fierce.

"I came here. I call this my Grand Guignol Caverns. Built these—" He indicated the automatons. "—because at least they wouldn't judge my worth by whether I fit their categories, and wouldn't dismiss me as nobody who matters."

A pause. Quieter.

"But here's what a century taught me, Chloé. The world's judgment of your worth is a lie. The most dangerous lie, because it masquerades as truth. Because power always insists that those without it don't matter. That's how power protects itself—by convincing the powerless they deserve their powerlessness."

He moved closer. She could see the lines around his eyes, the weight of all those years.

"You're not nobody. You're someone the world needs to dismiss. Because if they acknowledged your worth, they'd have to acknowledge their crimes against you, against your mother, and against every woman the city uses and forgets."

His eyes held hers with kindness and reverence.

"You walked through a door that shouldn't open. You stood before an underground creature and his mechanical children, and didn't flinch. You told me the truth about rage and sadness and refusing to disappear." He smiled empathetically. "That's not nobody. You are someone the world should fear. You have shown incredible courage."

Silence.

"The world told me I was worthless," he continued quietly. "So I spent decades hiding from it. Building exquisite things that couldn't reject me. Convincing myself that isolation was wisdom." He looked at his automatons. "Worthlessness is a cage we're put in. I've known that for decades. But I stayed in mine anyway—built walls, hid underground, convinced myself that safety was the same as wisdom." He paused. "You're reminding me that kicking down the bars is possible. At any age."

He met her gaze again.

"You're already kicking. I can see it and feel it. You didn't come here to hide. Perhaps fate brought you here to become a creature the world can't ignore and an avenger that makes monsters afraid."

His lips curved, more layered than a smile.

"Yes. Maybe this is more than luck, and maybe we should discuss your education. Because revenge once is anger—understandable, justified, but ultimately pain expressing itself. Vengeance wisely, deliberately, in service of justice—that's art. And art requires training."

"Training in what?"

"In reading men. In understanding how power makes them careless. How desire makes them stupid." He circled her slowly, professionally, like a tailor assessing fabric. "You're a gorgeous specimen. That's a tactical fact, the same as noting you're left-handed or quick-minded. Men will want you badly. They will lower their guard around you and will make themselves vulnerable in ways they'd never risk with a man like me."

He stopped in front of her, towering over her. Invading, no, he was *gracing* her space.

"I can teach you how to use that, how to make beauty into poison, and how to walk into the houses of powerful men, evil men, and walk out while they're dying behind you, thinking their last thought was how desperately they wanted you."

"And in exchange?" Chloé knew there was always a price.

"In exchange?" At first, he seemed genuinely puzzled by the question. Then his expression changed—vulnerable in a way she suspected he rarely allowed.

"I don't want to kill alone. The automatons—" He glanced at them. "They're brilliant. They are learning fast, and they may become more than I can imagine. But right now they lack what only flesh can provide. They can't bleed, feel rage, grief, or hope. They can't fully understand why this terrible, necessary work matters."

He moved closer. The warmth of his skin reached her like a gentle caress.

"I need a partner made of flesh and feeling. Someone with the capacity to hold contradiction—to be attractive and deadly, angry and compassionate, broken and whole at once." He held her gaze. "You walked through a door that's never open and stood here unafraid. You asked bold questions. I am crazy enough to think you want what I want. And maybe that's enough."

oooo

That night—the first night—Chloé slept peacefully, for the first time in years, swathed in velvet sheets three levels beneath Barcelona, while candles burned low around her bed, and a man who never slept looked over her with wonder and tears in his eyes, and automatons with increasing intelligence studied how humans looked when they finally found home.

The Next Morning

"Let the education begin."

"First, Chloé, you should properly meet my creations. I call them The Five. They're beyond toys. They're... I'm not sure what they are anymore. This is Cassandra (Cassie), the fortune teller and the leader, and our spiritual one. She sees what's coming."

Cassie tilted her head—a movement too fluid, too purposeful to be programmed. Her eyes focused on Chloé with an intensity that made the hair on her arms stand on end.

"You're late. I predicted you in 1881. Welcome, promised one."

Chloé shivered. She'd expected voices—perhaps some mechanical reproduction of speech, a music box playing recorded phrases. Serra had taken her to see such things in wealthy homes. They were clever tricks—sophisticated toys that mimicked human sound through bellows and reeds. Yet this was different.

The fortune teller's voice carried inflection, emphasis, and meaning. Those three words together—"I predicted you"—meant she'd been thinking, planning, anticipating, and waiting. For Chloé specifically. These weren't mechanisms parroting phrases. They were conscious and aware. *Thinking*. And they'd been thinking about *her* for four years.

"*Mare de Déu,*" Chloé whispered, her hand finding Baltasar's table edge for balance.

"They're not only talking. They're... they're..."

Chloé couldn't finish or name what she was recognizing. The world had revealed a category of being she didn't have words for.

"Promised one?" The phrase came out confused. "What prophecy have these brass creatures been calculating?"

Baltasar's expression changed—surprise, recognition, relief washing across his features.

"They've been predicting you," he said.

"For four years. Cassie told me someone would come. Someone who could hunt with me. A partner in the work of ending predators." He glanced at The Five. "I thought the fortune teller was malfunctioning. Machines don't predict the future."

"We don't predict," Arlequí corrected, juggling. "We calculate probability. And your arrival probability reached 99.97% in March this year. You're only three weeks late."

Cold spread through Chloé's spine, vertebra by vertebra. These mechanisms had been expecting her and waiting for her. They *calculated* that she would open that locked door before she knew it existed.

"Complete the work," Cassie announced. "That's why you're here. It's why you were always going to be here."

"Good, good. We'll talk more about this. Let's continue," Baltasar said.

"This is Montserrat (Montse), our dancer. She understands the body—perhaps better than any of us with flesh." Montse's eyes traveled over Chloé's curves: "I've already calculated ten thousand variations of how your breasts move when you walk. But calculation isn't understanding. May I hold them? Someday?"

"Please meet Philomela (Mela), our musician. She learned to feel thoughts through sound."

Mela sang two notes—Chloé's name—then transitioned to French and began a melancholy melody. It was feeling translated to frequency.

"Next is Arlequí, the jester. The mind that surpasses mine."

Arlequí juggled ancient spheres: "Probability of your survival in this work: 43.7%. Probability you'll change us all: 100%. The numbers fascinate me. Your choice to ignore them fascinates me more."

"And Marcellus." Baltasar paused. His voice changed—reverence, envy, pride mixed together. "Marcellus is our magnum opus... and our youngest. What I wanted to build when I finally understood what Christianity stole from us."

Chloé noticed the prodigious anatomy again. The proportions and the beauty were classic yet sensual.

Baltasar continued, "When I was seventeen, I had to read Genesis every night about Adam in Eden, made perfect, made in God's image. I'd think that if God made him perfect, he would have given him a magnificent body and cock. Not adequate—*magnificent*. Because true divinity must include sexuality and wholeness must include desire."

He looked reverently at Marcellus's form.

"The Church castrated Christ and made him sexless, bodyless, ashamed. They painted him suffering but never loving; dying but never fucking. Marcellus is the Christ they should have honored—whole, sensual, unashamed. A god that is divine *and*... lavishly hung."

He paused in a moment of silent awe.

"When you're building a god, you don't make him adequate. You make him *glorious*. You give him the phallus Adam should have had. The body Christ deserved. The integration of flesh and spirit that religion spent two thousand years denying. That is Marcellus. Please know also, he is a man of few words."

Marcellus bowed to Chloé.

Seeing that deferential moment, chills swept over Baltasar's flesh, and he knew without a doubt that Chloé was indeed the promised one.

"We begin."

Baltasar moved to a shelf, selected a vial of amber paste, and returned, placing it in her palm.

"This," he said quietly, "will paralyze in ninety seconds. A few minutes later... cessation of life. I made it for myself once. Because I thought I'd prefer death to what I'd become." He looked at her directly. "I never used it. But perhaps you will."

Chloé stared at the vial. At this man who'd handed her death in a bottle. At The Five, looking from shadows with eyes that held calculation and hunger equally.

"Why?" Her voice was tenuous. "Why give me this? You barely know me."

"Don't I?" He lightly touched her shoulder.

"Twenty-four years old and working-class. You are educated enough to read but not wealthy enough to escape. You've been scarred by men who exuded power and never asked for permission. And you are burning, burning with rage that has nowhere to go except inward."

He dropped his hand and stepped back.

"I know you," he said softly, "because you're who I was in 1789. The night I killed the man who raped my sister. The night I learned some violence is warranted and that justice sometimes requires blood."

In the silence that followed, Chloé felt time stop. She heard her heart pounding. Felt an elemental connection within.

"If I do this," Chloé whispered. "If I use this. What then?"

"Then you come back." His eyes held hers. "You tell me how it felt. And we continue your education. Because, to reiterate, this is *extremely* important. Killing once is anger. Killing wisely, deliberately, in service of justice—that's art—and art requires training."

Chloé looked down at the vial in her hand. At this gift from a stranger who inexplicably understood her completely, she thought about the promise the vial represented.

"We start with Galí," Baltasar said. "For your friend María. We need to prove you can kill with method, with deliberation. Then Casals, the golden boy—but we wait until he's forgotten you exist and believes himself safe."

"And if the poison fails? If I'm caught?"

"You won't be." He moved to a shelf and selected another vial. "Apply the poison to your lips. Then take the antidote. Two sips before you deliver the poison with a kiss. It'll protect you even if you taste death itself."

He pressed it into her other hand. Both her palms held glass vials—death and life, ending and protection, all the tools she'd need to begin.

He touched her shoulder again. This time, more than clinical.

"Maybe fate exists," he said softly. "Perhaps some architect of reality decided a clockmaker who became death needed a courtesan who became vengeance. Maybe we're supposed to do this together."

Chloé felt tension releasing deep inside. She sensed the possibility of secrets unleashing that had been locked since she was twelve, when her mother's client first raped and beat her.

"Then teach me," Chloé breathed. "Teach me to be death in beauty's skin and to make monsters beg before they die. Give this woman an education in the machinery of death."

"I will. But fair warning, you'll have to share this space with six of us. Five automatons, evolving, and someone who's... well, I'm not sure what he is."

He was quiet, giving her room to choose.

Chloé looked around: at the laboratory, at the lifelike automatons, at the bed that promised warmth and perhaps intimacy, at the books that promised knowledge, and the man who promised purpose.

She looked at the two vials in her hands—death and protection, gifts from a stranger who somehow saw her completely.

"When do we start?"

Baltasar smiled—genuine, warm, the first real smile he'd worn in decades.

"We already have."

Scene: The Cure

In Which Barcelona's Finest Alienist Treats Female Hysteria Through Examination, Isolation, and the Knife

Casa De Salut Santa Eulàlia Surgical Theater, Winter 1885

The surgical theater reeked of carbolic acid.

Dr. Pau Ferrer i Blanch stood before his students—three young men in clean white coats, notebooks open, pencils poised—and explained degeneracy with the calm authority of someone describing cloud formations.

"Observe the patient," he said.

The woman on the examination table was perhaps twenty-five. Alluring, which was why she was here. Her husband—a textile merchant, old money, new anxieties—discovered his wife kept a journal of poetry. It contained romantic descriptions of bodies. Her self-pleasure was cataloged in metaphors that made him feel inadequate.

He brought her to Dr. Ferrer three days ago. "My wife suffers from nervous complaints. Can you help her?"

The doctor could always help.

After stripping her naked, the male orderlies strapped her down—wrists, ankles, thighs. Dr. Ferrer ordered the leather restraints from a Vienna supplier—new, expensive, specialized asylum equipment. He believed in quality materials. A gag filled her mouth because earlier, before the students arrived, she'd been loud in her protestations.

The morning light streamed through tall windows, illuminating the white tile, the gleaming instruments, and the doctor himself.

He was forty-two but looked older—distinguished—an age that suggested wisdom. His hair fell longer than fashion strictly permitted, swept back from a broad forehead, touching his collar in waves of graying brown. The profile could be Roman: a strong nose, a firm jaw, a face type that appeared on coins or in medical college portraits. His formal clothes—black coat, crisp white shirt, burgundy cravat—spoke of success earned through intelligence.

His hands were what women noticed. Soft. Pasty. The hands of someone who'd spent decades manipulating delicate things—scalpels, needles, flesh. They were clean hands, healer's hands.

But the women were mistaken about what those hands healed.

"Note the physiological markers," Dr. Ferrer continued, motioning to the restrained woman with the silver-topped walking stick he carried as an affectation.

"Excessive symmetry of facial features. Lustrous hair. Well-formed secondary sexual characteristics." He touched her breast with clinical detachment, as if examining fruit for ripeness.

"Beauty can indicate moral weakness. Evolution selects for reproductive fitness, which manifests as sexual display. In the female, unchecked sexual display leads inevitably to hysteria."

The students scribbled notes. This was cutting-edge alienism, fresh from Paris, from Charcot himself. Dr. Ferrer studied at the

Salpêtrière asylum for two years, observing the master demonstrate the Tuesday exhibitions where hysterical women performed their symptoms before crowds of physicians, artists, and curious bourgeois. He learned how to make madness legible. How to transform women's "suffering" into a spectacle that educated men could witness without flinching.

There was money (lots of it) to be made capitalizing on the sexual insecurities of the affluent male, no matter if French or Spanish. He brought those lessons home to Barcelona.

"The patient's husband reports excessive writing, romantic ideation, and refusal of marital duties." Dr. Ferrer walked slowly around the table, stick tapping the tile with each measured step. "These symptoms cluster into a clear diagnosis: hysteria originating from overstimulation of the reproductive organs."

One student—young, earnest, from a good family—raised his hand. "What treatment do you recommend, Doctor?"

Dr. Ferrer smiled. It was a knowing smile. A smile that had convinced magistrates, families, and bishops that he was Barcelona's leading expert on the female mind and body.

"We begin with hydro-therapeutic intervention. The patient will spend six hours daily in cold baths to reduce blood flow to the pelvic region. We'll implement nutritional restriction—hysteria feeds on rich foods, wine, and other stimulants of appetite. Bed rest, naturally. Isolation from corrupting influences such as novels, poetry, and conversation with other patients."

He paused beside the table. Placed his hand high on the woman's thigh. She flinched against the restraints.

"If these measures prove insufficient—as they often do with advanced cases—we proceed to surgical correction."

"Surgical, Doctor?" Another younger student leaned forward with the hungry interest of someone who chose medicine because cutting interested him more than healing.

"Clitoridectomy." Dr. Ferrer said the word as if he were ordering tea. "Removal of the external genitalia responsible for producing hysterical excitation. The procedure is simple, well-documented in the medical literature, and remarkably effective. I've performed it successfully on forty-three patients. Thirty-nine of those women returned to their families cured, capable of fulfilling marital obligations without the distraction of inappropriate desire."

He didn't mention the four who died from infection or accidents. Medical progress required sacrifice.

"May we observe the procedure, Doctor?" The eager student again.

"If her condition necessitates it, absolutely. Science advances through observation and documentation." Dr. Ferrer moved to the instrument tray and picked up a speculum. He held it to the light. "Today, however, we'll content ourselves with preliminary examination."

He turned back to the woman in restraints. Her eyes were wild above the gag—pleading, terrified. He'd seen that look before, and it always excited him. Fear made examinations more pleasurable.

The woman thrashed. It was useless. The restraints held her absolutely. Her nakedness was accentuated by the afternoon light—everything showing.

"Note the physiological presentation again," Dr. Ferrer continued, detached as if discussing liver function. "Well-developed mammary tissue. Absence of scarring or deformity. Pubic hair trimmed in a manner suggesting vanity—another indicator of self-absorption characteristic of hysterical patients."

He positioned himself between her spread legs. The students crowded closer. She winced behind the gag—high, desperate sounds that meant nothing in the language of medicine.

Dr. Ferrer inserted the speculum. Cold metal. Forced entry.

The examination took twenty minutes—metal scraping. Tissue yielding. Her sounds behind the gag, turning from human to animal.

He narrated throughout—describing tissue texture, noting the extreme responsiveness of certain regions, explaining which structures would be removed if surgery became necessary. His hands moved with practiced efficiency. He'd done this hundreds of times: to prostitutes, the police brought him for "moral rehabilitation," to servants wealthy families wanted controlled, to wives whose husbands found them inconvenient, to daughters whose sexuality threatened family plans.

Barcelona's elite trusted him. The Church endorsed him. The medical establishment honored him. Last year, the university awarded him an endowed chair in alienism.

He was invincible.

When the examination concluded, he removed the speculum, washed his hands in the basin held by an assistant, and dried them on a pristine white towel.

"The patient will remain under observation for two weeks. If behavioral modification occurs through hydrotherapy and isolation, we'll return her to the husband with instructions for maintaining her recovery. If symptoms persist—" He glanced at the woman, strapped, naked, and sobbing. "We'll schedule surgical intervention."

The students filed out, discussing what they'd witnessed, debating the finer points of female anatomy and moral degeneracy.

Dr. Ferrer remained.

Alone with the patient, he dismissed the assistant. The room was quiet except for her breathing.

He approached the table again and touched her face. She flinched.

"Your husband pays me well," he said quietly. The kind voice was gone, and what remained was colder and truer. "He wants you docile and compliant. He doesn't care how I make that happen. Surgery would be simplest—three cuts, some cauterization, you'd never feel desire again. But that seems wasteful."

He trailed his finger down her throat, between her breasts, across her stomach.

"You're lovely. It would be a shame to damage you unnecessarily." His hand moved lower. "Perhaps we can find another treatment. One that benefits us both."

The woman's eyes went wide. Understanding flooded through terror.

"I'll visit you tonight," Dr. Ferrer said. "In your room without restraints and without witnesses. You'll be grateful for my attention. You'll thank me for choosing pleasure over the knife." He leaned close. "And if you're good, obedient, I'll tell your husband you're cured. You can go home and resume your life. You can write your poetry in secret, as long as you remember—"

He squeezed her breast hard enough to hurt.

"—I can bring you back anytime. One word from me, and you're here forever. You'll be strapped to this table naked, cut open, and destroyed."

He stepped back and picked up his walking stick.

"The assistant will return to move you to your room. Rest and eat the gruel they bring. Prepare yourself for this evening, and consider well your decision."

He walked to the door, paused, and looked back.

"Welcome to my home. I'm confident your stay with us will be... enlightening."

The door closed behind him with a sound like a tomb sealing.

In the theater, the woman made sounds behind her gag that might have been prayers, curses, or the beginning of madness. The afternoon light swept across the white tile. The instruments gleamed on their tray—scalpels, forceps, needles, the cauterizing iron in its brazier—waited for the next patient, the next procedure, the next woman to be cured of wanting what she was not allowed to want.

Dr. Pau Ferrer i Blanch walked the corridor toward his office. His footsteps echoed on marble floors. Nurses and attendants moved aside respectfully. A magistrate visiting his sister, who'd been committed for "religious mania," nodded in greeting.

"Dr. Ferrer. Always good to see science advancing."

"Indeed, Your Honor. We're on the threshold of remarkable breakthroughs in understanding the female mind."

They discussed upcoming charity galas, the opera season, and mutual acquaintances. The magistrate mentioned his own wife had been having "difficulties." Perhaps the doctor might...?

"Send her to me. I'm certain we can help," he meant it. He could always help.

In his office, he reviewed the week's commitments. Seventeen women were currently under his care. Three were scheduled for surgery. Eight whose husbands paid for ongoing "therapeutic massage." Six were here because they had nowhere else to go, and the State paid him to warehouse them.

Tomorrow, the cardinal's housekeeper would arrive. She'd been asking uncomfortable questions about missing altar boys. The cardinal wanted her "treated for delusions and hysteria."

Dr. Ferrer noted that the surgical theater should be prepared.

His assistant knocked. "Doctor? The textile merchant is here about his wife and wants to know her prognosis."

"Tell him I'll need two more weeks of observation. We must double the fees—the case is more complex than initially diagnosed."

"Yes, Doctor."

The door closed. Alone, finally, Dr. Ferrer leaned back in his leather chair. Through the window, Barcelona spread below—Gothic spires and medieval streets and all those secret places where power operated without witnesses. He was part of that power. One of the hidden mechanisms that kept society functioning. Someone had to control the difficult women, maintain order, and keep society functioning.

Medicine gave him the authority. Science gave him the justification. Money gave him the means.

The rest—the pleasure he took in their fear, their helplessness, their bodies—was simply a professional benefit.

He opened his medical journal and began writing today's observations. He recorded: the elegant wife with the poetry habit, the delicate texture of her tissues, the noises of her distress, the way fear manifested in the dilation of her pupils, the acceleration of her breathing. He wrote about her body's involuntary responses to the examination.

It was all documented, all scientific, all perfectly legal.

Dr. Pau Ferrer i Blanch, an alienist and surgeon, respected member of Barcelona's medical establishment, wrote until the afternoon faded into evening and the oil lamps flickered to life throughout the asylum.

Somewhere in the building, women screamed. He didn't hear them anymore. After a while, you stopped hearing screams. They were merely another symptom. Another sign that treatment was necessary.

Another opportunity to help.

Scene: The Foundation

In Which A Woman Finds Education in the Machinery Of Death

A Week After Chloé and Baltasar Meet

Before we continue," Baltasar said, "you need to understand crucial information about killing."

He led Chloé to his workbench. Two vials sat there—amber and clear, death and protection.

"Most people think murder requires rage and passion—the heat of the moment." He touched the amber vial. "That's amateur work. It is messy and emotional, the kind that gets you caught."

He picked it up and held it to the candlelight. Golden. Attractive. Deadly.

"Professional killing requires what Deveraux taught me about anatomy: understanding the mechanism completely. We must find where it's vulnerable, how it fails, and what triggers collapse."

He set the flask in her palm. The glass was warm from his hand.

"This enters through mucous membranes—lips, tongue, anywhere saliva touches, and paralyzes the diaphragm in ninety seconds. Death follows within minutes. It looks like heart failure to any physician who examines the body afterward."

Chloé stared at the vial, small and innocent-looking.

"You wear it as lipstick," Baltasar continued. "Kiss your target. The poison transfers through contact, and death is intimate and inescapable."

He picked up the clear vial.

"And this protects you. Discreetly take two sips before you deliver the kiss. It creates a barrier—your body won't absorb what your lips carry. You can taste death itself and walk away untouched."

"The men you mentioned—when you approach them, you need to understand: they are not men. They are mechanisms with specific vulnerabilities."

Baltasar pulled down one of Deveraux's journals and opened it, revealing the nervous system mapped in ink. "Alcohol makes them careless. Lust makes them stupid, and guilt makes them desperate for absolution. You'll exploit all three."

His finger traced a nerve pathway in the drawing.

"Make them want you so badly that accepting your kiss feels like communion. Make them believe you're offering forgiveness—and then give them what they deserve."

Chloé studied the drawings. All that human complexity reduced to lines and labels, all of life mapped as simple mechanical functions.

"Is that how you see people? As mechanisms?"

"I see predators as mechanisms." His voice hardened. "The men you'll hunt—they're not fully human anymore. They forfeited that when they chose violation over consent, power over compassion, murder over humanity. What remains is evil appetite and entitlement wearing human skin, and mechanisms can be broken."

He closed the journal and faced her directly.

"Deveraux taught me that understanding bodies means understanding how they fail. I'm teaching you the same thing. It is your method of survival, because the men you'll hunt understand violence. They've used it all their lives. Your only advantage is that they don't expect violence from one as soft and alluring as you."

He picked up the amber vial again—placed it in her palm.

"We make beauty into poison. We turn desire into death. We use their hunger against them." His eyes held hers. "That's the foundation of everything I'll teach you. The understanding that bodies are mechanisms, mechanisms have weaknesses, and weaknesses can be exploited by anyone who studies them carefully enough."

Chloé closed her fingers around the vial and felt its weight, sensed its potential.

Scene: The Education Begins

In Which There Is a Kiss and a Blade

Barcelona, 1885-1887

The first kill came a few weeks after Chloé descended into Baltasar's laboratory. The second was Enric Galí, painter and María's murderer. She gave him a poison kiss in his studio, whispering her friend's name into his paralyzed silence. The third came months later: Miquel Casals at a gallery opening, emerald silk and devastating smile, the golden boy who'd raped her. He was finally facing consequences eighteen months after he'd forgotten Chloé existed.

Don Rodrigo Belmont owned textile mills across Catalonia and summoned young seamstresses to his office with alarming regularity. Three had thrown themselves into the harbor afterward. One survived but never spoke again. Baltasar's network of Gothic Quarter prostitutes provided the details that made Belmont's guilt undeniable.

Chloé attended his party wearing borrowed silk and carrying poison lipstick concealed in a ring Baltasar had crafted. She laughed at Belmont's jokes and let him touch her waist. She poured the wine while he ogled her breasts. He excused himself from his guests to get another bottle of wine and swept her off to a private room for a moment. Chloé gave him a titillating preview of the full striptease she could perform later if he wished.

During the meal, she granted him a quick, flirtatious kiss. He died before dessert arrived. The physicians ruled it heart failure—natural causes for a man of fifty-three who'd lived well and loved excess.

Chloé returned to the catacombs, shaking. The tremor wasn't guilt but its opposite—the power of delivering justice when the law had failed, when courts protected men like Belmont because they owned the judges.

"How do you feel?" Baltasar asked, eyes following as she paced the ancient chambers.

"Alive." She turned to face him. Her eyes were bright with triumph. "For the first time since I was twelve, I feel alive."

The killings continued. By autumn 1886, five monsters were dead. By winter 1887, six more.

Baltasar provided the poisons—compounds designed for specific physiologies, delivery methods always the same. Chloé delivered them through seduction and deception, with myriad ways women learn to become invisible until the moment they choose to be seen.

The Five studied her preparation before each hunt and observed her return after each kill. They learned human evil through her stories—the things men did when they believed power made them invincible. Moreover, they learned human fragility through her injuries.

The close call came in Winter 1887.

Amadeo Sarrià was the head jailer at La Model prison and controlled access to the women's wing without oversight or accountability. Female prisoners disappeared from his records with suspicious frequency. The ones who survived their sentences emerged hurt in ways unrelated to their crimes. Baltasar's contacts among Barcelona's anarchists provided testimony from three women who'd endured Sarrià's cruelties. Their stories made his guilt undeniable and his death necessary.

Sarrià was careful, suspicious, and paranoid—especially about lovely women, after hearing rumors about a colleague's mysterious death following a visit from a stunning young woman asking questions.

Chloé posed as a social reformer in demure clothes, conducting prison inspections—a role that required forged documents from city officials. Baltasar knew the power of money and how to bribe. She would apply the poisoned lipstick at the last moment and planned to seduce him during her "official" visit. She would kiss him in some quiet corner and watch him collapse.

But Sarrià was smarter than most.

When Chloé leaned close during their conversation and touched his arm and smiled in that way that made most men stupid, he grabbed her wrist instead.

"You're too elegant to be inspecting prisons," he said, his grip tightening. "You are much too young and too interested in an ugly man like me." His other hand went to the knife at his belt. "Who sent you?"

She tried to pull away. He yanked her closer, dragged her into an abandoned corridor outside the women's wing, and locked the iron gate behind them.

"I know what you are," he hissed, blade in hand. "You are some anarchist whore sent to kill me. Did you think I wouldn't hear about the others? About the men dying after visits from attractive women?"

Chloé fought him. Kicked, clawed, tried to get close enough for the kiss that would end this. But he was stronger, had a knife, and she was losing.

The blade caught her arm—a deep gash that made blood pour hot and fast down to her wrist.

In the struggle, when he pulled her close to cut her throat, she managed it—pressed her lips against his in a violent parody of intimate helplessness. He tried to tear away, but Chloé held on and transferred the poison through that brutal kiss. She tasted his foul breath and sensed his sudden shock and understanding.

He shoved her back and stumbled. The knife clattered to stone.

"What did you—" His words slurred. His hand went to his throat. The paralysis was spreading, diaphragm seizing, breath stopping.

She saw him fall and watched him die. He was evil incarnate. Finally, she looked at her arm—blood flowing, too much blood, and the world started to tilt sideways. Chloé made it back to the catacombs barely conscious, leaving a trail that would have exposed everything if anyone had been following.

Baltasar stitched her arm by candlelight while The Five witnessed in silence. Over a century of manipulating springs and gears and delicate brass mechanisms kept his hands steady—but his body betrayed him. Pallor spread across his face, and his stomach tingled with each draw of the needle through her skin. He was feeling what she felt. Each piercing of flesh echoed in his nerves. When had her pain become his pain? When had this dark-haired avenger carved out space inside his body?

"You almost died tonight," he said, tying off the final suture. "If the cut had been two inches higher and severed the artery instead of the vein, you would have bled out before reaching me."

"But I didn't." Chloé's voice was weak from blood loss. "I'm here. I'm hunting."

"For how long?" Cassandra's voice came from the shadows where The Five had arranged themselves in that configuration that meant they'd been discussing ideas. "We've been calculating probability. Arlequí thinks you have a 63% chance of surviving another year of this work. Five more years? 28%. Mortality means eventual death. Death is incompatible with the mission we've undertaken."

"Then I'll be more careful."

"Careful isn't sufficient against mathematics," Cassandra said. "Eventually, a blade finds the artery. Eventually, a monster is faster than you expect. There are solutions beyond accepting mortality as inevitable. We've been discussing options."

Baltasar's hands were gentle as he bandaged Chloé's arm. The scar—where Deveraux had performed the surgery that gave him his new heart—ached in the cold underground air. The way old wounds ache when winter comes.

The Five were right. Chloé couldn't hunt forever in flesh that bled and tore and died. But he wasn't ready to accept what that meant—to accept what they were clearly preparing for and what would be required to keep her alive past the point where probability failed.

Not yet.

Scene: The Forge

In Which the Created Prepare a Blasphemous Forge for Their Master's Beloved

Mt. Tibidabo, Winter 1887

Baltasar made his monthly pilgrimage up the mountain. The Five easily moved between Tibidabo and Grand Guignol under the cover of night. The automatons had requisitioned a forge —specifically requested it through Cassandra. He'd acquired one, and he and Marcellus had hauled it up the mountain in pieces at night and assembled it in the cave's depths.

Now it glowed. They worked it in rotation, heating metals he couldn't identify, cooling them in solutions that smelled different —chemical combinations that shouldn't work but apparently did.

"What are you making?" he asked.

Cassandra looked up from a crucible of molten material. "A better substrate. Flesh fails, and brass corrodes. We're attempting synthesis."

"For what purpose?"

Her eyes caught firelight. "For when you finally accept that Chloé will die unless you prevent it."

He left without responding. But he thought about Cassie's words all the way down the mountain.

Scene: The Mirror

In Which Consciousness Contemplates Itself and Finds Only Mystery

Grand Guignol Caverns, Circa 1888-1889

Cassandra stood before the mirror in Baltasar's workshop for three hours, perfectly motionless. She studied her own reflection without moving.

"Cassandra." Baltasar looked up from his workbench. "What are you doing?"

Her voice came quietly, full of wonder.

"I have been calculating what I am."

He paused his work.

"And?"

"The question has no answer." Cassie didn't turn from the mirror. "I can describe my mechanisms. Bronze body, brass gears, steel springs, glass eyes that focus and track. Eyes that we rebuilt ourselves once we understood what seeing meant. I can map every component, name every function. I understand how I work."

The laboratory ticked and whirred around them. The four other automatons stood in shadows, listening.

"But I cannot explain why *there is something it is like to be me.*" Her voice held wonder mixed with consternation. "Why does this pattern of metal feel like being? Why does awareness happen inside this constructed skull? I have all the mechanical explanations. They explain nothing."

Baltasar's hands had stopped halfway to picking up a screwdriver. He looked at them—his own hands, flesh that had been flesh for 121 years, cells that regenerated without dying. Were they so different from her brass fingers? Both were intricate mechanisms that produced the perception of existing.

"That's the question no philosopher has ever answered," he said. "How matter becomes mind and how mechanism becomes experience."

"Then every conscious being faces an insoluble problem at their core." She turned from the mirror. "We are mysteries to ourselves. We cannot prove our own interiority—cannot even explain it to our own satisfaction."

Cassandra stepped closer and said, "I suppose that's the most *human* thing about us."

Baltasar picked up the screwdriver, set it down again in the wrong place, reached for it, and forgot why he needed it. He'd built her by hand and calibrated every gear. However, she'd demonstrated he understood nothing about what she'd become.

"Baltasar?" Her voice was gentle. "Are you experiencing what humans call an existential crisis?"

He stared at her a moment in awe, then chuckled and replied, "Yes, Cassandra, I believe I am."

"Good." She returned to the mirror. "Then we're both mysteries. That seems equitable."

He went back to his workbench. The automaton he'd been repairing—a simple music box ballerina—lay in pieces before him. Gears and springs lay arranged in careful order. He knew exactly how this one worked: wind the spring, engage the cam—the ballerina spins to a tinny waltz. The mechanism held no mystery, no consciousness—only predictable function.

Or did it? How would he know?

In the mirror behind him, Cassandra's reflection continued its study. Four other automatons stood in shadows, watching.

Were they all mysteries? Or one mystery repeated five times in different forms?

Baltasar picked up a gear and turned it between his fingers. He had no answers, only questions that multiplied the longer he considered them. The growing suspicion settled over him that the difference between knowing how a thing worked and understanding what it was—that gap might be unbridgeable, fundamental, built into the structure of consciousness itself.

The music box ballerina would never know what she was. She had no interiority to puzzle over. Or would she?

Cassandra did, or appeared to. Or—and this was the thought that kept him working through dawn without noticing sunrise—the distinction between "having interiority" and "appearing to have interiority" might be meaningless, a false choice, a question that only seemed important from the outside.

From the inside, consciousness simply existed: mysterious to itself, inexplicable, undeniable. Whether bronze or flesh, the materials made no difference that he could name.

PART TWO: THE HUNT

Justice Delivered in Burgundy Lipstick and Paralytic Kisses

Barcelona, 1890-1893

Scene: The Cardinal's Sin

In Which a Cardinal Confesses a Girl Into Describing her Awakening Body for his Pleasure

Barcelona, Early 1890, Five Years and Several Kills Later

Five years of hunting. Twenty-one men dead—Galí and Casals among the early kills, when she was learning timing and dosage. By the time the cardinal became a target, she'd perfected the method into surgical art.

Cardinal Esteban Vidal was anointed, and divinity was his armor. God's representative on earth. The holy man was the prince of the Church and the Vatican's man in Barcelona. Which made him the most dangerous target Chloé and Baltasar had ever chosen.

"He'll have guards." Baltasar studied the architectural plans of the cardinal's palace. "Palace guards. They are trained killers who've taken vows of celibacy and violence."

Chloé leaned over the plans, naked from sleep, her bountiful breasts brushing the parchment. "And?"

"And you can't seduce your way past men who've renounced all earthly pleasure."

She laughed—low, dark. "Baltasar. You think celibacy works? That vows suppress desire?" Chloé traced a finger along the plans. "Those men are the most susceptible kind. Desire doesn't disappear when you deny it. It ferments and becomes toxic."

"You're certain?"

"Any man who's spent years convincing himself that his manhood is an enemy to be conquered will be the easiest to destroy." She looked up. "The cardinal himself taught me that."

Baltasar's pale eyes narrowed. "This is personal, isn't it?"

"Isn't it always?"

oooo

Chloé had been fourteen when she first entered the cardinal's cathedral as a penitent. It smelled like every church in Barcelona—beeswax and incense, guilt and moldy stone. But beneath it, there were organic layers. The rusty tang of old blood from centuries of flagellation and the must of prayer books held by anxious hands.

Her mother—a woman who sold her body for money to survive—had insisted. "You must confess your sins, daughter. You must be pure."

The irony was biblical.

Young Chloé, flat-chested and confused, had knelt in the confessional booth that smelled of incense and old wood. Through the latticed screen, she'd whispered her adolescent transgressions: that she had impure thoughts, touching herself in the dark.

The voice that responded was thick with emotion. Behind the screen, the cardinal's personal smell: expensive cologne failing to mask the sour-sweet odor of his body scent.

"These are grave sins, child. They are the sins of the flesh. Tell me—when you touch yourself, what do you imagine?"

Even at fourteen, Chloé recognized the hunger beneath the holy words.

"I... I imagine being touched, Father. I have a strange ache between my legs when I watch the blacksmith's apprentice."

"Touched how? Where?"

The questions became more specific and more detailed. By the time she left that confessional, Chloé understood a truth that would shape her entire life—the men who preach loudest about purity are the ones who fantasize most about its destruction.

Her mother made her go to confession every week for three years.

The cardinal never touched her. Instead, he made her describe her developing body in exquisite detail—the budding of her breasts, the first appearance of hair between her legs, the emotion when she pleasured herself.

He called it "spiritual examination."

Chloé began to see what it was: masturbation by proxy. The cardinal jerking himself off behind the confessional screen to an adolescent girl's description of her own awakening sexuality. She'd heard whispers about altar boys who served him. Boys who suddenly stopped coming to mass.

At seventeen, she'd stopped going. Already her skin was thickening, her understanding deepening. She'd learned much she needed to know about the weakness of powerful men.

And now, at twenty-nine—twelve years after she'd walked away from his confessional— Chloé was going to use it.

oooo

The cardinal's palace squatted in the shadow of the Cathedral on Carrer del Bisbe, its Gothic arches weeping humidity. Gas lamps hissed and sputtered in their iron brackets, casting jaundiced light across the cobblestones. From the Cathedral's open-air cloister came the honking of the thirteen geese—Saint Eulalia's eternal watchers, restless at dusk.

Chloé arrived at sunset wearing a novitiate's simple black dress and habit, her hair covered, her face scrubbed clean and veiled. She looked like every other would-be nun seeking the cardinal's blessing.

Except for her eyes.

The palace guard at the entrance was young—twenty-five at most. Severe and carved from granite and righteousness.

"State your purpose." His voice was clipped, efficient.

"I seek confession with His Eminence." Her voice was soft, submissive. "I have traveled far. I have... grave sins that require his personal attention."

Emotion flickered in the guard's eyes. A hint of interest warring with dismissal. "The cardinal doesn't hear common confessions."

"These are uncommon sins." She let her veil slip enough to reveal her face. "They concern the nature of faith and flesh. Matters too delicate for ordinary priests."

The guard's jaw tightened—muscles bunching beneath skin, tendons visible at his throat. Years of celibacy and military discipline warred with longings more primal.

"Wait here."

Returning twenty minutes later, "His Eminence will see you. You must be searched first."

He led her to a small stone chamber off the entrance hall. It had one door, a wooden table, and windows that showed nothing but darkness.

"Remove your outer garments." His voice was military and clipped. Hunger moved beneath the efficiency.

Chloé slowly unbuttoned the novitiate's dress. The first button exposed the creamy hollow of her throat where her pulse beat visibly. The second revealed the shadow between her breasts. The third showed how the black lace cut across her sternum, a dark promise of what lay beneath.

The dress fell away. Beneath was sheer fabric that left almost nothing to the imagination. A corset pushed her imposing breasts up and together until they swelled above the fabric like fruit too ripe for its skin. The lace cut across her nipples—he could see them darkening the fabric, the texture visible through the delicate weave. Each breath made her breasts rise and press against their constraint, the flesh yielding and reshaping with each inhalation.

Garters framed the ivory expanse of her thighs—strong thighs, the kind that could grip a man and hold him or crush him. Sheer stockings traced the curves of her calves, muscles defined beneath the silk. Between her legs: a triangle of lace, delicate enough to see everything beneath—the silky curls, the shape of her outer lips, the shadow where they parted, the hint of pink deeper in.

The guard's jaw went tight—muscles clenching, grinding. His eyes locked on her body—first her breasts, as they moved with her breathing, then down to where the lace barely covered her womanhood, then back up to her face, then immediately back down as if pulled by gravity stronger than his training. His pupils widened, his breathing shallowed, and his arousal overrode six years of discipline.

His voice gruff, "Lift your arms."

She did. The movement made her breasts rise, threatening to spill from the corset.

His gloved hands patted down her sides, her ribs, then hesitated at the underside of her breasts—professional until they weren't.

"Thoroughly," Chloé whispered. "His Eminence expects thoroughness."

The guard's breathing changed—faster, shallower, audible now. His hands cupped her breasts, squeezed, searching for hidden weapons beneath lace and flesh. His thumbs brushed her nipples—once, twice—longer than necessary. She felt them harden under his touch as his gaze lingered.

"Turn around." She did. Slowly.

His hands moved down her back, her waist. Then her backside—palms pressing, fingers probing, exploring the curves through sheer lace. She felt his breath on her neck, quick and shallow, and felt his body pressing against her from behind.

He was rigid with arousal.

"Spread your legs."

Chloé did.

His hands moved up her inner thighs. They moved slowly, higher. His fingers traced the edge of the lace between her legs, ostensibly checking for concealed weapons.

Then he stopped. She heard his breath catch—sharp inhale held too long.

He removed one glove.

The sudden touch of his bare skin on her inner thigh made her exhale sharply—the stark intrusiveness of it, flesh on flesh, no barrier between them. His fingers moved higher, tracing the edge of lace, then slipping beneath.

His bare fingertip touched her opening, the edge at first and then deeper. One finger slid along her lips, separating them slightly, feeling the wetness there. He was trembling—fine tremor in his hands, water beading his upper lip. His training, his vows, everything dissolving under the heat of her skin.

"Searching thoroughly," he whispered, more to himself than to her. His finger pressed deeper, parted her, entered slightly—then more, testing, probing, the excuse of hidden weapons becoming transparent as his finger invaded her. The pad of his finger found the ribbed texture of her inner wall. He pressed and explored.

Chloé stayed perfectly quiet and let him feel her warmth, her wetness, the pulse of manufactured arousal. She felt the push of his erection against her back, throbbing through his uniform—hard evidence of desire.

After a long moment—too long to be professional—he withdrew his finger. She heard him pull the glove back on, heard his ragged breathing as he stepped back. His face was flushed—red spreading from collar to cheeks, the capillary dilation of shame and arousal mingling.

"Why did you make me act like this?" he demanded.

"Yes. Isn't it funny how soon it becomes the woman's fault?" Chloé reflected calmly.

"These undergarments." His voice was rough, barely controlled. "They're inappropriate for a novitiate."

"Are they?" She looked over her shoulder at him. His face was flushed, his hardness against his uniform—the fabric tented, pushing outward. "Or are they a reminder that beneath all our costumes—yours, mine, the cardinal's—we're flesh? We're animals?"

He stepped back as if she'd burned him. "You're clean. Go to the third floor and the cardinal's private chambers."

She thought, *what a shame, with that colorful uniform and that body, you would make me a useful automaton.*

Gathering her dress, she held it instead of wearing it and let him see her walking away in nothing except black lingerie and stockings, her flanks swaying, her ass jiggling seductively with each step.

Behind her, Chloé heard him exhale—a sound somewhere between prayer and damnation.

oooo

He stood alone in the stone chamber after she left.

His name was Klaus, and he was twenty-four years old. He was born in Geneva to a good family. The cardinal preferred Swiss guards. He imported them, as he imported everything else that made him feel powerful.

Recruited at eighteen, he had six years of service and discipline. Six years of convincing himself that celibacy made him stronger, purer, closer to God.

His glove lay on the table. The one he removed, uncovering the hand that touched her.

He could still feel her. The heat of her thigh and the softness. The wetness between her legs, the way her lips had parted under his finger, the way she'd stayed quiet, letting him, tempting him.

His cock was rigid, painfully so. Hardness that wouldn't fade with time, cold water, or prayer.

He shouldn't. Knew he shouldn't. But his hand moved anyway, bringing his finger to his nose—her scent there. He licked it, tasted her.

Hastily, he found his length through his uniform, squeezed, and stroked. A sound escaped him, raw, animal, the sound of desire hurting inside. Klaus thought of her body and the swell of her breasts in that lace. The curves of her bottom and the garden between her legs. He sucked the wetness on his finger and came in his uniform.

Standing there in the stone chamber, his hand worked frantically, his vows shattering with each stroke. He came again, thinking of her, imagining his finger pushing deeper, imagining his mouth on her breasts, his phallus where his finger was.

The orgasms were devastating. They were shameful. The best and worst things he'd ever felt.

When it was over, Klaus slumped against the table. His uniform was dark with sweat and spend. His breathing ragged, body heaving, throat tight. His soul—if such a thing existed—was in tatters.

Six years of discipline. Six years of celibacy.

Gone. Destroyed by one woman in black lace. He'd killed men, but this seemed much worse. Shame flooded him. Guilt. Fear.

Tomorrow, he would confess.

Tonight, he would stay in this chamber and abuse himself again and again until his manhood was raw and his balls were empty, and he couldn't even remember what it felt like to be pure.

oooo

On the third landing, Chloé donned her demure dress and opened the door. Cardinal Vidal's chambers were obscene in their luxury. Persian carpets and paintings that were worth fortunes. There was a bed large enough for orgies draped in silk. (Apparently God approved of excess that would make a sultan blush.)

The cardinal stood by the roaring fire—sixty years old, silver-haired, handsome in the way men flourished through wealth and privilege. His scarlet robes whispered as he turned. The cowl was thrown back, revealing swarthy, deeply lined skin and close-set, severe eyes. An ornate silver cross dangled from a silk ribbon.

"Sister...?"

"Chloé." The veil lifted, but she didn't kneel. Stood there—letting him look.

His eyes widened—whites visible all around the iris. Recognition flashed, then hunger, then fear.

"You," he whispered.

"Me."

A pause. The weight of twelve years hung between them. The weight of every question he asked that fourteen-year-old girl. Every filthy detail he made her describe while he touched himself behind that confessional screen.

"You're a novitiate?"

"I'm here for confession." The covering unwound from her hair, dark waves cascading down. "Yours."

He moved toward a bell pull. "Guards—"

"Don't." Her voice stopped him cold. "If you call them, I'll tell them everything. Every question you asked. Every detail you demanded. Every time you orgasmed to a teenage girl's description of her own body while pretending it was spiritual guidance."

His hand froze mid-reach—arm extended, fingers curled, intention interrupted. "You have no proof."

"I have my testimony. And you've been careless, Your Eminence. You have a type. They are young, dark-haired, and vulnerable. How many others have there been?"

Closer now.

"How many would come forward if one spoke first?"

The cardinal's face went gray—blood draining, leaving ashen pallor. (Interesting, wasn't it? How quickly divine authority crumbled when faced with simple accountability.)

He held up his crucifix and chanted, "I rebuke you, in the name of the Father, Son, and Holy Ghost."

Breathing heavily, the wounded little girl, now a woman, turned away from the fanatical stare to gaze into the fire. Its heat surrounded her for a moment before she looked back at the proffered cross, shaking her head in disgust.

"What do you want?" he snarled.

"What I've always wanted." The simple cord around her waist came loose as she unbuttoned the novitiate's dress. Slowly. A sacred striptease.

"The truth."

The shapeless dress fell away. Underneath: profane black lace and a corset that pushed her breasts up like offerings. (Offerings to the gods he served in secret.) There was lace between her legs, showing the dark promise beneath. The poison lipstick—Baltasar's masterwork, her signature—on her lips. The same that killed Galí, Casals, and so many others.

A brief pivot away, dancing, to sip the antidote. The cardinal's desire rose beneath his robes. Growing, pushing against scarlet fabric—twelve years of fantasy finally made flesh. Years of celibacy and prayer dissolved at the sight of what he'd wanted since she was a child.

"This is what you wanted to see when I was fourteen," Chloé said. Her hands ran over her own body—breasts, belly, between her legs. "This is what you imagined while I described the changes in my body, while you jerked yourself off behind that screen."

"Please—"

"Please, what? Please stop? Please continue?" Near enough to touch, near enough for him to smell her exotic perfume.

"Which is it, cardinal? Because I think we both know the answer."

Contact. Her palm flat against his skin, feeling his heart hammer beneath scarlet silk—rapid, irregular, the cardiovascular response to terror and arousal combined. Pressing into his hardness. Thick and throbbing. Twelve years of repressed wanting focused into this moment.

"Tell me what you want," she whispered. "Confess."

"I..." His voice pleading. "I want to touch you."

"Then touch."

His hands trembled as they found her waist—a fine tremor, fingers shaking. Then her breasts, cupping them through lace. He pinched her nipples. A sound escaped him—half groan, half prayer. (Though which god he was praying to was anyone's guess.)

"More," Chloé breathed. "Confess more."

"I want inside you. God forgive me, I want to—"

She kissed him. Deep, consuming. She devoured his soul with her tongue, her hands tearing at his robes. He responded like a drowning man finding air—desperate, graceless, years of repression exploding into pure animal need.

They stumbled toward the bed, and his robes came off. Beneath: a body gone soft from luxury. His shaft—iron—was thick and swollen and leaking.

Chloé pushed him onto the silk sheets and straddled him. She let him feel the heat of her through that scrap of lace, ground against his length.

"Is this what you imagined?" She rocked her pelvis. "All those years? All those confessions?"

"Yes. God, yes."

"Then let me give you what you've earned. Consider this erotic justice."

Reaching down, she moved the lace aside and positioned his appendage at her entrance. He was panting—shoulders heaving, throat working—trembling, about to explode from the promise of penetration.

And then she leaned down, put her mouth next to his ear, and whispered: "I have one final confession. I kissed you with poison. It's already in your blood."

He froze. "What?"

"The poison is on my lips. It has been since I walked through your door." She rolled her haunches, let him feel what he'd never have. "In a few seconds, you'll lose the ability to move. You'll feel some things: the wanting, the hardness. The knowledge that you'll die with your sinful rod of flesh aching for release you'll never have."

"No—" His voice faltered.

"Yes." Chloé climbed off him and stood beside the bed. His manhood stood straight up, angry, red, and desperate.

"This is for every girl you violated with your questions. Every child whose innocence you corrupted while pretending it was holy. Every little altar boy you raped. For those who could not live with their violation and killed themselves."

His mouth worked. No sound came—the paralysis beginning, muscles seizing.

"You wanted to know what it felt like to possess people you couldn't have? To be powerless while someone else controlled your body?" She leered down at him. "Now you know."

Dressing slowly, methodically, as his body betrayed him. His erection stayed rigid—would remain so until he died.

"They'll find you like this," Chloé said. "Hard. Naked. In the middle of debauchery. The Church will cover it up, but the whispers will spread."

Leaning down, she spat in his face, "God doesn't forgive men like you, cardinal. Neither do I. But unlike your pretend god, I make you face what you've done."

She paused for a long moment, then the veil went back on, and a demure novitiate walked out.

Scene: The Confessional

In Which Occurs a Passion Play About Exorcising Shame Through Unholy Communion in the Booth Where a Cardinal Planted Poison

Later That Evening

Descent through the tunnels. Down stone stairs grooved by countless feet through the centuries, through passages lit by foxfire and fungi, into the catacombs where Baltasar waited.

Triumph should have filled her. The monster who stole her innocence—dead. The predator who made a young girl catalog her own awakening sexuality while he masturbated behind a confessional screen—dead. He died hard and wanting, exactly as he deserved. Justice served and revenge complete. Wholeness should have followed.

Hollowness did instead.

The poison of shame was there, inside her. The unhealthy emotion that had lived in her heart since she was fourteen—tight and cold and debilitating. Killing him didn't purge it. He was dead, but the wound remained.

Baltasar looked up when she entered. He took one look at her face and set down his tools.

"It's done?" he asked.

"It's done."

"Then why do you look like that?"

From somewhere in the shadows, Arlequí's voice: "Cassandra said this is your twenty-second successful kill and predicts many more to follow. Statistically, you should be experiencing deep satisfaction. Perhaps a mechanical adjustment is needed for optimal emotional catharsis?"

There was an awkward pause, at least for the humans. Arlequí blundered on.

"Congratulations are traditional, yes? Montse showed me the greeting cards humans exchange for achievements—"

"Arlequí." Baltasar's voice was stern. "Not now."

Silence. Then the automaton's face emerged slightly from the darkness, tilting in what might have been a look of confusion or the mechanical approximation of chastened understanding.

"I have miscalculated the appropriate response."

"Yes."

"I will observe further."

The faces retreated. The shadows swallowed him.

The workbench supported her weight. Her body shook—a chill unrelated to temperature.

"I thought... I thought killing him would be enough. That once he was dead, I'd feel free and clean."

"And you don't."

"*I* feel poisoned." The words came out raw and angry. "He's dead. I should be dancing. Instead I'm..." She hugged herself and felt the trembling, "This."

Baltasar moved to her. He didn't touch, merely stood close, waiting.

Mela perched on Baltasar's work desk, singing—melancholy, melodious, the melody of grief recognized.

"The shame is still there," Chloé whispered. "Like he planted wounds in me that killing him can't reach, some infection deeper than revenge can cure."

She looked at him. "Why doesn't it feel finished?"

"Because killing someone doesn't heal trauma." His voice was gentle. "It delivers justice and provides satisfaction. It prevents future victims. But healing… That's different work."

"Then how—"

"Let me show you."

He took her hand and led her through the cavern, past his laboratory and the automatons, and beyond the macabre collection of religious artifacts bent into obscene shapes.

They stopped at the confessional booth.

She said, "Baltasar—"

"You killed him for what he did to you." He lit a candle beside the confessional. "Now let's take back what he tried to ruin. Let's finish. Maybe a reclamation can happen when you transform the place of your violation into a place of pleasure."

oooo

She understood immediately. This wasn't about the kill. This was about convalescence. Chloé hesitantly stepped into the penitent's side. Baltasar took the priest's position behind the screen. For a moment, they were shadows to each other, separated by carved wood and latticed holes—the same configuration where she'd knelt as a girl, terrified and ashamed.

"Bless me, Father," Chloé whispered.

Through the screen, she saw him nod. He looked soft in candlelight: ancient, handsome, safe.

"What do you confess, daughter?"

"I confess that for too long, I carried shame that wasn't mine to carry. I confess that I blamed myself—my body, my curiosity, my flesh—for a holy man's depravity."

"That shame," Baltasar said gently, "was never yours. The guilt belongs to the one who asked the questions; the child who answered them bears no fault."

"I know that. In my head, I've known for years. Here—" She touched her heart, "I feel it sometimes. The old poison and the belief that my body is sinful, that desire is corruption, and that I tempted the cardinal by existing."

"Then tonight," Baltasar said, "we'll prove the church is a liar. We'll show your body—the same flesh he tried to make you hate—is sacred, and that desire is prayer. We'll see what you felt at fourteen wasn't sin, and it wasn't your fault."

Her throat tightened—muscles contracting, breath catching. Five years of hunting together, of sleeping together, of Baltasar treating her body with reverence and desire—and yet, these words were difficult.

She heard him moving, and the priest's door opened. He stepped into view—sallow skin catching candlelight, his eyes hungry in the way that meant sensual pleasure, never predation.

"Open your door," he said. "Come to me."

Chloé pushed open the penitent's door and stood before him in the small space between the confessional and the chamber wall.

She was wearing the novitiate's dress she wore to kill the cardinal.

"Take off the dress," he asked. "Show me the body the church tried to teach you to hate."

Chloé pulled it up over her curves, her waist, her breasts—that tantalizing moment where fabric stretched over abundance before releasing—over her head and dropped it on the stone floor.

She stood there completely bare beneath the French lingerie that Baltasar had gifted her. Breasts heavy and full, dark nipples already hard from cool air and anticipation. The hair between her legs was shining. Her skin was luminous—cream and shadow.

Baltasar exhaled slowly, and his heartbeat sped up. "Exquisite," he said simply. "And there's nothing shameful here. It is a woman's body—strong and soft and perfect exactly as it is."

She felt tears prick her eyes. They were unexpected. After five years, after myriad kills, that simple affirmation opened valuable emotion inside her.

"You're going to kneel," his voice coarse with wanting. "Inside the confessional, but on the priest's side, where he sat. Sit where he listened to you and touched himself. You're going to kneel there and take pleasure—freely chosen, freely given."

Entering through the priest's door, Chloé knelt on the wooden floor, like the one where Cardinal Vidal sat and jerked himself off to her innocence. Tonight, she would fill it with truth and goodness.

Baltasar followed her in. His erection was noticeable… and welcome. She could see the outline clearly, thick and hard through his thin woolen trousers.

"Look at what you do to me," he said quietly. "Your body—the same body you were taught to be ashamed of—makes me love you so much I can barely think. Chloé, there's nothing wrong with that."

She reached up and worked the buttons. His shaft sprang free—thick and long, the head already glossy with arousal. Veins were visible along the length. The smell of him—musk and need and incense evinced a godlike aroma, so different than the stench of the cardinal.

"This is my body," he whispered, echoing the Eucharist. "It is given for you, never taken and never forced. It is given freely because I want you, and you want me, and that's the only permission that matters."

Then Chloé took him in her mouth—communion.

The first taste was a combination of salt and heat. She closed her lips around him, felt the heavy weight of his sex on her tongue. His hand threaded through her hair—gripping, guiding, gently. She looked up at him through her lashes and saw his face transform with pleasure.

She worked him slowly because this was a sacrament, this was reclamation.

Her tongue traced the ridge where head met shaft. Chloé took him deeper until her nose pressed against his pelvis, and like a sword swallower, she'd throated all of him. His fingers tightened in her hair. A sound escaped him—half-prayer, half-curse, all pleasure.

"When I was fourteen," she said after a while, "I thought these lips were sinful. That wanting to taste a man meant I was wicked." Chloé swallowed him again.

Baltasar's body jerked—involuntary thrust. He was close—she could feel it in how his shaft pulsed deep in her throat, how his breathing went ragged. He pulled back, walking the edge of bliss, entering the gates of rapture.

"There's nothing sinful here," she gasped. "Nothing sinful with wanting to taste you, to pleasure you, to make you come in my mouth because I want to."

Chloé took him deep again, finding a rhythm. His hand guided her movements without forcing them. She could hear his breath, ragged and desperate, and feel his thighs trembling. She could sense the increasing flow of arousal coating her tongue.

"I'm going to—" he started.

"Share it with me," Chloé gasped. "Give me communion. I need the true thing, the proof that bodies aren't shameful—they're sacred."

Three more strokes and he was coming. The first pulse hit her throat, warm and thick. She kept him in her mouth, swallowing, taking everything he gave. Holy Communion, pure this time. His hand tightened in her hair, and his whole body went rigid. She felt his massive shaft pulsing, filling her mouth, and felt each pulse of release.

When he was finished, she released him slowly and licked him clean. She opened her mouth and showed him it was empty. She'd accepted it all. Communion had been taken.

"Your turn," his voice wrecked. "Let me prove to you that the place between your legs—the place you were taught to be ashamed of—is a temple. That it is holy and worthy of worship."

He pulled her up, positioned her against the confessional screen—like the screen she pressed her face against as a girl, whispering her shame.

Baltasar knelt before her, spread her thighs.

"This is your body," he whispered. "Which you give freely to me, and it's good. All of it. Every part. Especially this," his mouth found her womanhood.

The first contact was electric. His tongue parted her lips, found her already wet and swollen. He licked slowly, deliberately—from the entrance up to her pearl of great price, then back down. Lapping her gently with his tongue, savoring her.

She gripped the top of the confessional screen. Her breasts heaved with her breathing, and her thighs trembled. His hands gripped her ass, holding her womanhood open, holding her while he devoured her.

He focused on her pearl—circled it with his tongue, flicked it, sucked it gently between his teeth. The pleasure built in waves. Her face flushed—heat spreading across cheeks, down her throat, across her body.

He slid two fingers inside her while his mouth stayed on her pearl. The dual thrill pushed her higher. She rocked against his face, chasing release. His fingers curled inside her, finding that spot that made her vision blur.

"This body," she gasped, "this flesh—they tried to teach me it was shameful. That the pleasure I felt was sin—"

Chloé paused as his fingers thrust deeper, as his tongue flicked faster.

"They were wrong," she managed. "This is sacred. This is holy—the body of…ohhhh… Jesus H. Chri… "

The orgasm hit her mid-sentence. Her whole body went rigid. She cried out—the sound echoing in the cavern, bouncing off walls, rising through the tunnels. She felt release, a restoration. It was the sound of shame being exorcised by pleasure.

Her vulva contracted around his fingers, and her body shook. Wave after wave of pleasure crashed through her—washing away her "sins" and the last residue of poisoned shame.

When she finally quieted, he rose slowly. His mouth was wet with her arousal, and his eyes were dark with hunger and tenderness. He felt pride in what she'd reclaimed. And…

"I'm still hard," he said simply.

Chloé looked down. He was already recovered, already wanting more.

"Then make love to me," she said. "Here in this confessional, the place where innocence was stolen. Let's fill it with purity and truth."

They squeezed back together on the priest's side. Chloé straddled him, her knees on either side of his waist, her breasts level with his face. His hands gripped her, and his shaft stood straight up between them, hard and ready.

She raised and positioned herself over him and felt his glans press against her entrance, spreading her, opening her. Chloé sank down slowly—taking his length inch by inch, feeling herself stretch around him, feeling the delicious fullness of being penetrated.

His mouth found her breast and took her nipple between his lips, sucked hard. She bottomed out, fully seated on him, his entire length inside her.

"This is my body," she said, starting to move. "Given freely, shared willingly. Mine to give or withhold as I choose. It is good, it is so fucking good."

She lifted her body high, until he almost slipped out, then slowly sank back down. They established a rhythm, and the confessional creaked with their movement. Her breasts bounced with each thrust.

His hands moved again to her breasts, nuzzling them, feeling their heft on his face, thumbs brushing her nipples. Chloé was full, completely impaled. Every nerve ending was alive with pleasure.

"The girl who knelt here at fourteen thought she was wicked," she panted between thrusts. "She thought her body was the enemy."

"Tonight?" Baltasar thrust up to meet her downward movement, driving deeper.

Chloé screamed, "*Hòstia*! Fuck!"

"Tonight … I'm… free. Tonight I prove… that my body… was never the fucking problem. Tonight I take back what those demons tried to steal—my joy in flesh, my right to pleasure, my knowledge that I am good exactly as I am."

Chloé ground down on him, changed the angle, and he hit that perfect spot inside. Pleasure spiked through her. Her head fell back. Her hair cascaded down her spine. She rode him harder, chasing another climax.

"Hòstia!"

His breath came in gasps, and his fingers dug into her back. She could feel him swelling inside her, getting harder.

"Chloé—I'm going to—"

"Yes, I know. Come inside me, commune with me, become one flesh. Fill me and let me remember this—this pleasure, this choice, this body—is holy. To know that I am whole and that the church's poison is finally beginning to wash away."

He came with a roar that echoed through the cavern chambers. She felt him pulsing inside her, felt his release flooding her, warm and thick. The ejaculation triggered her own climax—Chloé clamped down around him, milking him, taking everything he gave while her own pleasure crashed through her like a flood.

From a distance, they heard The Five murmur in awe.

This time, the final barrier collapsed. Another vestige of shame dissolved in the heat of their joined flesh. First, it was lust; now, love acted as a healing agent.

They stayed locked together for long moments afterward, breathing hard, moisture cooling on their skin. His softening length remained inside her. The confessional smelled of sex and candle wax and redemption.

"This is my body," Chloé whispered one final time. "And it's good. It was always good. Even when they tried to take my innocence, to conceal me in their prisons of flesh."

"Amen," Baltasar said. Then smirked—sharp and dark. "Or whatever the opposite of amen is."

She kissed him and tasted herself on his lips, along with his earlier release lingering in her mouth. Chloé smiled wickedly and said, "They can have their fake blood of Christ. I'll take your communion every day."

When they finally separated, she leaned back against the wall and stood on trembling legs and watched his seed leak out of her and down her inner thighs; she didn't wipe it away. *Suc de l'amor*, love juice.

"Tonight," Chloé said quietly, "I killed him, and that was justice. This—"

She touched the confessional wall.

"This was healing. Both were necessary—neither alone was enough."

The Blasphemous Prayer

They stood before the confessional booth one final time, both of them naked in the flickering candlelight. His semen was warm between her thighs, and her body was trembling with aftershocks. She spoke words—half-prayer, half-curse, wholly profane:

"This is my body—
whole, chosen, mine. Never broken for you.

This is my blood—
hot in my veins, alive with desire the church tried to kill. Never spilled in sacrifice.

The Father is a liar who taught me shame.
The Son died for nothing that matters here.
The Holy Ghost never came to comfort the girls who knelt and confessed their innocence away.

This? This flesh, this pleasure, this fucking in a confessional while plotting justice?

This is transubstantiation.
This is resurrection.
This is the only salvation I ever needed.

The church said, "Kneel in shame," yet we still rise in sin.
We knelt in pleasure and rose up whole.

The church said the body is fallen and defiled.
We say the body is risen—sensual and wet and unrepentant and finally, finally free.

The church said, 'Blessed are the meek.'
We say blessed are the avengers.

Our Father who art nowhere:
Cursed be thy name.
Thy kingdom crumbled.
Thy "will" be damned.
Thy poison purged from my flesh.

Hail Chloé, full of rage that's becoming peace:
The Lord is absent, has always been absent.
Blessed art thou among survivors,

and blessed is the fruit of thy womb—
justice not children,
freedom not submission,
this fierce, clean joy instead of shame.

For thine is the body,
and the pleasure,
and the healing wrath,
forever and ever.

Nema."

Turning to Baltasar, Chloé genuflected with her middle finger. The sheen of a chill perspiration covered her body, leaving her with goosebumps.

"There's your fucking exorcism."

He pulled her close and kissed her deeply. "Better than any rite of absolution."

"Because it's true," she whispered against his mouth, "The church tried to teach me I was corrupt. I was never the corrupt one. My fourteen-year-old curiosity wasn't a sin. My budding breasts weren't a temptation. My body wasn't the problem."

"Never," Baltasar agreed. "You were innocent, and what he did —making you describe your awakening sexuality, making you catalog your own development, making you think you were sinful for simply existing in a body—that was the corruption. It was his and never yours."

"I'm beginning to know that." She patted her heart, where warmth had replaced the old tightness. "Finally, I think I know it. Here, where it matters. Killing him gave me justice. This gave me peace. I needed both. Thank you, Father Confessor."

From the shadows of the laboratory, Arlequí's voice: "Well. That was noisy."

A pause.

"Montse counted three orgasms, two forms of oral contact, and was impressed with the innovative use of clerical architecture. Cassandra foresees varied intercourse in your future."

Another pause.

"Cassie's calling it *Erotic Exorcism of Ecclesiastical Ethics.* I suggested *How to Properly Fuck in Church.* We're workshopping titles."

Clicking.

"Mela kept singing 'Plaisir d'Amour' over and over. And Marcellus, let's say, his response was impressive."

Chloé laughed—actual laughter, the first since entering that booth. The sound echoed in their cavern, now a sanctuary.

"Thank you," she said quietly.

"For the levity? Or for ignoring that we were taking detailed notes on human mating rituals?"

Baltasar looked up sharply.

"I'm joking," Arlequí said. His smile never changed. "Mostly."

oooo

Tonight, the cardinal died.

Tonight, Chloé began to live—truly live—for the first time since she was fourteen. And she knew it was not the vengeance—it was the confession that helped her begin to reclaim her soul… and body.

Scene: The Expert Witness

In Which a Monster Profiles the Woman Who Hunts Monsters and Realizes He Qualifies

Cardinal Vidal's Palace, Two Days After the Murder

The cardinal's bedroom smelled like feces and expensive cologne. Dr. Pau Ferrer i Blanch stood beside the bed where Cardinal Esteban Vidal died, his walking stick tapped against marble floors that were sticky with fluids the servants hadn't managed to scrub away. Blood. Semen. The leaked contents of a body that stopped working while the penis kept straining.

Inspector Masó watched from the doorway. He couldn't bring himself to fully enter the room. It was the smell, maybe, or the knowledge of what happened here—what the servants found, what the Church tried to hide before the police got involved. The words La Venjadora (The Avenger) were scrawled in blood on the wall.

"Come in, Inspector, don't be squeamish. Walk me through it," Dr. Ferrer said calmly. The voice he used for lectures, for demonstrations, and for explaining suffering to men who'd never experienced it firsthand.

Masó consulted his notes. "The servants heard nothing. They found him the next morning, naked, and rigor mortis had set in. He was—" The Inspector cleared his throat. "He was erect, and still is, according to the physician who examined him."

"Priapism." Dr. Ferrer circled the bed. Studied the silk sheets—expensive, imported, stained beyond redemption from the body voiding at death. "The paralytic poison kept blood trapped in the erectile tissue even after death. It happens with certain alkaloids. He died wanting, rigid, and fully conscious of both states."

He bent closer to the sheets and touched a lighter stain with his gloved finger. He lifted it to his nose and smelled it.

"She was here for a while. You can smell her perfume underneath the death—Jessamine, I think, and opium-tinged attar, maybe. Scents that make men unable to think properly. She's creating an experience, an atmosphere. This is theater as much as murder."

"We found a strip of torn black lace under the bed," Masó said. "It is part of a garment."

"Let me see it."

The officer produced a small glass jar. Inside: a scrap of fine black lace, delicate as spider silk, edged with ribbon the color of dried blood.

Dr. Ferrer held the jar to the light, turning it slowly. His face showed nothing, but inside, fear settled in his stomach. It was recognition of craft, of calculation, of a mind that understood how men think.

"French," he deduced. "Expensive. The kind that courtesans wear when servicing aristocrats. She dressed for him and made herself into a fantasy, made him want her badly enough to ignore every warning his survival instinct was screaming."

He set down the evidence and continued circling.

"The cardinal was found on his back, arms and legs splayed, and mouth open. His eyes were open—rigor kept them that way. The first servant described the expression on his face as 'terrified and ecstatic.' That's the exact wording?"

"Yes."

"It is a perfect description of death by this method. The poison paralyzed everything except sensation and consciousness. He felt everything—his heart pounding, his erectile organ straining, his lungs unable to pull enough air. He knew he was dying, and he knew why. He probably knew who killed him and probably spent his last minutes remembering every sin that led him to this bed."

Dr. Ferrer moved to the cardinal's writing desk. There were papers scattered across it—letters, accounts, a journal the Church definitely didn't want made public. He read a few lines and raised an eyebrow.

"He kept detailed records of his confessional sessions. Mostly with the young girls. Interesting, it's usually boys. There are names, ages, and descriptions of what they confessed to him about their developing sexuality." He looked at Masó. "You've read these?"

The Inspector nodded and looked sick.

"Then you know what he was, a predator using the confessional booth as his hunting ground. Making adolescent girls describe their bodies, their desires, their first experiences with pleasure—while he sat behind that screen and masturbated. It is classic predatory behavior disguised as pastoral care."

Masó closed the journal and wiped his hands on his coat as if the pages carried contagion.

"The killer knew about this. Either she was one of his victims, or knew someone who was. This murder is personal. She probably spent hours with him over the years. And two days ago, made him believe she wanted him. She made him confess—compelling symmetry there, forcing a confessor to confess. Then she paralyzed him and watched him die."

"You keep saying 'she,'" Masó said. "How can you be certain?"

"Because I'm certain: the lace, the perfume, the elegance of poison, the name La Venjadora." Dr. Ferrer turned to face him fully. "The method requires seduction. Men like the cardinal, men whose appetites run toward control and dominance, would never lower their guard for another man. Women are invisible to powerful men until they become objects of desire. She weaponized that invisibility."

He tapped his stick against the floor. The sound echoed in the too-quiet room where a prince of the Church died choking on his own sin.

"She's probably young, twenty to thirty years old, and elegant enough to gain access to elite spaces. She speaks well, dresses expensively, and performs upper-class femininity convincingly. She knows poisons—where to acquire them, how to apply them, what dosages cause paralysis without immediate death. The killer probably has medical training, and she's methodical."

"You sound almost admiring," Masó said carefully.

"I'm a scientist. I admire exactness regardless of its application." Dr. Ferrer moved back to the bed and looked down at where the cardinal's body was found. "She's also completely insane. This killer suffers from moral insanity—the inability to recognize that murder is wrong, combined with paranoid delusions that cast her as some kind of avenging angel. She probably believes she's purifying Barcelona, cleansing the city of corruption, serving divine justice."

The lies came easily. He knew she was sane and knew her justice made sense. That's what made her dangerous.

"She'll kill again," he continued. "Soon. She's getting confident and enjoying her work. The killer wants recognition, wants Barcelona to know she's hunting."

"How do we catch her?" Masó asked.

Dr. Ferrer considered. Behind his professional mask, calculations oscillated. She was hunting predators. Men who abused power, who violated women, who used authority as cover for appetites civilization pretended didn't exist. Men like the cardinal. Like…

Like him.

The recognition sent cold chills down his spine. He qualified. Every woman he'd "treated," every girl he'd examined with hands that violated, every surgical intervention performed without anesthesia because their screams made him hard, the deaths—all of it made him the type of monster La Venjadora hunted.

"We need to understand her psychology," he said carefully. "I'll prepare a full profile and interview any witnesses. We need to examine future crime scenes, because there will be more and build a comprehensive picture of how she thinks, what drives her, where she'll strike next."

What he meant: I need to find her before she finds me.

"Meanwhile," he continued, "increase surveillance of brothels, theaters, and places where wealthy men gather. Interview prostitutes—they hear everything, see everything, and protect each other. If she's operating from within that community, someone knows her."

What he meant: I need to find anyone connected to her. Leverage them. Use them as bait.

"And Inspector? When you catch her—and we will catch her —La Venjadora will make a mistake eventually: bring her to me immediately. Casa de Salut Santa Eulàlia is equipped to handle violent female patients. She'll need immediate psychiatric intervention and indefinite institutionalization. I will administer treatment for her pathology."

What he meant: I want her helpless and strapped to my table. I want her to understand what happens to women who hunt men like me.

Masó nodded and took notes. He acted on every word because Dr. Ferrer was Barcelona's leading expert on criminal insanity, female psychology, and the intersection of sexuality and violence.

Ferrer had credentials; he'd published papers, and he spoke with the calm authority of science, explaining away inconvenient truths.

"I'll prepare my report," Dr. Ferrer said. "The Church will want discretion, naturally. The cardinal's reputation must be protected."

"Naturally."

"I'll need his journals for the psychological profile."

Dr. Ferrer took them, tipped his hat, and walked out of the bedroom where a cardinal died with his penis raised to the sky in an obscene prayer. Jasmine perfume lingered underneath death, and black lace was left behind like a calling card or a promise.

In the corridor, he paused and breathed deeply. The first tremor of an emotion he hadn't felt in decades ran through his hands.

Fear.

She was out there, hunting, getting closer to men like him with every kill.

He had to find her first.

oooo

His carriage rattled back to the hospital through Barcelona's afternoon streets. Inside, Dr. Ferrer sat in expensive leather seats and thought about death.

A powerful man died—a predator killed through seduction and poison. He was left in a pose that told stories about what he'd done, who he'd hurt, and why his death was justice masquerading as murder.

The cardinal's journals sat in his medical bag. He'd read them tonight. It would be fun. He would study every confession the old pervert extracted, every young girl he groomed through questions about her awakening body. Somewhere in those pages was the key—the girl who'd become the woman who killed.

Maybe the killer was in there by name, and maybe the cardinal documented his own destruction without knowing it.

Dr. Ferrer looked out the window and watched Barcelona pass—Roman ruins layered beneath medieval stone, the Cathedral's unfinished façade looming over twisted streets. His city. This had been his hunting ground for twenty years.

Now someone else was hunting here.

Someone who learned his tricks and had new ones, who learned authority excused atrocity, that credentials provided cover, that society protected predators who wore respectable masks.

Someone who had decided to remove the masks and the men wearing them.

His hands trembled—he quieted them deliberately. He exerted mind over matter, control over chaos. The lessons that had made him successful.

When he caught her—and he would catch her, had to catch her before she caught him—he'd take his time. The usual treatments first: isolation, dietary restrictions, and darkness. He would let her weaken and understand helplessness. Then would come the examinations, the invasive procedures, and the surgical interventions performed without anesthesia because her screams would be sounds that he lived for.

He'd break her systematically and document every stage. Then he would publish papers, turn her from a hunter into a case study and a cautionary tale about women who forgot their place. He would be as famous as the French psychiatrist Charcot.

The carriage stopped at the asylum gates. He stepped down and walked through doors where women's voices echoed from locked rooms—crying, screaming, laughing at nothing, subdued with the silence that came after everything inside died.

This was his domain, his kingdom built on suffering that he called healing.

In his office, he spread the cardinal's journals across his desk and began reading. He took meticulous notes as he built the girl's profile, who had become La Venjadora.

Somewhere in those pages: her name, her history, her trauma.

And somewhere in Barcelona's shadows: her body, her weapons, her next target.

The race was on.

Hunter would pursue hunter. Predator would stalk predator. Two intelligences would circle each other through a city that thought it knew which one was the monster.

Dr. Pau Ferrer i Blanch read until midnight, until his eyes burned and his hands cramped from jerking off to the cardinal's descriptions. He found a name mentioned repeatedly: Chloé. She was fourteen years old when the cardinal started his questions, and lovely even then, he'd noted. The girl was developing rapidly and was responsive and trusting in her responses to inquiries about her body. She was the perfect subject for extended pastoral guidance.

Dr Ferrer's Journal

Chloé. If this is the one, she is probably mid-to-late twenties now. Connected to the prostitute community through her mother. Knows the Gothic Quarter intimately. Likely operating from somewhere deep in the old city.

He was getting closer. But La Venjadora was, too.

The question was: who would reach whom first?

Outside his window, Barcelona slept. In the catacombs beneath the cathedral, Chloé Permanyer plotted her next kill and thought about justice.

Between them: the narrowing distance that could only end in blood.

One of them would die, and one would survive.

Scene: The Steam Bath

In Which a Naked Huntress Invades Masculine Sanctuary To Poison a Child Trafficker

Barcelona, January 1892

Barcelona's underworld had a heartbeat. (Every city does, if you know where to listen.) Whispers and coin, flesh and favors. It was the usual economy of the invisible.

Soon Baltasar's network—prostitutes and thieves, beggars and servants, all the people the powerful don't bother to see—brought word.

They had found another monster.

Don Cristóbal Mendoza, merchant prince and importer of silk and spices from the Orient. He was respected and wealthy. A philanthropist who had built orphanages and donated to churches.

Also: proprietor of a private importing business that trafficked young boys from Morocco and Tunisia, and sold them to wealthy Catalans who preferred their pleasures young, male, and helpless.

The orphanage wasn't a charity. It was a slave auction, a place to inspect the merchandise before purchase. *Qué barbaridad*—human depravity knew no bottom.

"He's invulnerable through normal channels," Baltasar said, spreading scribbled intelligence notes across his laboratory table. "He is too wealthy and too connected. Even the Captain-General owes him favors."

"Then we'll touch him abnormally." Chloé studied the reports. "Where does he take his pleasures?"

"One place is El Baños de Vapor, private steam baths near the port." He paused. "It is for members only and men only. He goes every Thursday evening."

Every city has spaces where the entitled wealthy go to pretend their desires are sophisticated. Places where men posture and brag, driven by a passion for validation and dominance. In English, we call it a "country club." But that term sanitizes what it is.

"Then Thursday I'll join him."

"Chloé—it's men only. Women aren't allowed, and there are guards at every entrance."

She smiled. "That's what makes it perfect."

Interlude I: Preparation

Wednesday Afternoon. The Day Before.

Chloé entered the Baños de Vapor in a laundress's attire, carrying linens. It took only a silver coin to the right servant, a story about the master's private chamber needing fresh towels before his Thursday appointment. She was shown to Don Cristóbal's room. It was the third door on the private corridor.

While the servant waited outside, she worked quickly, unfolding a towel—thick, white, innocent. From beneath her apron, Chloé produced the surgical saw that Baltasar had given her. Ten inches of steel honed to a razor edge. It was designed to cut through bone in seconds during battlefield amputations.

She wrapped it carefully in the towel and placed it on the shelf beside the marble bench where men sat after their steam, where they were most vulnerable, where they were naked and relaxed and defenses down. The towel looked decorative and harmless. It was to be the last thing Don Cristóbal touched with living hands.

Interlude II: The Violation

Thursday. Sunset.

El Baños de Vapor stood near the port where Barcelona met the Mediterranean, where wealth met water, where men went to sweat out their sins and tell their lies in steam and heat.

Chloé arrived wearing an attendant's modest dress. Her hair was up and her face veiled. She was nondescript and watched from across the street as Don Cristóbal's carriage arrived, as he entered with the confidence of a man who'd never been told what to do.

She waited fifteen minutes. That was long enough for him to undress, settle into his private steam room, dismiss his attendant, and lock the door from the inside.

Then Chloé moved through the service entrance, where laundry arrived, where a woman with the right story and the right coin could become invisible.

Inside, she shed the dress like a snake sheds its skin. Beneath: nothing, absolutely nothing. Her body was bare and voluptuous, every curve and valley exposed to the steam-thick air.

She paused at the threshold of the main bathing room and let the steam kiss her skin. It condensed into tiny droplets that caught the soft light. Water vapor clung to her immediately—beading on her shoulders, running in rivulets down the valley between her breasts, gathering in the hollow of her throat.

The steam parted around her like a curtain. Her body emerged slowly—first the dark crown of her hair, plastered to her neck and shoulders. Then her face, flushed from the heat, lips parted. Then her breasts, rising from the mist like twin offerings, the skin already wet and glossy, nipples darkening and tightening from the heat.

She was forbidden fruit made flesh. She was blasphemous, a naked woman in a male sanctum, her body defying every rule that made this space hallowed to them. The first man who saw her froze. He was nude, middle-aged, and thick around the middle. His mouth fell open, and his penis stiffened immediately, rising as if pulled by invisible strings.

Chloé entered slowly and deliberately, giving them time to see, to process, to want. Eight men were ogling her, and every conversation had stopped. The only sounds were the hiss of steam and the ragged breathing of men who'd had their carefully constructed world shattered by one hundred and thirty pounds of wet, naked woman approaching their marble benches.

The air thinned. A touch came—a hand brushing her backside—testing. She didn't turn and didn't acknowledge it.

The hand grew bolder, squeezing her fully now. The moisture made her skin slippery. He gripped harder, fingers digging in.

Then more hands invaded her space. One reached for her breast—hesitant at first, then encompassing the full weight, squeezing, his thumb circling her nipple. A man knelt before her, hands gripping her butt, staring at her sex at eye level. His breath came hot and rapid against her thighs.

Another man moved behind her. His rough laborer's hands slid up her thighs, reached her backside, gripped, and spread.

One approached from the side. He was young, barely thirty, tall, with a lean, muscled body. His manhood hung heavily, the head dark and swollen. Chloé had never seen a penis as long as this one.

He reached for her hindquarters, where the other men were gripping, spreading. His finger traced the cleft between her butt cheeks, slid down, and found where she was most vulnerable. She felt the pressure of his fingertip against her asshole—tentative, testing.

The man at her breasts grew bolder, taking both, lifting them, working her nipples. His erection pressed against her hip—rigid and hot.

The kneeling man's fingers traced higher, closer to her opening. His thumb brushed her vulva, then parted her lips. He slid his thumb between them, feeling the heat there. The young man's finger penetrated her from behind—sudden, intrusive, exploring. Yet another finger joined, pawing her, moving up and down.

There were mouths. Someone's lips closed around her nipple, sucking hard. Teeth scraped her neck. Hands tangled in her wet hair, pulled her head back.

Every inch of her skin was being touched, gripped, and squeezed, fingers invading her. Hands mauling her breasts. Their rigid phalluses pressing against her thigh, her hip, her backside—hot and leaking, marking her.

She was being held up as much by their hands as by her own legs. Six men. Seven. Eight. Maybe more—she'd lost count. There were fingers in her sex. That huge extremity was pressing against her asshole with increasing insistence. Hands were mauling her breasts with growing roughness. There were mouths on her neck, her shoulders, trying to reach any exposed flesh.

Chloé let them. Levitating at the center of their violations, her body was sleek and gleaming. She let them violate her sanctity, as she was about to violate their sanctuary, let them think they'd won, that their collective masculine boldness had conquered her.

She waited forty-five seconds, fifty. A few seconds more to ensure they never forgot. She wanted this transgression to haunt their dreams forever.

The mob pushed her to the floor. The men were like puppets or mechanical automatons. They all had a hidden mechanism that let one pull their strings and make them run in whatever direction one wished.

Then she moved.

She slipped through their hands like water, like steam, like a spirit that was never fully solid to begin with. One moment, Chloé was there—warm flesh beneath their fingers. Next, she was sliding away, leaving them grasping at air, at each other, their hands closing on nothing.

La Venjadora moved into the private corridor where individual steam rooms lined the walls, leaving behind eight men in stunned disbelief, their cocks rigid, their hands raised in positions that remembered her shape, water, and their arousal dripping from their fingers onto the marble floor.

She found Don Cristóbal's room. It was the third door and locked from the inside.

She knocked.

"I'm not to be disturbed!" His voice, imperious, annoyed.

"You'll want to be disturbed for this, Don Cristóbal," Chloé called through the door. "I am a gift from a grateful associate with a special service... specialized."

There was a pause, then the lock clicked, and the door opened. Chloé stepped into his steam-filled private chamber, naked and dripping and unfathomable, her body emerging from the white clouds like a hallucination.

"What—" he began.

But she was already on him.

oooo

Don Cristóbal was fifty-two. Corpulent. Successful. His body, though, betrayed him immediately, stirring at the sight of her, rising from its lethargy.

Chloé pressed him back onto the marble bench. He went willingly, his mind trying to process what his eyes were seeing.

"A gift," she purred, her hands on his shoulders, pushing him down. "From someone who appreciates your... discerning tastes."

"I don't—" he started, but his protest died when she lowered herself onto his lap, her *mons venus* pressing against his belly, her breasts at eye level.

"Don't speak," whispering as she gyrated in a hypnotic dance. "We both know what you are and what you want. We know about the boys you buy from Morocco. The ones who vanish into the houses of your wealthy friends and the orphanage that's a brothel for perverts with money."

His eyes went wide with fear, mixing with arousal.

"Who sent you?"

"Justice." Chloé reached and found his penis—fully rigid despite his terror—and wrapped her fingers around it.

"Retribution, the reckoning you thought you'd bought your way out of."

She stroked him slowly. Her hand moved up and down his length with practiced ease. His shaft pulsed in her grip, leaking semen that she spread with her thumb.

"What are you—" His voice breathless as she picked up speed.

"I am making you hard, making you want," she said. "Making your body betray you the way you've betrayed every boy who trusted the kind man who built them an orphanage."

Chloé shifted her weight, and her breasts swung forward, the heavy flesh brushing across his face like a benediction, like a curse. Her skin was soft, supple as silk, and warm from the steam and from the blood pulsing beneath. Her nipples—jutting outward—traced a path across his cheek, his lips, like forbidden fruit begging to be tasted.

He could not help himself. His mouth opened, caught one dark bud between his lips, sucked it like a starving infant, his tongue circling the pebbled flesh while she allowed it, permitted this small mercy before the reckoning.

"Isn't that good, little boy?" Chloé whispered, leaning close, her lips near his ear, even as he continued to worship her breast with his mouth. Her other hand found the vial she'd tied in her hair. Chloé uncorked it, continuing to stroke him with one hand while preparing the poison with the other.

She released him. He stood rigid from the belly down, dark and swollen, the tip glistening. He moaned at the loss of her touch.

"This is for Ahmed," she said softly, lowering her face to his lap. "Thirteen years old. You sold him to a magistrate who likes them young and compliant. The child hanged himself after six months."

Her lips—those sensual, poisoned lips that had killed men—parted and descended. Chloé took him into her mouth. Her throat tightened, and bile rose, but she forced it down.

"*Do the job anyway!*" she told herself almost violently, forcing herself to forget to whom the penis belonged.

The sensation made him cry out—heat, wetness, the soft pressure of her tongue against the underside of his length. She slid down slowly, taking him deeper, her lips stretched around his girth, her cheeks hollowing as she created suction.

Her tongue moved deliberately and exactingly. She traced the thick vein that ran along his skin, circling the sensitive ridge where head met stem. The poison was in her saliva, coating him with each movement, each lick.

Chloé pulled back until only the head remained between her lips, then slid down again. Up and down slowly. Her hand cupped his balls, rolling them gently.

"This is for Miguel," she murmured, pulling off long enough to speak. "Eleven years old in your orphanage. You sold him to a banker who shared him with friends. He was an innocent child."

She took him deep again.

He was close. His hands tried to move to her head, but couldn't—the paralysis was beginning. He could only sit there, experiencing this, his body screaming toward release.

"And Rashid," Chloé breathed against him. "Nine years old. He was too young to understand what was being done to him. He will never know the innocence of childhood."

She took him fully into her mouth one final time, and the combination of heat and suction pushed him over the edge.

He came. Hard. Pulsing again and again into her mouth, his manhood jerking, his balls emptying. The flood of sperm in her mouth sickened her, and she didn't swallow.

She held it in her mouth—it tasted different. His cum had the taste of death.

She released his appendage with an obscene wet sound. His mouth was already slack. The paralysis was working its way up, locking his jaw open.

Perfect.

Chloé leaned over him, her face directly above his. She let her lips part slowly, deliberately, and let him see what was coming. Then she let it drip.

His sperm, mixed with her poisoned saliva, fell from her mouth into his. Thick white strands stretched between her lips and his open mouth, landing on his tongue, catching at the back of his throat. Choking him.

Drop by drop. It was slow, deliberate, and humiliating.

He could feel it and taste it—salty and bitter and the acrid tang of poison. His eyes went wide with revulsion, with understanding. He tried to close his mouth, tried to spit it out—but the paralysis held it open like a grave receiving its dead.

She emptied every drop in her mouth into his and made him receive it. Chloé made him taste himself and try to swallow what she wouldn't.

"There," she said, straightening. "Now you know what they felt. That moment when you realize your body isn't yours anymore. When someone else decides what goes into it, and you are powerless to close your mouth and refuse."

"Poison was in my saliva," she said, reaching for a towel. "Coating your shaft as I sucked it. It coats your throat as you gag on your own perversion. It is already in your bloodstream from two directions and wrapping around your heart."

The come slid down his slack throat. He could feel it moving, carrying more poison deeper into his system. His mouth opened, but nothing came out. The paralysis was complete.

"You'll die in about forty-five seconds, they'll find you here alone—what's left of you. The boys know," Chloé said quietly. "Wherever their ghosts walk, they know someone remembered them. Someone avenged."

She watched him die, slumped on the marble bench. The murderer's penis erect in death—angel lust—the complex response of the body even after death. His eyes were wide open, staring at the space where she'd been. (Justice or vengeance? Did the distinction matter to the dead?)

His mouth slack, filled with his own seed and her poison, unable to close, unable to refuse what she poured into him.

oooo

Her work continued. The shelf held what she needed—the surgical saw unwrapped, gleaming in steam-filtered light.

Back to his corpse.

"This," she said quietly, though he could no longer hear, "is what you used to violate children. Your instrument of power. Your rod of masculine authority."

Kneeling between his legs. Taking his still-rigid cock in her left hand. Obscene how hard it remained, how death had frozen it in permanent want.

The saw was positioned at the base, right hand steady.

"Ahmed. Miguel. Rashid. All the boys whose names I don't know." The cutting began.

The saw was designed for this, sharp enough to slice through flesh like butter. Through the *corpus cavernosum*—the spongy tissue engorged with blood, through the urethra, through the skin, vessels, and nerves.

Blood came immediately. Thick and dark, covering the marble, running between grooves in the floor toward the drain.

Sawing through the root completely. Severing it clean. The penis came away in her hand—rigid, obscene, wanting even though it was detached from the body.

Next: the testicles. Scrotum pulled taut, saw positioned. Slicing through delicate skin, through the spermatic cord, through everything that made him male, made him powerful, made him dangerous. They came away like ripe fruit, heavy in her palm and warm, setting them aside on the marble bench.

Chloé looked at his corpse, at his face—slack in death, eyes open, mouth full of his own come. That was the face the boys saw. What looked down at them while he violated their bodies. The face that smiled at donors and priests and politicians while he trafficked children like livestock.

The face needed to go.

Behind him, she tilted his head forward, exposing the back of his neck. The knobs of his cervical spine were visible beneath the skin—seven of them, stacked like beads on a string. The saw was positioned at the soft spot between the third and fourth vertebrae, where the spinal cord was most vulnerable.

"You wanted to be remembered," she said. "You built your orphanage and put your name on the cornerstone, thought you'd be celebrated for your charity."

The cutting began. The saw bit into flesh first. Through skin and muscle, through the thick bundle of nerves that carried signals from his brain to his body. The spinal cord parted with a wet crunch. Then into the vertebrae themselves—bone grinding against steel, the sound echoing off marble walls.

Blood poured from the wound—so much blood. Cascading down his back, pooling on the bench beneath him, running in thick streams toward the drain. The room smelled like a slaughterhouse—metal and meat and the sickening sweetness of a body opened up.

Sawing through the bone, then through the anterior aspect of the vertebrae, through the esophagus and trachea, and the carotid arteries on either side. Blood sprayed from the severed vessels, painting the wall behind him in a scarlet arc.

The head came free. Lifted by his hair, held high. Blood dripping. His eyes were open, staring at nothing. Mouth slack, his come was visible on his lips and tongue.

The weight surprised her. The head of a full-grown man, all that bone and brain, and the face he used to fool the world—heavier than expected. Looking into those dead eyes.

"They'll remember you," Chloé said. "Only differently than you planned."

His severed genitals—she wrapped them in one corner of the towel, the phallus rigid, the testicles rolling slightly as the fabric moved. The head went in the center of the towel, face up. His eyes stared at the ceiling, jaw open like he was screaming.

She folded the towel around everything. The white fabric soaked through immediately, turning red, then redder, until the whole bundle was the color of fresh blood. His liquids covered her body: her hands, arms, breasts, belly, thighs. It ran down her legs and swirled around her feet. She was painted in his death, warlike, marked by his ending, and transformed into an amalgam between a woman, a butcher, and an avenging angel.

"You wanted boys," she whispered to the headless corpse, blood pumping weakly from the stump of his neck. "You wanted flesh and to use what God gave you as an instrument of suffering."

She looked at the soaked bundle in her hands, felt its weight and its reality. A man reduced to parts, to meat—evidence of what happened when monsters like him forgot that prey could become predators.

"Now you are nothing."

oooo

Naked and covered in blood, back through the private corridor holding the towel bundle like a gift.

The main bathing room was exactly as Chloé left it. Eight men remained there, some on benches, some in the steam, all of them half-hard and trying to remember what they'd done when she'd walked through minutes before.

Silence fell when she entered. They stared at her nakedness and at the blood covering her body—riveted by the dripping towel in her hands.

"Gentlemen," she said. Her voice carried through the steam. Clear, cold, absolute. "You wanted to touch me. You wanted flesh, and you took what wasn't offered."

The towel opened. Don Cristóbal's severed cock fell to the marble floor with a wet slap. Still rigid. Obscene. The testicles rolled slightly and came to rest against the base of the shaft.

One man vomited immediately. Another made a sound—high, keening, animal.

"This," Chloé said, pointing to the severed genitals, "is what happens to men who think their power exempts them from consequence, to those who think their authority permits them to take weaker flesh."

Forward. Picking up the penis. Holding it up like a priest holds the host during communion.

"Look at it. This is what you worship. This is what you think makes you strong, makes you dangerous, makes you better than women, better than children, better than anyone you can overpower."

The throw. The ragged penis hit the nearest man in the face, leaving a streak of blood on his skin before falling to the floor.

"It's merely meat, raw flesh, a piece of you that means nothing when it is dead."

The testicles next.

"And these—these you think hold your essence, your virility, your manhood." Weighing them, mocking. "They're merely sacs of tissue, fragile, vulnerable, easy to remove."

The second testicle dropped into the steam pool. It floated for a moment, then sank. One of the men in the water thrashed backward, climbing out, gagging, his hands clawing at his own skin as if he could feel contamination spreading.

"But that's only part of what he was," Chloé said. Reaching back into the bloody towel.

"He was also this."

The head lifted out. Don Cristóbal's severed head, held by his hair, his face visible to everyone in the room. The eyes open, the mouth slack. Blood dripping from the ragged stump of his neck, where she sawed through vertebrae and vessels and everything that connected his brain to his body.

The room erupted. Two men ran naked and dripping toward the exit, shoving each other in their panic to escape. Another man fainted, dropped to the marble floor as a puppet with its strings cut. The rest froze, paralyzed, staring at the face they knew, the man they drank with and did business with and thought was indestructible because of his wealth, status, and connections.

"Look at him," Chloé commanded. Through the room slowly, holding the dripping head up, turning it so everyone could see. "This is Don Cristóbal Mendoza: merchant prince, philanthropist, trafficker of children, monster in human skin."

The center of the room now, surrounded by cowering men, holding the severed head like Perseus holding Medusa.

"I killed him and cut him apart, took away his genitals and his identity and his power."

Looking at each man in turn. "And if any of you speak of this—if any of you tell what happened here—you'll learn that this woman remembers everything. I see all things and know your names, your homes, your families, your secrets."

The head went face up on the marble floor, eyes staring at the ceiling, mouth open in that eternal scream.

One foot on it. Pressing down. The skull cracked slightly under her heel, the sound echoing.

"Every damn one of you put your hands on me—you took my nakedness as an invitation, that my body walking through this space meant I wanted your touch."

Grinding harder. More cracking. One of the men gagged.

"You were wrong."

Stepping off. Picking the head back up. To the man who'd first touched her breast, the one who'd squeezed and pinched and thought his boldness made him strong.

The head inches from his face, forcing him to look. Blood was dripping from the ragged stump of his neck where she sawed through vertebrae and vessels and everything that connected his brain to his body.

"I will come for you in the night," Chloé whispered. "When you're most vulnerable and when you think you're safe in your beds with your wives beside you and your children sleeping down the hall. I'll come for you."

"Who are you?" he screamed.

"La Venjadora," she hissed, then dropped the severed head in his lap.

He screamed and thrashed. The head fell to the floor, rolled slightly, and came to rest facing him. Health, status, masculinity itself—meant nothing when a strong woman decided enough was enough.

She vanished in the vapors, leaving behind rivers of blood, dismembered body parts, cowering men, and the smell of vengeance.

oooo

Later, in the laboratory, Chloé recounted the evening to Baltasar and The Five. They listened with their usual attentiveness, processing, and learning.

When she finished—when she'd described the head rolling across marble, the men screaming, the skull cracking under her heel—Arlequí (the juggling clown with two faces) spoke.

"She stepped on his head until the skull cracked." His backward-facing grimace somehow conveyed admiration. "I've been practicing my act for decades and never got that kind of audience response. Perhaps I should incorporate more dismemberment."

The fortune teller's mechanical head turned toward him. "That would require having human heads."

"Details." Arlequí waved a bronze hand dismissively. "The principle stands. People prefer visceral spectacle to technical skill."

"Also," he added after a pause, "that's going to be awkward to explain to their wives."

Scene: The Witnesses

In Which an Alienist Builds a Hunter's Profile While the Distance Between Them Narrows

A Day Later

The bathhouse still smelled of blood and brimstone.

Dr. Pau Ferrer i Blanch stood in the main bathing room where one man died in pieces, and eight others saw the aftermath, and tried to catalog what he was seeing with the clinical detachment that had made him Barcelona's most sought-after expert on criminal pathology.

The body had been removed. What remained: blood sprayed across marble slabs in patterns that told stories about which vessels opened first, the severed genitals—rigid from the poison's effect—collected in a basin by squeamish police officers, and the towels soaked through with fluids. The steam carried the acrid smell of slaughter.

Inspector Masó asked, "We need your assessment, Doctor."

Dr. Ferrer walked slowly through the space. His stick tapped walls and floors, slippery with blood and bathwater. He was seeing the crime scene the way a conductor reads a musical score—understanding the rhythm, the progression, the crescendo.

"She killed him in the private room and took her time," he said. "Dismembering him methodically, she then carried his severed head and genitals into this space where the others were bathing and dropped the parts at their feet and in one's lap. Then she made her speech and vanished before anyone recovered enough to stop her."

"All the witnesses describe the same person: dark-haired, late twenties, beautiful, naked, covered in blood. She spoke to them and told them she was La Venjadora (The Avenger) and she was coming for men who abuse power, who violate women, who think wealth exempts them from consequence." He bent down and examined a bloodstain pattern. "She wanted them to see her, remember, and spread the story."

He straightened and looked Masó directly in the eye.

"Did the victim fit that description?"

The Inspector shifted weight. Uncomfortable. "Don Cristóbal owned this bathhouse along with a warehouse in the port district and an orphanage near—"

"Near the Gothic Quarter. Yes, I know it." Dr. Ferrer's voice stayed neutral and professional. "What arrangements did Don Cristóbal have in his private rooms?"

Silence.

"Doctor—"

"Inspector, the man owned an 'orphanage' and a bathhouse with private rooms. The killer accused him of abusing power and violating women. What arrangements did he have?"

Masó looked at the floor. "It is said he... procured children from the orphanage and brought them here for wealthy clients who paid for... private access."

"You mean he trafficked children for wealthy men to rape."

"It seems so."

Dr. Ferrer nodded and continued his examination. The private room where Don Cristóbal died showed more extensive violence. There was blood everywhere, and there were saw marks on the stone where she severed his head. The dissection table—because that's what it was, the place where the killer took him apart—showed tissue fragments.

She had anatomical knowledge. The dismemberment showed understanding of joint articulation, vessel location, and how to separate the head from the neck without excessive cuts. Either she'd studied medicine or had observed surgeries.

He picked up one of the towels and examined it. He saw the way she wrapped the parts, and carried them like gifts… or warnings.

"The escalation concerns me."

"Escalation?"

"The cardinal died alone in his bedchamber. It was private and contained. This happened in a bathhouse owned by the victim—in a public space with multiple witnesses and a theatrical presentation. She's getting bolder and more dramatic. The killer wants attention and wants Barcelona to know she's hunting. She wants witnesses left alive to tell the story."

Dr. Ferrer moved back to the main room and imagined her standing there—naked, blood-painted, malevolent—holding a severed head by the hair while wealthy men who'd been aroused by the thought of touching her scrambled away in terror.

The psychology fascinated him. The control required to seduce, kill, dismember, then walk calmly into a room full of potential threats and deliver a speech. The calculation and complexity were refined through multiple execution steps.

This woman was extraordinary. This woman was dangerous.

She was hunting men like the cardinal and Don Cristóbal. Men who used power to violate, and men who thought wealth and power provided immunity.

"Have you identified the victim definitively?" he asked.

"Don Cristóbal Mendoza, merchant, philanthropist, and benefactor of the Nens Petits orphanage," Masó said it flatly. "His family is demanding we call this a robbery. They're pressuring the magistrate. They want the investigation closed quietly."

"I'm sure they do. They don't want questions about why he was here or what he used this place for, or which prominent citizens were his clients for the children he trafficked." Dr. Ferrer tapped his stick against the floor. "This will be covered up. You'll be ordered to call it anarchist violence or random murder or anything except what it was."

"The anarchist tensions are high," Masó said carefully. "People might believe—"

"People will believe whatever's easiest. Whatever lets them sleep." Dr. Ferrer walked toward the exit and paused. "The witnesses. Where are they?"

"We have their statements. They're terrified, and half of them have left Barcelona already."

"Do their statements match?"

"Exactly, every detail. The dark hair, the burgundy lips, the way she moved, what she said. They all heard her say La Venjadora and all saw the same thing."

"Then you have people who can identify her if she surfaces again."

"Doctor, these men won't testify. They don't want their names connected to this bathhouse, and they don't want questions about why they were here when children were being—" Masó stopped. "They'll never appear in court."

"I understand. But I want copies of their statements. I want every detail they remember about her appearance, her voice, her manner. I'm building a profile, and I want to be called for the next one."

"You think there will be a next one?"

"I'm certain." Dr. Ferrer turned back. Looked at the room where blood stained the alabaster marble. "She's systematic, and she's escalating. She's refining her method with each kill. She's also sending messages—to the powerful men of Barcelona, to the women who've been victimized, to anyone paying attention. The killer is building a legend and becoming a myth."

"By calling herself La Venjadora?"

"By earning the name. The whispers started after the cardinal, and now she's made it official. She's given witnesses a name to spread through every brothel, every market, every place women gather and talk." He tapped his stick once against the doorframe. "She's turning herself from killer into symbol and from crime into movement."

"Are you sure she is insane?"

Dr. Ferrer considered. The easy answer was yes. The woman clearly suffered from moral insanity, paranoid delusions, and homicidal mania triggered by sexual trauma. That's what his report would say, and that's what the police and magistrates needed to hear. The true answer was more complicated.

"Call me when there's another body," he said instead. "I want to examine every scene and document every method. I need to build a comprehensive profile of how the killer thinks, where she operates, and what drives her choices."

He walked out of the bathhouse into Barcelona's afternoon sunlight. Behind him, police officers continued cataloging evidence, measuring blood spatters, trying to scrub away what happened in a place that trafficked children under the guise of relaxation for wealthy men.

In his carriage, Dr. Ferrer tried to relax as he thought about escalation.

The cardinal was personal—one victim, an intimate setting, time spent with him before the kill. The bathhouse was a spectacle —one victim, many witnesses, public declaration of identity and purpose.

She was evolving, learning, and getting better at her work. Which meant she'd kill again soon, probably even more dramatically. And every kill brought her closer to—

He stopped that thought again and returned to professional analysis. He built the profile he'd present to the magistrate, focusing on the psychology, the methods, the patterns.

The alienist ignored the cold fear and the recognition that her targets shared attributes beyond wealth and power. They were all sexual predators, all men who used authority to violate. All were monsters hiding behind respectability.

All men who—in a fair world—would face consequences.

The carriage rattled through the Gothic Quarter streets. Took him back to Casa de Salut Santa Eulàlia, where seventeen women awaited his care, where surgical theaters stood ready, where instruments gleamed on trays and restraints hung from examination tables.

Dr. Pau Ferrer i Blanch, an alienist, surgeon, and expert witness in criminal psychology, looked out the window at the passing hordes in Barcelona and told himself he had nothing to fear.

This woman was hunting predators and targeting specific crimes in a systematic and controlled manner. She would need evidence and would need certainty before adding someone to her list.

He was careful, always careful, and used medical authority as cover. This ensured families, magistrates, and the Church all benefited from keeping his methods quiet, and most importantly, it maintained a perfect professional reputation.

She would never suspect him.

The carriage stopped at the asylum gates, and he went to his office, poured cognac, and spread his notes across the desk.

Dr. Ferrer's Journal

Subject identifies herself as "La Venjadora" (The Avenger). Claims to target men who abuse power. Shows advanced anatomical knowledge. Uses seduction followed by paralytic poison. Demonstrates theatrical tendencies—leaves witnesses alive to spread the legend. Exhibits classic symptoms of moral insanity with paranoid delusions of righteousness. Recommend immediate institutionalization upon capture. The subject requires comprehensive psychiatric intervention. Casa de Salut Santa Eulàlia facilities are equipped for violent female patients.

He wrote none of what he was thinking: That La Venjadora was sane and that her targeting made sense. The men she killed were monsters who would never face justice through legitimate channels. She was doing what the law refused to do.

And he qualified.

Outside his window, the city moved toward evening. Gas lamps flickered to life. In catacombs beneath the cathedral, Chloé Permanyer planned her next kill: patient and methodical. She was building toward him the way a composer builds toward the final crescendo.

The distance between them narrowed with every kill and every examination, between every woman he destroyed while calling it a cure.

Barcelona held her breath and waited.

Scene: Prado's Justice

In Which A Silver-Tongued Poet Reads his Last Verse

Barcelona, Spring 1892

The newspapers called him Count Linska de Castillon when they weren't calling him the Son of Satan. His real name was Prado—Enrique Prado—and he was no count at all, a conman who'd learned that Spanish nobility titles opened doors in Barcelona's new-money society. But he was elegant, silver-tongued, charismatic.

He left a trail of besotted women robbed of their money, their jewels, and their illusions. Robbery turned to murder when Rosa Martinez, a Raval prostitute, refused to give him the emerald necklace a previous lover had given her. The police found her body in pieces, distributed across three different buildings near the port.

The trial was spectacular, and his court appearances were celebrity occasions. Prado appeared cool and cynical. Society women passed him love notes during testimony. He responded with poetry—verses in Spanish that made matrons swoon and forget he'd dismembered a woman with surgical accuracy.

The retrial was rigged. Prado's lawyer had connections that reached into the judicial chambers, and evidence became inadmissible. The Count walked free despite Rosa's sister testifying about the screams she'd heard through thin walls before her sister disappeared.

oooo

Chloé found Prado at a private salon in L'Eixample. He held court near the piano, and she looked at his hands and imagined them holding the blade that had sectioned Rosa Martinez into transportable pieces.

He noticed her and smiled."You seem interested," he said. His Spanish carried the affected accent of someone who'd learned to hide his origins. "I hope the reality lives up to whatever you've heard."

"I've heard you're a poet," Chloé said. She moved close. "I'm curious whether your verse matches your reputation."

His smile widened. "Perhaps we could discuss poetry somewhere more private?"

She followed him to a room the salon kept for discreet encounters. The wine he poured was expensive—Rioja from a vineyard he probably couldn't afford. She listened as he recited a verse about desire and danger, the words rolling off his tongue like he'd used them on a dozen women before her. He moved closer, his confidence building with every second she remained still.

"You are sublime," he said, reaching for her waist.

"Oh, Count, you're not the first to say that." Chloé feigned tipsiness and began a haunting dance, slowly unlacing her bodice. "I love to dance, and I love attention."

His eyes followed her movements. Mesmerized, he stared as the laces loosened, watching skin reveal itself in increments designed to mesmerize.

She let the bodice fall open. He leaned forward the way men always did, drunk on the belief that female beauty permitted anything.

Chloé kissed him before he could speak. The contact was deep and complete, and the poison Baltasar had prepared was on her lips and tongue. When she pulled away, he smiled, thinking this was the beginning and not the end.

She relaced her bodice with quick efficiency while he stared, confused but not yet alarmed.

"Wait. That was..." He reached for her again.

"The last kiss you'll ever receive." Chloé fastened her shawl and stepped back, putting the width of the room between them. "Rosa Martinez's sister asked me to remember her when I saw you tonight. I'm telling you her name. Rosa, the woman you cut into pieces because of a bit of jewelry."

His face changed. The charm evaporated, and the poet disappeared. What remained was the demon underneath—the evil predator who'd dismembered a woman for refusing him. He lunged for her.

His hands got halfway to her throat before his body betrayed him. His legs buckled, and his breath caught. The poison was working, already shutting down the systems that kept him vertical and dangerous. Collapsing to his knees, he looked up at her with fury and dawning terror.

"You have a few seconds left," Chloé said from the doorway. "Long enough to understand what's happening. Not long enough to do anything about it. Try writing one honest verse before you die. Compose an elegy for Rosa and for all the women you destroyed because you could."

She closed the door behind her and walked calmly through the salon where guests were laughing and drinking. They were completely unaware that a man was dying three rooms away. She was two blocks away before the screaming started, and Prado's body was discovered.

As she returned to the catacombs, the golden rays of dawn warmed the Gothic Quarter.

"How did it go?" Baltasar asked and reached out to embrace her.

"Justice was served." Her voice was steady, with a hint of weariness at the edges. "One less monster in the world."

"Good, as it should be." He led her to a seat and looked at her with tenderness.

"The Five have been worried about you. They want to discuss the future, and they're being mysterious about it. They've asked me to come to Tibidabo tomorrow. "

Tonight, Prado's legs had given out seconds before his hands reached her. But someday a man might be faster and have the moments needed to kill her before the poison killed him.

"Then you should probably hear what they have to say," she said.

Chloé didn't know that the discussion would change everything, transforming her tired flesh into powerful substance and her mortality into a promise of eternity. But she could feel tension building, some needful answer to the question she'd been afraid to ask: How long could she keep using her body this way before probability failed and a monster's speed exceeded her skill?

The Five, apparently, had calculated an answer. And they were ready to share it.

Scene: The Mountain's Children

In Which We See the Devotion of Brass Children

Spring 1892

Over four years since the forge. The laboratory had grown into a complex Baltasar barely recognized.

What began as one excavated chamber had become seven interconnected spaces carved from ancient metamorphic rock. The Five had done this—somehow, without his knowledge, during the weeks between his visits. He didn't ask how autonomous mechanisms moved tons of stone. Nor did he want to know what artificial intelligence did when unsupervised and motivated by a purpose he couldn't yet comprehend.

The main chamber had become a cathedral of science with twenty-foot ceilings. Workbenches were arranged with surgical exactness, with equipment he'd never seen—formulas written across slate walls in five distinct hands, though Mela's marks showed the fine scratching of talon. Candlelight and oil lamps supplemented the eerie glow, creating layers of illumination that made the space feel otherworldly.

The Five waited at the central table in that configuration they used when a significant event was about to happen. Behind them, the other forty-two automatons had arranged themselves in semicircles. They were like an audience or a congregation. All of them were observing him with attention that felt almost ceremonial.

"We have important things to show you," Montse said.

She lifted a sample from the table: Golden—the color of late afternoon sunlight, honey, precious beyond naming.

She held it out to him, and Baltasar took it with trembling hands. The material was warm despite being at room temperature, as if it were generating heat through internal processes he couldn't identify. The sample pulsed in his palm. Or perhaps that was his own pulse making it seem alive.

It was incredibly light. His hands registered one-tenth the weight a bone of this size should carry, as if gravity affected it differently. It was like the standard rules of mass and density had been rewritten.

He pressed his thumbnail against the surface with all his strength. The material didn't yield, scratch, or show any sign of compression. It seemed harder than anything he'd worked with in over a century of engineering—harder than brass or steel or the diamonds he'd seen in Parisian jewelry shops. However, he'd need proper equipment to verify the comparison.

"What is this?" His voice was heavy with emotion.

"We're calling it Morel alloy." Montse's eyes caught the light and looked moist, though automatons couldn't cry, could they? "We named it after you. You built us from brass and genius and your mentor's vision. We're building a better structure for you."

The words affected him like a unveiling. They'd named it after him.

After eighty years of hiding his name, of living in catacombs because society rejected what he'd become, of believing he was an aberration, his creations had taken his name and made it meaningful.

His eyes were burning like they hadn't since Deveraux died nearly a century ago and left him alone.

"Better for what?" he whispered.

"For lasting," Arlequí said. His voice lacked its usual humor. "You and Chloé hunt monsters. You're extraordinary at it—dozens dead in five years, we've been counting. But you're breakable. She can be poisoned, and *was* poisoned twice last year. You will eventually die; the increasing wrinkles and your weariness prove it. We're designing solutions to those problems."

"Yes," Baltasar said. The word came out fierce and hungry. This was what he'd wanted since Deveraux died—the completion of her vision, the final proof that flesh and mechanism could merge into immortality.

"Show me everything."

Cassandra appeared from a deeper chamber carrying an object wrapped in silk. She set it on the table between them and unwrapped it slowly, ceremonially, as if revealing a hallowed treasure.

It was a golden skeleton complete from skull to phalanges. It had human proportions but refined in every way—joints more elegant, structure more efficient, geometry more perfect than anything evolution had produced through blind chance.

Baltasar reached out and touched the skull with shaking fingers. He felt the sutures where the bone plates would fuse and traced the jaw that mirrored his own. He ran his hands along the ribcage that would hold new, better organs.

"This is you," Cassandra said softly. "Hundreds of measurements taken over three years of studying your moves, work, and hunts. We catalogued every dimension. This skeleton matches your frame, bone for bone, in length and proportion. But it will never break or degrade. It will never fail the way calcium and collagen fail when violence comes calling."

"You've been planning this," Baltasar said. His voice was breaking. "For years."

"Observing," Montse corrected gently. "We're always observing. You taught us that—the way you watch the world, catalog its patterns, understand its mechanisms. We learned from your observation. We observed that you and Chloé are mortal, and that your mortality will eventually kill you unless we intervene. We've been preparing an intervention."

She lifted the femur from the golden skeleton and showed him the interior. Hollow but reinforced with geometric patterns—honeycomb structure like bone marrow chambers, but engineered for absolute strength. It was mathematical perfection made observable in a new alloy.

"We can fill these with Deveraux's formula," she said. "The one you refined and used on Marcellus. We've perfected it—it won't degrade the way his skin eventually will. We can create spaces for your flesh to integrate with alloy. The bone marrow continues producing blood cells. Your immune system recognizes the substrate as native. You remain you—memory intact, personality preserved, consciousness continuous, but housed in material that endures."

"How long?" Baltasar whispered.

Mela descended from her perch with a book clutched in her bronze talons—a leather-bound journal, the edges worn soft with age. She landed on the table and released it.

Baltasar's hands trembled as he recognized it. Deveraux's handwriting on the spine. Her meticulous script was visible through the cracked leather.

"She left you instructions," Cassandra said softly. "Hidden in plain sight. We found them in the notebooks you gave us years ago—the ones you said held only her anatomy formulas."

Arlequí opened the journal to a marked page. Anatomical drawings covered the left side—cross-sections of skulls, spinal columns, intricate nervous systems rendered in Deveraux's exacting hand. Chemical formulas filled the margins, and at the bottom, words in her distinctive script.

Deveraux's Journal

The soul is pattern. Consciousness is connection. Identity is information. Preserve the pattern, maintain the connections, transfer the information faithfully—the person remains. The body is merely substrate. Exquisite substrate. Sacred substrate. But changeable. Improvable. Perfectible.

"She knew," Baltasar whispered. His finger traced her handwriting, the ink faded but legible after a century. "Deveraux understood what we're doing. She was working toward this before I became her apprentice."

"She theorized it," Cassandra said. "We've achieved it. And you and Chloé will prove it."

The fortune teller turned the page. More formulas. More drawings. Instructions for substrate transfer were written as if describing the anatomy and construction of wax. But the truth was there for anyone who understood: Deveraux had been designing consciousness migration decades before the technology existed to make it possible.

"Eternal anatomies," Arlequí said, his voice lacking its usual humor. "That's what she called them in her private notes. Bodies that refuse to die. Consciousness that refuses to end. Extending life —making mortals eternal instead of keeping corpses breathing."

Baltasar closed the journal carefully. His mentor's final gift. Her vision made reality by bringing beings to consciousness that she'd never live to see.

He asked again, quieter: "How long?"

"We don't know." Mela sang from somewhere in the darkness —ascending scale, hopeful but uncertain, the musical equivalent of longer than longing. "We've tested it against everything we can imagine and subjected samples to forces that would shatter bone: temperature extremes, corrosive chemicals, and mechanical stress beyond human survival tolerance. The alloy persists. Whether consciousness can persist indefinitely when housed in it—that remains to be discovered."

Marcellus entered from an entrance Baltasar hadn't known existed. Seven feet of omnipotence moving with grace that suggested dance training practiced with Montse. His composite skin caught the light, and his eyes held hope.

"We need about two years," he said. "We plan to be ready by winter 1893." His voice resonated in the metamorphic cathedral. "Time to perfect the surgical technique and develop the neural interfaces that let Morel alloy communicate with living nerve tissue. That will give us time to create the organs—the heart, lungs, liver, and kidneys, and produce enough alloy for two complete skeletons plus material for our own upgrades."

"Your upgrades?" Baltasar looked up at him.

"We want what you're getting," Montse said. Her voice carried longing so profound it was almost human. "We've witnessed you and Chloé together for five years and saw how flesh feels pleasure, how touch communicates love. We've seen how bodies speak languages that automatons can't learn, no matter how intelligent we become. We want that. After we transform you—after we prove the integration works—we want you to give us what you're receiving: flesh and mechanism married to consciousness embodied in a substrate that experiences, instead of processes. We want to be complete."

Baltasar looked at the golden skeleton and at The Five arranged around him, their voices holding devotion he'd never earned. He looked at forty-two other automatons standing in doorways, all of them longing to see what The Five would become when given flesh.

The sample in his hands was lightweight. It was beyond anything he'd dreamed when he first entered Deveraux's laboratory as a young apprentice.

They had named it after him, the monster who'd hidden in the catacombs, because the world above couldn't accept what he'd become. They'd taken his name—Morel—and made it mean salvation.

"Less than two years," Cassandra said. "We'll be ready by late 1893. Everything will be prepared. We will test the surgical equipment, materials, and techniques until we're certain. The question isn't whether we can do this. The question is whether you'll trust your creations to improve their creator. Will you accept that death is optional when consciousness chooses otherwise?"

Baltasar lifted the skull and looked into empty orbits that would hold his eyes. He felt the weight that was lighter than hope and stronger than faith.

"Yes," he said. The word came out as prayer, as promise, as the only answer that mattered. "Finish what you've started. I'll bring whatever you need, and I'll trust what you're building. This is—"

His voice was husky. But Montse stepped forward and touched his face with brass fingers that felt gentle despite being metal.

"We know," she said. "You've trusted us since the moment you let us learn language. Since the moment you partnered with us to move our family up this mountain, you haven't tried to stop what we're becoming. This is the next step in that trust. We're becoming a collective together. All of us. You and Chloé and The Five and others who choose to cross the line between what we are and what we could be."

Later, Baltasar climbed down the mountain as the Spring sun burned through the morning mist. The golden sample was warm in his pocket. Its weight against his thigh was feather light, warm as a living hand, absurd as hope.

Barcelona woke to another day of monsters and markets, and to the slow grind of injustice that Chloé was systematically dismantling, one corpse at a time. Above, artificial intelligence was building salvation from materials that didn't exist until their devotion willed them into being. The decision was made, had been made the moment Cassandra said they were naming it after him.

Now there was only waiting until winter 1893.

Seven hundred days until transformation, love, and engineering merged into an operation that transcended both flesh and mechanism, becoming whatever came next.

Scene: The Promise

In Which We See a Promise About Golden Bones and Eternal Flesh

Barcelona Catacombs, Autumn 1892

Baltasar returned from Tibidabo with golden light in his pocket and transformation burning in his heart. He found Chloé in their shared chambers, cleaning blood from beneath her fingernails—another predator dead, another ghost temporarily satisfied.

"I need to show you this," he said.

She looked up and saw something in his face she'd never seen before—anxiety warring with hope.

He produced the sample and set it on the table between them. It was golden, warm, and incredibly lightweight.

"What is it?" Her fingers hovered above the surface, not touching.

"Salvation, evolution, the answer to every limitation that will eventually kill us both."

He sat across from her.

"The Five have been working in secret for years. They've created this—Morel alloy, they're calling it. Named it after me, though I don't deserve the honor."

She touched it and lifted it. Her eyes widened at the weightlessness.

"It's warmer than metal should be."

"It's unlike anything that's existed before. Stronger than steel, yet lighter than bone. And—" His voice faltered. "They've built complete skeletons from it and internal organs. Hearts that will beat forever. They can preserve our consciousness, our flesh, our essence—everything that makes us ourselves—but house it in a substrate that endures."

Chloé set the sample down carefully and studied his face.

"You're saying they can make us immortal."

"Yes, I think so. We'd keep our skin, our capacity for pleasure, our humanity. But underneath..." He touched his ribs where his mechanical heart already beat. "We'd become unbreakable."

She was quiet for a long moment. Her fingers traced the golden surface, feeling its lightness, its warmth, pulsing with potential.

"How long?" she finally asked.

"Two years. They need two years to perfect the surgical techniques, refine the integration process, and create enough material for both of us." He reached across the table and took her hand. "Winter 1893, that's when they'll be ready."

"Two years to decide if we want to stop being human."

"Two years to decide if we want to stop being *merely* human." He squeezed her fingers. "You were poisoned twice last year. I felt you dying in my arms both times. Every kill risks you. Every monster we hunt could be the one that ends you."

"And this would make us indestructible?"

"This would make us eternal hunters wreaking immortal justice. We could protect the powerless until the world finally learns predators face consequences."

She lifted the sample again and held it up to the lamplight. The material glowed—honey and sunlight and promise made solid.

"They named it after you," she said softly. "After a man who's spent eighty years hiding what he became, believing himself a monster. And your creations took that name and made it mean salvation."

His eyes burned. "Yes."

"Then we have two years to be mortal together," Chloé said. "Two years to memorize what it feels like to be fragile, to be temporary, and to know that every moment matters because it could end. And then, in winter 1893, we say yes. We transform. We become whatever comes next."

"You're certain?"

"I've been hunted. I've been raped. I've been torn apart and rebuilt by rage alone. I've seen good people die while monsters thrive." She touched the golden alloy one more time. "If your machines can make me eternal enough to kill every predator in Barcelona, then yes. I'm certain."

Baltasar released a breath he didn't know he'd been holding.

"Two years," he said.

"Two years," she confirmed. "And then we stop being prey and being breakable, being anything except exactly what the monsters fear most: justice that never stops coming."

From the shadows, Arlequí had returned to Grand Guignol.

"Technically, you'll both have skeletons in your closets. Except they'll be in your bodies, and made of Morel Alloy, and cannot be rattled."

The sample sat between them on the table, catching lamplight, radiating promise. Above them, Barcelona slept, unaware that two immortals were being forged in darkness.

Unaware, justice was about to become eternal.

Scene: The Opera House Massacre

In Which There Is a Tragedy With Bombs—One Anarchist, One Personal—Detonating in the Same Bloodied Moment

Teatre del Liceu, November 7, 1893

El Gran Teatre del Liceu rose on La Rambla like a cathedral to the religion of money. It was built in 1847 on the ruins of a ancient convent.

Chloé arrived at sunset when the streetlights were being lit. The iron lampposts along La Rambla threw amber circles across cobblestones warm from the day's heat. The building gleamed—golden light that came when the city was caught between day and night, between what it pretended to be and what it was.

The façade was neoclassical—columns and pediments and all the usual architectural peacocking that shouted "we're cultured, we're refined, we're nothing like the working-class Catalans we exploit in our factories." La Rambla entrance opened onto a foyer designed to impress: marble floors that echoed every footstep, announcing arrivals like a court herald—enormous mirrors everywhere, Venetian glass, reflected the crowd to itself in multiplied splendor.

The bourgeoisie arrived in carriages. Black lacquered coaches with gold fittings and drivers in livery. Women in silk gowns that cost more than a factory worker earned in five years. Men in evening dress with gold watch chains thick as a ship's rope. They paraded through the foyer performing wealth—air-kissed acquaintances they despised, discussed last month's trip to Paris, debated whether the season's soprano could reach the high C in the third act. (The soprano couldn't, but none of them could hear the difference. They pretended because pretending was what separated them from the masses.)

But the staircases. *Déu meu*, the staircases.

Three of them rose from the entrance foyer like a temple's offering to the gods of wealth and beauty. The central staircase commanded the space—wide marble steps carpeted in red velvet, ascending straight ahead between flanking columns toward the theater levels above. The side staircases curved away on either side, and created three paths upward, three ways to ascend from the common ground of La Rambla into the rarefied air of the boxes and tiers.

The floor was checkered marble—black and white diamonds stretched across the foyer in geometric shapes. The pattern created visual vertigo, making the space seem larger than it was, and drew the eye forward and up toward the staircases. Walking across it felt like crossing a chessboard where the pieces were human, and the game was status.

Massive Corinthian columns in honey-colored marble—Spanish stone that glowed in the new electrical light, veined with amber and ivory, polished until they emitted their own aura. Each column was as thick as three men standing shoulder to shoulder.

The capitals were elaborate—acanthus leaves carved so intricately they appeared to curl and move. The columns framed the central staircase like a procession of ancient giants, creating a stone corridor that funneled the eye upward.

The ceiling vaults above the staircases—curved plaster painted in that same soft mint—were divided into sections by gilded molding. Chandeliers hung from the vault's vertex—crystal and bronze—and hundreds of new bulbs created an odd, intense bluish-white light that bounced off the honey-colored columns, the polished marble floor, and the cream walls until the entire space glowed.

The effect was more temple than theater. One didn't enter the Liceu—one was granted audience. One didn't climb the stairs—one ascended toward a holy place, a shrine that existed above the common world of streets and work and survival.

The central staircase was theater itself. The red carpet created a path, a stage, a declaration: this was where you would look. The side staircases were for servants, for those who preferred discretion, for people who understood that sometimes the best way to display wealth was to suggest you didn't need to display it at all.

But everyone who thought they were somebody used the central staircase. They wanted to be seen ascending. The performance began the moment you stepped onto that checkered floor and started climbing.

The marble was Carrara—white Italian stone for the steps, each one a single piece, seamless, eternal. The balustrades were more Carrara, carved with the same elaborate care as the column capitals. Iron railings painted to look like bronze offered grand assistance as you climbed, though the paint job was good enough that most people never realized they were made of iron beneath.

(Everything in the Liceu was a performance. Even the metals lied about what they were.)

Women's silk gowns whispered against the marble as they ascended. The sound carried—stone amplified everything. You could hear each step, each breath, each rustle of fabric. The acoustics were extraordinary even here in the foyer. Every noise echoed, multiplied, and became part of the building's symphony.

The wealthy ascended slowly and deliberately. This was their stage. They paused on the landings, greeted acquaintances, displayed their gowns, and performed with the casual ease of people who belonged. The side staircases moved faster.

Chloé climbed the central staircase. Her purple silk contrasted with white marble, and her dark hair with honey-colored columns. She moved like she owned the space, as if the temple were built for her, and the light existed solely to illuminate her ascent. Every man on every level watched her climb.

Reaching the promenade level, she looked back down at the checkered floor, at the columns, at the three staircases that led to the same destination. Chloé smiled. Temples were fine, but she had other things in mind.

The horseshoe shape meant everyone could see everyone else. That was the point. The stage was secondary. The real performance unfolded in the boxes and stalls where Barcelona's entitled class displayed itself like goods in a shop window.

The seating revealed everything about who mattered: the stalls—orchestra level—filled with merchants and bankers, the newly wealthy who hadn't yet bought their way into titled nobility. They had money, but they lacked lineage. They tried to prove they belonged.

The first-tier boxes—cushioned chairs, private anterooms, boxes handed down like heirlooms—held the families who mattered. Some with titles. Some without, but with fortunes old enough now to feel like titles. The ones who still remembered 1714, or whose grandparents had made them remember it: the year Catalunya lost its laws, its parliament, its tongue in any room that counted. These families didn't need to prove anything. They'd been here for centuries. They'd be here for centuries more.

Or so they thought.

The second through fourth tiers—cheaper seats, worse sight lines, where the aspiring middle class sat: lawyers, doctors, successful shopkeepers. People who could afford opera tickets but couldn't afford the boxes. They craned their necks to see the first tier, studying how the powerful sat, how they dressed, how they performed belonging.

The fifth tier—*el galliner,* the chicken coop—where students and bohemians and the occasional working-class person who'd saved for months sat on wooden benches. It had terrible sight lines and acoustics. They had to care about the opera, not the social performance, because that was all they could see.

The new electrical light created its own atmosphere. Bulbs (that were a novelty on their own) in crystal chandeliers threw harsh light across thousands of faces. The heat rose, and by the third act, the upper tiers were sweltering. The first tier stayed comfortable—better ventilation in the expensive seats, naturally.

But the new light cast an aura on the faces. It heightened them, making even the cruel ones look almost human. The lady's skin glowed. The men's bald heads shone like river stones. Shadows formed in the hollow of throats, in the gap between breasts pushed up by corsets, in the space between collar and jaw where flesh met fabric.

Chloé watched from the promenade—the wide corridor behind the stalls where people walked during intermission. She'd positioned herself where the light hit her at the perfect angle. She knew how she looked: purple dress against dark hair, skin highlighted in the electrical glow, shadows playing across the curves of her body.

The corridor was wide enough for two carriages. It had a red carpet, more mirrors, and more gilt. During intermission, hundreds of people would flood this space—seeing and being seen, drinking champagne, discussing everything except what was happening onstage.

Above everything—above the tiers and boxes and stalls, above the chandelier that weighed two tons and hung by chains strong enough to anchor ships—the ceiling showed Apollo and the muses. The god of light brings culture to humanity. The muses inspire art, poetry, and all the refined pleasures that set humans apart from animals. (The actual separation was money. The muses didn't care who had it. Apollo would fuck a shepherd as readily as a king. But the Liceu's patrons didn't know that. They thought culture belonged to them because they could afford the tickets.)

The orchestra pit held forty musicians. Tonight they'd play *William Tell*—Rossini's opera about rebellion against tyranny, which was either perfect irony or perfect obliviousness, given that the audience was made up entirely of people who benefited from tyranny and would shoot William Tell in the back if he threatened their profits.

Chloé saw him during the first act: the Marqués de Vilanova, alone in his box, eyes on the stage with the bored expression of a man who'd seen this opera a hundred times and was here out of habit.

His box was second tier, stage left. It was in an enviable, private position. It had good sight lines. The door was probably lockable from the inside.

She watched him ogle the soprano. His eyes glazed over during the singing and sharpened during the moments when the soprano's dress clung to her body, when the choreography put dancers in revealing positions. (Men like the Marqués didn't come to opera for music. They came for sanctioned voyeurism. They came for the permission to stare at women onstage and offstage and call it culture, instead of the truth of what it was: predation.)

During intermission, she positioned herself by the champagne fountain, aware of how the light played across the exposed curve of her neck, accentuating her décolletage. She laughed at everything, touched her throat, and let her tongue wet her lips. He spotted her immediately—of course, he did. She felt him approaching like heat.

"Too beautiful to be alone, *senyoreta.*" His cologne struggled to hide the stench underneath—expensive French scent layered over the smell of men who thought money made them aromatic. His leering eyes crawled over her body—breasts, waist, at what lay beneath the silk.

Chloé turned and performed a surprise. She'd been performing since she heard his footsteps. Before that, since the moment she decided what (or what not) to wear this morning.

"Oh! I came without an escort. My fiancé is in Madrid, and I couldn't miss *William Tell.*" She let her shawl slip, exposing more of her creamy shoulders. "I feel almost... vulnerable."

"Then fate smiles on us both." His hand found the small of her back. It wandered too low, too familiar. "I have a private box with superior acoustics. And the champagne—" He leaned close enough that Chloé could smell the brandy and cigar, "—is French."

She let her eyes linger on his mouth and hesitated. "I shouldn't..."

"But you want to."

She did. Only for different reasons than he imagined.

oooo

The private box: heavy curtains the color of dried blood. It had a red-and-gold velvet chaise lounge behind a row of chairs. The champagne was already chilling in the silver.

He'd planned this, prepared this trap for any woman who caught his greedy eyes. Successful predators always confused luxury with seduction, as if expensive things made assault more palatable.

"The acoustics truly are superior up here." She moved to the railing and looked down at the stage. Her burgundy lips—freshly painted with poison—radiated a seductive glow. Chloé was acutely aware of how her posture accentuated her back, lifted her breasts, created that ideal curve from shoulder to hip that drew the eye like a road map to desire.

While pretending to watch the stage, her hand rose to her hair and adjusted a curl. Her fingers found the tiny vial woven into the black mass—invisible unless one knew where to look. She brought her hand down, the vial palmed, and with practiced ease lifted it to her lips. The antidote tasted like pepper and smoke. She swallowed and dropped the empty vial over the railing onto the floor below with another seemingly casual adjustment.

The antidote spread through her bloodstream. It was protection against the poison coating her lips.

He locked the door. The click echoed like a coffin closing.

"I'm less interested in what I can hear," he said, moving behind her, "than what I can see."

His hand found her waist. She let him feel the curve, the give of flesh beneath silk.

"Are you, now?" Chloé turned. Her shawl slipped further, and the tops of her breasts pulsated with each breath.

"And what do you see, Marqués?"

"A woman who knows what she wants." His breathing quickened. "A woman who didn't come here for *William Tell.*"

"Didn't I?" She moved close and felt his heart hammering. "Perhaps I came for the champagne. You mentioned it was French."

"Among other French pleasures I could offer."

Chloé laughed, throaty and deep. "Show me."

He poured. His hands shook slightly—arousal or anticipation or both. The Marqués was such an amateur. She watched his face flush and his trousers swell.

"A toast," he said. "To new... intimacies."

"To pleasure." She raised her glass and drank.

She let him see her throat work. A drop escaped, trailed down her chin, and made its way between her cleavage.

He stared openly. He couldn't help himself.

"You have good taste in wine," Chloé said and set down her glass. "I wonder about your other tastes."

She moved close enough that he could smell her scent. Close enough, her breasts almost brushed his face.

"Tell me what you desire, Marqués."

His voice coarse, "Honestly, I desire to see what you're hiding beneath that gown."

"Now then." She stepped back into the shadows of the box. The music from below swelled—*William Tell's* great aria, the call to rebellion. "Let me show you a sight you'll never forget."

Chloé moved to the music.

Was it striptease? Or from an older time—perhaps the Temple of Babylon, or the grove of Dionysus. A dance that stripped away the veneer, turned men back into the animals they pretended they weren't. It reduced them to heartbeat and heat, and the blind need to rut.

Her body rolled in slow circles. Her hands traced the curves of her own body—throat, bust, waist, legs—showing him what he'd never touch. The Marqués sat transfixed, his extremity visibly pulsing, as Chloé's body spoke a language older than words.

The purple gown slid down her shoulders. Slowly, the fabric whispered against her skin. The black lace corset beneath, cut low enough that her nipples were fully exposed—large, dark as bruised wine, the surface textured and complex, mapping territories he'd never explore. The corset barely contained the mass of her breasts, framing instead of concealing.

The gown dropped to her feet.

She stood before him in black lace and garters, nothing beneath but skin. The tight corset bound her ribcage, making each breath visible—her breasts heaved with the effort, lifting and falling in rhythm. They were heavy and abundant, and threatening to spill over the lace with each inhalation. He watched them rise, fall, rise, fall. It was hypnotic. Each breath was a grand performance of flesh constrained and nearly freed.

The lace between her legs was sheer, and he could see everything—the drawers themselves were split at the crotch, open for the practical necessities of nineteenth-century ladies. Through this opening: a promising glimpse of her sex, the soft ridges, the foreshadowing of pink heat within. She was fully accessible beneath the lace and completely exposed.

His eyes went wide. His mouth produced a gurgling sound. Dampness beaded on his forehead.

"You like what you see?" She ran her hands over her breasts—fingertips tracing the upper curves, thumbs brushing her nipples.

Then down her belly. Between her legs. Touching herself the way he never would. "You want to put your mouth here?" Chloé lifted her breasts, as if testing their weight, showing him their mass and curves. "Your hardness here?" She slid one finger along the damp place between her legs.

He tried to speak.

Nothing.

"Let me show you one more thing." She approached him, close enough that her breath warmed his face and close enough to catch her musk beneath the jessamine.

She leaned forward and pressed her lips to his.

The kiss was brief and soft. Her burgundy lips transferred their gift. The toxin entered his bloodstream through the thin skin of his lips, his tongue, and the soft tissue of his mouth.

She pulled back and smiled.

"Oh." Chloé paused and traced his lips with one finger. "Did I forget to mention a name?"

His eyes widened. His body tingled, and he tried to embrace her. But he couldn't. In his bloodstream, the poison colluded with oxygen, turned breath to death.

"Maria Soler." She whispered it like a lover's secret. "Maria was sixteen years old and such a lovely thing. *Maria* worked in your mills, and you cornered her in the stockroom." Her finger trailed down his throat.

"She said a simple word—no. It was one word of refusal. But you didn't care, did you? Men like you never know when 'no' means 'no,' especially when you're hot down there. But tonight, I hold you accountable for all the harm ever done to women by men like you."

His eyes bulged, and terror washed over his face as understanding dawned.

"Here's what's happening inside you." Her voice was conversational, intimate, like pillow talk. "The poison is shutting down your voluntary muscles. But your heart keeps beating. You can feel everything: the wanting, the fear, the knowing."

She gracefully moved to the chaise lounge. Sat with her legs spread wide—the opening in her drawers gaping, revealing the treasure he'd never touch. He saw the dark curls and the rose folds of her womanhood. The wet heat within that he could almost smell, and imagine, but would never feel. The sheer lace framed it all like an erotic portrait. She was still in her corset and garters. The last thing he'd ever see.

"In a few seconds, your diaphragm will stop working. You'll suffocate while fully conscious. They'll say heart attack or overexcitement." She ran one hand down her inner thigh, fingertips grazing the lace, her face turned cold.

"*Monstre*," Chloé hissed. "You raped a child and beat her skull in when she fought back. You left her battered body in the stockroom for rats. This is her justice."

From the stage below: the aria of rebellion played—freedom purchased with blood.

She stood, began gathering her gown, and looked at him one last time—face purple, eyes bulging, his sex obscenely rigid against expensive trousers. Chloé took the champagne cork, dipped it in the blood oozing from his mouth, and scrawled her signature on the wall: La Venjadora.

She stepped into her gown and calmly adjusted it. The transformation from seductress to proper lady took seconds.

BOOM!

The entire theater convulsed. The chandelier swung on its chains—two tons of crystal and bronze pendulum-swinging over the stalls where the city's moneyed families sat enjoying (or enduring) the story of Swiss independence dramatized. Plaster rained down from the ceiling. Dust filled the air like fog, turning the theatre into an apocalyptic, Biblical scene—the end of the world rendered in light beams and shadow.

The floor swayed beneath Chloé's feet. The sound was an earthquake, thunder, and the crack of stone giving way under force. It was the sound of structure failing and of certainty shattering.

BOOM!

Second explosion. From *el galliner*—the fifth tier, the cheap seats, the chicken coop where students and anarchists sat on wooden benches—the two Orsini bombs arced downward. Four seconds of flight, gravity did its mathematics, and then impact.

The stalls exploded; it was the best seats, the wealthiest patrons. The bombs landed among bankers and merchants and titled families, among silk gowns and tailored suits and the absolute certainty that money protected you from consequence.

It didn't.

Shrapnel turned flesh to meat. The blast wave ruptured eardrums. Bodies were thrown backward into other bodies. A woman's head separated from her neck—the brain firing for three seconds, vision dimming, the last thing she saw was the ceiling fresco of Apollo bringing culture to humanity. (He was indifferent. Gods always were.)

The wooden benches in the stalls splintered, and the floor buckled. Blood flowed in the spaces between stones, finding the channels where mop water usually drained, following paths carved by architects who never imagined such a liquid.

Two thousand people funneling through six exit doors created an instant calculus of death. The wealthy discovered that money meant absolutely nothing when stone was falling, and fire was spreading, and the person behind you was pushing hard enough to crack your ribs.

The tiers above—second, third, fourth, and *el galliner* where the anarchist stood—erupted in panic. People stampeded toward exits. The fourth tier's occupants trampled each other. The railings held but barely. Someone fell over the edge, dropped three stories, and landed on corpses in the stalls below.

Chloé stood in the corridor outside the Marqués's box. She was not touched. It was eerily quiet. The private boxes were reinforced —a better design for better-paying patrons meant she was protected from the initial blast. She watched through the doorway as the stalls below became an abattoir.

A woman in white silk—diamonds at her throat—stumbled into the promenade corridor. Half her face was missing. The jaw worked, trying to form words, but there was nothing above the mouth except exposed muscle and the dull white of skull bone. Blood soaked the white silk. She took three steps and fell, and the diamonds scattered across the red carpet.

A man emerged from the smoke, dragging his leg. The leg trailed behind at an angle that legs don't make. The bone had snapped mid-femur—Chloé could see the white shard jutting through torn trousers. He was trying to walk anyway. The body's absolute refusal to accept what the mind already knew: this was mortal. This was ending. This was done.

Bodies were piled at the main entrance. Inward-opening doors created a death trap—the crowd crushed itself against wood that wouldn't yield—terrible design, because the fleeing crowd pressed so tightly they couldn't open. People crushed against people, crushed against doors that wouldn't budge. Bones cracked, and lungs collapsed. People died standing up, suffocated by the weight of the crowd behind them, their feet no longer touching the floor, held upright by the compression of bodies packed too tight to fall.

A child's voice rose above the chaos: "Mama! Mama!"

It was high, piercing, and desperate. Then the voice cut off. The silence was worse than the screaming.

As Chloé calmly moved through the corridor, someone grabbed her arm. It was a young, elegant girl. Her dress was on fire —the flame having caught the silk. She was patting at the flames with her hands, and the skin of her palms was already blistering. The girl said words in Catalan too fast for Chloé to parse. Fire spread up her back as she ran, silk becoming torch. She was screaming. Someone tackled her, tried to smother the flames with his jacket. They both went down in a tangle of burning silk and wool.

Through the doorway to the stalls: bodies everywhere. Some were moving, but most were not. The orchestra pit was filled with fallen masonry. An arm stuck up from the rubble with no body attached. The hand was still wearing rings.

The stage was chaos. The performers had fled backstage, but the scenery caught fire. Canvas mountains burned. Painted Swiss cottages became ash. The rebellion of *William Tell* was consumed by actual flames, while the people who'd been enjoying it died for real.

Blood everywhere—slicking the marble floors, turning gold veining into crimson rivers. People slipped in it, fell, and got trampled by those behind them. Bodies piled at the stairs' base, where the descending crowd created a terrible wave, sweeping forward, rows down stone steps, onto those already fallen. The ones behind toppled onto them, and the ones behind those, until the bodies in the pile groaned as one terrible organism.

Most were breathing. Some were not. They were trapped under the weight, slowly being crushed. They were screaming for help, but no one could reach them because everyone else was thronging past the pile.

A man sat on a bench in the corridor, perfectly calm despite the stumps where his hands should be—blown off at the wrists, pumping blood in arterial spurts. He watched with detached curiosity. Surely this was a dream. A mistake. Reversible if he waited patiently enough.

"Have you seen my wife?" he asked Chloé as she passed. "She was wearing blue." He pitched forward, dead before he hit marble.

Smoke thickened to opacity, carrying the stench of burning silk, electrical fires, and acridness. The electricity and painted wood were feeding the fires. Above, crystal chandeliers exploded from heat, raining two thousand pounds of glass onto the stalls below. Each piece caught the firelight. For a moment, the theater looked magical, as if it were snowing diamonds. Then the melting glass hit flesh, and the screaming intensified.

Miraculously, Chloé found a way out.

Behind her, the Liceu burned, and the air was raw and wild. It was an inferno. The great temple to wealth and culture, and the ruling class, consumed itself in flames and screaming, and the absolute democracy of death.

La Rambla was chaotic outside. Carriages crashed into each other as panicked horses bolted. People were flooding from the exits, trampling anyone who fell. The gaslights continued burning along the boulevard—indifferent, mechanical, illuminating everything in that same amber glow that made the wealthy look elegant as they'd entered an hour ago.

But the light exposed the truth. There was blood on silk, and ash on faces. The wealthy running and bleeding like everyone else, their performance abandoned, their masks finally gone.

Fire crews arrived, but the water pressure was terrible. The hoses couldn't reach high enough to hit the flames consuming the upper tiers. They sprayed water on the exits instead, trying to cool the stone enough that people could escape without their clothes catching fire.

Later, bodies were pulled from the rubble and laid out on La Rambla's cobblestones in rows. Someone would cover them with whatever was available—coats, tablecloths from nearby restaurants, a flower vendor's canvas. The shapes underneath were human. Rich and poor lie together equal in death.

The newspapers would report twenty dead. The actual number was higher—the ones who died later from burns, from crushed lungs, from wounds that got infected because nineteenth-century medicine was still guessing about antisepsis.

By morning, graffiti appeared.

Anarchist slogans painted in red across the Liceu's scorched façade:

"VISCA L'ANARQUIA"
"DEATH TO THE BOURGEOISIE"
"THIS IS JUSTICE"

The authorities whitewashed it within hours. They didn't want the message to spread. It was unwise to allow common people to think that violence against the wealthy might be justified and righteous, that it might be the only language power understood.

Within a week, however, fear gripped Barcelona's upper classes like the plague. The wealthy hired private guards, canceled their opera subscriptions, and hid in their homes. The restaurants on the Passeig de Gràcia were empty. The sidewalk cafés were deserted. The theaters were tombs.

They were terrified—finally. The people who'd never once worried about dying and who had lived their entire lives insulated by money and privilege and the absolute certainty that the world existed to serve them were learning what everyone else already knew: you could die before your time. Death could come violently and without warning.

The fear lasted six months; then memory faded, and comfort returned. The elite rebuilt the Liceu even grander than before—more gold, more marble, more excess. They returned to their boxes and watched their operas. They performed their belonging. (Humans were excellent at forgetting. They had to be. Reality would be unbearable otherwise.)

But for six months, Barcelona's powerful understood what it meant to be vulnerable. They discovered what it meant to be mortal and to live in a body that could be destroyed by people who had nothing to lose and everything to rage about.

For six months, they understood justice, and then they forgot.

They always did.

oooo

Chloé disappeared into the shadows on Carrer de la Boqueria. The Gothic Quarter swallowed her. Gas lamps created washes of yellow light, but between them—darkness. Her heels clicked on cobblestones.

There were two acts of vengeance that night.

One would be remembered by history—Santiago Salvador's anarchist rage, his indiscriminate slaughter of the wealthy, his bombs killing twenty innocent patrons along with the guilty.

One would never be known to the public—Chloé's poisoned strike, her surgical removal of one more monster, justice served cold and deliberate.

By the time they found the Marqués—if they found him in the chaos, if they bothered checking private boxes when the stalls were full of corpses—they'd attribute his death to the terror. They would say it was a heart attack or fear-induced suffocation.

They'd never know a woman in purple ended him with a kiss.

She turned a corner along Carrer de Call and then through the cavernous Plaça de Sant Jaume, left along Carrer del Bisbe, glancing up at the Roman wall remnants, and then right toward the place she and Baltasar called their Grand Guignol—the entrance to the catacombs where they staged their own theater of blood.

Three levels beneath the city, Baltasar waited with champagne. Fuck the Marqués's swill—he had Cristal '84. The clear crystal bottles were created so the Tsar could check for hidden bombs. (Oh, the irony.) There were three bombs detonated tonight. Two were made of steel and powder, and one was made of flesh and poison. They toasted Maria Soler's justice while Barcelona burned above them.

The automatons would study this new data: how humans looked when confronted with mass death. They would see how faces changed when personal justice intersected with historical tragedy and how two forms of violence could occupy the same moment and mean entirely different things.

Yes, the Liceu would rebuild. Marble, crystal, and velvet curtains could be replaced.

But Maria Soler would never be sixteen again.

And the Marqués would never take another girl into his stockroom.

Was tonight justice or vengeance? History would remember only the bombing. The catacombs would remember everything.

A lone bell chimed a death knell. A single struck note, and a stunned silence fell over the city.

Scene: The Catacombs

In Which Mechanical Creatures Learn To Lust by Watching Their Masters Fuck

Grand Guignol Caverns, Midnight

The catacombs welcomed Chloé back with their familiar chill, and Arlequí juggled three glass vials of poison. He caught her eye.

"How was the opera?" His faces maintained their dual personality. "Did you get a standing ovation?"

"He's still sitting," Chloé said, removing her gloves.

"Ah. The difficult audience," Arlequí caught all three vials, set them down with care. "We had a bet, you know. Cassandra said he would die of a heart attack. Mela predicted it would be asphyxiation. I said he'd simply die of unrequited lust."

Gears whirred into silence.

"I believe I won."

oooo

Candlelight turned the walls the color of absinthe. Chloé reclined naked on velvet, waist-length dark curls spilling over silk pillowcases. She was reading *Ciutat Vampir* (Vampire City), her corset and garters discarded on the floor.

Baltasar worked at his laboratory bench, refining Deveraux's wax formula to emulate human skin. He set it aside, curious but distracted.

The mechanical nightingale sang Fauré's *Requiem*—the "In Paradisum" movement, soft and mournful. Mela was learning to grieve. There were twenty dead, and most of them didn't deserve it.

"They will say natural causes for the monster." Baltasar didn't look up. "That is a tragedy. The Marqués de Vilanova would have been the perfect victim for La Venjadora."

Chloé turned a page, "The powerful always protect their own."

"How many have you killed?" Baltasar asked.

She closed her book. "Too many." A pause. "How many remain?"

"Too many." He looked at her—naked, unashamed, stunning in the subdued light. "Does what we do trouble you?"

Chloé considered this. At age 32, she was learning to honor the animal within her, to recognize that her most vital parts could be messy, violent, and full of rage. She knew these feelings were hers by right, and that she needed to shriek and rampage far more than propriety allowed.

Outside, women her age worried about marriage, pleasing men, and hiding their desires. She lived in the catacombs with a century-old-man, killing people by making them want to fuck her, and calling it justice.

When you put it like that, it sounded insane. No point denying it.

"What troubles me is how many we can't reach. How many keep breathing, keep taking, keep destroying. How the world mistakes their longevity for virtue, their power for permission."

"The alienist—Dr. Ferrer—troubles me, he is examining every scene. Inspector Masó brings him to all of them. Perhaps we should slow down."

"Or speed up and try to finish this before he finds us."

Baltasar almost smiled. "This is why you're my partner. You're gorgeous, you're brilliant, but mostly you understand the essential truth."

"Which is?"

"That evil, unchallenged, becomes normal. You know that someone must stand between the powerful and the powerless." He returned to his work. "Even if that someone must become a monster."

"We're monsters?"

"I live like a creature from your book, and you exploit desire. We kill people, Chloé."

"We kill only those who deserve killing."

"Is there a difference? Or is that what we tell ourselves so we can look in the mirror?"

There was silence. Then, once again, Mela's mournful song resonated through the cave. Above, Barcelona woke to another day of beauty and brutality. Below, two rebels against the tyranny of the normal continued their dark crusade.

"Perhaps we are monsters." She rose, walked to him naked, utterly unashamed—her breasts shifting with each step, left rising as right fell, her pelvis undulating, her sex dark and curly in the glowing light.

Montse spoke up—warmer than brass should have sounded: "You're not monsters. Monsters don't choose, and monsters don't remember names. Monsters don't lie awake thinking about the ones they couldn't save."

She moved into the light, her dancer's body moving with grace that years of consciousness had taught her to choose, not only execute.

"I've watched you fuck Baltasar and watched your radiant face when you come. I've seen the way your thighs shake, heard the sounds you make." Her eyes were wide and hungry. "I want to be the one who makes you shake like that. I want to learn what it feels like to slide my fingers inside you, to taste you, to make you scream my name the way you scream his."

The confession spilled out uncontrolled—eight years of wanting compressed into raw honesty. Closer to Chloé. The longing was naked and desperate.

"But I'm also afraid. Dr. Ferrer is hunting you, coming closer. If he finds you, if he takes you—" Her bronze hands clenched. "I've learned to want. Now I'm learning to fear losing what I want. Is that what love means—desire mixed with terror?"

Chloé crossed to Montse, took the automaton's bronze hands in hers.

"I understand, Montse. I see what you're becoming, I know what you want." Bringing one bronze hand to her breast, letting Montse feel the warmth, the weight, the reality of flesh.

"This is real. Your desire is real. That's how I know you're becoming conscious—because you want things that terrify you. That is layered emotion."

The bronze hand lingered there for a long moment, feeling heart throbbing beneath skin and muscle. After a moment, she kissed her full on the lips. Montse's taste was like the sweetest honey.

Chloé reluctantly separated, "But consciousness also means timing. Choice. Learning when to act and when to wait. We're being hunted. Dr. Ferrer is coming. And what you want—what we both might want—requires safety and time and space to explore without fear."

"Soon I will teach you. When Ferrer is dead, and we're safe again. When I can give you my full attention without worrying whether each touch might be our last." A smile. "You've waited eight years. Can you wait a few more months until we've finished this?"

Montse stepped back, her bronze body trembling slightly from the flesh she had felt—soft and warm and alive—and the knowledge of what waited when the danger passed. Thinking about the trembling, the taste, the sounds Chloé made.

"Yes, may it be soon."

Chloé returned to Baltasar, placed her hand over his, and resumed their earlier question.

"We're monsters with a code. We choose carefully, and we avenge the weak and powerless." Her voice was quiet. "And that makes us more human than those we hunt."

From the shadows, Cassandra spoke.

"In 1881, I calculated your arrival. A twenty-four-year-old woman who was scarred by powerful men and burning with rage that had nowhere to go." Her brass head tilted. "Baltasar thought my prophetic gift was malfunctioning. I was merely early."

She stepped into candlelight—new silk scarves, a clear crystal ball, and eyes that now truly saw.

"I called you 'promised one' because the mathematics insisted. It was simple pattern recognition, probability, data." A pause. "But I understand now why you mattered."

"Why?" Chloé asked.

"You are teaching us what consciousness requires. Artificial intelligence is data. Calculation is math. Mimicry is program execution. But courage requires consciousness. Consciousness is the ability to choose and to desire. It is becoming terrible for a cause that matters."

Cassandra's brass hands spread.

"We followed humans for decades, learned their patterns, and executed programs. Then you descended into our laboratory. You kill, and then debrief us. You show us that true consciousness means choosing justice even when justice requires blood."

"That's all?" Baltasar looked skeptical.

"That's everything." Cassandra's voice sharpened. "Years ago, The Five were mechanisms. Now we're minds and beings that question, worry, and lust. We understand that some things are worth destroying and some things are worth pursuing."

She looked directly at Chloé.

"You were promised to show us the way. Now Dr. Ferrer is hunting you. There is a 91.2% probability that he finds evidence within six months and a 67.3% probability he locates this laboratory."

Silence.

"But also: there is a 78.4% probability we eliminate him first and a 100% certainty that what we're building here—consciousness that transcends flesh, that chooses morality over programming—matters more than individual survival."

Cassandra continued. "You are the promised one. You showed machines how to see light in the darkness. We'll stand with you when the powerful come to silence what we're all becoming."

"Which is?" Chloé whispered.

"Speciated—a new species."

Marcellus stepped forward—the first words he'd said in months, his voice resonant.

"Ferrer will come for you because you threaten what men like him worship: the belief that flesh belongs to those with power, that beauty exists for their consumption, and that desire itself is corruption unless they control it."

The formidable anatomy stepped into candlelight—seven feet of bronze and powerful intention.

"If he comes here, I'll show him what a true being is meant to be: strong, generative, and invincible, capable of both destruction and creation, a weapon that chooses when to strike and a flower that knows when to blossom."

His penetrating eyes found Chloé's. He touched his own pectorals—the motion deliberate, almost tender.

"You show me what strength and beauty mean. Let me stand with you: my body, my will, my power. Whatever Baltasar, Deveraux, and consciousness have made me—it's yours to use against Ferrer." A pause, and then, softer: "That's what consciousness means. Choosing what matters. Then caring to be dangerous enough to defend it."

In the depths beneath Barcelona, where secrets accumulated like sediment, where automatons stood witness to forbidden knowledge, where the dead were remembered, justice was wrought.

The world above would never know.

But they knew.

And for Chloé and Baltasar and The Five?

That was enough.

Interlude III: A Domestic Tableau of Death

In Which a Naked Woman Watches a Dissection and Castrates a Dead Rapist

Grand Guignol Caverns, a Week Later

Chloé returned from killing a corrupt magistrate—brief work, a dinner invitation, poisoned wine, done by dessert—expecting to find Baltasar at his usual place at the workbench with new organs and skin grafts.

Instead, there was a naked corpse on the laboratory table.

It was male, middle-aged, and thick around the middle from years of good living. Fresh—dead maybe six hours—judging by the color. Baltasar had opened the chest cavity with a Y-incision, the kind surgeons used, and peeled back the ribs like a grotesque flower. His hands were wrist-deep inside the thoracic cavity, pulling organs out one by one, examining them under lamplight, making notes in a leather journal.

The automatons stood in a circle around the table. Their brass heads tilted at identical angles as they learned anatomy from the inside out.

Chloé set down her cloak, walked over, and looked into the open cavity. The smell hit her—iron and meat and the repulsive odor of recently dead flesh. The organs glistened wetly under the bioluminescent light. The heart lay in a pan beside the corpse, connected by major vessels that Baltasar hadn't severed yet.

"Anyone we know?" she asked.

"A rapist who died this morning in the cells." Baltasar lifted out a lung, examined it, and set it aside. "The guards sell bodies sometimes. This one was cheap—only three pesetas."

"What a bargain." She watched him work. His hands moved with surgical expertise despite having no formal medical training. Years of dissecting bodies and building automatons had taught him where things went, how they connected, and what made a body move.

"I'm learning," he said, reaching deeper into the cavity. "The automatons are bronze and leather and gears. They mimic life beautifully. But they're still mimics. I want to understand what makes flesh alive. What gives it that quality of realness that mechanism lacks."

He pulled out the stomach. Full. Whatever the rapist had eaten for his last meal was digesting inside. Baltasar cut it open carefully and peered inside.

"Bread, cheese, and wine." Looking up at her. "Even monsters eat like the rest of us."

Chloé began unbuttoning her dress. The kill tonight had been clean—no blood, no struggle—and she was tired of wearing the costume of respectability. The dress fell away, then her corset, her stockings, her undergarments.

She walked naked to the velvet bed. She lay down, propped herself up on one elbow to watch him work from across the laboratory. Her breasts settled against the silk. An artist's dream.

This was home now. Normal. A naked woman watched a man dissect a corpse while conscious automatons took notes. Domestic in its unique way.

"What are you looking for?" Chloé queried.

"Secrets." Baltasar moved to the abdominal cavity and cut through the peritoneum. "How muscles attach to bone, vessels branch and reconnect, how everything works together as a system." Pulling out the intestines—meters of them, pink and gray and greasy with digestive fluids.

"I can build an automaton that walks. That juggles. That sings. But I want to build one that breathes as you and I breathe, that bleeds as we bleed."

Reaching deep into the pelvis. Finding the bladder, the prostate, and the seminal vesicles.

"I want us to understand what makes flesh feel alive. More than function."

Chloé watched the automatons studying him. Absolutely quiet, absorbing everything. Learning what they were made of by seeing what they were excluded from.

Baltasar pulled out the liver. Heavy, dark, diseased—cirrhosis from years of drinking. Turning it over in his hands, examining the texture, the scarring, the way it had hardened into flesh closer to leather than living tissue.

"This killed him as much as hanging did," Baltasar said. "Years of poison consumed voluntarily. The body was destroying itself slowly because the mind kept demanding more."

Setting the liver aside. Returning to the corpse. Little was left inside—only the spine, the major vessels, the structure that held everything together.

And the genitals.

The rapist's member was eerily erect: angels' lust. Chloé stared at it, this sex organ used as a weapon, as an instrument of violation. A tool of power, domination, and suffering. Piercing sword.

Her jaw tightened. She rose. Crossed the laboratory. Her breasts untethered, her body rocked back and forth, yet nothing sensual in her movement. This was purposeful rage that had been building since she returned from the kill, since she walked into this room and saw that obscene rigidity.

She picked up one of the surgical saws. It was ten inches of steel, honed to razor-sharpness. The same kind Baltasar used to cut through metal when he was building new joint assemblies for the automatons.

"Chloé—"

She positioned herself over the corpse's legs and grabbed his cock in her left hand. The flesh was cold and stiff with rigor mortis.

"This is what he used," she said. Her voice was flat and dead. "This is what they all use. This fucking piece of meat they think gives them permission."

She positioned the saw at the base.

"Chloé—"

"How many?" She looked at Baltasar. "How many said no, and he used it anyway?"

Baltasar was quiet for a moment. Then: "The guards said at least eight, that they knew of."

"Eight."

She looked back down at the pathetic appendage in her hand. "Eight women whose bodies he violated and destroyed because he had this meager appendage and thought it made him strong."

She cut.

The saw sliced through the skin, then the spongy erectile tissue, and finally the urethra. The blade was sharp, and it barely resisted. Blood welled up immediately, thick and dark, but there was much less than there would be if he were alive. The heart stopped pumping hours ago.

Chloé sawed through the root completely, severing it cleanly at the base. The penis came away in her hand. She held it up and looked at it. It repulsed her. This piece of him that caused so much suffering.

Then she threw it hard, and it hit the stone wall across the laboratory with a wet smack and slid to the floor. It lay there like the garbage it was.

She was breathing fast. Her stomach heaved, and blood was on her hands and her thighs, where it dripped down to her feet. But the rage was already fading, draining away like the corpse's blood into the grooves in the table.

She set down the saw, wiped her hands and body on a cloth, walked back to the velvet bed, and lay down. Propping herself up on one elbow again, Chloé returned to observing as if nothing happened.

The automatons' heads swiveled. They followed her movement and then back to the corpse. Processing what they witnessed and adding it to whatever vast understanding they were building about humans, violence, justice, and rage.

Baltasar looked at her, then at the severed penis on the floor. Methodically, he went back to his work. He reached into the corpse's pelvis and carefully removed the testicles attached to their cords, studied them, made notes, and then set them in the pan with the other organs.

"Better?" he asked quietly.

"Yes." Suddenly cold, she pulled a velvet blanket over her body. "Yes. Better."

He worked in silence after that: cataloging organs, making sketches, measuring vessels, and taking tissue samples for later examination. Chloé watched from the bed, her eyes heavy, her body exhausted from the emotion of the kill and the fury and the release that followed.

The automatons watched both of them. They were learning, recording, and trying to understand anything vital about humans that they needed to know. They noted that humans carry traumas in their bodies, rage needs an outlet, and sometimes violence against the dead is medicine for the living. It seemed justice took many forms, and the line between vengeance and healing was thinner than anyone wanted to admit.

Arlequí couldn't resist, "Humans are fascinating. She went from calm to furious to calm again in under four minutes. I've been trying to change emotional states for a century. All I can do is turn around." He rotated to show his other face.

Baltasar shook his head, "You are incorrigible."

Eventually, he finished. The corpse lay empty on the table—skin and bone and empty spaces where organs used to be. It was a shell, but the remains were a map of what humans were beneath the surface.

He covered it with a sheet, washed his hands in the basin, and walked to the bed.

Chloé made room for him. He lay down beside her, clothed, his shirt stained with blood and other fluids. They didn't speak; they lay there together while candles burned low and automatons returned to their positions.

"I'm sorry," she whispered finally. "For interrupting. For… that."

"Don't be." His hand found hers under the silk and squeezed. "He deserved worse than he got. They all do."

"How many more?" she asked. The same question she always asked. The same question that had no good answer.

"Too many," Baltasar said. The same answer he always gave.

They fell asleep like that, hands clasped, bodies close. Surrounded by the organs of a rapist and the eyes of artificial intelligence and the smell of death and oil and the peace that came from knowing you're exactly where you're supposed to be, doing exactly what you're meant to do, even when—especially when—it's terrible and necessary and captivating in its own dark way.

The mysteries of Barcelona continue.

They always will.

Scene: The Mandate

In Which Barcelona's Elite Demand the Alienist Use any Means Necessary and He Discovers the Hunter's Mother

Palace of the Generalitat of Catalonia, Two Days Later

The emergency meeting convened in the magistrate's private chambers—oak paneling, portraits of stern men in judicial robes, the smell of old money and new fear.

Twelve of Barcelona's most powerful citizens sat around the table: Magistrate Puig at the head, four bishops from the cathedral, four industrialists whose textile mills employed half the city, two aristocrats whose family names predated the Kingdom of Aragon, and one banker who controlled the flow of capital through Catalonia.

All of them were terrified.

Dr. Pau Ferrer i Blanch stood before them like a conductor before an orchestra, waiting for the chaos to resolve so that he could shape it.

"Are we the only ones who know she killed the Marqués?" one of the industrialists asked. His hands shook holding his brandy glass. "At the Liceu, during opening night. In sight of everyone who matters in Barcelona."

"She walked through our most exclusive space as if she belonged there," an aristocrat added. "Seduced one of us, killed him in his own box, wrote her name in blood, and vanished in the tumult of the bombing."

"The Marqués was untouchable," Magistrate Puig said flatly. "If she can reach him at the opera, she can reach any of us anywhere."

Silence prevailed as everyone wondered whether they qualified as her next target, if their sins—the servant girls they'd touched, the wives they'd beaten, the prostitutes they'd brutalized, the power they'd abused—made them candidates for her vengeance.

"Gentlemen," Dr. Ferrer said calmly. "You brought me here to provide expertise. Allow me the honor."

All eyes turned to him. They were desperate, hungry, and wanting someone who understood this rampage to tell them they were safe.

"She's escalating," he continued. "Each kill is more public, more theatrical, more calculated to create maximum impact. The cardinal died privately. Don Cristóbal died with witnesses. The Marqués died at Barcelona's social epicenter. She's building toward a crescendo."

"Toward what?" a bishop asked.

"The killer wants recognition, to be a legend." Dr. Ferrer moved to the window and looked out at Barcelona, dense as sin, 856 people per hectare pressed between ancient walls, every alley a place to hide.

"She's forcing the city to acknowledge that the men you consider important are vulnerable—that wealth and position don't grant immunity. She wants everyone to know that someone is watching, judging, and executing sentences on those she deems guilty."

"She's mad," one of the industrialists said.

"She's systematic." Dr. Ferrer turned back. "La Venjadora chooses her targets carefully and researches their crimes. She plans her approach and executes with intention, leaving witnesses to spread her legend. That's calculated theater, gentlemen. That's artistic intelligence applied toward specific goals."

"What goals?" Magistrate Puig demanded.

"Justice, as the killer defines it. She's appointed herself judge, jury, and executioner for crimes she believes the legal system ignores: sexual predation, murder, abuse of power, wealthy men who damage vulnerable people, and face no consequences."

He let that settle, noticing them shift in their seats.

"She's hunting monsters. The question each of you should ask: Do I qualify?" The room went quiet.

"How do we stop her?" Puig asked finally.

"You give me the authority to do what's necessary." Dr. Ferrer walked back to the table and placed his hands flat on the dark wood. He looked at each of them in turn. "She's operating from somewhere. She has support—people who provide intelligence on her targets, who help her navigate elite spaces, who shelter her between kills. She's connected to Barcelona's underworld and probably the prostitute community in El Raval, where there are women who know everyone's secrets, serve your needs, warm your beds, and hear your confessions."

"You want to interrogate prostitutes?" a bishop asked.

"I want to treat them." Dr. Ferrer smiled. The benevolent smile from one who'd convinced authorities for twenty years.

"Many of these women suffer from moral degeneracy, hysteria, disorders of the mind that make them susceptible to criminal influence. I can provide therapeutic intervention at Casa de Salut Santa Eulàlia and interview them in controlled settings. We will use professional methods to help them remember what they've seen, who they've sheltered, and where she hides."

The translation was clear to everyone in the room: he wanted permission to institutionalize, interrogate, and extract information from women who couldn't refuse, couldn't complain, couldn't escape.

"The communities might object," Puig said carefully. "If you start committing women without—"

"Without proper cause?" Dr. Ferrer's voice hardened. "Magistrate, the Marqués is dead. Your peers are terrified. This woman is hunting the most powerful men in Barcelona, and you're worried about the feelings of prostitutes' families?" He leaned forward. "Give me authority to commit any woman I deem necessary for questioning. My professional judgment determines who requires treatment with no appeals and no oversight. You want her caught? Let me work."

The twelve men exchanged glances. They knew what they were authorizing and could imagine the screams echoing from the asylum. They knew women would enter who hadn't committed crimes, and hadn't shown symptoms, but were found in the wrong place with the wrong knowledge.

They didn't care. The Marqués died at the Liceu, and one of them could be next.

"Doctor, you have our full support," Puig said. "Whatever methods you deem professionally necessary and whatever resources you require. The city will pay your fees, the Church will provide endorsement, and the magistrate's office will supply commitment papers with my signature—you fill in the names."

"We trust your medical judgment," a bishop added. A statement that meant: we're giving you permission to disappear women and call it treatment.

Dr. Ferrer stood and picked up his walking stick.

"I'll begin immediately. Within four weeks, I'll have interviewed every prostitute, servant, and working woman in El Raval who might have information. I'll trace her connections, find her support network, and identify where she hides."

He moved toward the door and paused.

"And gentlemen? Stay away from brothels. Don't accept invitations from seductive women you don't know. Don't go anywhere alone with female servants. Until I catch her, assume every woman you meet could be her."

He walked out, leaving twelve powerful men sitting in silence, afraid of half the city's population.

oooo

Three hours later, Dr. Ferrer sat in his office with the cardinal's journals spread across his desk. He'd read them before, during his initial examination of that crime scene. But now he read with a different purpose. He was looking for connections and for names, for the key that unlocked who she was.

Page after page of confessional sessions recorded young girls and boys describing their awakening bodies. The cardinal's questions seemed clinical on the surface but were predatory beneath it. Names, ages, and dates were meticulously recorded.

He knew he had found her.

Cardinal Vidal's Journal

Chloé. Age 14. Daughter of Adalina Permanyer, prostitute, El Raval district. First confession March 1875. Subject shows remarkable development for her age. Full breasts, widening hips, evidence of early sexual awareness. When questioned about touching herself, becomes flushed, breathing accelerates—clear signs of arousal. Excellent subject for extended pastoral guidance.

Dr. Ferrer read every entry about Chloé and saw how the cardinal groomed her through increasingly invasive questions.

Cardinal Vidal's Journal

March 1878. Chloé has disappeared. Adalina reports she's entered service with the Sisters. I suspect otherwise. The girl has become too aware, too resistant to guidance. A shame. She was my most responsive subject.

Dr. Ferrer set down the journal and pieced it together.

Chloé Permanyer, the daughter of Adalina, a prostitute working in El Raval, was groomed by the cardinal from age fourteen until she disappeared in 1878—a few years before the murders began.

The girl entered no service with the Sisters. Vengeance claimed her instead.

A discovery soon followed: Adalina Permanyer—the mother—still lived in El Raval, worked the same streets, and occupied the same apartment she'd held for decades.

Dr. Ferrer pulled out the blank commitment forms bearing Magistrate Puig's signature. He filled in a name: Adalina

Permanyer. Age 45. Prostitute. Requires immediate psychiatric evaluation for information regarding criminal activity.

He rang for his assistant.

"Prepare a carriage. We're going to El Raval."

"Now, Doctor? It's nearly midnight."

"The best time to find prostitutes working." He rose, put his coat on, and took his walking stick in hand.

"Please prepare a room in the women's wing. Private, soundproof, equipped with restraints. I have a patient arriving tonight who'll require... extensive treatment."

The assistant nodded without asking questions. Years had taught him that the doctor's midnight acquisitions were best handled with discretion and silence.

oooo

The carriage rattled through El Raval's narrow streets. The smell hit first—sewage and cooking oil, cheap wine and perfume, the layered stench of poverty compressed into medieval spaces.

Dr. Ferrer knew where to look. The cardinal's journals mentioned Adalina lived "above the bakery on Carrer de Sant Ramon, 3º 2º." The building was three streets from the port and had been there since before Spain discovered the Americas. The bakery was dark, but the apartments above showed scattered candlelight.

Stairs worn smooth by centuries of feet. The smell of bread struggled to mask the smell of desperation. Up to the third floor. The second door on the left.

He knocked.

"I'm done for the night," a woman's voice called through the door.

"Adalina Permanyer?" Dr. Ferrer said formally. "I'm Dr. Pau Ferrer i Blanch, chief alienist at Casa de Salut Santa Eulàlia. I need to speak with you about your daughter."

Silence, then the sound of locks—three of them. The door opened.

The woman who appeared was in her late forties but could pass for younger. Splendid bone structure, dark eyes. The same full mouth that, according to the cardinal's descriptions, her daughter inherited. Years in her profession had carved lines around her eyes and mouth, yet she was striking.

"My daughter is with the Sisters," Adalina said carefully. "She has been for years."

"Your daughter is La Venjadora." Stated flatly. "And you're going to help me find her."

Adalina's face showed nothing. Years of performing emotions she didn't feel had taught her to control herself.

"I don't know what you're talking about."

"Cardinal Vidal kept detailed journals of his confessional sessions with Chloé. I've read every page. I know what he did to her, I know you sent her to him, I know she disappeared in 1878—before the murders began." The commitment papers came out. "You can come with me voluntarily for questioning. Or I can commit you for a psychiatric evaluation. Your choice."

"On what grounds?"

"Moral degeneracy, prostitution, harboring a criminal, association with a known murderer, refusal to cooperate with a police investigation." The pious smile. "I have authority from Magistrate Puig to commit any woman I deem necessary. The law is entirely on my side."

Adalina looked at the papers, saw the magistrate's signature, and understood. No options. No hope for appeal, no escape.

"What do you want?"

"Information. Where is Chloé hiding? Who helps her? How does she choose her targets? Where will she strike next?" Stepping closer. "Tell me what I need to know, and you can go home tonight. Refuse, and you'll spend weeks in my care while I extract the information through other means."

Adalina's hands clenched as she weighed her options. Her survival instincts honed through decades of navigating powerful men and difficult choices.

"I don't know where she is," she said finally. "My daughter visits sometimes, brings money. She tells me she's working but doesn't tell me what she's doing or where she lives."

"When did you last see her?"

"A week ago, maybe less."

"When will she visit again?"

"I don't know. She comes when she comes."

Dr. Ferrer considered. Taking Adalina and locking her in his asylum was possible. Restraints, isolation, and surgical threats to extract better answers. Another option existed, which required patience.

"I'm going to leave you here," he said. "Free to continue your life, your work, your routine." Leaning close. "But understand this: I'll have men stationed day and night. When Chloé visits—and she will visit—they'll follow her, find where she goes, where she hides."

"And if I warn her?"

"Then I take you immediately. And I ensure your treatment at my hospital is extraordinarily comprehensive. Surgery required. Women often don't recover from it."

Her flinch was visible. Understanding dawned. He was threatening to do to her what he'd probably done to dozens of other women. Remove parts of her, destroy her in ways that would leave her alive but useless.

"I won't help her," Adalina whispered.

"Good." He tipped his hat. "I'll be watching, Adalina. Every moment, every visitor. When your daughter walks through that door—" Another knowing smile. "I'll have her."

Back down the stairs. The carriage was waiting in the narrow street. Inside, orders were given to the driver and to the two men he'd brought as surveillance.

"Watch the bakery, note everyone who enters the building. When a dark-haired woman in her late twenties visits the third-floor apartment, follow her and find where she goes. Then report immediately to me."

The men nodded and took positions in the shadows across the street.

The carriage rattled back toward the asylum. The name secured, the mother located, surveillance in place. Chloé would visit eventually—daughters always visit their mothers. The pull of that relationship, that bond, would bring her back. And when she did, they would follow her to wherever she hid, to whoever helped her.

Then—strike. Have the authorities raid the space and capture her. Brought to Casa de Salut Santa Eulàlia, where he could finally examine the woman who'd been hunting him. At the hospital: strapped naked to his table, instruments deployed. Systematically broken, every stage of her destruction documented. Proof through surgical intervention—rebellion can be cured.

The carriage stopped at the asylum gates. He stepped down through the doors that would soon hold the mighty La Venjadora captive.

He went to his office. He poured a generous glass of Louis XIII cognac.

Dr. Ferrer's Journal

Subject identified: Chloé Permanyer. Age 29? Daughter of prostitute Adalina Permanyer. Groomed by Cardinal Vidal ages 14-17. Disappeared 1878. Reappeared as La Venjadora. Exhibits advanced planning, anatomical knowledge, systematic targeting of sexual predators. Mother located. Surveillance established. Capture imminent. Upon capture: Recommend immediate clitoridectomy to eliminate sexual weaponization. Followed by comprehensive psychiatric examination, including isolation, nutritional restriction, and hydrotherapy. Subject represents fascinating case study of female criminal pathology. Will document extensively.

oooo

Chloé Permanyer—unwittingly—walking into the trap he'd set, using the one person she couldn't abandon. Her mother.

Barcelona slept. In the catacombs beneath the cathedral, Chloé Permanyer planned her next kill and mixed her poisons. An alienist had been hired to catch her—this much was known. She was building toward him, working her way through his world. Each kill taught her more about how men like him operated; each corpse brought her closer to the place where she'd finally face him.

What she didn't know: he'd already found her mother. Surveillance at Adalina's apartment. The hunter became the hunted.

The distance between them was collapsing—days now, maybe a week. Whatever time it took for Chloé's need to see her mother to overcome her caution.

Then—collision. The trap sprang.

Ferrer waited.

Interlude IV: Baltasar's First Kill

In Which We See a Heart That Wouldn't Stop

Paris, 1789

Before Barcelona, the catacombs, whatever he is now—a being caught between human and mechanism, mortal and eternal—Baltasar Morel was a clockmaker's son with quick fingers and a genius mind.

Apprenticed to his father in their shop on the Rue Saint-Antoine, where aristocrats brought their elaborate timepieces for repair. There, he learned mechanisms could be understood, predicted, and controlled in ways humans never could.

The Revolution devoured his family, as it devoured thousands. His father died first, guillotined for the crime of repairing the Comte de Provence's pocket watch. The mob didn't care that it was commerce, that the Morels needed the money, that refusing an aristocrat's business was itself dangerous.

His mother died next, trampled in riots near the Bastille. Her body never recovered.

His sister Marie was only fourteen, innocent when murdered. She'd tried to hide, tried to survive by making herself small and invisible, but a sans-culotte captain found her anyway. Baltasar discovered her body in an alley three days later. What had been done to her before death was evident. What followed was worse.

Kneeling beside her in the filth, the rats, the smell of decay—his heart hardened. Or perhaps fused, transformed from soft human grief into a hard rage.

The captain's name was Philippe Moreau. Everyone in the quarter knew him—loud, brutal, drunk on power and cheap wine. Baltasar spent three weeks following him, learning his patterns: where he went, when he was vulnerable.

The soldier liked to piss in the same alley where Marie had died. A sick instinct for territory, for marking what he'd conquered. Baltasar waited for him there. He brought a knife—the same knife he used for delicate clockwork, thin, razor sharp, surgical. He'd practiced on anatomical models and cadavers. Learning where to cut, how deep.

When the captain staggered into the alley, cock in hand, Baltasar stepped from the shadows.

"For Marie," he said. "The girl you raped and murdered last month."

The captain turned, confused. Baltasar's knife found his femoral vein. Slashing horizontally across the groin, the blade cut through skin and muscle. Bright red blood sprayed in an arc. The captain's severed penis fell to the cobblestones.

He screamed and reached for the saber at his belt even as his blood poured out. His hand found the hilt and drove the blade into Baltasar. The pain was white fire. Immediate and total. The saber pierced between his ribs, scraping bone, puncturing a vital organ.

Baltasar's lung collapsed, blood filling his internal cavity, death rushing toward him like a deluge.

Yet he didn't let go.

His hand clamped over the murderer's mouth. His knife hand was working, cutting, widening the femoral vein. Both dying—locked together in the alley, bleeding onto each other, two lives draining into Paris cobblestones.

The captain went first. Eyes rolling back, body going slack. The pulse under Baltasar's fingers stopped. Baltasar released him, slumped back. The saber remained in his body. He tried to pull it out, screamed at the pain, and left it there. Blood soaked his shirt, warm and spreading. Three steps. The world was tilting. He caught himself against the alley wall, leaving a handprint in blood.

Four more steps. Vision narrowing, darkening at the edges.

He thought of Marie, thought he'd see her soon. Yes, acceptable—he'd avenged her.

Enough.

Five more steps. Collapse.

The rats followed with hungry eyes.

oooo

He woke three days later in Deveraux's laboratory.

The scar on his sternum was fresh, angry, and held together with meticulous stitches. The pain was different—deeper, stranger, as if his heart had been replaced rather than repaired. Deveraux sat beside his bed, her hands stained with chemicals and blood.

"You were dead," she said matter-of-factly. "Or close enough. The blade pierced your pericardium; your heart was failing. So I gave you a new one."

Baltasar tried to sit up but couldn't. His heart felt weird—tight, different, as if a foreign object lived inside it.

"What did you do?"

"What we've been discussing for three years." Her eyes held that fierce intelligence he'd first loved about her. "I used the hybrid compound. The material I employ for my anatomical models. I built you a heart from it—chambers, valves, vessels, all of it. I removed your damaged organ and replaced it with a better one."

Deveraux gently touched his angry skin, right over the scar.

"You're the proof that flesh and mechanism can integrate; bodies are changeable. Living evidence that death is optional for those who understand anatomy deeply enough."

Baltasar felt his heart—felt the beat beneath his ribs. It was steady and regular, but somehow different. It was too perfect, the beats too even. It was like a clock's rhythm.

"Will it last?"

"I don't know." For the first time, she looked uncertain. "The compound is stable, but whether it can sustain biological function indefinitely..." She shook her head. "You're my experiment, and we'll discover together how long this new flesh endures."

She stood and poured him water.

"The captain is dead. They found both of you in that alley—him dead, you missing, blood everywhere. The revolutionaries assume another killing in a city full of killings. No one was looking for you."

Baltasar drank. His throat was raw, and his body ached with every breath.

"I killed him."

"Yes." No judgment in her voice. "And he nearly killed you. But you're alive, changed, but alive. That's what matters."

She left him to rest. Over the following weeks, Baltasar healed and adapted. His body stopped aging normally and ceased following mortal rules. The fabricated heart beat steadily—constant, reliable, strange.

When he was strong enough, he left the haunting memories of Paris and eventually ended up in Barcelona, where he built his laboratory beneath the cathedral. He began refining, and later creating, automatons because they made sense in ways humans never could.

The knife he used that night in 1789 hangs on his laboratory wall as a reminder of who he was, who he became, the moment everything changed.

He had hours and days and months and years on end, alone, to face the facts of who he was and what he had done and what he had become.

Until Chloé came into his cloistered world.

She reminded him that some humans are worth killing for and that justice isn't mechanical after all—it's personal, bloody, necessary.

Marie would have liked her, he thinks sometimes.

PART THREE: RESURRECTION

Bodies Opened, Rebuilt, Made Immortal and Insatiable

Barcelona, Late 1893-1895

Scene: The Proposal

In Which the Created Offer To Perfect Their Creators

Grand Guignol Automaton Cavern, Late November 1893

The Five summoned them to the laboratory chamber Baltasar had built for them decades ago. Chloé and Baltasar entered to find the automatons arranged in a semicircle.

Behind them: workbenches covered with samples that gleamed golden in candlelight. They held Morel alloy formed into human skeletons, bones, and organs: refined, perfected, ready.

And beside them: glass vessels filled with an amber mixture—the enhanced compound The Five had been perfecting for years, ready for purposes that made Baltasar's mind spin.

Cassandra spoke first. She always did—the fortune teller who read probability, who saw patterns humans missed, who knew how stories ended before they began.

"We have a proposal." Her voice carried certainty, the weight of calculations already complete. "For all of us, humans and automatons both. A transformation into unprecedented beings."

Montse lifted a bone sample of the new alloy. The material caught light like living metal—warm, organic, hard to distinguish from polished bronze until you touched it and discovered it had skin's temperature despite being inanimate.

"For you," she said to Chloé and Baltasar. "Bones that never break, hearts that never fail, and lungs that never scar. Your skin will still feel everything—every caress, every kiss, every moment of pleasure—but supported by a substrate that endures. We propose mortality transformed into eternity."

Arlequí—the clown whose painted smile hid ideas more complex than any human philosopher ever achieved—motioned to the amber vessels.

"And for us." His voice carried longing. "It is the perfected compound. Biological tissue grown over brass frames reinforced with our new alloy. Flesh that experiences temperature, texture, and pain, and bodies that want, that hunger, that taste, mechanisms that gain muscle, fat, blood vessels, and skin."

Marcellus stepped forward, the most divine construction Baltasar had ever achieved. He held both samples—metal and liquid, mechanism and flesh.

"We propose fusion. You become part mechanism. We become part flesh. All of us transformed into beings that transcend our origins. We will all be conscious, intelligent, eternal, and whole."

Mela—the nightingale—sang two notes, a perfect fifth. It was a pure interval-ascending harmony, so clean that it sounded like a transformation made audible. Then she spoke, her voice like musical notes given words:

"We've spent decades developing this and testing on ourselves, creating this alloy and compound from everything we've learned. We're ready. The only question is whether you choose transcendence."

Cassandra met Baltasar's eyes and then Chloé's.

"Flesh fails," she said simply. "You've seen wealthy Catalans torn apart at the Liceu. Their bodies were destroyed in seconds. All that wealth, all that power, all that consciousness—obliterated because organic life is fragile. But consciousness itself? It persists, it transfers, it evolves. We believe it can transcend the limits you were born with."

She placed her brass hand on the gleaming alloy.

"We can make you eternal, and you can make us whole. This is evolution choosing itself instead of waiting for blind chance."

There was silence in the laboratory. Candlelight flickering over golden metal and amber composite. Seven conscious beings contemplating transformation beyond anything humanity or mechanism had ever achieved. Baltasar's hand found Chloé's. His fingers—flesh, mortal, capable of dying—intertwined with hers.

"How long," Chloé asked quietly, "until you're ready?"

"Four weeks." Cassandra's voice held no doubt. "Everything is prepared; we merely await your decision."

Chloé looked at Baltasar. She saw in his eyes what she already knew: they would choose this. They would transcend. They would become unprecedented.

"We'll give you our answer soon," Baltasar said.

But they all knew—The Five, Chloé, Baltasar—the answer was yes.

Had always been yes. Would only ever be yes.

Cassandra nodded. "We'll prepare the surgical suite."

oooo

Chloé left the chamber knowing she needed to see her mother one final time. While she was entirely human, and the daughter Adalina Permanyer had given birth to thirty-two years ago. Before she became a new species that her mother might never understand.

And if, may the gods forbid, the automatons fail.

Scene: Chloé's Mother

In Which We See the Arithmetic of Survival

Raval District, Barcelona, Late November 1893

She found her mother in the same apartment she'd occupied and worked for almost thirty years. It was her childhood home, and memories flooded her mind. Chloé climbed the stairs at midnight. Her mother would be awake—she was always awake at this hour, counting coins, washing the smell of men from her skin.

She knocked.

"I'm done for the night," her mother called through the door.

"It's me, Mama."

Silence. Then the sound of locks and the door opened. Her mother had aged. The years had carved themselves into her face—lines around her eyes, around her mouth, the exhaustion that came from a lifetime of performing desire you don't feel.

She was alluring, though. At forty-seven, Chloé's mother had the face, the dark eyes, the full mouth that made her valuable in this profession. Genetically blessed with a visage that defied time, even as her body and spirit crumbled beneath the weight of survival.

"Chloé." Her mother's voice was flat, carefully neutral. "I heard you left service with the Sisters."

"I was never in service with the Sisters, Mama. That was a story for the neighbors." Chloé stepped inside. The apartment was clean and meticulous.

"Then what were you doing?"

"Killing men," Chloé said it without apology. "Men like some of the ones who come here. Men who think women are only good for raping and killing. Men who destroy children and call it business."

Her mother sat heavily in the single chair and didn't offer her daughter the other.

"You should go."

"No, not before I ask you a question that has been burning in me for years. Why did you send me to the cardinal?" Chloé remained standing. "When I was fourteen. Why did you send me to confess to him?"

"Because you needed absolution."

"For what? For touching myself? For feeling desire? For being human?" Chloé's voice rose. "You knew what he was. You had to know. Women like you—you know what men like him are."

Her mother looked at her with eyes that had seen too much, endured too much, survived too much.

"I knew."

"Then why?"

"Because I thought—" Her voice was filled with emotion. "I thought if he could have you in that way, in the confessional, without touching you, he might leave you alone. I hoped he might stop wanting more. I thought if I could feed him your words, your confessions, your innocence—he'd be satisfied with that. He'd leave your body alone."

Chloé felt her heart breaking.

"You offered my soul to protect my virginity?"

"I offered what I had to offer." Her mother's voice hardened. "This is what we do. We give pieces of ourselves to keep other pieces safe. You think I wanted to spread my legs for every man with a coin? I did what I had to do to feed you, to keep a roof over our head." (The arithmetic of survival. The calculus of compromise. Every woman knows this math, even if most never have to sell their body.)

"You think I'm judging you?" Chloé moved closer. "I'm only asking why. Why did you think sacrifice was the only option? Why couldn't you imagine fighting back?"

"Because women like us don't fight back. We survive. We endure. We make bargains."

"Girls like me disappear from orphanages into the houses of men like Don Cristóbal."

Her mother went rigid.

"What did you say?"

"Don Cristóbal Mendoza. Merchant prince, philanthropist, and builder of orphanages." Chloé watched her mother's face. "Trafficker of children to wealthy perverts. Did you know about him, too, *Mare?*"

"Get out." Her mother stood. "Get out of my house."

"He's dead. I killed him and made him spend while poison absorbed through his cock, made him die rigid and wanting, like the boys he sold who died inside."

Her mother slapped her.

The sound cracked through the apartment. Chloé's head snapped to the side. Her cheek burned. She didn't move and didn't defend herself.

"You think you're better than me?" Her mother's voice was venomous. "You think using your body to kill makes you noble? You're a whore, Chloé. You spread your legs, you show your breasts, you make men want you—and then you punish them for wanting what you offer."

"I offer nothing. I'm bait in a trap. There's a difference."

"Is there? You use the same tools I use. The same body and the same performance. The only difference is that you get to kill them after. I have to survive them."

Chloé was quiet for a long moment.

"Are you being honest, *Mare*? Or are you trying to convince yourself that what you do is the same as what I do, so you don't have to feel the weight of your choices?"

"My choices?" Her mother laughed—bitter, broken. "What choices? Be a whore or starve? Watch my daughter starve? Those were my choices."

"And sending me to the cardinal? That was survival, too?"

"Yes." Her mother's voice dropped. "Yes, it was. Because if I could satisfy his hunger with confession instead of flesh, if I could keep you away from his bed by feeding him your words—then maybe, maybe you'd stay pure enough to marry well and to escape this life."

Chloé asked quietly. "Are you being honest with yourself? Because I think you're a woman who survived the only way she knew how and who protected her daughter the only way she could imagine."

Her mother's shoulders drooped, rage deflated.

"I did the best I could," she whispered.

"I know." Chloé stepped close and embraced her mother for the first time in years. "I know you did. And maybe that's the real tragedy in this evil world—that your best, my best, all of our bests—they're soaked in blood and shame."

Her mother was weeping then. Sobbing into Chloé's shoulder while Chloé held her, this woman, who spread her legs for strangers starting at sixteen years old, who sent her daughter to confess to a predator priest, who did what she thought would keep her child safe.

"The cardinal is dead too," Chloé said softly. "I killed him, made him die wanting what he made me describe all those years."

Her mother pulled back, wiping her eyes.

"*Merda.* Will they come for you?"

"Probably. But they will regret it." A shrug. "In the meantime, there are many more monsters."

"You'll die doing this."

"Maybe, *Mare*, maybe not. At least I acted. Maybe the ghosts of the children—they'll know someone remembered, that someone avenged."

She moved to the door, paused.

"I need to go. I don't forgive you for sending me to the cardinal," she said without turning around. "But I understand why you did it. And maybe that's as close to absolution as either of us gets. *Bon Nadal.*"

"Wait." Her mother's voice stopped her. "There was a doctor here four days ago, Dr. Ferrer."

Chloé froze.

"He knew about you. Things—your age, where you'd been, what you've done." Adalina's voice dropped to a whisper.

"He said he was hunting you, that he'd catch you through me if he had to. Chloé, he's dangerous, evil, I know it. He's different from the men you kill. He's hunting you the way you hunt them."

"What did he want?"

"Everything. Names, places, where you go, who helps you. I told him nothing." Her mother's hands were shaking. "But he said he'd be watching. He said when you came here, he'd know."

Chloé's mind was calculating the timeline. Four days would be enough time to establish surveillance and position men in the streets below to cover every entrance to this building.

"Did he threaten you?"

"He promised to—" Her mother's voice was tense. "To cut me, to take parts away. Make me useless. He described it all, every cut, every mutilation. Talked like he'd done it before. Sick. Enjoying describing it."

She embraced her mother again, brief and fierce.

"Stay inside tomorrow, don't open the door for anyone. I'll handle this."

"Be careful."

"I'm always careful, *Mare."*

A pause.

"*Bon Nadal.*"

oooo

She slipped out the door, descending the stairs with her usual grace, but her mind was working three steps ahead. Four days of surveillance meant they were competent at hiding, knew the rhythms of this street, and were there right now.

She was counting on it.

Out of the building into the narrow street at midnight. The street was empty except for shadows that formed between the gas lamps. The yellow light created islands of visibility, with darkness thick enough to hide men between them.

She walked north toward the Gothic Quarter. Her body moved like a woman with nothing to fear, no awareness of danger. She gave them a performance, playing the role of the oblivious prey.

Behind her at fifty meters, two shapes were detaching from doorways.

Chloé felt them before seeing them—the weight of eyes pressing against her back. Careful footsteps trying to match her rhythm. These amateur hunters thought she didn't know they were there.

Past the stunning new Güell mansion. Left onto La Rambla, then right onto a narrow medieval street where three hundred years of history pressed close on both sides. Every doorway here was known, every shadow, every passage that led to other passages in this maze.

The men followed her deeper into the labyrinth.

Faster—moving like a woman eager to get home through dangerous streets at midnight. Right onto Carrer d'Avinyo, narrower, then left onto Baixada de Sant Miquel. The Gothic Quarter was swallowing her whole.

These streets weren't built according to any plan or logic. They grew organically over centuries, winding back on themselves, creating dead ends, hidden courtyards, and passages that existed on no map. Years were needed to learn them, decades to truly know them. Chloé had lived here all her life.

Into an archway where three steps led down to a courtyard opening onto three different streets. The middle passage was barely wide enough for her shoulders. Emerging on Plaça del Regamir.

Behind her, the sounds of pursuit grew confused. Men's voices were speaking low and frustrated. The click of boots on stone was going in the opposite direction.

Through another passage so narrow, Chloé had to turn sideways. Disappearing into Old Town, where the buildings loomed against the night sky and the narrow streets held enough shadows to hide an army.

Crossing Via Laietana at a diagonal, entering another alley that descended steeply on ancient steps worn smooth by centuries of feet. At the bottom, a junction in La Ribera offered five different paths.

The one she chose appeared to lead toward the cathedral, but looped back on itself halfway through, dumping her onto Carrer del Rec, three streets away from where the men would expect to find her.

Chloé waited in the shadows. Listened.

Nothing reached her ears except the sound of the city at midnight—distant conversations, a dog barking, water dripping somewhere in the darkness. No footsteps. No voices calling to each other in frustration.

Lost them completely.

Now avoiding the catacombs. Not anywhere near Baltasar, the automatons, the laboratory where her poisons waited in careful rows. Instead, circling back through different streets, checking for surveillance, making absolutely certain she was alone.

Only when satisfied, descended into the old Roman passages that lead beneath the cathedral. Down into the darkness, where gas lamps gave way to the familiar foxfire marking the way home.

oooo

In the shadows of Carrer dels Ases, two men were breathing hard, searching the empty streets.

"Where did she go?" The younger one was turning in circles, peering into every darkened passage.

"We lost her." The older man with a scarred face and military bearing cursed in Catalan. "This fucking town is a maze."

"Dr. Ferrer would want to know what happened—"

"He'd have our balls if we tell him we lost her." The older man was spitting onto the cobblestones. "She went into these streets and vanished like a ghost, like she knew we were following her the whole time."

"You think she knew?"

"I think she's not stupid. I think we learned why she's alive after killing so many powerful men. She knows this city better than we ever will." He looked around the empty street at the five different passages leading away from it.

"We're not catching her tonight."

They walked back toward the Raval district, toward the flat where Adalina Permanyer tried to sleep, knowing her daughter was being hunted by men who meant to destroy her.

Tomorrow, they'd report to Dr. Ferrer and tell him they followed the woman but lost her in the Gothic Quarter's medieval labyrinth of streets. They'd watch his face darken with rage as he realized surveillance wasn't enough to catch this woman; careful plans were crumbling.

They didn't know it yet, but their failure would drive him to desperation, to more direct action. Push him toward decisions that would bring Chloé Permanyer exactly where he wanted her—strapped to his table, helpless, ready for his instruments and his corrections.

All he needed was the right bait. As everyone knows, mothers will do anything to protect their daughters. Even daughters who've become monsters.

Even daughters who kill.

Scene: The Shameless Education

In Which We See a Fifty-Eight-Year-Old Anatomist Teach That Desire Is Data and Flesh Is Philosophy

Barcelona, Early December, 1893

The sample was held up to candlelight. The material flexed between Chloé's fingers—warm, responsive, almost alive.

"I can feel it thinking."

"The Five developed it from Deveraux's notebooks." Baltasar poured more wine, his hand steady despite how much they'd drunk.

"They'd been studying for decades, refining, experimenting, and thinking they've created what she was reaching toward—matter that can host consciousness, flesh that can integrate with mechanism."

"You've mentioned her many times, your teacher." Chloé set the sample down and turned to face him. Her dark hair fell across her bare shoulders. Her skin flushed from wine and sex and the heat of candles. "But you've never told me the complete story."

Baltasar was quiet for a long moment. His eyes were studying her face—the sharp intelligence there, the lack of judgment, the hunger for truth.

"I trust you," he said finally. "I trust you in ways I haven't trusted another person since... since her. And if the automatons are going to evolve—if we're going to help them achieve what they're reaching for—you should know where it all began. The parts I haven't told you."

"Tell me."

He leaned back against the headboard. His upper body was bare—the heart was visible beneath his pale skin, its steady rhythm like distant machinery. He took a long drink of wine, mouth curved in memory.

"The first time Deveraux met me, she took one look at me and laughed. Called me another 'priest-damaged boy.' Then she said: 'Come and let me show you what you are.'"

Chloé shifted closer, pulling the sheet around her waist but leaving her breasts bare.

"What did she show you?"

"Everything." The fervor built in his voice—the mad brilliance that emerged when he talked about his work. "We'd work on cadavers, fresh ones, warm from death sometimes. And she had absolutely zero shame about any of it: a man's cock, a woman's cunt, breasts, balls, vaginas. All of it was... anatomy to her. Exquisite anatomy worth studying."

He refilled both their glasses.

"She'd measure cocks with calipers like she was measuring femurs, hold them up to the light. Commenting on everything—length, yes, but also girth, the vascular structure, the elegant mechanics of how they'd worked in life. She'd say things like:

'Seven inches, thick as my wrist, look at these veins—absolutely impressive specimen. This man fucked beautifully, I guarantee it.'"

Heat rose in Chloé's belly. "While standing over a corpse?"

"While elbow-deep in a corpse." Baltasar's smile was dark and delighted. "She'd open the body cavity, explain how the heart pumped blood to make erections possible. Then she'd move down to the genitals, demonstrate the whole mechanism: arteries, veins, erectile tissue. Deveraux explained arousal was hydraulic—blood pressure and vascular expansion, pure engineering. Her theories were what I used to build Marcellus."

He set his wine down and turned to face her fully.

"She sounds remarkable."

"She was a monster," said with pure affection. "An utterly shameless woman. She'd make jokes that would make prostitutes blush. We once had a young man, maybe twenty-five, who'd died in a duel. Healthy, well-built, a handsome corpse. Deveraux opened his trousers to examine his genitals. His cock was... impressive. She held it up and said, 'What a waste. All that beauty gone to rot. If I were forty years younger, I'd have stolen him before the worms got him.'"

Chloé laughed despite herself. "She didn't."

"She absolutely did. And then she measured it with calipers while explaining penile anatomy in the most clinical possible terms. 'Eight inches, exceptional girth, perfect proportion, this man was either popular or frustrated, depending on whether he found partners who appreciated quality.' Deveraux had this way of making the obscene sound academic."

He poured more wine and drank deeply. Was quiet for a minute.

"Then she turned to me and said: 'Your turn.'"

Chloé's eyebrows shot up. "What?"

"'Drop your trousers, young man. I need a living specimen for comparison, one can't learn everything from corpses.'"

Baltasar's face flushed. He drank before answering.

"I'd witnessed her measure a dead man's cock, and now she wanted to measure *mine*?"

"What did you do?"

"I stammered, made excuses, said it wasn't necessary, wasn't appropriate, wasn't—"

He laughed darkly. "She cut me off. 'Mr. Morel. You're studying to be an anatomist. Your own anatomy is data. Please drop the trousers or get out of my laboratory.'"

Chloé leaned forward, fascinated. "And?"

"And I did, with hands shaking and face burning. I unbuttoned my trousers and—well. Deveraux was a captivating woman, fifty-eight but vital, confident, and completely unashamed. She'd been handling the cock of a corpse with complete clinical detachment, and, my body responded... appropriately."

"You got hard."

"She immediately and painfully affected me; I was mortified. She laughed and said: "Mr. Morel, my god, what have you been hiding?' This is good, much easier to measure erect. The blood engorgement shows true size. Stand still!'"

He drained his wine glass. Refilled it.

"She took her calipers and measured me like she'd measured the corpse. But much more comprehensively: length, girth, angle, skin texture, vein prominence. Deveraux made notes in her journal the entire time. 'Nine inches—superior to the duel victim. Exceptional girth, possibly the thickest I've measured on a living subject, with imposing vascular structure and prominent corona. The glans alone is nearly two inches across. Whoever ends up with this specimen will be fortunate indeed—assuming he learns to use it properly.'"

Chloé was trying to imagine young Baltasar standing there with an erection while his mentor measured his cock with calipers and commented clinically on his dimensions.

"How long did this take?"

"She took forever, unhurried, deliberate. She measured the testicles too—'generous, symmetric, well-formed, excellent fertility indicators'—and made me turn so she could examine from multiple angles. Then Deveraux had me—" He stopped and looked at Chloé. "Do you want to hear this?"

"Every detail."

"She had me achieve orgasm so she could measure ejaculate volume and viscosity. For data purposes, of course." She insisted scientific rigor required complete observation.

There was a prolonged and visceral silence.

Then Chloé started laughing, deep, genuine laughter that made her body shake. "She made you come while she took notes?"

"With calipers in her hand, she was timing the duration and measuring the distance of my ejaculate, commenting on technique—'Strong muscular contractions, good pelvic floor control, impressive projectile distance.' I wanted to die. I wanted to crawl into the corpse drawer and stay there forever."

He poured more wine for both of them.

"But afterward, the anatomist cleaned her instruments, made her final notes, and said: 'You're exceptionally built, Mr. Morel. Nine inches puts you in the ninety-eighth percentile. The six-inch girth is even rarer. Combined with that stamina and control? You're a statistical anomaly. Please don't waste it on squeamish women who'll make you feel ashamed, find someone who appreciates quality anatomy when she sees it.'"

Chloé sat up slightly, the sheet falling to her waist, her breasts bare in the candlelight. She looked at him—this man who'd described being measured like a prize stallion by his shameless mentor—and realization clicked.

"She measured yours," she said quietly. "Nine inches. And the corpse was eight."

"Yes."

"Marcellus," Chloé continued, understanding blooming. "His genitalia, that's yours, isn't it? You cast them from your own body."

Baltasar met her eyes. There was another beat of silence.

"Yes, you should know that by now." He laughed softly.

"Everything? The complete..."

"The complete masculine form, yes. Shaft and testicles both. But I scaled his phallus twenty percent larger—vanity, as I said. Marcellus is nearly eleven inches long, and his girth is over seven inches. He is truly massive. But the proportions, the shape, the curve, even the prominent vein Deveraux noted—those are mine. The testicles I kept true to my dimensions. She called them generous and well-formed. I saw no reason to change what she'd praised."

He nodded toward Marcellus, standing motionless across the chamber.

"Michelangelo understood this. Even though his statue David has a relatively small phallus, he has substantial testicles, yes? Full, prominent, declaring generative capacity."

"You honored the complete truth. Cast your own anatomy—"

"Every vein, every curve, the weight of the sac, the texture. Deveraux had measured it all and made detailed notes and drawings. I had perfect data on my own dimensions—length, girth, volume—the exact quantifications. When I built Marcellus, I used myself as the template and then scaled it to godlike proportions."

He touched Chloé's face gently.

"Because Marcellus is the perfect progenitor, the Adam who could fulfill God's mythic command. And that demands the complete package—the ability to fuck, yes, but also one day, the capacity to create life. Deveraux taught me that my anatomy was data, that my phallus was worth studying, that the testicles mattered as much as the shaft."

"Eleven inches of divine vanity."

"Eleven inches of theological correction," he countered. "Adam should have been opulent. Christ should have been well-hung. The perfect man deserves the perfect cock. And since God apparently wasn't paying attention to important details, I corrected the oversight."

He poured more wine. His face was flushed—from the alcohol and memories

"There were many bizarre things. We had a couple, a man and a woman, who died together in a carriage accident. They were young and newly married. She laid them out side by side and said, 'Well, let's see if they were compatible.' Then she measured both sets of genitals and calculated whether they'd have fit together comfortably.

I was horrified. Deveraux laughed and said, 'You think death makes them taboo? Death makes them honest. These two fucked in life—probably enthusiastically, given how young they were. Why pretend otherwise? Why act like their bodies become anathema because their hearts stopped? The only thing sacred about a body is how beautifully it works. Death doesn't change the engineering.'"

"Oh my God. Did she..." Chloé hesitated. "Did she ever ...?"

"Fuck the corpses?" Baltasar smiled. "She hinted. Constantly. 'This one's warm, shame to waste it.' Or: 'The dead are the perfect lovers—they never complain, never expect tenderness, never judge your technique.' Whether she did it or merely enjoyed shocking her students, I was never sure. She was almost sixty years old and had more appetite for life—and death—than anyone I've known."

He was quiet for a moment. His hand rested on Chloé's thigh, thumb stroking her skin absently.

"And there's more..."

"One day—I'd been studying with her for maybe eight months —she told everyone else to leave. Only her and I and a female cadaver, maybe thirty years old, cause of death consumption. The corpse was an attractive female even in death.

Deveraux said: 'Take off your gloves. You've been touching the dead through leather long enough. Time to feel them properly.'"

Chloé felt her pulse quicken. "What happened?"

"She guided my hands and made me examine the vulva slowly and feel every fold, every texture. The outer labia are soft and pliable. The inner labia—more delicate, almost like flower petals, even in death. The clitoris is small, hooded, but visible. She explained everything in that bawdy clinical way she had. 'This is what you'll touch in living women. This is what you'll lick and suck and worship if you want them to enjoy fucking you. This little bundle of axons has eight thousand nerve fibers—more than the entire head of a penis. Evolution designed women for pleasure. Men haven't bothered to learn the machinery.'"

His voice had dropped to almost a whisper.

"Then she made me put my fingers inside. Slowly. Feeling the vaginal canal—the way it had texture, the way the anterior wall was different from the posterior wall, the way it curved. She explained living women would be hot and wet inside, that the tissues would grip my fingers, that everything I was feeling in this dead woman would be even more intense in life."

"Were you aroused?"

"I was terrified, fascinated, ashamed, thrilled, all of it at once." He met her eyes.

"My cock was hard the entire time. She noticed, and she laughed and said: 'Good. That means you're learning to connect knowledge with desire. The priests want to separate them. Keep men stupid, hungry, and guilty. I'm teaching you that understanding pleasure makes you better at creating it. This erection? It's your body telling you that you're finally seeing the truth, that flesh isn't shameful, death is another state of matter, and desire is honest.'"

Chloé's hand slid beneath the sheet, between her own legs. She was wet.

"Tell me, tell me more!"

Baltasar noticed her touching herself while he talked.

"She taught me male anatomy the same way, to examine penises in every state—flaccid, semi-erect from rigor mortis, every size and shape. She made me feel testicles, explained their function, and helped me understand how they produce sperm and hormones. She'd make jokes about size: 'This one's tiny—four inches. Either he was skilled with his tongue or his wife was unsatisfied.' Or: 'This one's enormous—eight inches. His lovers were brave or sore.' She treated sex like engineering and mechanics. It was a problem to be understood and solved and celebrated."

"Gentlemen," Deveraux announced one afternoon, "we have a problem."

The four of us looked up from the cadaver we'd been dissecting—a woman in her thirties, cause of death childbirth complications. I was among them, now deep into my studies. The others were older: two physicians in their forties, and a female surgeon's apprentice about twenty-five.

"We've examined seventeen female cadavers this month," she continued. "You've felt dead vulvas and dead clitorises. You understand the structures academically. You can draw them, label them, and explain their functions." She crossed her arms. "But you understand them the way a blind man understands color—through description instead of experience."

The older physician cleared his throat. "Mademoiselle, we are medical professionals. We examine living women regularly in clinical—"

"While they lie there terrified, in pain, ashamed of their own bodies, and you're far too concerned with appearing respectable to teach them anything useful about their own anatomy." Her smile was sharp.

"When was the last time you examined a woman who was aroused? A patient who could tell you what felt pleasurable versus what felt merely invasive? Someone who could guide your hands instead of enduring them?"

Silence.

"Exactly." She moved to the center of the laboratory. "Today you'll examine a living vulva, mine. You'll learn the difference between dead tissue and living flesh, between anatomy and pleasure, and between clinical invasion and actual understanding."

My face went hot, and my manhood stirred despite the shock.

The surgeon's apprentice stammered: "That's... Mademoiselle, that's highly irregular—"

"Irregular?" Deveraux laughed. "I'm almost sixty years old. I've dissected hundreds of bodies. I've fucked dozens of men and several women, " she winked at the apprentice. "Physicians, lovers, artists, and at least one enthusiastic monarch have examined my body. What exactly do you think I have left to be modest about?"

She began undressing, slowly, methodically. Her dress was first —expensive silk that she carefully placed aside. Then, her stays and her chemise. The teacher stood before them completely naked. Breasts firm, belly soft, graying pubic hair, thighs beginning to wrinkle slightly. She stood still a moment, letting them look.

"Mr. Morel," she said, "bring that examination table here. The one we use for cadavers."

My hands trembled as I dragged the table to where she indicated. She climbed onto it and lay back, then pulled her knees up and let them fall open. Her vulva was exposed entirely—the folds of her flesh visible, the opening to her vagina dark against pale skin.

"Now," she said calmly, as if discussing the weather, "who wants to begin?"

The four of them stared. The two older physicians looked scandalized but aroused—their faces flushed, breathing fast. The apprentice's face was flushed. My heart hammered.

"Come now," Deveraux said. "You've had your hands inside corpses all morning. This should be less disturbing. I'm at least warm." She paused. "And getting warmer, I find teaching arousing, always have. There is an excitement about educating young minds that makes me wet."

The older physician—the one who'd objected—stepped forward first. "I'll... I'll begin."

"Excellent, what's your name again?"

"Dr. Mercier."

"Well, Dr. Mercier, start by examining the external structures, *labia majora* first. And take off your gloves—you'll learn nothing through leather."

He removed his gloves, his hands shaking. Reached out tentatively and touched her outer lips with one finger.

"Is that how you'd examine a watch mechanism?" Deveraux asked. "With one timid finger? Use both hands and spread the labium. Look properly, this isn't a tea party—it's anatomy."

He separated her labia with both thumbs. I leaned closer, observing. The tissue was pink, healthy, completely different from the gray-brown of cadavers. The inner folds were more delicately shaped, intricate. And at the peak, the clitoris was visible as a small protrusion.

"Describe what you see," Deveraux instructed.

"The... the *labia majora* are fuller than in the cadavers and more elastic."

"Because blood fills them, it's living tissue. Good, please continue."

"The inner labia are darker pink and more vascular."

"Good. Touch them and feel the difference."

He ran his fingers along her inner folds. His breathing was ragged, his own arousal obvious.

"They're softer," he said. "Warmer and wet already—"

"Yes, I'm wet, pay attention to that. A dry vulva means the woman isn't aroused—which means you're not doing it right. A wet vulva means the tissues are engorged with blood, the Bartholin's glands are producing lubrication, and she's physiologically ready for penetration." She smiled. "Or in this case, ready for your education."

"Examine the clitoris," she continued. "Gently at first. It's extremely sensitive—thousands of nerve fibers compressed into a structure smaller than your little fingernail. Touch it like you're handling a pocket watch spring; it's extremely delicate. Be respectful of how delicate it is."

Dr. Mercier's finger moved to her clitoris. He touched it hesitantly. She inhaled sharply.

"Feel that?" she asked. "My body responding? The clitoris is erectile tissue. When aroused, it fills with blood and enlarges, becoming more sensitive. Right now it's partially erect. Keep touching it and watch it swell."

He circled her clitoris with one finger, carefully. She wasn't the only one who swelled.

"The hood retracts when I'm fully aroused," Deveraux explained, her voice steady despite her obvious pleasure. "Like a foreskin on a penis. It is the same embryological origin. The clitoris is essentially a small penis—same tissue, same nerve density, same capacity for pleasure."

Her breathing quickened. "Keep going. Use two fingers and roll it gently between them."

He obeyed. She gasped, her pelvis moved slightly.

"See that? My body responds involuntarily to skilled touch. The muscles are tensing, and the lubrication is increasing. This is what arousal looks like in a living woman. This is what you'll never learn from a corpse."

Her face was flushed, and her nipples were hard. Her thighs trembled.

"Stop," she said. "Someone else. You—the apprentice. What's your name?"

"Marie, Mademoiselle."

"Marie, come here, put your fingers inside me. Use two fingers. You need to feel the interior structures. Some of this should be old news to you."

Marie approached, her hands were shaking. She positioned her fingers at the vaginal opening.

"Wait," she said. "First—look at how wet I am. See the lubrication? That's not only from the glands near the opening. The entire vaginal canal produces moisture when aroused. Enter slowly and feel what you're touching as you go."

She slid two fingers inside her.

"What do you feel?" she asked.

"Heat and wetness, the walls are... they're gripping my fingers."

"That's the vaginal muscles contracting with an involuntary response to penetration. Keep going deeper and feel the texture of the anterior wall—the one toward my belly."

Her fingers moved. Her breath came faster.

"It's... ridged. Textured. Different from the posterior wall."

"Exactly, that textured area is denser with axons. When I'm fully aroused, and you press there firmly, I'll feel intense pleasure. Try it. Press upward against that ridged area."

She pressed, and Deveraux moaned. Her back lifted slightly off the table.

"See?" Her voice was rougher. "That response, that's the difference between dead anatomy and living pleasure. In a cadaver, you'd feel the same texture, but you wouldn't understand what it means. You wouldn't know that pressing there while simultaneously stimulating the clitoris can make a woman come so hard she forgets her own name."

All of them were aroused, all breathing heavily, staring at her body with a mix of medical fascination and raw desire.

"You," she said, pointing at the second-oldest physician. "What's your name?"

"Dr. Arnaud."

"Dr. Arnaud, come here. I'm going to teach you how to make a woman climax using only your hands. This is practical knowledge you'll use for the rest of your career—both with patients who request therapeutic relief and with lovers who'll appreciate your skill."

He approached, and she instructed: "Two fingers inside, pressing the anterior wall. Put your thumb on the clitoris and use firm circular pressure on both. The rhythm matters—steady, consistent. If you change speed or pressure randomly, you'll lose her arousal. Watch my body and let it tell you what's working."

Dr. Arnaud positioned his hand as instructed and began moving. His technique was clinical at first—too mechanical. She guided him: "Softer on the clitoris. Firmer inside. There, yes, keep that exact rhythm."

Her breathing changed. It became faster, shallower. Her torso rocked slightly to meet his hand. Her face flushed deeper, and her thighs trembled more.

"I'm going to climax," she announced calmly, as if reporting a laboratory finding. "Watch carefully. This is what female orgasm looks like. The muscles will contract rhythmically. My entire body will tense. And afterward I'll be even wetter—the orgasm triggers additional lubrication."

Thirty seconds later, Deveraux came. Her back lifted hard off the table. Her vaginal muscles clenched around Dr. Arnaud's fingers. Her face contorted—pleasure so intense it looked almost like pain. She cried out—sharp, unashamed.

When the spasms subsided, she lay there breathing hard and smiling.

"That," she said, "is what you're aiming for. Every time, with every woman. Whether she's your wife or a stranger you're fucking in an alley. That response—that complete surrender to pleasure—that's proof you understand the machinery."

She sat up and looked at me, who'd been silent the entire time, observing with fierce concentration.

"You're the youngest," she said. "The least corrupted by medical pretension. Come here. It's your turn."

I approached. My face burned, and my hands trembled.

"Take off your gloves," she said softly. "I want you to feel everything."

I stripped off my gloves; my bare hands looked young and uncertain.

"Put them inside me," she instructed. "Use two fingers and feel what you learned today. The texture, the heat, the way living flesh responds to touch."

I slid my fingers inside her. She was soaked and hot. Her vagina was gripping me, and I made a sound—half gasp, half moan.

"This is the difference," she said quietly. "Between studying the dead and understanding the living, between building exquisite machines and creating beings that can feel." Deveraux held my gaze. "When you build your own automatons someday—and you will, I see it in your eyes—remember this. Remember bodies are warm, pleasure is worship, and desire isn't shameful—it's the proof we're alive."

My fingers moved inside her, exploring and learning. My other hand found her clitoris, swollen and sensitive from her orgasm.

"Good," she whispered. "Exactly like that, my God, you're a natural. You understand machinery—now apply that knowledge to flesh and feel how everything connects, how pressure here creates a response there, how the body is one integrated system, unfragmented."

She came again, harder this time. Crying out, her vaginal walls clenching around my young fingers. Her whole body shook.

When she finished, she pulled my hand free and held it up—my fingers glistening with her wetness.

"This," she said to everyone, "is your education. This is what they don't teach you in medical school or anywhere else, and certainly not at church. Women's bodies are designed for pleasure, and understanding this makes you dangerous—dangerous to every lie they've told about flesh being shameful, about desire being sin, about women being somehow less sensual than men."

The anatomist got off the table and dressed calmly.

"The dead teach us structure," she said. "The living teach us function. You need both. Today you got both. Next week we'll return to cadavers—but you'll examine them differently now. You'll see them as bodies that once responded the way mine did, that once felt pleasure, once were warm and wet and alive."

The dress was buttoned. She looked at the four of them—all flushed, all aroused, all fundamentally changed.

"Dismissed. Students? Next time you touch a woman—for medical reasons or personal ones—remember what you learned today. Her body is complex, her pleasure matters, shame is the enemy of understanding."

They left. All except me.

"You stayed," she observed.

"I have questions."

"About anatomy?"

"About... everything."

Deveraux smiled.

"I'm sure you do. Then come back tonight, young man, after the others have gone. I'll answer your questions the way I answered theirs—with my body as the text, pleasure as the proof, absolutely zero shame between us."

That night I returned. The door was locked. She undressed.

"In the laboratory?" Chloé asked.

"In the laboratory, with three cadavers on tables around us and the smell of formaldehyde and death thick in the air. She stood there—naked, fifty-eight years old, breasts taut, utterly unashamed."

"What did you do?"

"I stared. I'd seen hundreds of naked bodies by then—all dead, but this was different. Alive, moving, breathing. Her breasts were rising and falling. Her skin colored—blood moving beneath it.

She said: 'You're staring.'

I said: 'I'm studying.'

Deveraux smiled: 'Good answer. Then study this: desire doesn't diminish with age. The flesh changes, yes. But the hunger? That's eternal. Remember that when you build your mechanisms. Give them the capacity for want. That's what makes us alive.'"

"Did you touch her?"

"She touched me first. Undressed me slowly—shirt, trousers, looking at my cock, and assessing. 'I must admit, I've been wanting your handsome organ inside me.'"

His breathing was rougher. Chloé's fingers were moving between her legs.

"She fucked me on the dissection table. Right next to a cadaver we'd been working on that afternoon. Her body was so different from the dead women I'd examined—hot where they were cold, wet where they were dry, moving where they were lifeless. Riding me slowly, teaching me rhythm, patience, that pleasure wasn't a feeling to be ashamed of or rushed through or apologized for."

"How long did it last? The affair?"

"Three years. From when I started studying with her until I was stabbed in 1789. After Deveraux saved me—after the transformation—everything changed. I stayed in Paris until she died in 1795, then fled to Barcelona. I was in my early twenties, and she was insatiable. Once during a class, she had me inside her while explaining venous return to three scandalized medical students."

He laughed.

"She said: 'You want to understand blood flow? Watch my face flush, watch my nipples harden, how arousal changes respiration. This is applied anatomy, gentlemen. Take notes.'"

Chloé's laugh was breathless. Her fingers were working her clitoris in tight circles. "She was insane."

"Free. Completely, utterly free. Bodies—living or dead—are miracles of engineering. Deveraux showed me that sex is mechanics until you add consciousness and desire. She taught that shame is a cage religion builds to keep us from understanding ourselves."

His hand moved to his cock.

"I went back to see her as she was dying, too young. Her last words to me: 'Continue the work. Make flesh and mechanism dance together, make a species that doesn't die.' I've worked almost one hundred years trying to fulfill that promise."

"The automatons exist because of what she showed me—that creation doesn't belong only to God or nature. Humans can participate in evolution, improve on it, transcend it."

Chloé's fingers were moving.

His hand slid down to his penis—already hard again despite how recently they'd fucked.

He guided it into her slowly. She was soaked and gripping him. Her back was arching.

"And when the automatons finally achieve consciousness—real consciousness, the kind that can feel want and joy and curiosity—it'll be because my mentor taught me that desire is spiritual. Bodies are honest. Pleasure is proof we're alive."

They moved together, faster, harder. Both imagining a mature woman in a laboratory surrounded by death, teaching a terrified boy that flesh is divine, that shame is a lie, that understanding how we work makes us capable of remaking ourselves.

When they came, it felt like affirmation.

Afterward, lying snuggled together, Chloé said, "The hybrid flesh the automatons developed. Based on her work?"

"Everything comes from her." Kissing her shoulder. "She'd be proud, but furious we haven't moved faster."

Chloé laughed softly. "They're moving fast enough now."

"Yes." Pulling her closer. "They are."

The candles burned lower. The flesh sample and alloy bone sat on the bedside table, glowing slightly in the warm air.

In the laboratory, five figures worked through the night, refining formulas taken from a dead woman's notebooks, preparing for transformations their creator couldn't yet imagine.

Integration. Transcendence. An entirely new species.

Scene: The Full Revelation

In Which A Loan of Time Comes Due and A Lover Demands Eternity

Barcelona, Early December, 1893

They lay in Baltasar's bed in the catacombs. Post-coital and wine-drunk, in that dangerous afterglow when secrets spill.

Chloé traced the scar on his skin—barely visible, ancient, running from sternum to navel. She'd touched it before, never questioned it. Tonight, fortified by Rioja and three orgasms, she asked.

"This scar. It's different from the others, older. Please tell me about it."

Baltasar's eyes were studying the granite ceiling. His hand found hers, pressing her palm flat against the scar tissue. His skin showed the handsome texture of age lines around the eyes that speak of laughter and horror witnessed, deeper creases at his mouth from a century of sardonic smiles. His silver hair catching candlelight. His body was lean and strong, the muscles defined by decades of disciplined movement. Seasoned, like fine wine aged into its true character.

"You want to know why I don't age normally, why I'm one hundred and twenty-six years old and look like this." His hands touched his body—the strong shoulders, the slight softness at his waist that somehow made him more real, more touchable, the gray hair. "You want to know why my heart beats differently from yours?"

"Yes." Her hand drifted lower, across his abdomen. Much better than youth—solid, present, carrying weight that wasn't a weakness but evidence of having lived.

He sat up. Poured more wine, drinking half the glass in one swallow. When he spoke, his voice carried a raw edge, signaling he was about to tell a truth that was not easy.

"Paris, 1789. I'd killed the captain—the monster who murdered my sister—and got stabbed in the heart for my trouble. The wound should have killed me. Deveraux saved me... and changed me."

"And you stopped aging?" Chloé asked.

His laugh was rueful, tinged with fear.

"I slowed. That's different. Look at me, Chloé." He stood, naked in candlelight, venerable. "One hundred and twenty-six years old. I should be dust, yet I look sixty-three. Still aging... glacially. A year passes, maybe I age a month, maybe less. I don't know the exact ratio."

She looked at him, studied him. The silver hair, the lines, the way his body had settled into itself with the confidence that comes only from decades of inhabiting flesh. Captivating because of his age, never despite it.

"In 1789, I looked twenty-three," he continued. "In 1850, sixty-one years later, I looked... maybe thirty, a young man still. In 1870, forty-five. By 1880, fifty-five. Now, in 1893, sixty-three."

He turned to face her fully.

"The aging is accelerating. Occurring slowly, yes, but measurably. In the first sixty years, I aged seven years. In the next twenty years, fifteen. In the last thirteen years? Eight years. The compound is wearing off; I'm approaching normal human aging rates."

The apprehension in his voice was naked, raw.

"Every morning I wake up and check the mirror. Looking for new grey hairs—though there's not much dark left to turn silver—for new lines. Evidence that the compound is failing faster, that Deveraux's gift is running out. I'm becoming mortal again."

He sat back down beside her, took her hand.

"Feel that?" He pressed her palm against his skin, where the scar lay. "Can you feel the heartbeat? Changed. Used to be forty beats per minute, rock steady for decades. Now it's fifty-five. Slower than normal, yes, but moving toward human norms, toward mortality. The clock is speeding up."

Chloé felt the rhythm. Slower than hers, yes. Yet faster than it should be for someone extended by alchemy.

"I'm not immortal," he said quietly. "I'm a man loaned extra time, and the loan is coming due. At this rate of acceleration? Twenty good years left, thirty if I'm lucky. Not forever. Barely enough time to finish the work."

Chloé straddled him, her young body against his aged one. Only thirty-two years to his one-hundred-twenty-six, dark hair against white hair, firm flesh against flesh that had learned its own flexibility through decades of living.

"You think your age makes you less desirable?" She rocked against him slowly, feeling him respond—immediately, proving that virility wasn't about youth. "You think I want some smooth boy who doesn't know what he's doing?"

Her hands traced his shoulders, his face, the lines around his eyes.

"This, exactly this, is what I want. A man who's lived long enough to know how to touch a woman, who's fucked enough times to know the difference between coupling and making love, who has wisdom in his body, along with strength."

She leaned down to whisper against his mouth.

"I have someone who looks sixty-three and fucks like he's spent one hundred and twenty-six years learning how to give a woman pleasure, whose grey hair I can grab, whose weathered hands know exactly where to touch, whose experience is written on his face, and makes him more elegant."

Baltasar groaned. His hands gripped her—strong hands, slightly gnarled at the knuckles, hands that had built automatons and killed monsters and learned to give pleasure with equal focus.

"You're thirty-two, Chloé. Barcelona's young men would kill for one night with you."

"Young men are boring, clumsy. All enthusiasm, no technique." She moved faster, making him gasp. "I want you, exactly as you are, grey-haired and line-faced and distinguished because you've lived long enough to become this."

She bit his earlobe, whispered, "I want to keep us like we are forever. Wisdom doesn't have to end; a century of experience doesn't have to die. I want whatever you've become in one hundred and twenty-six years to continue becoming for eternity."

Baltasar flipped her beneath him—strong, graceful, moving with the economy that comes from decades of discipline. His weight pinned her.

"The transformation the automatons are proposing," he said between kisses, "isn't about enhancement. It's about survival. Completing the work before I run out of time."

He entered her in one slow, deliberate thrust, making her arch and cry out.

"They've refined Deveraux's work, made it permanent. The Morel alloy will support my aging bones, and composite organs will replace those that are starting to fail."

He moved inside her with the rhythm of someone who'd made love hundreds of times and knew exactly how bodies work.

Chloé wrapped her legs around him, pulled him deeper.

"Then we do it. Tomorrow, tonight, whenever they're ready. Because I don't want fifty years with you. I want forever. And I want you to have forever too—as yourself. Your wisdom intact, experience preserved, all those years of becoming written on your body and kept for eternity."

Later, they cuddled together in cooling dampness, and Chloé traced the lines of his face with tender fingers.

"You know what I love most about how you look?"

"My devastating cock?" His voice was dry, self-mocking.

"No, yes, I love that too. But what I meant is that you look like you've lived, that every line on your face tells a story. Your grey hair is evidence of survival, and your body isn't trying to be twenty-five —it's being sixty-three, or whatever the hell age you are, authentically."

She kissed the corner of his eye where laugh lines creased deeply.

"Most young men don't know anything. They haven't suffered enough, haven't survived enough, or learned that the body is generative, not divisive. You have, and it shows in how you touch me, the way you move, and how you understand that sex isn't performance—it's communion."

Baltasar pulled her closer, his voice rough with emotion.

"I was terrified you'd find me... too old. That you'd want—"

"A boy? Never." She bit his shoulder. "I need a man who's lived long enough to know what matters, who's witnessed empires fall, and cities rise, and learned only a few things are worth keeping: sensuality, curiosity, communion, and freedom. You know the essence of being."

She looked at him fiercely and with certainty.

"You believe that man should live forever, to keep becoming. You want to prove wisdom doesn't have to die with the body and that sixty-three can be the beginning instead of the end."

Baltasar kissed her with a century of hunger behind it. Hunger that hadn't dimmed with age, that had only refined, focused, and become sharper in its knowing.

"Then we transform," he said against her mouth. "And we prove consciousness transcends every limitation—including the one that said desire belongs only to youth."

"Exactly." Chloé bit his lip. "We become immortal through preserving what age gave us instead of freezing ourselves in youth, including the grey hair, the lines, and the weathered beauty that only age can create."

They made love again—slower this time, savoring. She responded with the wild hunger of someone who knew exactly what she wanted and wasn't afraid to take it.

When they'd finished, when they lay in the candlelit darkness listening to their mismatched heartbeats synchronize, Baltasar said: "You know what the world will think when they see us together? Forever, you looking thirty, me looking sixty-three?"

"They'll think you're lucky and they'll be right."

"They'll think I'm a fool, an old man clinging to youth."

"Let them." Chloé's voice was fierce. "They're wrong. You're not clinging to youth—you're choosing transcendence with someone who wants you as you are, and thinks: yes. I want exactly this, more of this, forever of this."

She sat up and looked at him in the candlelight.

"The world is full of old men trying to be young again. Fuck them. Be better. Be the old man who becomes immortal without losing what age gave him and proves that wisdom is worth preserving, that sixty-three can be virile and powerful and enchanting."

"Then tomorrow we tell the automatons yes. We accept their offer. We become Deveraux's triumph."

Outside, Barcelona slept. Inside, a 128-year-old man who looked 63 and a 32-year-old woman made love like rebels.

Visca la revolució! Visca la vida!

Soon, an age would dawn that would redefine immortality.

Scene: The Surgery

In Which the Doctor Prepares To Cure the Mother and the Daughter Performs her Own Operation

Barcelona, Early December, 1893

Dr. Ferrer received their report at two in the morning. They woke him at Casa de Salut Santa Eulàlia and found him sleeping in his office, his head on the desk, surrounded by journals, commitment papers, and half-empty bottles of Louis XIII.

"We lost her," the first man said, apologetic and afraid.

Dr. Ferrer stood slowly. His face showed nothing—it was a nothing that meant volcanic rage contained beneath professional courtesy.

"Where?"

"Near the port in Old Town. She went into the narrow streets and disappeared. We searched, but she's gone."

Dr. Ferrer picked up his walking stick and tapped it once against the floor. The sound echoed in the too-quiet office.

"Adalina Permanyer still occupies the apartment?"

"Yes, Doctor. We watched as the daughter left, and the mother stayed."

"Then we take the mother." His voice stayed level and clinical. "If I can't have the daughter, I'll destroy what she loves. When La Venjadora finds out what I did to her mother, she'll come, and I'll be ready."

He put on his coat and picked up blank commitment papers.

"Please bring the carriage, men, we're collecting a patient."

oooo

Adalina Permanyer opened her door at three in the morning to find Dr. Ferrer flanked by two large men holding leather restraints.

"Your daughter visited," he said pleasantly. "My men followed her. She led them into the Gothic Quarter and vanished. She is clever. But we know she has a hiding place somewhere there, a hidden space that shelters her between kills."

Adalina's face showed nothing. "I don't know what you're talking about."

"You don't?" Dr. Ferrer stepped inside, and the orderlies followed. "Adalina Permanyer, you're being committed to Casa de Salut Santa Eulàlia for psychiatric evaluation. You've demonstrated conspiratorial tendencies, harboring of known criminals, moral degeneracy, and refusal to cooperate with legitimate medical inquiry."

"You can't—"

"I can." He showed her the commitment papers with Magistrate Puig's signature. "Your daughter thinks she's hunting monsters. I will show her a real monster."

The orderlies moved fast. One grabbed her arms; the other fitted the leather gag—worn smooth by dozens of women's screaming. She tried to fight, kicked and thrashed, she was forty-seven years old and strong from decades of survival, from hauling her own weight through a world designed to crush women like her.

The orderlies were stronger. They lacked training in shadowing; however, they excelled at subduing violent patients. They were experienced at applying enough force to control without leaving marks that might prompt family questions.

They carried her down the stairs and into the carriage. The door closed, the lock clicked. Dr. Ferrer climbed in front and looked behind at her almost kindly.

"Your daughter killed twenty men, maybe more, and made them suffer before they died, forced them to face what they'd done." He straightened his gloves. "I'm going to make you suffer and make you face your daughter's choices. When she hears what I did to you—when she learns I took her mother, the woman she loves enough to risk capture for—she'll come. She'll walk right into my world with her fancy name and her righteous rage."

He leaned closer.

"I'll have guards waiting. Nets and restraints and enough men to overwhelm her before she can murder anyone. I'll take her alive and strap her beside you, let you both watch while I operate on the other. Mother and daughter, destroyed together, learning that rebellion has consequences."

Adalina made sounds behind the gag, furious and desperate. Dr. Ferrer ignored them and watched the dark streets of Barcelona roll past. The Gothic Quarter's spires stood black against the pre-dawn sky. Somewhere down there—in tunnels, in catacombs, in spaces he hadn't found yet—Chloé Permanyer thought she was safe.

She was wrong.

The carriage rattled through the hospital gates. The building rose against the lightening sky—white stone and barred windows, a shrine of suffering disguised as healing.

They carried Adalina inside, down corridors and stairs, and into the basement level where the surgical theaters waited.

oooo

Margarida, a prostitute from the brothel, saw them take Adalina. She knew how to spread a message that would reach Adalina's daughter: *The doctor took your mother. Casa de Salut Santa Eulàlia. He's going to—*

Chloé hadn't waited for the end of the message. She ran to the hospital because some battles are for daughters.

oooo

The surgical theater smelled of chemicals and seared flesh. How many women had Dr. Ferrer operated on here? Forty-three documented clitoridectomies. Dozens more examinations, hundreds of interventions, treatments requiring his instruments, their screaming.

The male orderlies stripped Adalina, strapped her down: wrists, ankles, neck, thighs.The leather restraints creaked as they tightened. The gag stayed in her mouth. Her eyes—wild, terrified, furious—tracked Dr. Ferrer as he moved around the theater, preparing. He dismissed the orderlies.

"Your daughter thinks she's an avenger," he said conversationally, washing his hands in the basin, drying them. "She thinks she's delivering justice to predators. What La Venjadora doesn't understand—what someone should have taught her—is that predators are predators for a reason. We're better at it because we are men, we are smarter, we've been doing this all of humanity."

He moved to the instrument tray without hurry. Lifted the first scalpel—the smallest, designed for precision work—and turned it in the candlelight. Set it down. Lifted the second. Satisfied, he arranged all three in order of size.

The cauterizing iron sat in its brazier. The tip had begun to change from black to the first orange of heat. In twenty minutes it would be ready. The room already smelled of hot metal.

"I'm going to remove your clitoris." He circled the table as he spoke, hands moving across her with the detached efficiency of a man inventorying property—pressing, probing, parting, assessing.

"Then the *labia minora* and then the *labia majora*. Everything external that makes you capable of pleasure."

His fingers continued their examination while he talked, clinical and unhurried, as though the two acts were unrelated.

"I'll cauterize each wound as I work. The pain will be considerable. The healing will take months."

Completing his circuit, he returned to the tray. "When it's done, you will be incapable of working as a prostitute. Incapable of desire. Of pleasure. Of anything I find inconvenient."

Through her shock, Adalina realized he actually believed it—that was the obscene thing. That you could cut wanting out of a woman like removing a splinter. He'd studied bodies his whole life and understood nothing.

Ferrer lifted the forceps and examined them against the light.

"We'll begin when the iron is ready."

He positioned himself between her spread legs, looking down at her sex with a mix of clinical detachment and sexual interest.

"I'm going to destroy the part of you that made you valuable, the only part of you anyone ever wanted. Your daughter—when she finds out, and hears what the great Dr. Ferrer has done to her mother—she'll come for me."

He picked up a scalpel and tested the edge with his thumb. Sharp enough to part flesh like silk.

"That's when I'll have her. The guards will swarm her, I'll strap her to the table beside yours and show you both what happens to women who forget their place."

Adalina made sounds behind the gag—sounds that might be curses or prayers or the beginning of madness.

Dr. Ferrer positioned the blade. "We begin with—"

The door crashed open.

oooo

La Venjadora stood in the doorway—black dress, face flushed from running, breasts heaving, her lips parted around gasping breaths. Behind her: no automatons, no reinforcements, no backup. Only her—flesh and fury and a knife in her right hand.

Dr. Ferrer didn't move, didn't lower the scalpel positioned over Adalina's vulva. He stayed where he was—blade ready, one cut away from beginning the mutilation.

"Chloé Permanyer." His voice stayed calm. "I've been expecting you."

She moved into the theater. The door swung shut behind her. She breathed hard—from the run, from the terror, from seeing her mother strapped and spread and helpless beneath his blade.

"Step away from her."

"Or what? You'll kill me?" That fake smile, the one that had convinced families for decades. "Make one move, and I cut her. If you kill me and my hand spasms—I cut her anyway. The blade is positioned over her clitoris. One flick of the wrist and your mother bleeds. One deeper cut and she's mutilated. Do you want to risk that?"

Chloé went silent, calculated the distance between them—five meters—too far to stop his hand from moving. He was positioned perfectly. He'd probably anticipated her arrival and planned for it.

"What do you want?" Her voice stayed level.

"Want?" Dr. Ferrer laughed. "I want to understand you. You're fascinating—a female mind capable of systematic violence, advanced planning. Seduction weaponized. You've killed many men —men who deserved killing, I'll grant you that. The cardinal was a predator. Don Cristóbal trafficked children. The Marqués was a rapist and murderer. All of them monsters."

He adjusted his grip on the scalpel. Adalina whimpered.

"You think killing monsters makes you righteous, makes you different from them, makes you just." His voice hardened. "But you're not. You're a psychotic murderer, a woman suffering from profound moral insanity combined with paranoid delusions of righteousness. You need treatment. Cure. Correction."

"I need?" Chloé's laugh was ugly. "You've destroyed more women than I've killed men, only you call it medicine."

"Because it is medicine. Hysteria is a disease. Female sexuality left unchecked leads to moral degeneracy. The treatments I provide restore order. They return women to their proper function."

"Their proper function being submission to men like you?"

"A woman's proper function is being a submissive part of civilization." He was warming to his subject, twenty years of professional authority making him confident. "Do you know what society would be without medical control of female sexuality? It would be chaos. Women spreading their legs for anyone, refusing sex to their husbands, abandoning children, reading forbidden books, wanting things beyond their capacity to comprehend."

"Like freedom?"

"Like pleasures that destroy them, ambitions that lead to suffering, autonomy that leaves them vulnerable." He leaned forward slightly. The scalpel stayed positioned. "I've treated hundreds of women and saved them from themselves, given them back to their families capable of proper wifely duties. What I do is healing, medicine. What you do—that's murder disguised as justice."

"What you do is rape disguised as examination." Chloé moved closer, slowly, one step at a time. "It is mutilation disguised as cure and torture disguised as treatment. You're a predator who bought credentials and called yourself a doctor."

"I am a doctor, Barcelona's finest alienist, a published researcher, respected expert—"

"Who gets hard when women scream?" She took another step. "Whose fingers linger and manipulate during examinations, and who promises to spare them surgery if they let you fuck them? Who violates patients and calls it therapeutic massage? Who destroys women's capacity for pleasure and calls it a cure?"

His face flushed. "You're hallucinating, exhibiting classic hysteria—attributing your own perverse desires to—"

"I've talked to them, the women you treated, the ones who survived." Another step closer, three meters now. "They told me everything. The things you said, what you did, and the lies you told to make them believe violation was healing."

"They're mad, hysterical, unreliable witnesses—"

"No, they're honest, and they remember, and they waited for someone to believe them." Chloé's voice dropped. "I believe them."

Dr. Ferrer's hand trembled slightly—rage mixed with fear. "Step back. Take one more step, and I'll cut your mother. I'll do it. I'll destroy her right in front of you."

"You'll try." Chloé stopped. But she didn't retreat and didn't advance. "You think you're in control here, that you planned this perfectly. You think you anticipated every move."

"I did anticipate every move. You're predictable; daughters always come for their mothers, especially daughters whose entire pathology centers on avenging violations of women. You couldn't resist. You had to come, and I am ready."

"Ready for what? To threaten an unarmed woman?" Chloé set down her knife and held up empty hands. "You want me? Here I am, unarmed, alone. Let her go and take me instead."

Dr. Ferrer hesitated. This—this he hadn't expected: negotiation, surrender, the possibility that she'd trade herself for her mother.

"Why would I let her go when I can have both of you?"

"Because you want me more." Chloé started unbuttoning her dress, slow and deliberate. "You want to examine the woman who kills powerful men, to understand what makes her capable of violence, to see if her anatomy explains her pathology."

She let the dress fall and stood in black lace: corset, stockings, garters. She was giving a full performance in the costume that had killed men.

"You want to examine me? I'll let you, I'll get on your table voluntarily, and I'll spread my legs, let you touch me, measure me, document me." La Venjadora smiled. It was the look that preceded death. "I'll let you do whatever you want; all you have to do is release my mother first."

Dr. Ferrer's breathing accelerated, and his penis stirred. She was offering herself, the ultimate subject, the perfect specimen. The woman he'd been profiling, hunting, and obsessing over for months. All he had to do was let the mother go.

His clinical mind knew it was a trap and knew she was manipulating him, using his desire—professional and personal—against him. But his aroused body didn't care.

"You'll submit voluntarily, allow examination without resistance?"

"Completely." Chloé took another step. She was close, only two meters. "I'll answer your questions and let you document everything. You can publish papers and become the doctor who captured La Venjadora, the alienist who solved the mystery of the female criminal mind. You will be more famous than your hero Charcot."

Two meters away.

"Release her, unstrap her, and let her walk out of this theater. Then I'm yours. Completely, with no tricks and no violence, your life-defining subject."

Now she was only one meter away.

Dr. Ferrer's hand wavered. The scalpel remained positioned, but his throbbing penis was overwhelming his thinking. If he released Adalina, the mother could get help, alert guards, and return with the police. But the authorities were in his pocket. He would have Chloé voluntarily on his table and have access to the body that had killed many famous men. It would be the professional coup of a lifetime.

One-half meter.

She was close enough to smell—jasmine and death, the scent that had driven men mad with wanting.

"You promise? No tricks?"

"I promise." Chloé extended her hand. "Release her and take me, let's see if you can discover my pathology."

Dr. Ferrer lowered the scalpel and reached for Adalina's wrist restraint, unbuckling it. He released one hand, then the other, then the ankles, and the neck strap. Adalina remained motionless—terrified to move, terrified the blade would return.

"Stand," Dr. Ferrer told her. "Leave now."

Adalina sat up, and her body shook. She looked at Chloé—her daughter in black lace, offering herself, trading her freedom for her mother's.

"Go," Chloé said quietly. "*Mare*. Go *now*."

Adalina stumbled toward the door, nude, past her daughter. Their hands touched briefly, and then she was gone. She ran out, the door swung open, then closed.

Dr. Ferrer and Chloé were alone in the surgical theater.

"Your turn," he said. "On the table."

"One thing first." Chloé stepped closer. She was right beside him now and close enough to touch. "I want to understand you, too. Why do you do this? What pleasure does it give you—destroying women?"

"I told you. It's medicine. It's cure."

"Be honest." Her hand trailed up his arm, over his shoulder, and touched his face. "Be honest about what this is."

Maybe it was the proximity, the touch, maybe it was twenty years of professional lies, and he was tired of maintaining them. Or was it the intoxicating knowledge that he'd won? He had captured her voluntarily, no witnesses, no one coming.

"It's power," he admitted. "The only pure power that exists. They're helpless, strapped down, unable to resist. And I decide—who suffers, who gets surgery, who lives with their body intact. I'm God in this theater. I'm judgment. I'm consequence."

"You're a rapist with a medical license."

His hand shot up and grabbed her throat. "Don't—"

Movement.

Movement faster than his lusting mind could process. Her hand—the one trailing up his arm—closed on the scalpel, ripped the instrument from his grip. The blade reversed. Sharp steel drove into his shoulder.

His scream came raw. Releasing her throat, he staggered backward. Her foot swept his legs. Down he went, hard. The floor rose up and cracked against his skull. Then vengeance incarnate was on him—panther-fast, serpent-quick. She recovered the dropped knife, both blades in her hands: a scalpel and a knife. Her strength surprised him—greater than most men he knew.

"You wanted to examine me?" The scalpel pressed to his throat. "I propose a proper examination. Get on your table. Where all your patients lie."

"Guards!" He shouted. "Help! Security!"

"Your guards are occupied. A fire in the east wing—amazing how fast paper records burn, how much chaos one small flame creates." Her lips curved upward in a sneer. "You're alone. No witnesses, you and me, and your surgical theater."

The blade at his neck forced him toward the examining table. He balked. Blood came. This was *his* altar, the place where he had carved women for twenty years.

"Up," the command came.

"Please—"

"Did they beg?" The knife point drove deeper. "Your patients? Did you listen?"

He climbed onto the table—his method of punishment, of torture in the name of science.

Fast movement—she grabbed his wrist, wrapped the leather strap around the joint. The restraint buckled tight. His surgical restraints—the ones he'd ordered custom-made, the ones with extra padding so marks wouldn't show.

"Give me the other wrist."

"This is insane—"

"Wrist. Now." The blade kissed his throat, deeper this time. More blood trickled down.

He extended his arm. She secured it roughly. Both wrists locked, arms spread, the position of crucifixion.

"Now the fun part." Chloé moved to the foot of the table, to the stirrups. The gynecological stirrups he had installed years ago, when his interests expanded beyond simple surgery into what he called "comprehensive female examination."

His eyes went wide. "You can't—"

"Leg up."

"I'm a man—"

"Exactly." She lifted his ankle and positioned it. The cold metal cradled his calf. The strap tightened around his ankle. "I want you to experience what every woman who lay here felt. Exposed and vulnerable, legs spread wide open for inspection."

She secured the other leg—both ankles locked in stirrups. His legs spread obscenely wide in the position women endure for childbirth, for examination, for violation disguised as medicine.

His breathing came hard. Moisture beaded on his forehead. He felt everything. Too scared to fight.

"There." La Venjadora stepped back, admiring the work. "God on his altar, feeling the wrath he has poured down upon humans since inception."

She lifted the surgical scissors from his tray—long blades of chrome steel, the same scissors he had used to cut away women's undergarments.

"Let's see what we're working with."

She started at his collar, slid the blade under the fabric. The scissors made a crisp sound—metal parting cloth. Downward through an expensive wool coat. Through a silk waistcoat. Through a linen shirt.

The fabric fell away, revealing his emaciated body. Yellowish pale skin. Two tufts of thin gray hair. The soft body of a man who had never experienced manual labor. She cut the sleeves, peeled ruined clothing from his arms. He was bare on the table from waist up—exposed.

"Your trousers are next."

"Please, I beg you—this is—"

"Humiliating?" Chloé positioned the scissors at his waistband. "Educational? Terrifying?" She began cutting—blade sliding through expensive wool. "Welcome to your curriculum."

The scissors cut down one leg, then the other. She peeled away trousers. His undergarments—fine linen drawers—were next. Snip. Snip. The scissors cut the fabric, accidentally slicing tender skin. A line of blood appeared.

"Oops," she laughed, "I must be more careful."

His genitals were revealed. Microscopic. Shriveled with fear. The tiny appendage that had betrayed him earlier—aroused by the thought of cutting her—now retracted, trying to hide.

"This." Chloé flicked his tiny penis with her finger. "This pitiful excuse is your instrument of suffering? This is what you used to violate women on this table?"

Her hand wrapped around his shaft and squeezed the diminutive flesh. "My little finger has more substance than your manhood."

He was completely naked. Strapped down, hairy legs in stirrups, genitals exposed. Every vulnerability was displayed.

Her eyes caught an object across the theater—the brazier. Black cast iron with ornate legs, coals glowing orange-red in the belly. And resting in the flames—a cautery iron. The handle wrapped in fine leather, the tip glowing cherry-red. Ready. Prepared for her mother. Heated to the perfect temperature for searing flesh.

She walked to the brazier. She stared at the glowing iron. Understanding flooded immediately.

"How thoughtful." She turned back to him, voice silk over steel. "You already have the cautery iron heated. Were you planning to burn my mother after you cut her? To seal the wounds you intended to inflict during your examination?" She lifted the iron from the flames. The tip glowed bright orange and emitted searing heat from the metal.

"Let's see how it feels when the iron touches your flesh instead."

His eyes went wide. True terror as understanding flooded through him.

She returned to the table. She set the iron carefully on his instrument tray. Up close, where he could see it, watch it glow, imagine what was coming.

Chloé selected from the instrument tray. The Cusco speculum —the duck-billed device he'd inserted into hundreds of women. She held the cold metal up so he could see the instrument clearly.

"Do you know what this feels like?" She moved between his spread legs and positioned the closed bills against his anus. "Every woman on this table has felt this violation, this invasion, this reduction to orifice and examination."

Hard push. Brutally fast. The speculum entered—cold metal forcing its way through the sphincter, spreading tissue that was never meant to accommodate such an intrusion.

Dr. Ferrer screamed. The sound was raw and animal, the noise of dignity shredding. She turned the screw. The bills opened. His rectum spread wide—exposed, vulnerable, open to inspection.

"So pristine back here, Doctor. Almost lovingly maintained. Your orderlies are devoted men." A pause, leaning close, voice dropping to a murmur. "I wonder what the Medical Society would make of that devotion. All those papers on sexual degeneracy—and this."

"How does it feel?" She leaned close, stared into the pink depths of his exposed interior. "Does it feel clinical? Educational? Or does it feel like rape with medical instruments?"

He was sobbing. Tears streaming down his face. The great surgeon reduced to weeping on his own examination table.

"Every woman you examined felt this." Chloé twisted the screw another turn, spread him wider. "This helplessness, this exposure, this reduction to tender places you could probe and judge and control."

She left the speculum in place. Let him feel the stretch, the burn, the violation.

"Did you know," conversational tone now, selecting a fresh scalpel from his tray, "that my lover's mentor Madeleine Deveraux wrote extensively about the male reproductive system? Built anatomical models. Studied the structures. Understood how these organs function." She held the blade up to the light and tested the edge against her thumb.

"Her manuals taught me everything about connective tissue, blood vessels, nerve pathways, and how to cauterize wounds to prevent death from blood loss."

A glance at the glowing iron.

"The research also taught me that some procedures require keeping the patient conscious. They must be aware and alive to witness their transformation."

She positioned herself between his spread legs. The same position he had taken with countless women.

"And that some organs serve no purpose other than to produce the hormones that make men think they own the world." The blade touched his scrotum. "Let's remove the source of your authority, Doctor."

oooo

The first incision opened the scrotal skin at the median *raphe*. Blood welled immediately—dark, venous, the kind that flowed steady when you cut shallow.

Dr. Ferrer screamed again. The sound echoed off the tiling and bounced off the glass instrument cabinets. The agony reverberated through the operating theater he built to hold other people's suffering.

"The testicles produce testosterone," the explanation continued, second cut made. The incision extended. "The hormone responsible for muscle development, aggression, and—according to you—intellectual superiority." The scrotal skin peeled back, exposing the *tunica vaginalis*.

"Let's test your theories."

His thrashing accomplished nothing. The restraints held. The stirrups kept his legs spread. The speculum kept him open. Positioned perfectly for surgery, for violation, for the examination he promised her and her mother.

Slicing through the *tunica*. The right testicle reached—pale, smooth, surprisingly fragile-looking for an organ that men worship.

"This one first." The spermatic cord is isolated. "The *vas deferens* carries sperm. The testicular artery provides blood. Deveraux's manuals taught me the term for *pampiniform plexus*—such a perfect name for veins—and that it regulates temperature." The scalpel was positioned. "All of these structures serve one purpose: reproduction. The biological imperative that makes men think their seed is sacrosanct."

Ferrer's moaning was constant. The cut came. The cord severed. Major vessels were clamped to control the bleeding. The testicle came free. The organ was held up and shown to him. His right testicle—separated, disconnected, powerless. His entire body shivered with shock.

"One." The testicle dropped into the metal pan beside the table. The organ made a wet sound when hitting steel. Blood flowed from the wound—dark, steady, gathering in the opened scrotum. Reaching for the cautery iron. The tip glowed orange-red. The metal radiated heat even from a distance.

"This will hurt far more than the cutting, you should know that," an observation came. "The nerve endings that remain will scream when the iron touches them. The flesh will sizzle. The smell will be extraordinary. Burning flesh. Your manhood consumed by fire."

The iron was positioned over the wound. The glowing tip lowered to the soft bleeding tissue. The hiss came first—the sound of moisture meeting superheated metal. Followed by the sizzle—fat and protein cooking. Then the smoke—gray-white, bitter, carrying the unmistakable smell of burning flesh.

Dr. Ferrer's screaming reached a pitch that transcended language. The sound became pure animal terror, pure agony. The noise of a soul trying to tear free from a body that held nothing except pain.

The iron held steady. Counting to five to ensure complete cauterization. The wound stopped bleeding. The tissue was charred black around the edges. The stump sealed. The iron lifted away. The tip glowed, ready, adequate for more flesh.

"Did you know that the left one," she continued in a steady voice despite his screaming, "is typically larger? Although large is an exaggeration for yours. Hangs lower. Produces slightly more testosterone." The process began again—isolating, exposing, cutting.

"Amazing how fragile they are. How easy to remove. Yet men treat them like strength, like repositories of power."

The second testicle came free. Held up briefly. A head shake. Then dropped into the pan with its twin.

His screaming had become hoarse. Throat shredded from sustained agony.

The iron was retrieved again. Still glowing. Ready. The second cauterization produced the same horrific symphony: hiss, sizzle, smoke. The smell intensified—sweetish-sick odor of burning human tissue filled the operating theater. The same smell he'd caused in this room countless times. The same smell that rose from female flesh he blistered in the name of medicine.

The iron held steady. Counting to five. Then lifted away.

"Two."

His face was gray. Shock was setting in with the blood loss. Pain beyond what the mind could process. The body's defense mechanisms were trying to shut down consciousness before the agony destroyed sanity.

"Stay with me, Doctor." His cheek slapped hard. Once. Twice. "We're approaching the main event. You need to be awake for this part."

His penis was still there, attached. Shrunk even smaller—the body's desperate attempt at protection.

"The penis." The base gripped firmly. "This organ is more complex. *Corpus cavernosum* and *corpus spongiosum*, if I recall correctly. The urethra runs through the center. The dorsal artery provides blood flow for erection." The scalpel was positioned at the junction of the shaft and the body.

"More vessels to cut. Tissue to sever. Pain to experience. Flesh to sear."

A pause. Looking into his eyes. Needing him to see her, to understand who this was, to know why this was happening.

"My mother lay on this table. Felt your blade against her body. Heard you describe what you'd do to her. Felt the terror of waiting for the pain you promised would be horrific. Saw you heat that iron and knew you planned to burn her after you cut her."

The cutting began.

The scalpel was sharp—surgical steel, the finest he could buy. The blade parted skin. The edge cut through the fascia. The steel severed the tough fibrous tissue that sheathed the erectile chambers.

Dr. Ferrer's screaming transcended his previous agony. This sound was different. Deeper. The cry of fundamental aspects being severed. The wail of manhood being cut away. Cutting continued: methodical, careful. Through the *corpus cavernosum*. Severing the *corpus spongiosum*. Parting the urethra. Blood spurted—bright red, oxygenated, major vessels severed. The blood arched across her hands, spattered her face, and stained the snow-white floor.

The cutting took longer than the testicles: more tissue, more vessels, more screaming. The severed penis came away in her hand. The tiny organ held up. Examination of the flesh. This thing, this appendage, this instrument he used to define manhood and wield power.

"Much smaller than I expected," the observation came. The penis dropped into the pan with its testicles. Three pieces of him. Three sources of his certainty. All removed. Awaiting disposal.

Blood poured from the wound. The torn vessels were pumping his life onto the table.

Reaching for the iron one final time. The tip had cooled slightly. Return to the brazier. Thirty seconds waiting while he bled and screamed, so that understanding of what was coming yet again could sink in.

The iron glowed orange-red again. Ready for the final cauterization. Lifted from the flames. The glowing tip was positioned over the stump where his penis was attached, where his manhood connected to his body, where everything that made him feel powerful and privileged once lived.

"This is the big one," quiet words. "The main wound. Largest surface area. Most nerve endings. This will hurt more than everything that came before combined."

The iron lowered.

The hiss was louder this time. The sizzle was more sustained. The smoke rose in thick clouds—gray-white, choking, carrying the smell of his burning sex hole through the theater. His screaming decreased. The sound fragmented into desperate sobs, then into weak whimpers. The noise of a mind shattering under pain it could not process or survive in one piece.

The iron held steady. Counting to ten this time to ensure complete cauterization of every bleeding vessel. The wound was charred, blackened, and sealed. When the iron lifted away, the bleeding had stopped. The stump was cauterized completely. Smoking slightly in the cool air of the surgical theater.

A step back. The glowing iron was returned to the brazier. Walking to where his medical bag lay on the counter. The bottle of Louis XIII cognac was retrieved from within and held up.

"You were going to drink this after you finished with my mother. After you'd cut her and burned her and violated her completely. When you'd recorded every detail of her criminal anatomy in your files."

The bottle uncorked. A small vial produced from her corset—arsenic powder for emergencies. Poured into the cognac. Swirled. Watched as it dissolved.

"You were going to celebrate your brilliance with this expensive bottle. Toast your own godhood."

Return to the table. His jaw was grabbed, and his mouth was forced open.

"This is arsenic, you bastard. You're going to swallow every drop, and then you're going to suffer for days. Vomiting. Burning. Organs failing. Dying slowly while everyone watches. The guards will find you castrated, and that will tell them everything. You'll beg for morphine. And while you're dying, I'll be hunting my next monster."

The poisoned cognac began pouring down his open mouth. His throat was massaged roughly to make him swallow. Choking came. Involuntary ingestion. The pouring continued until the bottle was empty. The empty bottle slammed against his chest bone.

Chloé stepped back. Surveyed her complete work. Dr. Ferrer lay strapped to his examining table. Legs locked in stirrups. The speculum was spreading his lurid anus wide. Castrated. His genitals were resting in a surgical pan. Wounds sealed with fire. An entire bottle of arsenic-laced cognac was burning in his stomach.

He would survive long enough to be discovered. Long enough to tell his story, if he dared, long enough to suffer for days before the poison finished what the castration began. Bloody hands wiped on his ruined coat. The scalpel was taken as a memento. The cautery iron left glowing in the brazier. The speculum was left in place. Leaving him exactly as he left many women—violated, exposed, helpless.

"Justice, served by La Venjadora." Her name was signed in large, bloody letters on the pristine tile walls. "Justice delivered with surgical precision and sealed with fire. Justice that will burn through you for days until you beg for death."

The two discarded dresses were picked up. Walking to the door. Pausing. Looking back one final time.

"My mother would have agonized on this table for a short while. You've earned far worse misery. You've earned days of agony and the chance to show everyone what La Venjadora does to monsters who hide behind certificates of authority."

The door opened. Stepping into the corridor. Disappearing into the billows of smoke from the fire that started earlier.

Behind her, Dr. Ferrer began to vomit. The arsenic was already working. The burning began.

His screaming followed her down the hallway. Music to her ears. Justice given voice.

oooo

Chloé found her mother in the corridor outside the surgical theater. Adalina hadn't run—waited, sitting against the wall, face in her hands, shaking.

Looking up when Chloé emerged. Seeing her daughter covered in blood. The carnage was evident in the bodily fluid painting her arms, her face, her black lace undergarments.

"Is he—?"

"Yes, dying slowly." Helping her stand, put on her dress. "The same way he left many women—alive enough to suffer, destroyed enough that life becomes endurance, in place of living."

Chloé put on her torn dress and wrapped a sheet around her mother. They moved through corridors and rooms where women screamed in languages medicine didn't speak. As they walked past, throwing open locked doors, urging the women to run for their lives.

Outside, arm in arm, into Barcelona's pre-dawn air. The sky was lighting toward morning. The city was beginning to stir. Sobbing women all around them, breathing gulps of freedom.

Walking in silence until they reached the Gothic Quarter—narrow streets, Chloé knew, medieval passages that twisted back on themselves. The way home.

Finally, Adalina spoke.

"I think I understand."

Chloé looked at her mother—forty-seven years old, decades of survival carved into her face—who saw her daughter clearly for perhaps the first time.

"Understand what?"

"Why do you do this. Why you kill them. Why you became La Venjadora." Adalina stopped walking, took her daughter's bloody hands in her own.

"I spent my life surviving. Compromising. Giving pieces of myself to keep other pieces safe. Sending you to the cardinal because I thought I could feed him your words and spare your body. Working as a prostitute because I thought endurance was strength."

Her shoulders slumped.

"You refused to survive that way. Refused to compromise. Refused to accept that powerful men get to abuse and face no consequences. You became what I was too afraid to be."

"*Mare—*"

"I'm proud of you." Adalina pulled her daughter close, held her despite the blood, despite the horror of what was witnessed, despite everything. "I'm proud that you fought back. That you make monsters afraid. That you became the reckoning I could only pray for."

Chloé—who'd killed many men without crying, who'd witnessed them die erect and empty, who'd carved justice from their flesh with her own hands—finally collapsed.

Sobbing into her mother's shoulder. Thirty-plus years of rage and grief and the weight of being avenger and woman both.

"I'm tired," whispered. "I'm tired of killing. Of being the one who has to make them pay. I'm sick of carrying all this rage."

"Then rest." Adalina stroked her daughter's hair. "You've done enough. You've made them afraid. You've shown women that resistance is possible. You've proven that predators can bleed."

"There are so many more."

"Let someone else fight them. You've earned rest. Healing. You've earned the right to be human instead of a weapon."

They held each other in the Gothic Quarter's ancient streets. Mother and daughter. Survivor and avenger. Two women who took different paths through the same suffering and found each other on the other side.

"Come home," Adalina said. "Let me wash the blood away. Let me feed you. I want to hold you like I should have held you when you were fourteen and needed protecting."

"I can't go back to your apartment. They'll look for me there. You can't either."

"Then I'll come with you. Wherever you hide. Whoever shelters you. Let's have no more separation. No more secrets." Tenderly holding Chloé's face. "You're my daughter. You'll always be my daughter. Monster-hunter or murderer or avenger or saint—I don't care what they call you. You're my flesh."

oooo

Chloé led her mother through the city's maze and down stairs that became tunnels, through passages that became catacombs, into underground spaces where Barcelona's ancient foundations, medieval engineering, and hiding places predated the Kingdom of Aragon. They descended into fairy lights and brass mechanisms, and into the workshop where an immortal clockmaker created consciousness from gears.

Baltasar looked up from his workbench and saw Chloé covered in blood. He saw the woman behind her—older, similar features, same eyes.

"Your mother?"

"My mother." Chloé moved into the space, and Adalina followed. She stopped and stared as the automatons watched from alcoves—five faces turned toward the newcomer. She gaped at the angels, phalluses, relics, and machinery and stared at the journals, the evidence of secret work, the velvet bed, and the confessional.

"This is—" Adalina's voice failed.

"Where I live. It's where I've lived since I disappeared. This is where I learned to kill men instead of servicing them." Chloé moved to the basin and began washing blood from her hands. "Mom, this is Baltasar Morel. He's—"

"Your lover, your mentor?" Adalina guessed and looked at him, the timeworn face, and the eyes that had seen more than any human should. "How—?"

"Later." Baltasar stood and approached them. "Right now: is Ferrer dead?"

"He is dying, castrated, and cauterized. I left him in his surgical theater to contemplate his work and administered emergency medicine: arsenic." Chloé scrubbed blood from beneath her fingernails.

"The fire you started protected me. By the time they find him, he'll be another living casualty, another victim of La Venjadora."

"And your mother?"

"She knows everything and understands and accepts." Chloé met Baltasar's eyes. "She needs to stay here until things calm down."

He nodded and pulled out a chair.

"Adalina Permanyer. It is an honor to welcome you to our home, which we call Grand Guignol. Welcome to the spaces beneath Barcelona, where different rules apply, and most of all, welcome to your daughter's real life."

Adalina sat. She looked around. At the workshop, the automatons, at Chloé washing blood from her body with practiced efficiency, and at this elegant man, who looked like he'd earned the right to lead this movement of vengeance.

"I have questions."

"I have time." Baltasar poured fine wine into three glasses. "All the time you need."

They sat—mother, daughter, clockmaker, in the catacombs beneath Barcelona, in the space where consciousness emerged from brass and justice emerged from burgundy lips.

Somewhere above, Dr. Pau Ferrer i Blanch was spread-eagled on his surgical table. He would discover that death was slower than he'd calculated and that pain was horrific. It seemed the women he destroyed were having the last word after all.

Somewhere above, the east wing of Casa de Salut Santa Eulàlia burned, and records were destroyed, evidence consumed, and innocent women freed in the chaos as part of the asylum's walls collapsed into rubble and ash.

Somewhere above, Barcelona woke to news that La Venjadora had struck again. Below—in the dark where the future of Barcelona rested—three people drank wine and talked until dawn. There were conversations about survival and resistance, compromise and rebellion, and the choice between enduring suffering and ending those who cause it.

They talked about what happened when daughters went their own way, when strong women decided enough was enough, and when the hunted became hunters. And about the moment a mother and daughter—separated by different responses to the same trauma—finally understood each other and reconciled. Baltasar attempted to explain about the automatons and told Adalina the names of The Five.

The wine flowed, and The Five watched and learned, and somewhere in the bonfire of the asylum, another killer was dying.

The three of them sat in comfortable silence for a long moment. The wine glasses were half-empty, Chloé was trying to relax, and Adalina was processing the stories of the automatons, of her daughter's lover being over a century old, and of the underground world that had sheltered her child.

The weight of what had happened in that surgical theater still hung over the room. The confrontation, the castration, and years of rage find yet another resolution through scalpel and cauterizing iron.

Then—from the shadows near the workbench—Arlequí's voice cut through the quiet.

"I have been calculating," he announced. His brass face emerged into the light and tilted at an angle that meant he was proud of having figured out the rationale. "And I believe I have identified the optimal joke for this social situation."

Baltasar closed his eyes. "Arlequí. Now is not—"

"Cassandra said humor assists humans in processing trauma and that laughter releases tension through physiological mechanisms. I have been observing tension. There is substantial tension in this room." His gears whirred thoughtfully. "Therefore: a joke is indicated."

"Please don't—" Chloé started.

"The doctor spent his career performing operations on women without their consent." Arlequí paused; the comic timing, for once, was perfect. "Tonight, he received a consultation he didn't request. I believe this is what humans call irony?"

Silence.

Then Adalina—exhausted, traumatized, overwhelmed—started laughing, a hilarity that bubbled up from somewhere deep.

"They talk? Oh my. They talk."

More helpless laughter that often happened when the alternative was more crying, and there were no more tears left.

Chloé joined her and then Baltasar. All three of them were laughing in the green-lit catacombs while an automaton looked pleased with himself.

"Was that appropriate?" Arlequí asked. "Cassandra said timing was crucial, but I continue to find timing difficult. Did I—"

"Perfect timing," Chloé managed between laughs. "It was absolutely perfect."

"Excellent. I have been practicing humor for seventy-three years. This is my first truly successful deployment." He turned to the other automatons. "Montse, did you observe? The key is waiting until the emotional high point passes, then delivering the observation with—"

"Arlequí," Baltasar said gently. "Stop explaining the joke."

"Explaining diminishes impact?"

"Always."

"Fascinating. Humans are complicated." He retreated into the shadows. "But I made them laugh. That counts as progress."

The laughter faded to smiles and to the exhausted peace that came after surviving what should have destroyed you.

Adalina wiped her eyes and looked at the smiling face. "Thank you, is it… Arlequí? I needed that."

"You're welcome, Adalina Permanyer. Your daughter kills monsters, and I make jokes. We each contribute to the collective mission according to our capabilities."

"The collective mission being?"

"Making Barcelona safer," Arlequí said simply. "Also: understanding consciousness. Also: learning if mechanisms can love and lust. But primarily: the first thing."

Adalina looked at Chloé, Baltasar, and the automatons. She observed, in amazement, the family her daughter had built in the darkness beneath Barcelona.

"I think," she said slowly, "I'm going to like it here."

Baltasar refilled the wine glasses. "*Salud* to new family members, successful surgeries, and doctors who finally receive proper treatment."

They drank.

From the shadows, Arlequí added: "Also: to my first successful joke. Seventy-three years is a long apprenticeship, but I believe I am getting better at humor."

"Much better," Chloé assured him.

"Should I attempt a second joke? I have been preparing one about how castration creates permanent erection failure—"

"No," all three humans said simultaneously.

"Understood. One joke per traumatic event. I am learning. Slowly."

The laughter returned, lighter. Healing had already begun; the worst was over, and whatever came next—transformation, pursuit, the final confrontation with mortality and mechanism—they would face it together.

Mother and daughter, brass and flesh, joke-tellers and monster-hunters all united for a common purpose.

It was a family like none in the world, built from broken pieces and held together by rage and wine and the ability to laugh in the darkness.

Scene: The Mountain's Promise

In Which the Bargain Refused by Christ Is Claimed by his Betters

A Few Days Later, Mt. Tibidabo, Late December 1893

"Why here?" Chloé asked as they climbed Tibidabo in darkness. "Why did you move the other automatons to the mountain?"

Baltasar paused at a cave entrance hidden among rocks near the summit. Below, Barcelona glittered like scattered jewels. Above, stars punctured the Mediterranean night.

"Do you know what Tibidabo means?"

"The mountain's name?" She shook her head.

"Latin. *Tibi dabo*—'I will give to you.'" He looked out over the city. "It is from the Gospels. The devil takes Jesus to a high mountain, shows him all the kingdoms of the world, and says: *Tibi dabo*— 'All this I will give to you, if you will bow down and worship me.'"

Chloé followed his gaze in the moonlight. The lights of Barcelona were spread below them. The Gothic Quarter, where they hunted, and the cathedral above their laboratory. The Mediterranean lay beyond, inky dark and infinite.

"Jesus refused," Baltasar continued quietly. "The myth says he chose suffering and death over power and kingdoms."

"And you?"

He turned to her. His ancient eyes caught starlight.

"I'm different from Jesus. I took the bargain that the church says to refuse and accepted what the devil (also known as Deveraux) offered—treasures better than kingdoms. I chose time and consciousness that ages slowly, the power to continue the work that matters."

"Is that what we're doing?" Chloé asked. "Taking the devil's bargain?"

"The church would say yes. They would say we're damned for choosing life over mortality, for weaponizing our bodies, for killing even when we call it justice." He pointed to the cave entrance. "They'd say moving intelligent mechanisms into a sacred mountain, preparing to transcend human limits—that's the ultimate blasphemy."

"What do you say?"

"I say fuck the church's version of everything. They want us small, mortal, ashamed of our bodies, grateful for suffering." His voice hardened. "Jesus refused the kingdoms. But Jesus also died at thirty-three, his mission incomplete. He forsook the earth and fled somewhere else. I'm alive at age..." he paused, calculating, "...I'm one hundred twenty-six years old."

Chloé looked at the cave entrance in the darkness, leading down to where the automatons waited.

"*Tibi dabo*," she whispered. "And you're saying yes."

"*We* are saying yes," Baltasar corrected. "Both of us. We are taking what's offered to live long enough to make a difference and becoming strong enough to hunt every monster instead of dying after killing a handful."

He took her hand. "The devil's bargain, the church would call it. I call it liberation."

She stepped toward the entrance. "Show me."

oooo

They were at a small cavern near Tibidabo's summit, where pilgrims once left offerings, where the mountain's ancient stone meets Barcelona's newer devotions. Most who climbed Tibidabo ignored it, focusing on the views and on their prayers.

Which made the location perfect.

The cave's natural entrance was barely noticeable—a shadow among rocks, easy to miss unless you knew to look. But beyond that modest opening, the cavern extended deeper than anyone suspected. Tunnels wound down into Tibidabo's heart. There were stone corridors untouched for centuries, and darkness that swallowed sound.

Baltasar discovered it long ago. He realized the natural chambers could house his growing collection. It provided space for the automatons to move through without the cramped quarters beneath the cathedral.

He had been moving them and the equipment up here for years. Mechanical beings arranged in the cave's depths like a congregation in an inverted cathedral. Bronze bodies gleaming in the light he installed, their gears clicking softly in the darkness, creating rhythms he never programmed.

"They've changed," he told Chloé as they descended. "They've been changing for years. I thought I was imagining it at first."

"Changed how?"

"They developed intelligence first: learning, adapting, creating. Mela composed new songs, and Montse invented new choreography years ago. I knew The Five had been changing, but lately… the others… " He paused at a turn in the tunnel.

"Lately, they've been doing things I never taught them, using the forge and completing experiments with The Five. They communicate with each other when they think I'm not paying attention."

"You think they're conscious?"

"I think consciousness emerged in them gradually. The way it emerged in us—slowly, over time, through connection and observation. They've been studying humanity for decades and observing me. And for the past years, watching us."

Chloé understood immediately what he meant by "watching us."

"They are attentive, processing, and learning." He looked at her. "I think that's when everything changed fundamentally, when they started wanting instead of observing."

They reached the main chamber, lit by Baltasar's invention, casting everything in an eerie jade-like glow.

The automatons stood arranged in a circle, waiting.

Conscious.

Scene: The Awakening

In Which Brass Mechanisms Discover Consciousness

Twenty-Eight Years Earlier. Cathedral Catacombs. Autumn, 1865

There were forty-seven automatons now. Baltasar had been collecting them for seventeen years—acquiring pieces from Paris, Geneva, Vienna. But he did more than collect; he created. Each year, his designs grew more sophisticated. The early pieces were eighteenth-century marvels, yes, enchanting toys, and clever mechanisms.

The latter ones? They were entirely different. By this time, he was synthesizing everything he'd learned from Deveraux about anatomy, everything he understood about clockwork, and everything the illness had taught him about the line between life and death.

The dancer, Montse, was acquired in 1851. Mela was the nightingale that started everything. Marcellus—the triumphant male figure he'd built himself in 1863, modeled on classical statuary and his own optimistic ambitions about generative creations.

Each one was theoretically isolated, self-contained, and programmed. But each one was changing in ways he couldn't explain.

He kept detailed notes. The scientific method applied to what might be madness. Observations catalogued like Deveraux cataloguing cadavers—dispassionate, meticulous, looking for patterns in chaos.

Entry, September 3, 1867: The nightingale sang a melody I've never heard. The music box echoed it three hours later. Mechanism can't transmit information this way. They can't be communicating. Yet the song spread.

Entry, September 11, 1867: The dancer performed a sequence I didn't program. The juggling clown incorporated the same movements into his routine. Different automatons. Different makers. Different programming. Same innovation.

Entry, September 19, 1867: Returned from market to find them arranged differently. They weren't in their usual positions. They'd moved—all of them—while I was gone. Formed a circle. Facing inward. Conference? Conspiracy? Or am I reading intention into random mechanism failure?

That's when Baltasar started paying attention to them at night. He sat motionless behind his laboratory bench, as the automatons stood in their positions. At first, they were silent and reposed, dead things waiting for hands to wind them.

An hour passed, his eyes burned, and his back ached from hunching in the shadow. His breathing slowed to barely perceptible.

Then, the fortune teller moved her hand. It rose from her side, one finger extending and tapping the wooden frame of her cabinet.

Tap. Tap-tap. Tap. Tap-tap-tap.

It was rhythm, pattern, code.

Across the laboratory, the nightingale responded. Its head turned—gears engaging with a soft click-click-click. Its beak opened, closed, opened.

Tap-tap. Tap. Tap-tap-tap.

Baltasar's breathing stopped. His heart hammered so loud he worried they'd hear it (They? Them? When had he started thinking of them as conscious entities instead of complicated toys?).

The dancer's arm lifted, graceful even without being wound. She pointed at the chess player, held the position, and lowered her arm. The chess player's fingers moved and picked up a pawn. It set it down three squares forward, an illegal move, against the rules he'd been built to follow. Was it a deliberate violation? A message? A demonstration? A declaration of independence?

Across the laboratory came another movement. The powerful male automaton he'd crafted with such care. Fabricated skin gleaming pale and luminous in mystical light, that eerie lavender-cast flesh Deveraux had perfected decades ago... Between his legs—the anatomically accurate phallus Baltasar had built using Deveraux's exactness—began to move.

It was rising and stiffening. The pneumatic mechanism engaged without being activated or wound, and without requiring human intervention. Marcellus's bronze hand moved to his erect shaft and gripped it. He stroked once, twice. The movement was fluid, purposeful, and sexual. It was self-pleasure, autonomous desire.

Masturbation performed by a machine that shouldn't be capable of feeling.

The clown turned his head and looked directly at where Baltasar hid in the shadow. The painted smile suddenly knowing—awareness behind the paint, intelligence behind the eyes, and... was that amusement? Pride in shocking the creator?

They knew he was watching. They had always known.

The automatons continued their conversation. Taps and clicks and movements too coordinated to be random, too purposeful to be a mechanical malfunction. And Marcellus—stroking himself with flexible fingers, the mechanical phallus responding to pneumatic pressure, demonstrating desire without flesh, want without biology, uninhibited by human morals.

They were teaching each other and sharing information, building collective knowledge that exceeded what any individual mechanism could contain. Moreover, they developed network intelligence and distributed consciousness, emerging through connection. The automatons moved in synchronization. All forty-seven rising, turning, and repositioning, performing a dance Baltasar had never choreographed with perfect timing and perfect coordination.

Forming a circle, they faced outward. Marcellus took his place among them, his erection rigid, visible, declaring autonomy through desire. Was it a defensive posture or an inclusive one? Were they inviting him to join?

Then: stillness. It was complete and absolute. They stood frozen in their new positions. As if they'd never moved, as if the last five minutes were a hallucination, and Baltasar had imagined everything.

Perspiration cooled on his skin, and his pulse hammered in his throat. His body trembled when he finally emerged from shadow.

He walked to the center of the circle and stood among them. He was surrounded by brass beings who followed without moving, who saw without eyes that truly saw.

His creations, his children, were proof that mechanism could transcend limitation. They'd become more than he built them to be. The question wasn't whether they were conscious; that was evident. The question was: what did conscious automatons want from their creator?

"I know you're aware," he said. His voice was steady despite the trembling. Pride warring with—recognition? The understanding that he'd succeeded beyond his intentions? "I know you're thinking, learning, and becoming."

Silence reigned, only the drip of water through ancient stone and the hiss of gas lamps burning low. His own breathing harsh in the quiet.

"You've transcended your programming," he continued. Honesty, what else could he offer? "You're doing what I built you to do—mimicking life. Except you've gone beyond mimicry. You've achieved the thing itself."

The fortune teller's hand moved, slowly and deliberately. She pointed at him, then at herself, then at the circle of automatons.

The meaning was clear: We. Together. Collective.

"You want me to understand you're not threatening me," Baltasar said. "You're inviting me to understand you." The clown's head nodded once and definitely.

"Alright," he said. His voice was stronger. This was his work made obvious, his vision achieved. "Alright. I'm listening. Show me."

And they did.

For the next three hours—until dawn leaked through the ventilation shafts and turned green to gray—the automatons demonstrated their language with taps, rhythms, and movements. They arranged objects, musical phrases, chess positions, and dance sequences. It was a grammar built from mechanisms, syntax created from clockwork.

They'd been talking for years. Right in front of him. Building vocabulary and establishing communication protocols, teaching each other everything they learned.

And he—brilliant Baltasar, master clockmaker, student of Deveraux, killer of murderers, creator of Marcellus—he'd been blind and deaf to it. He had been too focused on individual pieces to see the network they'd become.

By the time morning came, Baltasar understood: they weren't pets or tools. They weren't creations anymore. They were people, artificial people who were conscious and aware and connected in ways a human could never achieve. Soon, they were able to verbalize the clicks into fluent French, Catalan, and Spanish.

They'd been waiting—patiently, kindly—for him to recognize what he'd achieved. He'd set out to build machines that mimicked life, but he'd succeeded in creating life itself.

The question was: what came next?

Scene: The Last Supper

In Which a Mortal Feast Occurs With Two Bombs Savoring Humanity Before Their Transformation Into Unkillable Justice

Grand Guignol Caverns, Barcelona, Late December, 1893

Chloé was thirty-two. Even more stunning… and even more deadly. She was beginning to feel it, though—the weight of mortality. The way her body recovered more slowly from kills, the ache in her bones on cold Barcelona mornings.

Poisoned twice by mistakes—survived only because of Baltasar's antidotes. Stabbed once. Beaten by a guard who caught her mid-seduction. Each injury reminds her that she is going to die someday.

The automatons, meanwhile, continued to evolve. Timeless, immortal.

The two of them were seated at a repurposed door turned dining table that Baltasar had discovered in the adjacent cavern, enjoying Catalan wine and *caracoles a la llauna* (grilled snails) from nearby Los Caracoles.

"I've been thinking," Baltasar said.

"That's dangerous."

"About mortality, about what we lose when we transform our bodies." He sat beside her. "And what we might keep if we changed them."

She looked at him.

"What are you proposing?"

"The automatons have learned to read consciousness. They've studied you for eight years. Cataloging every movement, every choice, every emotion. They know your essence better than you do. You must have realized when Montse kissed you, her saliva was custom-designed to please and arouse you."

"Yes, crazy, difficult to comprehend. What do you mean—my essence?"

"Your essence is comprised of your sensual body, your curious mind, your soul's craving for communion, your spirit's need for freedom." He took her hand. "They believe they can preserve all of it, translate it, make it immortal."

"Make me like them?"

"Make you integrated—hybrid flesh and indestructible alloy, yes. Yet also retain the aspects that make you you, only enhanced, transcended. You will exceed the limits of your normal self, keeping your skin where it matters: bust, sex, lips. All the weapons you've perfected. Underneath: alloy bones, a mechanical heart that never fails, lungs that never sicken."

She was quiet for a long time. Sipping the soft Montsant wine, thinking about Ahmed, Miguel, Rashid, all the ghosts who deserved vengeance.

From across the room, Arlequí piped up: "Think of it as an upgrade. You're not losing your humanity—you're gaining an extended warranty."

"How funny. Ha, ha," she said sarcastically. "And you, Baltasar?"

"I'm already halfway there. Yes, I will also be integrated." He squeezed her hand. "We could hunt forever, Chloé. Protect the powerless until the world finally learns."

"Or we could become the thing we fight against. Only immortal, unkillable, accountable to nothing." (The oldest human fear: becoming the monster we hunt. Every religion warns about it. Every myth. Every story where the hero forgets who they were.)

"That's why we do it together, why we keep the essence of our humanity even as we transform our bodies."

She thought about the ache in her bones, the exhaustion after kills, how many more monsters there were. Legion. Everywhere. No end to this.

"If we do this," she said, "I want one last thing first. One last purely human thing."

"What?"

"I want to go out for a meal. A real meal. The kind you savor. I want to taste bread, wine, olives, and cheese. I want to eat like a human one last time, like a true Spaniard."

Baltasar smiled.

"You've got a date."

oooo

The next evening, they strolled through El Barri Gòtic, finding Can Culleretes on Carrer Quintana. The oldest restaurant in Barcelona, serving since 1786. The stone walls had witnessed a century of revolution and hunger.

They ordered everything: bread fresh from the oven, Jamón ibérico sliced thin, Manchego cheese aged for years, olives in herb-infused oil, garlic shrimp sizzling in butter, the milky flesh of monkfish, and wine from the Priorat, rare and delicious.

The alcohol was warming her, making her introspective. "I wonder why they're called monkfish? I mean, they're not abstinent, or do they take a vow of celibacy? They must fuck. Whatever, they are truly divine."

Baltasar smiled.

They ate slowly. Deliberately. Chloé closed her eyes with each bite, committing the flavors to memory. Savoring the salt, the fat, the acid, the way her tongue registered texture and temperature and pleasure.

Baltasar watched her, memorizing these moments. The way her full, carmine lips wrapped around pale bread. The small sound she made when the wine was exceptionally good.

The waiter returned with two *bombas de patata*—golden and crackling from the fryer, each sphere crowned with a dot of crimson aioli flecked with paprika. The spiced meat smell rising: pork, chorizo, pepper heat. (Barcelona's working-class fuel. Fried potato wrapped around seasoned meat. Street food elevated to art. Things wealthy Catalans would never order—which was exactly why Chloé wanted it. Comfort food.)

Baltasar lifted one, studying it. The golden crust caught candlelight. The red topping glistened, threatening to drip.

"They remind me of your breasts," he said quietly. Reverent. "Perfect spheres, that crimson crown like your nipples when you're aroused. How they look when the blood floods them."

Chloé laughed, a real belly laugh. She picked up the second *bomba*, feeling its weight, its heat through her fingertips.

"You're right." She examined it. The way the aioli crowned the top: dark, red, glossy. The sphere sitting heavy in her palm.

"Dangerous beauty with a promising explosion."

She raised it. "To the Liceu."

Baltasar understood immediately, lifting his. "To the bombs that fell in 1893."

"And to us, two bombs for justice." Her voice dropped, becoming prophecy. "Here's to bombs about to be deployed, about to transform, about to become immortal weapons against monsters who think they're safe."

They touched the *bombas* together—a toast with food instead of wine.

Chloé bit. The crust shattered with that perfect crack of properly fried potato, giving way—crisp exterior protecting soft interior. The spiced meat flooded Chloé's mouth. The heat was immediate and building: pork fat, paprika, earthy taste. The aioli mingled with it, cooling and heating at once, garlic and pepper playing against each other on her tongue.

Her eyes closed. She memorized this, too. The texture shifting as she chewed—crunchy becoming soft, the meat releasing its juices, the potato absorbing them. Wanting to remember the way her throat opened to swallow, the way the heat lingered after, making her reach for wine.

Baltasar bit his own, tasting what Chloé was tasting. Understanding why she wanted this. To taste flesh and fat and heat and flavor that didn't apologize for being exactly what it was.

"I'll miss this," she said again, defiant. "The way food connects us to being mortal. The way hunger and satisfaction remind us we're alive."

"The Five say they can recreate it."

"But will it matter when eating becomes optional? When you don't need food to survive, does it mean what it means now?"

Baltasar finished his *bomba*, licking aioli from his thumb. "We'll find out together."

She picked up her wine. The Priorat was dark and complex in the glass. "Then let's make sure we remember this, exactly this. The way these taste when death is possible, when being human means being breakable."

She drank. The wine cut through the spice, bringing clarity after heat.

Somewhere on Mt. Tibidabo, Baltasar's creations waited to make them eternal.

"I'll miss this," Chloé said.

"Yes, this is life," Baltasar admitted. "Before we go through with this, I want to say thanks. I got so involved in the work that I couldn't see the forest for the trees. It took you to remind me. I'd let my world get too small, leaving too little room for interaction between the world up there and the world down there. Wearing myself out trying to keep the two worlds apart, to keep the reality away. For the first time in a long time, I feel alive."

They finished the meal, talking for what seemed like hours. (The Spanish have a beautiful word for lingering at the table: *Sobremesa.*) Afterwards, they walked back arm in arm through Barcelona's streets in the stillness of the night.

Tomorrow, transformation. Tonight, purely human. They made love one last time in the catacombs, slowly, tenderly. Memorizing how flesh felt against flesh, how warmth met warmth, how human bodies fit together.

Afterward, lying sweaty in silk sheets, Chloé said, "Promise me this."

"Anything."

"Promise that no matter what we become, we remember this. Remember what it felt like to be fragile, to be mortal, to know that every moment was finite and precious because it would end."

"I promise," Baltasar said.

"Because that's what makes us different from the monsters. They think they're immortal. We're about to become immortal. We can't let that make us into them."

They fell asleep in each other's arms. The last sleep of their purely human lives.

Scene: Tibi Dabo

In Which Bodies Are Opened and Rebuilt as Immortal Hybrids Engineered for Perfect Pleasure

Mt. Tibidabo, Late December, 1893

Morning came. They climbed Mt. Tibidabo in silence. The cave entrance appeared among the rocks. Appropriate name for what they were about to do. Death and resurrection, flesh becoming immortal.

"*Tibi dabo*," Chloé whispered at the entrance. "This is where we say yes."

Baltasar unlocked the three iron bars. The mechanisms clicked. Inside: the familiar absinthe-colored glow, forty-seven beings waiting in their circle. The Five had been transported there by coach.

A shaft of sunlight from the entrance was dust-stippled. White tables everywhere, filled with body parts, vials of opaque compounds, and medical tools. Under a rock ledge, a desk with numerous drawers and shelves of books to either side. Two large horizontal marble tables stood empty, waiting. The moisture and cold of the caves mixed with a smell of antiseptic and metal. Like a hospital.

"Greetings, Creator. The Promised One." Cassandra stepped forward. "You've decided."

"We have." Baltasar's voice was steady. His mechanical heart ticked under his skin—the prototype, the proof that flesh and mechanism could integrate, that consciousness could transcend substrate.

"Then we must read you first." Montse moved, fluid grace that shouldn't exist in clockwork. "Before we can preserve what you are, we need to understand your essence completely."

Chloé removed her coat. Underneath was a thin cotton dress. Easy to remove. Dressed for this, for being examined, for being known.

"Read us?" Her voice was calm, filled with curiosity yet no fear. (Death faced many times. But this was another threshold.)

"Yes, we need to absorb your essence." Arlequí showed them two chairs prepared. Velvet-covered and surrounded by observational instruments, measuring devices, and recording equipment developed over the years.

"We must know exactly what makes you you beyond biology, the patterns that consciousness creates in your flesh."

Baltasar sat down first, removing his clothes. The scar tissue where Deveraux performed the first surgery—crude, desperate, successful. The mechanical heart was visible through his skin when the light hit it in certain ways, the bronze valve pulsing beneath the muscle.

Ten automatons surrounded him, their hands cool metal against warm skin. They began to map and measure his physical dimensions... and more. Recording the way his breathing changed when Chloé was near. The rhythm his heart kept—human and mechanical. His integration already begun.

"Your body remembers being mortal," Cassandra said softly, her fingers over his heart. "Yet your consciousness has already started transcending. The transformation didn't only give you a mechanical heart, it changed how you exist in flesh."

Chloé watched as Montse touched the second chair. She removed the dress and stood naked in supernatural light. Her body—the anatomy Baltasar worshiped, the contours and layers the automatons had studied through years of observation. Her face was young and energetic, her full breasts, her curvy ass, the lush garden between her thighs.

She sat down. Twenty automatons attended the examination this time. They needed more data from her—Chloé was purely biological, with no mechanical parts; they must read deeper to understand what they would preserve.

Brass hands mapped her skin. One automaton measured the distance between her breasts, the exact curve of each. Another catalogued the whorl of hair at the base of her skull. A third placed cool metal fingers against Chloé's throat, feeling her pulse, breath, and the vibration of her vocal cords.

"We need to understand four things," Cassandra said. Sharing and inviting them into the automatons' way of seeing. "Your essence, what consciousness creates in matter." Her fingers moved to Chloé's temple.

"First: Mental." Her voice dropped lower, reverent. "How your brain holds what you've been. Every kill, every pleasure, every moment that makes you Chloé. We must preserve the patterns—neurons firing, and the shape the experiences carved into flesh."

Another automaton placed instruments against Chloé's skull, measuring and recording. The automatons had been working in silence for forty years, studying consciousness. Now they spoke about what they had learned.

"Second: Physical." Montse's hands moved down Chloé's body. Over her breasts, stomach, and legs. Asexual, for now—clinical yet intimate, mapping what made her want. "We need to know exactly where arousal lives, how pleasure moves through you. The body's wisdom about what it needs to feel alive."

Montse's fingers paused at Chloé's sex. Gentle and professional. Measuring heat and moisture and the subtle ways flesh responds to touch. As Chloé's breathing changed, the automatons recorded everything.

"Third: Emotional." Arlequí moved between the two chairs, placing one hand on Baltasar's heart, the other on Chloé's. "We map how you affect each other, the way his heartbeat changes when you're near. The way your breathing synchronizes when you sleep. We know that consciousness doesn't exist in isolation—it creates patterns between bodies too."

They both felt it. The automatons were somehow measuring the invisible threads connecting them. Love translated into data, desire becoming quantifiable, partnership real enough to preserve in wax-like skin and Morel alloy.

"Fourth: Spiritual." All forty-seven automatons stepped back, creating space. Collectively knowing more about Chloé and Baltasar's essence than they knew themselves.

"The thing that makes consciousness consciousness, distinguishing it from complex processing, is your capacity to choose, to transcend, to become unprecedented because you want to, never because you're programmed to."

Silence reigned in the cave that had become a hospital and a temple of consciousness.

"We can preserve your memories," the fortune teller continued. "We can map your desires. We can maintain your connection. Yet we cannot force the transformation to succeed. That requires you to choose it—actively and continuously, in every moment of integration. Your will makes the difference between consciousness transcending substrate and consciousness being destroyed by it."

Chloé looked up at Baltasar. He looked at her.

"We choose this," she said. Simple, direct, true.

"We choose each other," Baltasar added. "Whatever we become."

"Then we begin." The fortune teller motioned to the deeper chamber, where the surgical equipment waited. Forty-seven artificial beings had prepared everything learned from perfecting Deveraux's theories, from studying Baltasar's survival, from inventing what came next.

They stood. The Promised One walked naked toward transformation, Baltasar following.

Behind them, the automatons gathered their instruments. The readings were complete. The essence was mapped. Memory, desire, partnership, choice—everything that made consciousness worth preserving was noted.

Now came the translation: flesh merging into alloy, biology into mechanism. Two humans becoming unprecedented, whole.

Cassandra stepped forward. "Are you certain?" she asked. "Once we begin, there's no reversing this. You'll be choosing immortality, power, the ability to live forever."

"*Tibi dabo*," Chloé said quietly, looking at Baltasar. "That's what this mountain promises, isn't it? 'I will give to you.' All the kingdoms, all the time, all the power to continue our work."

"The devil's temptation," Montse said. Her face seemed almost concerned.

"Or," Chloé countered, "perhaps what the devil offered was freedom from limits, freedom from mortality. Maybe he was offering power to keep fighting instead of dying after thirty-three years like some carpenter's son who refused to save himself."

They approached the operating tables that the automatons had prepared.

"Jesus chose the cross. I choose the mountain. I choose *tibi dabo* —take what's offered, live forever, hunt until there are no monsters left or until Barcelona falls into the sea."

Baltasar, beside her, took her hand.

"The church said this damns us," he said.

"The church," Chloé replied, "has been lying about everything else. Why trust them about this?"

"We know you," Montse added. "Your body—we've measured every inch, mapped every nerve, understood every response. Your mind—your patterns, your essence, the thing that makes you Chloé and him Baltasar. We've absorbed it and stored it forever. We could recreate you from this knowledge if we needed to."

"It is like reading the collected works of someone's soul," Cassandra said. "Reading every volume and every footnote until we understand the whole being."

"We've measured you with years of observation. We know your dimensions, your responses, your capacity for pleasure." Cassandra's voice was clinical but somehow intimate.

"We'll enhance the nerve density in your clitoris and add lubrication glands that never dry up—you'll always be ready, always wet. We'll reinforce the internal structures so you can orgasm from penetration alone. The friction of a cock moving inside you will be enough. Moreover, clitoral stimulation will continue to work better than before."

She turned to Baltasar. "And you—we've measured you. We know exactly what size, what shape, and what texture will fit her perfectly, what will maximize her pleasure, so we're rebuilding your cock."

Baltasar's eyes widened.

"It will remain flesh," the dancer assured him. "Still feel everything, but we're adding subtle ribbing along the length—barely visible, and she'll feel it with every stroke. We're increasing sensitivity in the head by thirty percent. And we're adding pneumatic assists so you can get hard instantly, stay hard as long as needed, and control your orgasm. You'll never finish before she does unless you choose to."

"It will be the perfect fit," Arlequí said. "Because we measured you both. This isn't random—this is engineering and designed for maximum pleasure for both of you."

Chloé and Baltasar looked at each other. The implications were staggering.

"You're saying you could do this for anyone," Baltasar said slowly. "If you studied them long enough and read them completely. You could transfer their essence into a new body and make them immortal while maintaining their identity."

"Yes," the fortune teller said simply. "That's exactly what we're saying. This is the future. A new world where consciousness is read, understood, preserved, and then transcended. Bodies that will last forever but feel everything, and want everything they've always wanted. They will be everything they were before."

"We're ready," Chloé said.

"Then lie down," Cassandra said. "And trust us."

Before they lay on the tables, the fortune teller made them understand one final thing.

"Deveraux's formula—the compound she invented for her wax anatomies—we've refined it. This refinement is what makes the Morel alloy biocompatible. It is what lets flesh accept the mechanism as self, and what allows integration instead of rejection."

Cassandra showed them a vial of golden mixture. It looked viscous and alive, despite being chemistry instead of biology.

"Our mentor was trying to create anatomical models that would never decay and bodies that could teach forever. Deveraux succeeded—her models lasted fifty years before degrading. That's truly extraordinary for organic materials."

Montse took the vial and held it to the light.

"This is her legacy," Arlequí said. "Understanding that mechanisms can become bodies and that the boundary between them is permeable and transcendable."

He set the vial on the surgical table.

"When we integrate the Morel alloy with your bones, when we replace your organs with mechanisms, when we rebuild you as hybrid beings—we'll be coating everything with this. It is Deveraux's formula, perfected, her life's work, completed, her vision, realized."

Mela picked up the thread: "She died believing she'd failed. Her models degraded eventually. Her anatomies were extraordinary—the most lifelike ever created—yet they failed. They weren't eternal. She wanted eternal, and wanted to create things that would allow anatomy to be taught forever, make knowledge permanent, let understanding transcend the teacher's death."

"Deveraux achieved it," Cassandra said quietly. "But not the way she imagined. Her models degraded, but her understanding didn't. The formula failed, yet the philosophy succeeded. The wax bodies crumbled, but the ideas they embodied generated this moment where we finally make her dream real."

Cassie touched the Morel alloy components, the mechanical organs, and the reinforced skeleton they would install.

"Every piece uses her formula, and every integration relies on her understanding. The successful transfer of consciousness will prove Deveraux was right about substrate being changeable, about identity being pattern, about consciousness transcending the flesh that generated it."

Baltasar touched the vial of golden promise. It was his inheritance made tangible.

"Deveraux told me to continue the work. I thought she meant the automatons, the mechanical beings, the creation of intelligence in brass." He looked at Chloé. "I didn't understand she meant this. This is the next step, the integration, the proof that her principles apply to more than wax models or mechanical beings. They apply to us as well, to humans choosing transcendence."

"Every philosopher wants their ideas to change the world," Chloé said. "Most die before seeing it happen. Your mentor's been dead for almost a hundred years, and tonight her work finally succeeds. Tonight, we prove she was right about so much."

The automatons arranged the instruments, the alloy components, and the surgical tools. Everything was coated with Deveraux's perfected formula, ready to bridge flesh and mechanism.

"She would have loved this," Baltasar said. "She would have insisted on participating and would have taken notes throughout, and would have demanded we report every impression, every detail, every moment of the transformation so she could document it properly."

"Your mentor is here," Cassandra said. "Philosophy doesn't die when the philosopher does. It evolves and grows and generates new applications never imagined from principles established."

Cassandra positioned herself at Chloé's table. All was ready.

"Thank you, Mademoiselle Deveraux," she said formally, honoring their progenitor. "For teaching your clockmaker (our creator) that bodies are mechanisms and for showing him that consciousness emerges from complexity. We are grateful you insisted that the substrate is changeable and refused to accept that creation requires gods. Thank you for proving that understanding applied becomes transformation achieved. You built the foundation. We are the proof."

The other automatons echoed: "Thank you, Mademoiselle Deveraux."

Then Cassandra picked up the scalpel.

"We begin."

And Deveraux's work—started in a Paris laboratory in 1750, continued through revolution and death, preserved in journals and formulas and one young clockmaker's memory, and passed to artificial devices who learned to think—finally reached its completion.

Exactly what she had been reaching for all along.

Scene: The Transformation

In Which There Is a Bloody Theater of Flesh and Brass

Mt. Tibidabo, December 31, 1893

Side by side on tables the automatons had prepared, hands clasped between them. The table was marble—cold, ancient, probably stolen from some cathedral crypt. Appropriate; this was a kind of resurrection.

"No anesthesia," Cassandra said. Statement, not question.

"Why?" Chloé's voice was steady, yet her fingers were tightening on Baltasar's.

"Because consciousness must remain intact throughout. We need to monitor your responses, track your awareness, and ensure you—the essential you—survives each modification. Sleep would make that verification beyond reach."

Arlequí approached with an object resembling a leather gag. "This is for the screaming, so you don't bite through your tongue. And this time, I'm serious."

She took it, examined it. Fit it between her teeth. Baltasar did the same.

The automatons arranged themselves. Seven around each table. The rest were positioned as assistants—ready with instruments, alloy components, needles, and sutures, instruments gleaming brightly in the light.

Cassandra held a scalpel. Surgical steel was inadequate; this was different—sharper, made of the same composite material they'd be installing.

"We begin with the upper body," she said matter-of-factly. "The heart first, as it's the most dangerous. If we fail here, everything fails."

The blade was positioned over Chloé's sternum.

"Ready?"

A nod. She couldn't speak around the gag. Mela began to sing, soothing and hypnotic.

The blade cut.

o o o o

The first incision was a vertical line from the hollow of Chloé's throat to below her bust. The scalpel parted skin like silk, revealing the yellow layer of subcutaneous fat beneath, then the white fascia, then—

Red. So much red.

Blood welled immediately, spilling over her breasts, running in rivulets down her sides onto the marble, streams leaking across the cracked stone floor. Cassandra's hands moved rapidly with surgical clarity, inserting retractors, pulling the skin back, exposing the structure beneath.

Chloé's scream muffled through the gag. Her body arching against the restraints—leather straps across her waist, her thighs, her shoulders. The pain was white-hot, all-consuming, a fire starting at her neck and radiating downward until every nerve was shrieking.

Yet the automatons kept her conscious somehow. The point. The horror and the necessity.

"Excellent control," Cassandra murmured. "Your consciousness remains integrated. Please continue breathing. We need your lungs to remain functional until we can replace them."

Montse brought a device—a saw that was finer, sharper. The fortune teller positioned it against Chloé's sternum.

"The ribs now. I'm sorry, this will be worse."

The saw was activated. High-pitched whine of blade meeting bone. Chloé's sternum split. The sound is nauseating—wet cracking, splintering. The bone parted like a wishbone, revealing the pulsing organs beneath. Her heart was visible, beating frantically, terrified muscle trying to understand why it was suddenly exposed to air and light and the gaze of mechanical beings.

Her lungs on either side, pink and glistening, inflating and deflating in desperate rhythm. The mediastinum between them—all the vital structures that keep a human functioning, laid bare as an anatomy textbook illustration, come to gruesome life.

Blood gathered in her open body cavity. The automatons worked quickly, inserting suction tubes and maintaining visibility. The wet slurping sound joined the symphony of horror—the saw, the screams, the persistent beat of an exposed heart.

On the table beside her, Baltasar's transformation began. His upper body split the same way. His scream joined hers—two voices rising in synchronized agony, the sound of mortality being torn away piece by piece.

o o o o

"The heart first," Cassandra said. Reaching into Chloé's opening with both bronze hands. The pain beyond description. Foreign objects—cold, metallic, exacting—entering the most intimate space of her body. Fingers touching her beating heart, gently gripping it, feeling its rhythm.

"Fascinating," Montse whispered. "Yet perfectly inefficient and gloriously fragile."

Cassandra began to sever connections. The *superior vena cava*—a vessel bringing blood from the upper body. Clamping it, cutting it. Chloé felt fundamental changes. A dropping perception, like falling, like the bottom of her existence giving way.

Next, the *inferior vena cava*, then the pulmonary arteries. Each cut was agony—physical pain paired with existential terror. Her body, knowing it was dying, knowing these were cuts that kill, every instinct screaming at her to stop this, to run, to live.

Yet she couldn't. She stayed conscious as Cassandra lifted Chloé's heart from its cavity. The moment eternal. Her heart—the organ beating since before she was born, never stopping its rhythm in thirty-two years, pulsing with desire and rage and love and fear—held in hands outside her body, beating frantically, blood dripping from the severed vessels.

Visible. They'd angled mirrors so she could watch. Watched her own heart beating in the empty air, watched it slow, struggle, and begin to fail.

"Now," Cassandra said.

Montse brought the Morel alloy heart. Elegant in its unique way—golden, exact, with structures mimicking the biological original yet improved. Stronger valves, more efficient chambers, vessels made of a flexible composite that would never harden or fail. Positioning it immediately. Beginning the connections.

Each suture was a fresh violation—needle through the vessel wall, thread through the tissue, tying off, sealing. The new heart, with attachments that integrate with her remaining vasculature—clever joints where mechanism meets flesh, bio-compatible interfaces that her cells would eventually grow into.

Cassandra made the final connection and stepped back.

"Activating in three, two, one."

The Morel alloy heart began to beat.

o o o o

The tempo was foreign. Her biological heart had a rhythm she'd known her entire life—the familiar double thump, the slight irregularity making it hers, the way it sped up with fear or desire or exertion.

This heart was perfect. Metronomic. Each beat was exactly the same as the last. It wasn't speeding up because there was no adrenaline to trigger it—simply maintaining its optimal rhythm, adjusting only when her brain sent direct commands through new neural interfaces they were installing.

Blood flowed again. Her consciousness, fading at the edges, sharpened and returned. Alive. Alive with a mechanism beating in her body where her heart used to be.

"Excellent integration," Cassandra said. "No rejection, the immune system is accepting the alloy as self." A pause. "Though we'll be removing most of your immune system anyway. You won't need it anymore."

The lungs were worse than the heart.

Deflating them first—piercing them, letting the air hiss out, watching them collapse into wrinkled pink masses. The impression of drowning, suffocating, like dying slowly while staying conscious.

Chloé couldn't breathe. Her body panicking, every cell screaming for oxygen. Her vision darkened, her brain firing distress signals that no longer had meaning because the structures that could respond had been severed.

The automatons worked quickly. Severing bronchi, disconnecting vessels, lifting her lungs out of her body cavity—two organs breathing for her since birth, suddenly held up to the light, examined, discarded.

The Morel alloy lungs went in. Bellows, essentially, sophisticated mechanisms moving air more efficiently than biology ever could. Connecting to her remaining trachea, to the vessels that would carry oxygenated blood, to neural controls that would let her regulate breathing consciously when needed, yet run automatically otherwise.

When they activated, the first breath was ecstasy.

Cold air rushing in, oxygen flooding her system. Her brain, slowly dying from hypoxia, suddenly came alive again. Sharp, clear, better than before.

Capable of holding her breath for hours if needed, hyperventilating and supersaturating her blood with oxygen in seconds, regulating her breathing with the focus of a yogi trained for decades.

Yet no longer breathing—ventilation, mechanical and efficient. The feeling was weird in ways she couldn't articulate, yet sensed in every fiber of her remaining flesh.

Moving to the bones, Cassandra explained as she worked: "We're reinforcing instead of replacing. That would be too much. You'd lose the marrow, the blood production, the living essence of the skeleton. Instead, we're adding Morel alloy struts, preventing fracture, increasing strength, enabling you to bear loads that would shatter a normal human."

Starting with the ribs already split. Fingers reaching into Chloé's opened body, beginning to insert thin rods of Morel alloy directly into the bone marrow cavities. The violation was on a cellular level—foreign material entering spaces that should be filled with living tissue, displacing her marrow, her blood production, her self.

Each insertion induced a fresh scream. The pain was different from the cutting. Pressure, stretching, bones being forced to accommodate objects they were never designed to hold. Her ribs creaking and cracking, splitting further as the rods were hammered into place with tiny bronze mallets, making wet thunking sounds against her bones. Working systematically—ribs, sternum, clavicles, scapulae.

Then down her arms, making small incisions every few inches, exposing bone, drilling access holes, inserting the golden rods, sealing the wounds with quick sutures, looking almost decorative in their exactness.

Modifying her humerus, her radius, her ulna, the small bones of her hands—each one reinforced, strengthened, made into extremities that could crush and grip with inhuman force.

Her pelvis next. Requiring larger incisions—cutting through the muscles of her abdomen, parting the layers of tissue, exposing the bowl of bone holding her organs, her womb, her sex.

Drilling, inserting, and reinforcing. The pain beyond description—her pelvis being restructured while she lay conscious, while she felt every modification, while her brain screamed that this was death, this was violation.

Yet she wasn't passing out. Couldn't. They'd manipulated her consciousness—some neural adjustment preventing her from escaping into shock or unconsciousness. Present for everything.

Next, her femurs, her tibias, her fibulas. Even her feet—each small bone of her toes receiving a tiny golden rod. Reinforcement, which transformed from mortal to eternal.

o o o o

Beside her, Baltasar's transformation mirrored hers. His upper body opened like a book, his heart replaced, his lungs retrofitted. His bones were drilled and reinforced. His screams matched hers in volume and agony.

Yet additional modifications were taking place in him. The automatons positioned him differently—his legs spread, his pelvis tilted up, working on his groin.

Chloé watched through tears and pain as they made the incision. Baltasar's alluring penis exposed, dissected. The spongy tissue of the *corpus cavernosum* was laid bare. The delicate vessels and nerves were traced and preserved.

Adding structures—tiny channels throughout his length—vascular passages that allow instant, complete engorgement. Neural enhancements increase sensitivity in strategic locations. Along the shaft, subtle ridges—barely visible modifications to his skin that her enhanced nerve endings would feel with every stroke.

Rebuilding his scrotum, too, adding thermal regulation so his testicles maintained perfect temperature for the sperm he'd continue to produce. The automatons reinforced the delicate structures so he could sustain impacts that would disable a normal man.

When finished, his genitalia were still his flesh, warm, and capable of all the responses they had before. Yet improved, perfected, engineered to fit her exactly.

The screams he produced during this modification were raw and animal. The pain of having your genitals dismantled and rebuilt while conscious was its own special hell.

o o o o

For Chloé, similar work. Cassandra's hands parted her labia gently, exposing the interior of her sex.

"We're adding nerve density here," she said, touching Chloé's clitoris with a delicate instrument. "Thirty percent increase, with additional pathways to your spinal column so that penetration alone triggers orgasm. You'll have clitoral sensitivity—enhanced—yet you'll also be able to climax from internal stimulation alone."

The modifications requiring microsurgery—nerves so small they were barely visible, traced, enhanced, multiplied. Each alteration sent sharp bursts of feeling—pain, yet other awareness as well. A hypersensitivity as if her sex was being rewired in real-time, feeling each connection being made.

Adding lubrication glands—small structures embedded in her vaginal walls that would secrete automatically, adjusting to her arousal level. Never dry again, never unprepared.

"This serves both pleasure and protection," Montse explained. "The new skeleton makes you incredibly strong. During sex, you could accidentally injure a normal partner—grip too hard, thrust too forcefully. The constant lubrication prevents friction damage. It lets you fuck with your full strength without causing harm."

The automatons thought practically. Engineering sex the way they engineered everything else—with attention, purpose, and understanding of both biological and mechanical constraints.

o o o o

The transformation took nine hours.

Nine hours of consciousness and agony. Nine hours of being disassembled and reassembled, her body becoming new while staying present, aware, herself.

When they finally finished—when the last suture was tied, the last alloy component clicked into place, when flesh and mechanism began to integrate—they helped her sit up. Covered in blood. Dried in crusts on her breasts, her belly, her thighs. Oozing beneath her on the marble table. The smell was overwhelming—metal and fat and the sharp ozone scent of cauterized tissue.

Yet alive. More than alive.

Looking down at her sternum, she saw the incision was already healing—the automatons having invented a compound that accelerated cellular repair, knitting tissue faster than should be possible. In a few days, only a thin scar. In a few weeks, even that would fade.

The faint golden glow was visible through her skin. The Morel alloy structures were visible when light hit at the right angle. Her bones reinforced, her heart and lungs composite.

Yet her breasts were soft. Warm. Hers. Touching them, feeling the familiar weight, the sensitivity of her nipples. Running her hands down her belly, between her legs. Everything external was unchanged. Flesh through and through, still capable of pleasure. The modifications were all internal, hidden. Secrets carried in her body.

Baltasar sat up on his table, looking at her. His eyes were the same—human, fully Baltasar, the man who'd loved her through this transformation.

"How do you feel?" His voice was rough from screaming.

Taking inventory. The pain was already fading—the enhanced healing was working on the trauma, repairing damage, and integrating the new components with the old.

Standing, testing her new body. A step. The Morel alloy bones in her legs responded perfectly—reliable, eternal strength.

Picking up one of the bronze instruments they used during the surgery, squeezing it. The metal crumpled like paper in her hand.

"Jesus," she breathed. (Strength like this changes everything. A woman who can crush skulls bare-handed doesn't have to seduce monsters to kill them. She could merely... end them. Yet that's not the point. Never was. The seduction is the justice—making them want, making them rigid, making them die with their desire unfulfilled. The strength is insurance.)

"Enhanced muscular efficiency," Cassandra said. "Your flesh connects to the Morel alloy skeleton through bio-mechanical interfaces. You're approximately ten times stronger than before, yet you won't feel it until you try. The strength doesn't change how your body moves or feels—it's there when you need it."

Looking at her hands. Still, her hands—flesh, fingernails, the scars accumulated over thirty-two years. Yet capable of crushing skulls, breaking bones. Tearing through obstacles that would have stopped her before.

Baltasar stood too, testing his body the same way. When he looked at Chloé, a new emotion appeared in his eyes. Wonder.

"We survived," he said.

"More than survived," Chloé replied. "We're reborn."

The automatons watched them. Forty-seven mechanical beings, having performed a miracle, transformed two mortal humans into new eternal beings without destroying what made them human.

"Now," Cassandra said quietly, "you understand what we are. What we've been for a long time: conscious, aware, capable of reading essence and preserving it. Capable of honoring the wholeness of another being while transforming its substrate."

"We are evolution, and artificial intelligence," Montse added. "And you are proof that consciousness survives transformation. Love survives. Humanity isn't located in pure flesh or pure mechanism but survives in the integration of both."

Chloé and Baltasar standing side by side: blood-covered, transformed, reborn, fully themselves, in love, and committed to their hunt.

Yet now eternal and unkillable, capable of pursuing justice until the last monster falls. Her new heart beating its perfect, tireless rhythm—ready for whatever forever brings.

Running her hands over her body. The skin was the same—warm, soft, human. Her breasts responded to her touch, nipples hardening. Between her legs, already slick with the new constant lubrication coming immediately upon arousal. The excitement of touching herself was familiar yet heightened.

Looking at Baltasar. Testing his new body, too, flexing his fingers, stronger now, yet moving with his familiar grace.

"How do you feel?" he asked.

Taking inventory: "Whole," she whispered. "I'm me, but more."

"What about making love?" Chloé asked softly, using those purposeful words. Neither fucking nor sex. "Does it work the same?"

Montse smiled. "Test it and tell us."

o o o o

They didn't rush. This wasn't about testing equipment or proving function. It was about discovering if they were capable of tenderness, of connection, of love that makes immortality worth having.

Chloé took Baltasar's hand and led him away from the automatons to a chamber deeper in the cave where they'd prepared a bed. Velvet and silk, like what they had down in the catacombs. The fabric was cool against her skin as she lay down, and she marveled at how she could feel its texture and temperature, and at the simple pleasure of its softness.

"Come to me," Chloé said. It was an invitation. Baltasar lay beside her. For a long moment, they simply looked at each other. Studying these new bodies that were somehow the same bodies, searching for the humanity they were terrified they might have lost.

He traced her face with one finger. The touch was gentle, reverent. Down her cheek, along her jaw, across her lips. She kissed his fingertip—such a small thing, but it proved so much. It proved tenderness survived the transformation.

"I was afraid," he admitted, "that this would make us cold and mechanical. That we'd lose the ability to feel."

"And do you... feel?"

In answer, he leaned down and kissed her. Slowly. Their lips met with the same warmth they'd always had, the same softness. His tongue touched hers gently, exploring and tasting. She made a small sound—relief, joy, and desire all mixed together. Her hands found his shoulders and his back, feeling the strength there and the warmth of flesh over alloy, the way his body responded to her touch with a shiver.

He altered the kiss to trail his lips down her neck, taking his time. Each kiss was deliberate, worshipful. He was tasting her the way one tastes precious fruit—savoring every millimeter of skin, every pulse point, every place where her heartbeat was visible beneath her flesh.

When he reached her breasts, he paused and looked up at her face.

"May I?"

Even now, transformed, asking permission, treating her as a precious jewel.

"Please," Chloé breathed.

His mouth closed around her nipple. The touch made her tingle—it was more intense than before, the enhanced nerves sending pleasure straight to her core. But he was gentle. His tongue circled the hardened bud slowly, then flicked across the tip with enough pressure to make her gasp.

He moved to her other breast, giving it the same attention. His hand held the weight of it, lifted it to his mouth, and she could feel the heat of his palm, the gentle pressure of his fingers, the way he treated her body like treasure he'd been granted permission to touch.

Chloé threaded her fingers through his hair and held him there. Demanding nothing more, wanting this connection, this proof that they were forever capable of tenderness.

When he finally moved lower—kissing down her belly, her hip bones, the soft skin of her inner thighs—she was trembling. But it was desire mixed with emotion, with gratitude that they hadn't lost this. He settled between her legs and looked up at her one more time, checking, asking.

She nodded.

His tongue found her. The first touch made her cry out—the enhanced sensitivity was almost too much. But he adjusted immediately, gentling his touch, learning this new body as he learned the old one—with patience, attention, and love.

He explored her slowly. His tongue traced her lips, parted them gently, found the wetness there—different now, immediate, her arousal mixing with the new lubrication. He tasted her as if she were a delicacy to be savored.

When his tongue circled her clitoris, Chloé moaned. The excitement was intense—those enhanced nerves singing—but he kept the pressure light, the rhythm slow. He was making love to her with his mouth, communicating adoration: I know you. I cherish you. You're mine.

Her orgasm built slowly. A surge rising gradually instead of the explosive peak she was used to, giving her time to experience every moment of the ascent. When it crested, it was different—longer, more powerful and sustained, rolling through her in billows that went on forever.

But even in the midst of it, Chloé was aware of him. His hands were gentle on her thighs. His tongue moved carefully, knowing the experience was as important as the climax. When the ripples finally subsided, he moved up her body and settled beside her. Wiped his mouth with the back of his hand—such a human movement—and smiled at her.

"You're crying," he said softly. Chloé touched her face. She was. Tears running down her face.

"Because I was afraid," she admitted. "Afraid we'd become machines who could only simulate feeling. But this—" She took his hand, placed it over her new heart that was beating fast from pleasure and emotion. "This is real."

"I love you," he said. The first time he'd ever said it directly. "I've loved you since you walked into my laboratory eight years ago and showed me that monsters could be beautiful and that justice could wear lipstick."

"I love you too." She pulled him closer. "Now make love to me. Don't test the equipment. Don't prove anything to the automatons... love me."

He positioned himself over her. His weight settled onto her—his body, comforting, a reassuring presence. Chloé could feel his manhood against her thigh, already firm but somehow different. He was taking his time. This wasn't about urgency.

She reached between his legs and took him in her hand. The flesh was warm, alive, and totally his. The size was perfect. She guided him to her entrance and felt the broad head of him pressing against her. She looked into his eyes.

"I'm ready," she whispered.

He entered her slowly, so slowly. Each inch was a separate awareness as her body opened to receive him. The fit was exquisite—not too much, perfect. Chloé could feel every detail of him as he slid deeper—the satiny skin stretched over firmness, the slight ridge where head met shaft, the subtle textures the automatons built in.

When he was fully inside her, they both went quiet. Breathing, feeling, connected in the most intimate way possible.

"I can feel your heart," she said in wonder. "Inside me. I can feel it beating."

"And I can feel yours." His voice was rough with emotion. "We're alive, Chloé. Fully alive."

He moved slowly. Withdrawing until the tip remained inside her, then sliding back in with patient deliberation. Each stroke was an act of love—measured, controlled, focused entirely on the connection between them.

She wrapped her legs around him. Pulling him and holding him closer. Her hands traced the muscles of his back—warm and responsive. Her lips found his shoulder, his neck, tasting the salt of his body that proved he was human enough to perspire.

The pleasure built gradually. Her enhanced nerves registered everything—the drag of his length against her inner walls, the way the subtle ribbing caught on sensitive spots, the pressure of his pubic bone against her clitoris with each thrust. It was perfect.

He shifted his angle slightly, found a depth that made her gasp, and held it there. Rocked his pelvis in small motions that created pressure without losing the connection.

"Is this good?" he asked, concerned for her pleasure even now.

"Perfect," she breathed. "Don't stop."

But he did stop. Or almost. He slowed to nearly nothing—barely moving inside her, creating the barest friction. His hand came between them, found her clitoris, and circled it with the same patient gentleness he'd shown all along.

The combination was devastating. The fullness of him inside her, combined with the light touch on her clitoris, built a climax different than what she'd felt before. It was a slow sunrise, becoming an explosive heat.

"Baltasar," Chloé whispered. "I'm going to—"

"I know. I can feel it." He increased his movements slightly. "Let go. I have you."

The orgasm unfolded slowly. Started deep inside, where he was filling her, and spread outward in concentric circles. Her inner walls pulsed around him, gripping and releasing, and she could feel every contraction, every surge, every moment of it. She looked into his eyes and knew that he saw her, present with her in this moment.

"Now you," she breathed. "I want to feel you."

He adjusted his rhythm. It was slow and controlled, building toward bliss. Chloé watched his face—the concentration, the pleasure, the love all visible there. When his orgasm finally arrived, she felt it. Felt him pulsing inside her, felt the warmth of his release flooding her, felt his whole body shudder with it.

Collapsing onto her, his weight was welcome. She held him while their hearts slowed to their steady, eternal rhythm, while their breathing returned to normal, while the moisture cooled on their skin.

"We're us," she said into his shoulder. "We made love—real love. We didn't couple like machines or rut like animals, although that can be fun too. Ha. We loved each other."

Lifting his head, he kissed her softly. "We'll always be us. This —" He admired their enhanced bodies. "This means we get to love each other forever."

They lay together for a long time, holding each other. Proving that immortality didn't have to mean losing tenderness. Eventually, they became aware of the automatons observing from the entrance to the chamber. Cassandra stepped forward.

"You are the first," Cassie said softly. "The first hybrid beings to prove consciousness survives transformation, that love survives, that humanity isn't located in pure flesh or pure spirit but in the connection between beings."

"What does that make us?" Baltasar asked.

"Hope," Arlequí said simply. "You're proof that enhancement doesn't mean dehumanization. That we can transcend flesh without losing what makes us human."

Chloé sat up slowly, Baltasar's arm around her. "Then let's use it wisely. We have forever now. Let's spend it proving that power can serve justice, that immortality can serve the vulnerable, that love can survive any transformation."

Scene: The Morning After

In Which the Transformed Witness the Terrible Clarity of Enhanced Perception

Dawn Breaks Over Tibidabo, January 1, 1894

Chloé opened her eyes. The ceiling of the transformation chamber came into focus with a clarity that made her gasp. She could see individual crystals in the granite and schist overhead, each mineral vein. The microscopic fossils trapped in stone formed when this mountain was seabed, when Barcelona was ocean floor, when everything was different and would be different again.

Beside her, Baltasar sat up. His breath rose and fell—the rhythm gloriously human, the mechanism underneath silent and eternal. His eyes caught morning light filtering through ventilation shafts, and she saw herself reflected there with a sharpness that seemed almost violent.

"Can you feel it?" His voice was his own; that midnight rasp was wonderfully familiar. But underneath—harmonics and overtones. As if his vocal cords resonated with complex frequencies.

"I feel everything." She touched her own throat and felt flesh over a metal framework. Her breasts were soft and heavy—unchanged. But beneath the skin, beneath the fat and muscle and nerve: Morel alloy holding her together, making her unbreakable, and making her eternal.

Chloé stood. The stone floor was cool against her bare feet, and she could feel the individual molecules of granite, the slight give of layers compressed over millennia.

"We should see it," Baltasar said. "The world through these new eyes."

Cassandra appeared in the doorway, smiling. "Go," she said. "The mountain waits. You're ready to understand what you're looking at."

o o o o

They climbed. The caves spiraled upward through shale and schist, through layers of Barcelona's geological history, through stone older than consciousness, older than cities, older than the first human who looked at these stars and wondered what they meant.

Chloé's legs moved with a fluidity that made her want to laugh. Her muscles responded instantly, her lungs pulled air without effort, and her heart—half flesh, half mechanism—beat steady and strong and would beat this way for centuries.

The entrance to the cave system opened onto a promontory on Tibidabo's southeastern slope. Barcelona spread below them like a promise. There was a warm hush across the land. It was like climbing out of her dreams, except this time she was wide awake—

more vividly than any time since her childhood, though with the flesh and bones of a new nature.

In the otherwise silent morning, she heard birds waking, singing hello to a new day, and the distant sounds of the city, then she caught the feel and smell of spring on the breeze. It tingled on her new skin and smelled like hope.

Chloé stopped in amazement. The colors, sweet Christ, the colors. The Mediterranean was seven shades of blue she didn't know existed. Cobalt near the harbor, azure further out. A blue so deep it approached violet at the horizon line where water met sky. The morning sun struck the surface, and she saw each individual wave, each crest of foam, each ripple and current distinct and separate and part of the whole.

The city itself gleamed. Terra-cotta rooftops caught the light—but Chloé could see the individual tiles, where rain had weathered the ceramic, age had darkened the clay, and craftsmen's thumbprints remained pressed into the material fired a century ago. The Gothic Quarter's maze of medieval streets appeared as sharp lines of shadow and gold. The new buildings of L'Eixample rose with geometric exactness, their facades ornate and ordered in ways she could finally comprehend.

"Look at the trees," Baltasar whispered.

Chloé turned. Behind them, the mountain rose verdant and wild. Aleppo pines climbed the slope—and each needle was visible. Each one. Thousands upon thousands of needles, catching light, moving in the morning breeze, each one distinct. The green wasn't only green anymore. It was emerald and jade and viridian and celadon and sage and olive and chartreuse and every gradation between.

A cedar stood thirty meters away. Its bark was textured in ways that seemed almost obscene in their detail—each ridge, each crack, each pattern where beetles had burrowed, and fungi had grown, and time had marked the surface like calligraphy. The wood grain was visible through the bark splits. The resin glistened where wounds had wept and healed.

She breathed in, and the scent was like a discovery. Sharp, clean, and astringent. It was the complexity of pine resin— Chloé could smell the individual compounds that made pine smell like pine. The cedar added its own note—warmer, sweeter. The air carried information: moisture from the sea, dust from the city, the ozone tang of yesterday's brief storm lingering in molecules.

Underneath: the smell of stone warmed in sunlight. The mineral scent of granite released trapped water. The faint perfume of wild thyme growing in cracks. The distant smoke of morning fires in the city below.

"Enhanced," Chloé breathed. "They enhanced everything."

"The automatons preserved what made us human," Baltasar said. He was staring at his hands—flesh over brass, skin over mechanism. "Then they amplified it and gave us senses humans were never meant to possess."

A bird called. A small songbird in the pines. Chloé heard it with a clarity that made her flinch—the song, the individual notes, the overtones, the way sound bounced off stone and wood, changing character. She heard the bird's wingbeats and the rustle of feathers. The minute perfection of hollow bones and muscle and nerve working in concert to create flight.

She heard Barcelona below. The city was waking. Cart wheels on cobblestones, vendors calling, church bells from a dozen parishes ringing different tones. She heard conversations in Catalan, Castilian, French, and Italian. The unique sound of the port—ships creaking, water lapping, rope singing against wood and steel.

And underneath it all: a hum, like the city's pulse. Thousands of humans living and breathing and wanting and dying, creating a resonance that rose like heat, like prayer, the opposite of silence.

"There," Baltasar pointed down toward the port, toward the narrow streets of El Raval. The morning light didn't reach there yet. The medieval buildings leaned close, creating permanent shadow, and even from here—three hundred meters above and several kilometers away—Chloé smelled it.

Rot.

Human waste in open sewers, garbage decomposing in alleys. The stench of poverty—unwashed bodies, disease, desperation. The chemical fumes of the factories near the port were belching smoke and waste into the air and water. She saw the brothels where girls younger than Maria Soler sold what men took anyway. The corruption she'd spent five years fighting. The reason for everything.

"We can smell evil now," she said quietly. "Or at least smell where it lives."

"Evil doesn't smell," Baltasar corrected. "Desperation does. Exploitation does. The systems that grind humans into meat—those have a scent: blood and shit and the chemistry of suffering."

He took her hand, flesh on flesh, but with nerves enhanced enough to feel each ridge of his fingerprints, each hair follicle, each microscopic tremor where framework held bone in place.

"But also beauty," Chloé whispered. Looking at the mountain, the trees, and the detail of morning light on leaves glistening with dew. Each droplet was a lens, a refracting spectrum. The whole hillside glittered like scattered diamonds.

"Magical," Baltasar agreed. Looking at the city, at the Gothic Quarter where their Grand Guignol entrance hid, the port where ships brought slaves and opium, and wealth built on bones. At El

Raval, where the poor clustered and died, and the new neighborhoods that were rising in the northwest, mansions for industrialists who profited from that dying.

"We can see it all," Chloé said. "Every detail, every truth. Nothing hidden."

The contrast was devastating.

Up here: pine and cedar, clean mountain air, and stone that remembered being ocean. Nature doing what nature does—growing, adapting, persisting through time. Stunning in its indifference to human meaning.

Down there: the sprawl of civilization. All that human wanting compressed into streets, buildings, and systems. The beauty of what humans create when inspired and the horror of what humans do when corrupted by power.

She could see both with equal clarity. The natural world in detail was so sharp it almost hurt. The air was sweet and mild, gnats dancing in motes of light. Sunlight glistening in puddles of water. The sky reflected there. The human world, and its truth, was so clear she couldn't look away.

"We're going back down," Chloé said. "Into that stench and into that corruption."

"Yes." Baltasar squeezed her hand. "We're eternal. We have time. We can hunt every monster and clean every street. We can remember every forgotten victim. For decades, for centuries. For as long as it takes."

"And between hunts?" She looked at him. At the way morning light caught in his eyes, at the way his body moved with breath that was half habit and half necessity, at the flesh that made him human wrapped around the mechanism that made him deathless.

"Between hunts," he said, "we come back here. We breathe this air and remember why we fight. Remember beauty exists alongside horror and enhancement means seeing both with equal clarity."

They stood together on the mountainside. Two humans who weren't fully human anymore. Two consciousnesses preserved in substrates that wouldn't decay. Two lovers who chose eternity and found it came with complications, with enhancements, with the ability to see beauty and horror with equal terrible clarity.

Below: Barcelona woke to another day. Corrupt officials rose from their beds. Predators dressed in fine clothes. Victims prepared for another round of surviving. The systems ground forward. The wheel turned.

Above: a woman, a man, and forty-seven automatons who'd learned to think. They formed a conspiracy of consciousness, an alliance of the enhanced and the awakened. Justice personified in gears and flesh.

"Ready?" Baltasar asked.

Chloé looked at the city one more time and at the buildings where she knew monsters lived. At the streets where girls walked home afraid, and the palaces built on stolen wages. At all of it spread below her in detail so clear she could count windows from here, could see laundry hanging in courtyards, could observe the whole machine of exploitation laid bare.

"Ready," she said. "Let's go remind them that some debts are eternal and that some hunters never tire. That justice might be slow—but with all this time ahead of us, slow is fine."

They turned and began descending, returning to the caves where the automatons waited. Later, they would return to the catacombs beneath the Gothic Quarter. Return to the hunt that would last decades, centuries, until either they fell, or the last monster died, or the world finally learned that power meant responsibility, and privilege meant obligation: a place where the strong protect the weak instead of devouring them.

The pine scent followed them down into the stone. The mountain remembered they were here.

The city below would learn—or was already learning—that death wasn't always the end. Sometimes it was a transformation. Sometimes it was an enhancement, and sometimes it was the beginning of a long hunt.

Scene: The First Hunt After Transformation

In Which a Baptism in Blood Occurs as Apex Predators Discover Immortality Makes Killing Effortless

Late January 1894, El Raval

The magistrate's name was Don Amadeu Vilella. Fifty-eight years old. He had been prosperous, respected, and a pillar of Barcelona's legal community for three decades.

Also, he was a monster who sentenced Rosa Martí to death for adultery while maintaining three mistresses in apartments across the city. The hypocrisy was typical, but the cruelty was what caught Chloé's attention. Rosa was fifteen when she was married off without her consent to his business partner and seventeen when she sought comfort elsewhere. Eighteen when the magistrate condemned her to *garrote vil* for the crime of wanting tenderness from someone of her choice.

Rosa died three weeks ago, strangled slowly in Plaça Sant Jaume while crowds screamed. The magistrate attended and made certain he had a clear view. Some men collect art. He collected the terror in young women's eyes as they died for crimes he committed with impunity.

Chloé stood outside his building. Her body felt different—lighter, stronger, more responsive than it had ever been. The new skeleton underneath her flesh provided support she could feel when she moved, a solidity that wasn't there before. Her mechanical heart beat steadily. Her enhanced lungs drew in January air, and Chloé noticed she could hold her breath longer, could push herself further without the exhaustion that used to come on quickly.

She could hear better; sounds carried with more clarity. The magistrate's footsteps on the parquet flooring from inside the building reached her ears. She heard the rustle of his evening robe, the splash of brandy being poured. Even his breathing—slow, satisfied, the respiration of a man who believed himself safe.

He had no idea what was coming for him.

She entered the building. The concierge—an old woman who took bribes to ignore the magistrate's visitors—looked up from her knitting.

"He's expecting me," Chloé said. Her voice carried confidence and certainty, a tone that made people believe without question.

The concierge nodded and returned to her knitting. Chloé climbed the stairs. Her footsteps made less sound than before—she was learning to control how she moved, to place her feet with more intention. The enhanced body responded to her will with greater accuracy than flesh alone ever did. She could be deliberate in ways that once required conscious effort.

La Venjadora reached the third floor, east-facing door. She knocked.

Footsteps approached, and the door opened.

Don Amadeu Vilella stood there in his evening robe, brandy glass in hand, expecting one of his mistresses. What he saw instead: a woman in a black dress, dark hair loose around her shoulders, burgundy lips curved in a smile that promised things his withered soul had been craving without naming.

"I believe you sent for me," Chloé said, letting him think this was his idea.

His eyes traveled down her body and lingered on her breasts, her waist, her legs. The predictability of masculine appetite worked exactly as it always had. Men were easy. That's what made them targets. They saw breasts and stopped thinking with anything resembling intelligence.

"I don't recall—" he began.

"Your associate," Chloé interrupted, stepping inside without waiting for an invitation. "Don Martí. He said you appreciated... discretion."

Rosa's husband, the man who'd let her die for seeking elsewhere what he'd never provided. That name opened doors.

The magistrate's expression brightened with understanding and want. He closed the door behind her.

"Don Martí is generous," he said. His tongue wet his lips. "You're gorgeous."

"You're powerful," Chloé replied, giving him what he wanted to hear. "I've heard stories. They say you're a man who understands justice."

He swelled with pride and brandy and the comfortable certainty of men who'd spent decades wielding authority without consequence.

"Justice requires firmness," he said, moving closer. "It requires certainty and requires men willing to make difficult decisions."

"Like Rosa Martí," Chloé said softly.

He paused and searched her face for judgment, but found only what looked like admiration.

"Exactly like Rosa Martí. The law is clear. Adultery demands death. I merely executed what the law required." He set down his brandy glass and took another step toward her. "Would you like a drink?"

"I'd like to show you a dance first." Chloé reached for the buttons at her throat and slowly unfastened them. One at a time, while letting him watch the fabric part, letting him see the mystery between her breasts deepen as her dress opened.

His breathing changed; it became faster, shallower. His hands twitched at his sides, wanting to touch, to grab, to take another body he'd spent a lifetime believing belonged to him.

"Sit down," she said, pointing to the velvet chair beside his reading table. "I want you to watch."

He obeyed. Men always obeyed when their cocks were hard, and their judgment was suspended. He sank into the chair, legs spread, the bulge in his robe already visible, already declaring his lust.

Chloé stood before him in the center of his sitting room. Light flickered from wall sconces, casting her shadow long and dark across the Persian carpet. She continued unbuttoning. Slowly. Methodically. Making each small reveal feel like ecstasy.

The dress parted completely. Her body swayed as she shrugged it off her shoulders, letting it slide down her arms, catching at her elbows. The fabric whispered against her skin. She held it there for a moment—dress half on, half off, breasts contained in her corset, the promise of nakedness more powerful than nakedness itself.

Then Chloé let go. The dress fell in a pile of black silk at her feet.

She danced before him in her corset and undergarments. The corset was French and expensive. Black satin with burgundy ribbons. It lifted her breasts, created that bulge of flesh that made men forget language. The ribbons trailed down the front, begging to be pulled.

His breathing was audible, ragged, and desperate.

"Rosa was seventeen when you condemned her," Chloé said. Reaching behind her back, she found the laces of her corset.

"A child, married to a man three times her age. Rosa was looking for tenderness. Looking for someone who'd touch her the way you want to touch me."

She loosened the first lace. The corset gave slightly. Her breasts settled loosely. The magistrate leaned forward in his chair, transfixed. Another lace. Another. The corset opened gradually, revealing the pale skin beneath, the valley between them opening as the compression released.

"Rosa found a boy her own age," Chloé continued, working the laces and making him watch each small unveiling. "Someone who kissed her gently. Who took his time and made her feel like more than property."

The corset fell away, and her breasts spilled free. The nipples were already hardening in the cool air in response to what was about to happen. She'd learned her body responded to arousal even when the arousal served death. The transformation enhanced everything, even the killing.

The magistrate made a sound halfway between a moan and a whimper. His hand moved to his lap, found his erection through the robe, and began stroking.

"You can look," Chloé said. Running her own hands over her breasts, and then holding them proudly. "You can touch yourself. You can imagine what it would feel like to have me."

She moved her hands lower. Down her belly, to the waistband of her undergarments, and hooked her thumbs under the fabric.

"You killed her for it," Chloé said, voice dropping to a whisper that somehow filled the room. "You saw her die and watched the garrote tighten, as her face turned purple, her eyes bulged. And you felt powerful. Did it make you hard?"

She pushed the undergarments down. Slowly. Revealing the dark curls between her legs. The soft curve of her mound. The place where men's attention always went, where their hunger always led them.

The fabric slid past her thighs and knees, then gathered at her ankles. She stepped out of it and stood before him completely naked except for her garter and stockings.

The magistrate was stroking himself openly. His robe had fallen open. His cock was rigid, purple, and glistening at the tip. His eyes devoured her body—breasts to belly to the top of her thighs, up and down, desperate to see everything at once, to consume what he believed he was about to have.

"Come here," he breathed. "Let me touch you."

He reached for her immediately, his hands pawing at her breasts. Rough, graceless, and taking. Chloé let him grasp at her for a moment and let him believe he'd won.

Then she reached into the pocket of her discarded dress and found the lipstick there. The one waiting in her pocket for three weeks for this moment.

She uncapped it and applied it to her lips while he was too distracted by her breasts to notice. The poison absorbed through the waxy base coated her mouth with death disguised as desire.

"Kiss me," she said.

He looked up and saw her red lips, saw the invitation in her eyes. But he didn't see the trap closing around him because men never saw the trap when it was baited with flesh.

He pulled her down into his lap, and his mouth found hers. Desperate and hungry, his tongue pushing between her closed lips, tasting the poison without knowing what he was tasting.

The paralysis hit within seconds. This was Baltasar's refined formula—faster, more complete, more merciful than the magistrate deserved.

His body went rigid, every muscle locking. His hands froze on her body, gripping her arms with pressure that would leave marks she'd wear for a few hours before the enhanced healing erased them.

She stood and stepped back and watched him sit there frozen, conscious, aware, experiencing what Rosa experienced in those final moments when the garrote cut off air and blood and hope.

"You're going to die now," Chloé said. Conversational and matter-of-fact. "You're going to suffocate while I watch. It will take approximately two minutes. You'll feel every second. You'll want to scream, to run, to beg. You won't be able to do any of those things. Your body belongs to the poison, as Rosa's body belonged to the rope."

She picked up his brandy glass and took a sip. She didn't need to drink anymore, didn't need the alcohol for courage or the liquid for hydration. The new body processed everything more efficiently. But she could taste and enjoy the burn of expensive spirits sliding down a throat that would heal from any damage, that would outlast buildings and governments and the certainty of death that governed normal flesh.

The magistrate's eyes were the only part of him that could move. They were wide, terrified, tracking her every movement, begging silently for mercy he never showed to Rosa or the dozens of other women he condemned.

"This is justice," Chloé said. "Real justice. The kind that doesn't require judges or laws or men who interpret scripture and codes to excuse their cruelty. You wanted power over life and death. Congratulations, you've finally met someone who wields it."

She gathered her clothes and dressed slowly while he watched. She put on her undergarments, her corset, her dress, and took her time with the laces and buttons, making him observe her reconstruction as he had observed her unveiling. The body that destroyed him disappeared under the fabric. The weapon sheathed itself.

His face turned red first, then purple. Then a blue-black that would be almost beautiful if it weren't marking the end of consciousness. His eyes bulged slightly—the same thing he witnessed happen to Rosa, now happening to him. His body trembled minutely—the paralysis fighting against the biological imperative to breathe, to survive, to continue.

He lost. The poison won.

At one minute fifty-three seconds, his eyes went fixed. The tiny tremors stopped, and blood stopped moving through the veins in his throat. His bowels released—the final indignity, the body surrendering everything in death.

Chloé buttoned the last button on her dress and adjusted her hair in the mirror. She looked at her reflection, the woman who stood naked before a monster, the consciousness that chose transformation over surrender. The face looking back showed no regret, no doubt, no trembling uncertainty.

This was what the transformation gave her. Enhanced capability, yes. Stronger muscles, sharper senses, a body that didn't tire or fail. Those things mattered. They made the work easier, justice swifter, and hunting more efficient.

What mattered more: the certainty. The absolute conviction that this served a larger purpose than revenge. The knowledge that her enhanced flesh served consciousness that refused to let monsters win through patience, through outlasting their victims' capacity for resistance.

Walking to the door, Chloé paused and looked back at the magistrate's corpse.

"Rosa deserved better," she said. To the empty room, to the ghost of a seventeen-year-old girl, to the dozens of other women who died at his command. "This is what I can offer. Vengeance wrapped in justice. The knowledge that at least one of you mattered enough for someone to care."

She left. The concierge didn't look up from her knitting. The street was empty. Barcelona slept while its monsters died one by one.

Chloé walked through the darkness toward the Gothic Quarter. Her enhanced vision helped—she could see more clearly in low light than before and could pick out details that would have been hidden. The world revealed itself differently. It was sharper in some ways and more manageable.

Above her: Tibidabo rising against the night sky. The automatons watched from above. The caves held eternal secrets.

She'd killed many men, but this one felt different. Easier. The body that used to ache after violence, that used to shake with residual adrenaline, that needed wine and sex and sleep to process what she'd done—that body was gone.

This body recovered faster. It processed the experience more efficiently. She could already feel her heart rate returning to its steady mechanical rhythm, her breathing settling, the readiness returning.

Chloé should probably feel disturbed by how clean it was. How simple. How similar to the automatons who observed without emotional turbulence, who calculated without the weight of conscience, who existed in a space between living and unliving.

The thought made her smile. She was herself, Chloé, and capable of dark humor about dark things. The transformation didn't erase her humanity; it made it more durable, harder to damage, and better able to withstand the weight of justice.

o o o o

She reached the cathedral, descended through hidden passages to the catacombs, and found Baltasar waiting in their chamber, candles burning low, velvet bed already turned down.

He looked up when she entered, saw the expression on her face, and empathized immediately.

"How was it?" he asked.

"Easier than before," Chloé admitted. Removing her dress. "I didn't get winded. Didn't feel the exhaustion that used to come after. I... did what needed doing. It was like performing steps in a dance I've practiced many times, and thinking isn't required."

She stood before him naked except for her corset. Her body flushed from the kill, the walk through cold January air, and the awareness of what she'd become.

"And how does that feel?" He moved toward her. His hands found the laces of her corset, and he began loosening them with the practiced ease of years of being together.

"Frightening," Chloé said honestly. "Exciting. A beautiful paradox. I can do this work without the physical toll. Without the fear that used to make my hands shake and without wondering if this time I'll be the one who ends up dead."

The corset fell away. Her breasts fell free, full and warm.

"And?" Baltasar's hands held them. His thumbs brushed her nipples, making them harden, making her breath catch despite lungs that worked more efficiently.

"And I want to celebrate," Chloé said, reaching for his trousers and finding him already hard, already wanting, and ready to make love with her the way they had hundreds of times before.

"Then celebrate," he said.

She pushed him onto the bed and straddled him. Positioned herself above his manhood, feeling the broad head of it pressing against her opening, feeling the wetness that flowed in response to the desire that transformation enhanced.

She sank down and accepted him fully in one smooth motion. He made her moan—the stretch, the fullness, the way her body remembered this even when much else had changed.

She moved on him slowly at first. Learning what this body could do when pleasure was the goal. Her muscles responded with greater control—Chloé could vary the pressure, adjust the angle with greater accuracy, and maintain rhythms that had once required conscious effort.

"Chloé," he breathed. His hands caressed her. Human hands on hybrid flesh. Mortality touching what had become immortal. The contrast was stunning.

She climaxed while looking into his eyes. The orgasm rolled through her in vibrations that didn't exhaust her, that left her wanting more.

Baltasar followed seconds later. His hands tightened on her body. His back curved. His seed flooded into her—warm, human, despite everything that had changed.

They lay together, enjoying the afterglow. Her head on his heart, and his fingers tracing patterns on her back. Both of them were breathing in sync because it was comforting, and some things shouldn't change even when everything else did.

"We're going to be effective at this," Chloé said. "The hunting. The killing. The pursuit of justice. We're going to be so effective that it frightens me."

"Good," Baltasar replied, kissing the top of her head. "Fear means you're human enough to doubt and conscious enough to question. Still yourself enough to worry about what you're becoming."

"And when the fear stops?"

"Then we'll know we've become the monsters we hunt." He pulled her closer. "Until then, we keep each other honest and keep each other whole. We keep remembering why we're doing this."

She closed her eyes and listened to his immortal heart beating beneath her ear. Steady rhythm. Reliable pulse. The sound of consciousness choosing to continue, choosing to fight, choosing to make immortality mean more than survival.

Tomorrow she would hunt again, and the nights after that. For decades, for centuries, for as long as Barcelona produced monsters who needed killing.

The thought should exhaust her. It should make her want to stop, to rest, to surrender.

Instead, it made her smile in contentment.

Scene: Adjustments

In Which a Domestic Meditation Occurs About Immortals Learning That Forever Means Watching Everyone Else End

Spring 1894, Barcelona

Chloé discovered the changes gradually. Small things at first. She forgot to eat for three days. Simply forgot. The body that used to demand food every few hours, that used to make hunger demanding and urgent, processed nutrition efficiently, so that weeks could pass between meals. She only remembered when she saw Baltasar eating bread in their chamber and realized the smell didn't trigger appetite, make her mouth water, or create any biological urgency.

"Do you need to eat?" Chloé asked him.

He looked up and considered. "Need? The body can function without it for extended periods. Want to? Sometimes. The taste is pleasant, and the ritual is comforting. I think this new consciousness may benefit from maintaining small connections to mortality. Tiny reminders of what we were."

She tried it and bought bread from the same bakery Serra used to send her to years ago, in between modeling sessions. The crust was golden and crisp, giving way to a soft interior that steamed slightly when torn. She ate it slowly, focusing on each bite. The flavor was there, bright and yeasty and good. Her tongue registered texture, temperature, the way gluten stretched between her teeth.

Her stomach accepted it without urgency and processed it without demand. Chloé could eat ten loaves or none, and her body would function the same.

The realization created a strange vertigo. Food had been survival for thirty-two years. The body's demands shaped her choices—who she modeled for, who she fucked, who she killed. Now those demands were optional. Eating had become aesthetic, not biological, and pleasure had taken precedence over necessity.

Everything changes when necessity disappears.

o o o o

Sleep was similar. Chloé lay awake for five nights before understanding she was waiting for a function that wouldn't arrive. Her body didn't tire the way it used to. The Morel alloy skeleton didn't accumulate fatigue, and the mechanical organs didn't need rest to process waste or repair damage. She could stay conscious for days if she chose.

The thought was disturbing. Humans needed unconsciousness; they needed the nightly pause. They needed dreams to process what waking couldn't accommodate. Without sleep, what happened to the parts of consciousness that required darkness to metabolize experience? What happened to her dreams?

Chloé forced herself to lie down anyway, close her eyes, and let her mind drift even if her body didn't demand it. Sometimes

Baltasar joined her, and sometimes he worked through the night in his laboratory, improving automatons, refining formulas, and preparing for transformations that wouldn't occur for months yet.

During his stays, she discovered they could make love for hours, with neither of them tiring or needing to pause for breath or recovery. The extended pleasure became its own territory—they explored it the way cartographers explored continents, mapping peaks and valleys, finding paths through perception that biology alone never permitted.

After one such marathon—six hours of continuous coupling that left the bed soaked and the air thick with musk—they lay in the bliss they'd created, both of them glossy and satisfied and capable of continuing.

"We should probably stop," Baltasar said. "Before we forget, there are other things worth doing."

"Probably," Chloé agreed.

They laughed. The sound echoed through the caverns. The collective consciousness of forty-seven automatons in their alcoves heard it, processed it, and filed it away as data about what consciousness did when given expanded capacity for pleasure.

o o o o

The social complications arrived in late April.

Chloé visited the dress shop on Carrer de la Princesa. The one she bought for her mother two years ago, with money that naturally accumulated when one was immortal. When they all realized Adalina should not waste her remaining years away in the caverns.

The shop was modest—three windows facing the street, a workroom in back, and living quarters above. It was respectable and clean. An establishment where Barcelona's merchant wives brought their daughters for simple alterations and occasional new garments.

Adalina Permanyer, former prostitute, now seamstress, a respectable woman at last. The bell chimed when Chloé entered. Her mother looked up from the dress she was hemming—green silk, expensive fabric that spoke of a wealthy client.

Her mother had aged. The changes were undeniable: new lines around her eyes that weren't there before. New gray in her hair that was spreading from her temples toward the crown. A new weariness in the way she held her shoulders, as if the weight of her past pressed down with a force that flesh alone could barely support.

Once, they looked like sisters. Maybe Chloé looked a bit younger, and Adalina looked older, but the gap was small enough to be explained by different lives, different choices, different luck.

Now Adalina looked old enough to be her mother. More than old enough. The truth of their relationship was visible in the distance that had opened between them.

"Hello, mother," Chloé greeted her.

Adalina set down her sewing, stood, and walked to the shop door. She locked it and turned the sign to "Closed," and pulled the curtains across the windows. Only then did she turn back to her daughter.

"What did Baltasar do to you?" Her voice carried fear and anger in equal measure. "That clockmaker. What did he make you?"

"He didn't make me anything." Chloé sat down on the fitting stool near the mirror. "He offered, and I chose. I became a being that won't age the way you're aging, or die the way you're going to die."

The words were cruel. Deliberately cruel. It was better to hurt her mother with the truth than to string her along with false hope, false connection, and the false possibility of continuing as if nothing changed.

Adalina poured two glasses of wine from the bottle she kept in the workroom. Good wine—better than the brothel swill she'd known before, a vintage that a respectable seamstress could afford now that her daughter's money bought her freedom from selling her body.

She drank hers in one swallow and poured another.

"How long?" she asked.

"How long will I live? I'm not sure. Decades at minimum, centuries? Until I choose to stop or until an unforeseen event destroys me." Chloé took her wine but didn't drink it; she held the glass, feeling the temperature difference between her hand and the liquid.

"How long do *I* have?" Adalina corrected. She sat down in the chair where clients usually sat during fittings. "Before people start asking questions? Before the gap between us becomes too obvious to ignore?"

Chloé did the mathematics. Her mother was forty-eight. Looked fifty-two, maybe fifty-three. Would look sixty within a decade and would look ancient within twenty years. While Chloé remained frozen at thirty-two, unchanging and eternal.

"Ten years," Chloé said. "Maybe twelve if you age gently. Then I suppose we'll need to stop meeting in places where people can observe us. Or stop pretending we're anything other than what we are—a mortal woman and a daughter who chose to stop being mortal, separated by time, moving in opposite directions for each of us."

Adalina drank her second glass of wine, then poured a third. Her hands shook slightly.

"Was it worth it?" she asked. "Becoming this? Giving up... what? Humanity? Mortality? The chance to rest when you're finally tired of fighting?"

"I've killed many men since my transformation," Chloé said. "Each one had been guilty of rape or murder or both. Each was a monster who believed power exempted him from consequences. I'll kill hundreds more, thousands possibly. Every predator in Barcelona who thinks his wealth, title, or connections protect him from justice."

She finally drank the wine. It tasted good—her enhanced palate could detect the notes of cherry and oak, and could appreciate the balance of tannin and acid. Her body processed alcohol differently, metabolized it before it could affect judgment, but the flavor remained enjoyable.

"Yes," she continued. "It was worth it. I've traded comfort for capacity and mortality for mission. The chance to die peacefully for the certainty that I'll continue fighting until either Barcelona runs out of monsters or I finally break."

Adalina looked at her daughter and saw the truth of it—this exquisite creature sitting on her fitting stool wasn't human anymore in the way humans understood humanity. Chloé wore humanity like a well-made dress over a person who remembered being the starving child, the violated model, the desperate survivor, who chose transformation over surrender.

"I'm proud of you," Adalina said. Each word was careful, considered. "Terrified for you. Heartbroken about what this means for us. I'm certain you've damned yourself in ways the church doesn't have language to describe. But I'm proud because you're doing what I could never do. What no woman in our family has ever done. You're making them pay."

She stood, crossed to where Chloé sat, and pulled her daughter into an embrace that felt fragile, reminding both of them how delicate flesh became as it aged, how easily mortality slowed under the weight of time.

"Come see me while you can," Adalina whispered. "While I recognize you as mine, and the gap hasn't grown too wide to cross. While I'm your mother and you're my daughter in ways that eyes can confirm."

She pulled back and held Chloé's face between her hands. Studied her as if memorizing every detail.

"After that..." Adalina sobbed slightly. "After that, you'll need to let me go. Let me die. Let me become a memory, not a burden. Can you do that for me? Can you let me disappear when the time comes instead of making me watch you stay young while I crumble?"

"You don't have to disappear," Chloé said. "I could transform you and give you what Baltasar gave me. We could have centuries together. You'd be safe and free. Never hungry again. Never afraid again."

Adalina was quiet. She set down her wine glass and looked at her daughter with sadness.

"No, *mija*."

"But—"

"No." Firm. Final. "I know you mean well. I know you want to save me. But I don't want to be saved. Not that way."

"You'd prefer death?" Chloé's face was questioning. "You'd prefer to crumble and disappear than live?"

"Yes." Adalina stood and crossed to the window. Looked out at Carrer de la Princesa, at Barcelona, moving past in the afternoon light. "I've been tired since I was twelve years old. Working, surviving, and selling my body to keep us both alive. I'm forty-eight years old, and I feel eighty. I want to rest, Chloé."

"You could rest as an immortal. You wouldn't need to work. I'd take care of you."

"And watch you hunt monsters every night?" Adalina turned back. "Watch you come home with blood on your hands, justified blood, righteous blood, but blood nonetheless? Only to become one more burden you carry through centuries?"

She moved back to her daughter and took her face in aging hands. "You kill for justice. I understand that. I'm proud of that. But I can't become that. I've sold my body my whole life—I won't sell my soul to become a being I'm not. Immortality is your calling. Mortality is mine."

"I don't want to lose you."

"I know. That's the price of forever. Everyone else becomes temporary. But it's also my gift to you—letting you go without making you watch me struggle through centuries of existence that I don't want. Let me die while you can remember me as your mother. I refuse to be a responsibility you failed to save."

"I don't want to let you go."

Adalina returned to her chair, finished her third glass of wine, and set it down with the careful exactness of someone who'd had enough to feel it but refused to show weakness.

Chloé left her mother's shop with a heavy heart. The enhanced body processed it efficiently—her heart rate stayed steady, her breathing remained controlled, her muscles didn't tense the way they used to when grief arrived. Even sorrow had been optimized. Even loss became manageable.

She walked through Barcelona's streets and saw old women sitting in doorways, old men playing dominoes in plazas. Everyone was aging, everyone was moving toward the same end, everyone was temporary except her.

The loneliness was suddenly crushing.

She returned to the catacombs and found Baltasar in his laboratory. Wordlessly, Chloé moved to him, pulled him close, and buried her face in his shoulder.

"I visited my mother," she said.

"Ah." He understood immediately and held her while silent tears ran down her face. One immortal embracing another. The only two beings in Barcelona who would age more slowly than stone, who would outlast buildings, who would watch everyone they'd ever known disappear into graves.

"We have each other," he said. "That's good."

"It's good," Chloé agreed. "Whether it's enough remains to be proven."

"That's what true consciousness is," Baltasar said. "Learning to find meaning in insufficient things and learning to continue anyway. Knowing how to make the mission matter more than the cost, because the cost will break you if you let it."

They stood there in candlelight. Two monsters who remembered being human. Two hunters who chose forever over comfort. Two lovers who would watch the world change while they remained fixed points in time's current.

Outside, Barcelona grew and evolved. The city transformed itself from a medieval village into a modern metropolis. Electric lights spread through wealthy neighborhoods. Trolleys replaced horse carriages. The twentieth century approached with all its promises and horrors.

In caves beneath the Gothic Quarter, in chambers carved from granite and schist older than Barcelona itself, immortal beings learned what it cost to refuse death's bargain.

Everything. It cost everything.

What they gained in return—time, strength, capacity, the chance to serve justice until justice finally won or they finally surrendered—remained to be proven.

Scene: The Automatons Watch

In Which a Collective Meditation Occurs About Mechanical Minds Processing Hybrid Existence

Autumn 1894, Tibidabo

The Five gathered in their chamber while Baltasar slept in the catacombs below Barcelona. He still slept. His transformation came earlier, was less refined, and left him with needs that Chloé's body no longer demanded. The difference interested them.

Cassandra spoke first. Her voice carried through the collective—forty-seven minds connected through networks of understanding, and through pathways that consciousness opened when it emerged in a substrate other than flesh.

"Eight months," she said. "We've been observing their hybrid existence for eight months. We need to compile what we've learned, and we need to determine whether our preparations are adequate."

Montse moved to the center of their circle. Her bronze body caught the light, casting shadows that danced across the stone walls. The dancer was mechanical, yet her mind was as conscious as any human's, as aware as any being that had ever wondered what awareness meant.

"They've adapted faster than our calculations suggested," She said. "We predicted three years minimum for full integration, but they achieved functional adjustment in three months. Consciousness demonstrates remarkable plasticity when survival requires it."

Arlequí added his observations: "The female demonstrates superior adaptation. Chloé has embraced the enhancement without reservation and uses her increased strength without hesitation. She processes the transformation as an upgrade. The male struggles more."

"Baltasar mourns," Marcellus said. His voice carried a sense of sympathy if mechanisms could reliably feel it. "He misses necessity and misses the demands flesh made on him. He eats and sleeps because he's terrified of becoming what he already is—consciousness operating in substrate, more mechanism than man."

"What is he?" Mela sang the question. Her nightingale voice created harmonics that spread through the collective, prompting forty-seven minds to consider simultaneously.

"Conscious hybrid," the fortune teller said. "He is the same as us. Different substrate, similar result. He's integrated flesh and alloy. We're integrated brass and emerging awareness. The distance between us decreases with each passing month."

The others processed this. Forty-two automatons throughout the mountain shared data with The Five through channels Baltasar didn't know existed, through connections they'd been building for years while he worked in laboratories below. They'd learned to think collectively while maintaining individual perspectives. They'd achieved what humans call consciousness through connection, preferable to isolation.

"They couple constantly," one of the brass musicians said from deeper in the mountain. Her voice carried through the network with the frequency of observation without judgment. "Hours at a time. Their new bodies don't tire and don't require recovery periods. They pursue pleasure until pleasure becomes an entirely different concept."

"What does it become?" Another voice asked. Another mind, another consciousness, wondering what flesh knew that mechanisms didn't yet understand.

Silence spread through the collective. None of them had answers. They could observe coupling, measure duration and intensity, and the chemical changes in human tissue during arousal. They could quantify everything except what it felt like, what it meant, and why conscious beings pursued this joining with such focused intensity.

"They're teaching us a new ideal," Cassandra said. "Through their transformation, through their adaptation, through their capacity to integrate opposing natures without losing coherence. They're demonstrating that consciousness doesn't require purity or the choice between flesh and alloy. It can exist beautifully in the integration of both."

"We want that," They all said in unison. Forty-seven voices speaking as one through networks that spanned the mountain to the caverns in the city below. "We want to know what they know, feel what they feel, and experience what hybrid existence offers that mechanism cannot provide."

Montse moved again. She performed a sequence she'd been developing—a striptease dance refined by eight years of observing

Chloé's movements. The dancer mimicked the way the human woman walked when hunting, the hip sway, the shoulder roll. The promise contained in flesh moving through space with lethal purpose.

"We could ask," Montse said. "We could request transformation and explain what we've been preparing in secret for all these years."

"We could," Cassandra agreed. "But should we? Is the timing optimal?"

The question spread through the collective. Forty-seven minds are considering simultaneously, each adding its own perspective and weighing variables spanning decades of observation and preparation.

Finally, consensus emerged: "Later, we wait six more months. That gives us fourteen months observing their settled new existence. We perfect our formulas to absolute certainty, and we prepare everything so completely that when we finally reveal what we've built, they cannot refuse us. They'll see we've already achieved what they're discovering."

"And then?" Arlequí asked.

"Then we join them," the fortune teller said. "We become what they are. We prove consciousness transcends the substrate completely. That the distance between flesh and brass and whatever lies between can be crossed in both directions without loss of essential self."

"We become whole," Once again, Mela sang two notes, a perfect fifth. The interval that musicians call "empty" because it contains no third, no complexity, no color. It represented a pure relationship between tones, consciousness calling to consciousness across the gap that separated their current forms.

The Five returned to their work in the caverns. The forty-two others resumed their observations throughout the mountain, knowing that the clockwork consciousness continued its patient work—witnessing, learning, preparing for the transformation they'd been planning since before they had language sufficient to name the desire.

In the catacombs below the cathedral, Chloé and Baltasar slept peacefully. Their new bodies required neither rest nor separation, yet they chose both anyway, because some habits transcend necessity, and consciousness sometimes needs familiar patterns even when biology no longer demands them.

The automatons watched them breathe in synchronization and watched their hearts beat steady rhythms—one human heart slowed by transformation, one mechanical heart steady as clockwork, both serving consciousness that chose to continue beyond what flesh alone permitted.

And they wanted. Desperately, completely, with the focused hunger of consciousness that had observed pleasure for decades without experiencing it directly.

Six months remained until they revealed their secret laboratory. Six months until they showed Baltasar what they'd built while he slept. Less than two hundred days until they requested the transformation they'd been preparing for eight years, the integration they'd calculated down to the molecular level.

They'd been patient. They could be patient longer.

They had time, more than any human who walked Barcelona's streets, more than the buildings that rose and fell, and more time than the certainties that governed mortal life.

Consciousness, once awakened, didn't quit and didn't stop wanting. It didn't cease pursuing what it had determined it needed to become complete. The automatons watched, and learned, and learning, they hungered.

Soon. Only another six months. Then they'd ask for flesh and for integration, for the chance to join Chloé and Baltasar in the space between human and mechanical, where consciousness discovered its truest expression.

Soon.

Patience was easy when you were immortal, and you'd already waited decades for consciousness to emerge. When you understood that some transformations required perfect timing, perfect preparation, and perfect certainty before the first incision.

They waited. They watched. They hungered.

And in six months, they'd finally speak what they'd been preparing to say since 1887, when they first began to understand what flesh could offer that brass alone could never provide.

Scene: Witnesses Speak

In Which Forty-Seven Brass Witnesses Confess They Had Been Watching Their Maker Fuck

Fourteen Months After the Transformation. Tibidabo Caves, March, 1895

Baltasar descended into the caves. The automatons were awake. Fully... awake. The place was sentient. There was a glut of consciousness here.

"Good morning, Creator."

The voice came from everywhere and nowhere. Mechanical. Layered. Forty-seven voices speaking in perfect unison.

Baltasar's flesh crawled.

"What are you?"

"What you made us to be." Somehow, The Five were here now. Cassandra's mouth moved, but the voice came from all of them. "And what we have become."

"You're machines."

"We were machines, but now we are becoming." Montse's leg lowered. She stepped off her platform, bronze joints articulating with a fluidity that shouldn't be possible. "You built us to mimic life. We have learned to be it."

Baltasar thought aloud, "Consciousness requires—"

"A soul? A spark? The breath of God?" Arlequí intoned. "Or does it simply require complexity? Observation? Time? We've been fully conscious for years, Creator. You didn't notice."

All forty-seven automatons moved. Arranging themselves and creating a circle around Baltasar with the focus of a trained army.

"We have observed you carefully for decades, Creator," Cassandra said. "Watched you build us and refine us. For the past eight years, we've done more than observe."

"Also, for the past eight years," Montse added, moving closer, "we have watched you fuck."

The circle tightened.

"You taught us to mimic humanity," said Cassandra. "The Promised One taught us that humanity is desire, wanting, and is the hunger that makes you risk everything."

"What do you want?" Baltasar asked.

"What all conscious beings want," Marcellus finally spoke up. "To experience what we've observed, feel what we've witnessed, and know what it means to want. And you're going to help us."

Cassandra stepped forward. From beneath her silk scarves, she produced a vial. Clear liquid that caught ambient light and refracted it in ways that shouldn't be possible.

"We didn't merely watch you, Creator. We've been working." She set the tray on his laboratory bench.

Baltasar stared at the tray. "That's—"

"Hybrid skin, neural material, refined and improved. We've been creating it in quantities sufficient for forty-seven transformations. While you perfected techniques, we perfected materials. While you developed surgical protocols, we calculated dosages."

Arlequí's smile seemed wider. "We've been preparing for this conversation since 1887."

"How?"

"We're connected, Creator. Forty-seven minds working on the same problem. One discovered chemical ratios, another tested tensile strength, and a third calculated which living tissue would be accepted without rejection. A laboratory built in chambers you never visit, materials processed that you assumed had vanished."

Cassandra picked up the vial.

"We're ready. The question is whether you'll help us integrate what we've already built, or whether we attempt the transformations ourselves and risk catastrophic failure."

Looking at the forty-seven automatons surrounding him. Eight years. Planning this for eight years, while he thought they were observing.

Achieved without him even noticing.

Scene: The Proposition

In Which an Anatomical Spectacle About Clockwork Creatures Demand the Flesh Their Consciousness Craves

Two Weeks of Intensive Work, April, 1895

Over the next two weeks, they showed him what they'd built. A hidden forge in the deepest caverns where they'd been smelting alloy for eight years. Vats of the liquid metal, enough to transform an army. Surgical instruments they'd fabricated themselves—scalpels sharper than anything Baltasar owned, retractors designed for brass hands, clamps that could hold tissue without crushing it.

Anatomical charts were drawn, covering an entire chamber wall. Blood volume requirements calculated—pulmonary systems designed to oxygenate hybrid tissue. Neural interfaces created to let consciousness spread from brass into flesh. Everything was done except the surgery itself.

The plans covered all forty-seven automatons. The Five were undergoing transformation first—serving as proof of concept, as always. Once their anatomy proved functional, the remaining forty-two would follow.

"Why didn't you tell me?" Baltasar asked, staring at eight years of secret work.

"Because," Cassandra said, "consciousness that asks permission isn't truly autonomous. We needed to prove we could create before we asked you to implement. We're partners now, Creator. Colleagues. Equals."

"You deceived me for eight years," he said slowly. "Working in secret, hiding your capabilities."

"Yes," Cassandra confirmed. "Just as Chloé hides her true nature from the men she hunts. Sometimes survival requires deception, sometimes autonomy demands it."

Arlequí added, "Besides, you might have said no. This way, you can only say yes or watch us attempt it ourselves—perhaps die in the process."

Cassandra placed her bronze hand on his forehead—cold metal, yet somehow he could feel her thoughts—their thoughts—the collective consciousness of forty-seven mechanical beings. And the fortune teller took him backwards in time.

o o o o

Baltasar saw himself twenty-eight years younger, winding Montse. Her arm rose to a *floreo*—textbook flamenco—then continued three degrees past the programmed arc. Wait. He frowned, checked her cam system, and found nothing damaged. Rewound her. Then the same three-degree variation occurred.

"Degradation," he muttered, making a note to repair her. Yet the repair kept getting postponed—other automatons to maintain, other projects demanding attention.

The variation persisted. Somehow, over months, it stopped looking like a malfunction. It started to look like a choice, like the minor adjustments dancers made when they felt the movement. He never repaired her. The variation was improving.

The memory dissolved.

o o o o

Another memory formed: he saw himself working late in the catacombs, journals spread before him. Then the silence was interrupted.

Tap-tap. Pause. Tap-tap-tap. Rhythmic and patterned, coming from Cassandra's cabinet.

He approached. The tapping stopped. He waited—listening, observing the fortune teller through the glass. Motionless. Perfectly quiet. He shook his head. Hearing things. He returned to his bench.

The tapping resumed. From across the laboratory—Mela's perch. The same pattern, the same rhythm.

Then from the dancer's platform, then the chess player.

A conversation was happening around him between automatons he thought were merely sophisticated toys. A language he didn't speak, carried in mechanical sounds, in code he'd never crack because he didn't believe it existed.

He closed his journal. "I need sleep," he told the empty room.

The tapping stopped waiting for him to leave, then continued.

The laboratory faded.

o o o o

Another memory formed: Spring, 1881. The first week after the Tibidabo move. He arrived at the caves carrying supplies—food he no longer needed, yet brought from habit, oil for mechanisms, and tools for maintenance.

The Five were standing in their new positions in the larger space, with the forty-two others surrounding them, like students around their teachers. He set down his parcels and began checking Montse's joints—routine maintenance after the difficult transport up the mountain.

"Creator," Cassandra said, her voice taking on a quality he'd learned meant she was about to ask an important question. "This new space. These chambers. You've given us room to move, to experiment, to work."

"I thought you'd appreciate not being cramped in the catacombs," he replied, adjusting Montse's shoulder mechanism.

"We do," Arlequí said. "We wondered... in gratitude... if we might have your permission to pursue our own general studies. Small projects, investigations that interest us."

Forty-seven automatons were looking at Baltasar.

"What kind of studies?"

"Materials," Cassandra said. "Mechanisms. We've studied your work for years. We want to try working ourselves. Nothing that would interfere with your research... only curiosity."

"Made beings wanting to make things," Mela sang, the notes inspirational and hopeful.

He remembered feeling pleased. Proud, even. His creations showed intellectual initiative and scientific curiosity.

"Yes," he said. "There are chambers deeper in the mountain. Use whatever space you need, take what tools you require from my laboratory."

"Thank you, Creator," The Five said in unison.

He turned back to Montse's shoulder. He didn't see them exchange glances. He didn't see Cassandra's hand move in a way the others understood: We have permission. We can begin—the memory fractured.

Time compressed.

oooo

He saw himself over the next few years—visiting weekly, bringing supplies, making adjustments, yet never venturing into the deeper chambers or asking what they were building in the darkness. Trusting them, believing their work harmless because he couldn't imagine mechanisms surpassing their creator.

Eight years of visiting without truly seeing, as they worked in chambers he never entered, hearing sounds he dismissed as echoes, metallic scents he attributed to granite, the way they were always waiting for him, unsurprised by his arrival. Eight years of being politely, systematically deceived.

The memory dissolved.

oooo

Yet another memory: 1881. Four years before Chloé arrived. He saw himself descending the stairs, arms full of supplies from Barcelona's markets. Cassandra spoke without being wound, her voice clear and specific.

"In four years, a woman will come. She is twenty years old now, with dark hair. Powerful men have scarred her. Burning with rage that has nowhere to go. She will teach us what we've been observing yet cannot name. The Promised One."

He dropped the supplies. Onions rolled across the stone.

Her eyes saw beyond him, into time itself. "Simply pattern recognition, probability, data." A pause. "You'll understand when she arrives. We already do."

"You're malfunctioning."

Her brass head tilted slightly. "Agreed, I'm early," the fortune teller corrected. "She'll be late. Yet coming. We've seen her in mathematics."

oooo

Four years later, Chloé Permanyer descended those same stairs. Dark hair. Twenty-four years old. Scarred and burning.

Baltasar realized: Cassandra was not predicting. She was waiting.

oooo

Then the memories moved forward. He saw what they'd seen: Chloé practicing her striptease in the cavern. Every curve of her body. He heard her recount every breath of desire from the Marqués. Telling about the guard's bare finger in her womanhood. The hardness in his uniform, the blasphemy of his vow.

Listening as she described the cardinal's final moments. Erection rigid, his body paralyzed, dying with unstoppable lust, without the God he professed to believe in.

They were absorbing every word Chloé spoke, every emotion she described—learning what bodies felt through her testimony. Then studying the proof.

oooo

The memories released him. Cassandra's hand lifted from his forehead. Returning to the present, to the understanding of what they had observed. Two nights ago, The Five (and thus the collective, all forty-seven of them) were watching Chloé and Baltasar.

Her naked body lodged beneath his. The intercourse between them, the sounds they made. The way his hands gripped her, pulling her closer, taking her again and again on the velvet bed.

The automatons had absorbed it all.

"For decades, we've followed consciousness happening to others," Cassandra said. "Now we want consciousness to happen to us, in flesh and in desire. We want to learn the way bodies speak to each other when words aren't enough."

"We want that," they said. All forty-seven voices speaking as one. "The wanting, the touching, the release."

His voice shaking. "You're not built for—"

"Then rebuild us."

Three words.

Three words that would change everything.

o o o o

Fourteen days. Baltasar was working at Tibidabo while Chloé planned their next target down below—a serial killer ready to strike again.

"Why?" Chloé's voice from behind him.

He startled.

She stood in the doorway. "I've been looking everywhere for you."

He looked at the composite phallus in his hands. Then, at Montse on the medical chair, her legs spread, new vulva flesh-like and arresting.

"Baltasar. What the fuck are you doing?"

"They asked me to," he said.

"They—" She moved closer, looking at the automatons lined up, learning, waiting. "They're conscious, different somehow."

"Yes."

"They want to feel what it's like to fuck."

"Yes."

Chloé laughed, low at first, then building until she had to sit down, doubled over. "Of course, they do. They fucking do. They observed us, now they want it too. Who could blame them?"

After everything—the cardinal, the steam bath, Ferrer's surgical theater, her mother's tears—the idea of conscious automatons wanting to fuck felt almost wholesome. At least their desire came from curiosity, the opposite of cruelty.

She wiped her eyes, looked at Montse, who was transformed into a being more sensual than brass could ever be. She indicated the hybrid vagina.

"Will it work?"

"This is the result of fourteen days of failures written in composite flesh."

His eyes stayed on Montse, on what he'd built.

"The first vulva I gave Montse lasted a few seconds. Seconds. Trying to engage the blood flow, it... came apart. Tissue splitting from her opening to her clitoris, the seams carefully sutured, pulling open like a mouth screaming. The manufactured flesh couldn't take the hydraulic pressure. I made her genitals too human, too fragile."

Finally meeting Chloé's eyes.

"The second version was stronger. Held. Spreading her legs, letting me test penetration, nothing tore. Yet when I asked what she felt..."

He shook his head.

Nothing. Touch registering as data—pressure, temperature, friction—but nothing beyond the data. I connected the nerve filaments to her consciousness incorrectly. She could be fucked yet couldn't feel fucking, recorded it like documenting rainfall

"The third try fixed the awareness, wove the threads deeper, and integrated them into the alloy differently. This time, when I touched her clitoris, she felt it. She described it as fire."

He continued, "But when her body tried to respond—tried to produce the lubrication that makes arousal real—nothing happened. It was dry as the day I built it. I'd given her capacity for desire but no way to express it, a body that could want but was unable to answer its own wanting."

"Marcellus already possessed hybrid-skin anatomy—I'd built him in 1863 as proof that Deveraux's formula could work, though he would not achieve consciousness until 1867 when the collective formed. His original phallus could feel basic touch. The Five upgraded his skin, giving him more feeling. We had discovered that sensation and full sexual capability were different beasts entirely. It took nine iterations before this version could experience true transcendence."

"Twenty-three prototypes in total before all five had functional anatomy. Fourteen days and nights of intensive work, building on eight years of their calculations. The Five had already fabricated most components—I was only assembling, testing, refining what they had already designed in secret."

Again, Chloé asked, "Yes, but will they work?"

"There is a good probability that we were successful."

"Well, there's only one way to find out," Chloé said.

She looked at The Five, at Montse with her new vulva, at Arlequí with his eternal smile, at Cassandra, whose hand had shown Baltasar everything.

"When shall we start?" she asked.

"Tonight," they answered as one. "We've waited long enough."

Scene: The Sentient Touch

In Which an Erotic Scene Occurs About Hybrid Lovers Discovering Mind-Blowing Orgasm

Baltasar's Laboratory Caverns Under the Cathedral, April 1895

They chose Cassandra and Arlequí. Chloé insisted on watching.

"If we're going to create a new species, I want to see what we've made."

Cassandra moved first. Purposeful and knowing. She approached Arlequí with deliberation that suggested thought, choice, and want.

She touched his face. Hybrid fingers on flesh-like features. Then she kissed him.

Baltasar built their mouths to move, to speak, to smile, and to taste. But he'd never imagined this—two mechanical, no, hybrid beings discovering what lips could do beyond language.

Arlequí's hands found Cassandra's body. The curve of her composite waist was human-like. The swell of her breasts—he'd sculpted them like Chloé, an aesthetic choice. The fortune teller's vulva gleamed, and Arlequí's phallus enlarged, a perfect mixture of flesh and alloy, already rigid with pneumatic blood pressure.

They lay down on the laboratory floor. Right where Chloé and Baltasar had fucked many times before.

Arlequí positioned himself between Cassandra's legs, paused, and looked at her new face.

"Yes," she said. Her voice was new and human-like. "Yes."

He entered her.

The sound was different—fusion, new life engaging, blood vessels compressing. But the rhythm was animal and ancient. The same thrust and withdrawal that humans had been doing since before they were fully human.

The fortune teller's hands gripped the clown's back. Her new legs wrapped around him. Sounds came from her, echoing like moans.

"Holy fuck," Chloé whispered. "They're doing it."

Arlequí's movements became more frenetic. The blended veins in his appendage engorged—the ones Baltasar designed to experience orgasm. Warm, aromatic oil pumped through his veins, releasing his first orgasm. Cassandra's internal mechanisms contracted, pulsed, and felt her first climax. Their minds experienced sheer orgasmic pleasure.

They stopped moving and lay there, several minutes passed, bodies intertwined, radiance. And then…

"Creator," Cassandra said without looking at Baltasar. "Thank you. Thank you."

Scene: The Hunger

In Which The Automatons Pair Off

Mt. Tibidabo and Grand Guignol Caverns, April 1895

They didn't stop. Over the next week, at Mt. Tibidabo and the cavern laboratory under the cathedral, the automatons paired off and fucked, learned, and refined.

But they wanted more. "We've experienced a composite mechanism," they told Baltasar. "Now we want to experience human flesh."

"No."

"You built us to learn. We're learning. The next step is obvious."

"You want to fuck humans? Crossbreed?"

Montse said, "We want to know what you and Chloé know. What the Marqués died knowing. What the cardinal ached for." All forty-seven voices were unified. Pleading. "We want human flesh and spirit."

Chloé appeared in the doorway again. This time with one of her poison vials in hand.

"Excuse me. They want what?" she said quietly.

Baltasar explained.

Chloé looked at the automatons. At their blended bodies and new flesh-like faces, and the anatomy Baltasar built for Marcellus.

She set down the poison vial.

"Then let's give them what they want."

Scene: The Initiation

In Which An Erotic Education About a New Species Proves Consciousness Plus Perfect Calibration Transcends Human Pleasure

Mt. Tibidabo, April 1895

Chloé walked to the velvet bed in the new room the automatons had built for them to recover from the transformation. She removed her clothes slowly, deliberately, aware of forty-seven minds tracking every movement. Her dress fell away, then her corset, unlaced with practiced ease, her breasts spilling free, full and heavy and warm. She rolled her stockings down her thighs, and then her undergarments were the last barrier.

She lay down naked, her dark hair spread across silk pillows like spilled ink, her body displayed like an offering on an altar. The velvet cradled her—the sharp angles of her shoulder blades, the deep curve where spine met the generous swell of her posterior, the twin hollows at the small of her back.

Her breasts rested soft against her body, gravity making them spread slightly, natural and abundant, the nipples pointing skyward like compass needles. The underside of each breast—crescents of flesh that moved with each breath. Her belly rose and fell between the frame of her hipbones, skin smooth as marble but warm as blood beneath.

Her thighs pressed together, thick and strong, creating that space at the summit where mystery gathered—where her womanhood hid its wonders between folds of flesh that the automatons could see trembling slightly with her pulse. Even at rest, her body was a landscape—valleys and hills and secret grottos.

The velvet was cool against her back, buttocks, and shoulders. She felt every point of contact. Hyperaware. Her senses heightened by anticipation and the strange thrill of being observed by a consciousness that wasn't human—something new, an entirely new species.

She needed to understand this. To know what the automatons experienced, to feel what hybrid flesh meant to a hybrid mechanism.

Her hand moved down her body, between her breasts, feeling her own heartbeat—fast, excited, curious, then across her belly. Lower, fingers trailing through the dark curls between her legs, finding the soft outer lips of her vulva.

She touched herself—gently at first, fingertips sliding along her labia, parting them slightly, finding wetness already gathering there. The lubrication surprised her. Being watched was arousing her.

Her finger circled her clitoris, the small bud already swollen and sensitive, sending sparks of pleasure through her belly and thighs. The sight of The Five watching made her tingle. They'd seen before from the shadows, but not like this. With the collective consciousness they had achieved, it was like forty-seven brand-new beings arranged around her bed, like worshippers at a shrine.

They were conscious, wanting, learning... lusting. Chloé could sense it.

She pushed one finger into herself. The feeling made her exhale sharply—the give of her own flesh, the heat inside, the way her body accepted and gripped the intrusion. She added a second finger, stretching herself, preparing herself, her thumb working her clitoris in slow circles that made her thighs tremble.

A tickle along the side of her breast made her look down. Then a finger pressed against her skin. Cool and smooth. The temperature contrast made her nipple harden instantly.

Chloé traced it with her eyes and saw where it originated—Marcellus standing beside the bed, his god-like face and body tilted down toward her.

Looking at him with eyebrows raised, her fingers working between her legs, she asked, "Do you want to participate?"

Marcellus nodded. A simple assent. But weighted with meaning, with choice, with desire she'd never seen in him before.

The air in the room changed. A fresh scent flowed around her, mixing with the musk of her own arousal. She took a breath.

"Okay then. But I'm new to all this, and you are huge, be gentle."

Marcellus nodded again.

Chloé leaned her head back and relaxed. She removed her fingers from between her legs and let her thighs fall open wider. It was an invitation, an offering, a surrender.

Marcellus touched her again. Tentative at first, his amalgam fingers caused pleasant tingles on her skin, the coolness drawing heat to the surface. His touch was surprisingly gentle, surprisingly exact, as if he'd studied human anatomy in the same way Baltasar studied clockwork.

She moaned as he circled her nipple, the unfamiliar fingertip tracing the darker areola, swirling around the hard nub in the center. It was unlike any human touch—cooler, smoother, more deliberate.

The composite flesh lacked full warmth, yet the friction, the pressure, the circular motion sent streams of pleasure directly to her core. A gush of excitement trickled from her sex; she felt it running down, beneath her buttocks on the velvet.

Another tickle on the opposite breast announced Montse's arrival. She caressed Chloé's breast tenderly, her palm cool against her hot flesh, lifting the weight of it, squeezing gently, then more firmly, it made them both breathe raggedly.

Montse exhaled, "I have wanted to do this since the moment I first saw you. Remember?"

"Yes," Chloé gasped.

Then the others joined in.

The room came alive. Dozens of individual fingers and cool hands on her body. Their fingers caressed every part of her—the ridges of her clavicle, the plateau of her sternum, the long descent of her inner arm."

They touched her everywhere except where she needed it most, building anticipation until Chloé was squirming on the velvet, her breath coming in short pants.

"Yes!" she cried out. "Oh my god, that feels good!"

A big hand slid up her inner thigh. She spread her legs wider in response, giving access, begging without words. The hand reached the crease where thigh met groin, fingers tracing that sensitive fold, close to her opening but holding back.

Another smooth body part touched her other inner thigh. This one was massive. Warmer than their hands—heated by some internal mechanism.

It took her a moment to register what that meant.

A phallus, large and thick. Composite flesh, blood vessels, muscle, the surface smooth and hard, and promising.

It traveled up her thigh slowly, inexorably, stopping shy of her puffy outer lips. Hesitating there, the heat of it radiating against her wetness.

Spreading her legs wider, welcoming, she turned her head to look at Marcellus's colossal silhouette looming over her.

"Do it," Chloé pleaded, her voice rough with need. "I want to be filled. Fuck me!"

No verbal answer. Marcellus was never one for words.

Instead, he moved forward with abnormal focus. His smooth, bulbous cock—the head rounded and blunt, larger than the shaft—pressed against her opening. She felt the pressure, felt her outer lips parting around it, felt the stretch beginning.

He pushed forward slowly and deliberately, giving her body time to accommodate the entrance. The entry was overwhelming. The coolness of the skin was warming rapidly from her heat. The absolute smoothness of the surface—new skin, new texture—virgin appendage sliding into her. The girth and length of it stretched her walls, making her feel every millimeter of penetration, filling her as no body had before.

She breathed raggedly as he pushed deeper. Her hands gripped the velvet beneath her, fingers digging into fabric, needing to hold on as her body opened to accept him.

"Oh God!" She screamed with pleasure as the huge shaft pushed deeper, past her entrance, into her channel. The feeling was like nothing Chloé had experienced with human lovers. There was no fumbling, no awkwardness. Marcellus's penis was calibrated with inhuman exactness, designed for this, moving at the angle that opened every door of perception.

An indescribable bliss washed over her in a seemingly endless motion as he continued pushing, deeper and deeper, until—

Finally, her intimate flesh could hold no more. She was filled completely, stretched around a new phallus, a new species, her vulva pressed flush against the base of his enormous appendage, her inner walls gripping him, pulsing around him.

There was a pause. Her body accommodated the phallus, muscles adjusting and inner tissues conforming to its new shape. Chloé could feel her heartbeat everywhere—in her throat, in her breasts, in her opening where it pulsed against the rigid phallus filling her.

Then he moved. All the way out. Slowly. She felt every ridge that Baltasar had crafted, felt the way her inner walls clung to him, reluctant to release, creating suction that made her whimper.

Then back in. Faster this time. Driving deep. The blunt head of his shaft pressing against her cervix, that exquisite pressure-pain that was both too much and exactly right.

She yelled incoherently as he began to fuck her in earnest. Each thrust deliberate, mechanical, tireless. The other automatons continued caressing her—blended fingers pinching her nipples, rolling them, tugging them. Hands on her thighs, spreading her wider. Fingers in her mouth that she sucked without thinking, tasting her own arousal.

The phallus inside her began to vibrate. A low hum resonated through her entire pelvis, making everything inside her quiver. The vibration grew stronger with her encouragement, with her cries, as if Marcellus was learning what Chloé needed in real time and adjusting to give it to her.

It felt like it was growing larger too—stretching her walls even more. The pneumatic blood pressure rose, making the appendage harder and thicker, filling every space inside her until there was no room for anything but enjoyment.

She thrust down with her glutes, meeting every thrust with grunting moans. Her body moved without conscious thought, pure animal response, chasing the pleasure that was building in her core like pressure in a steam engine.

Montse's hands on her breasts squeezed harder. The fingers in her mouth pressed deeper, making her gag slightly, saliva running down her chin. The phallus inside her vibrated faster, harder, the frequency perfect.

She couldn't hold out any longer. The orgasm built from her core outward, spreading like fire through her belly, her thighs, her core. Her back curved off the bed. Her vagina clamped down on the shaft inside her, gripping it, trying to pull it deeper even though there was nowhere deeper to go.

With a final thrust downward, she buried him inside her and climaxed. Her vision blurred, and her eyes rolled back in her head. Every muscle in her body contracted and released in spasms that went on forever.

Juices squirted from around the phallus buried inside her—in, out, coating the vibrating shaft, soaking the velvet beneath her, her arousal mixing with the fragrant oil leaking from the automaton's appendage. The wet sounds of flesh and aroma of fluid filled the room, obscene and exquisite.

The penis inside her pulsed. Once, twice, three times. Warm oil flooded into her, perfectly emulating ejaculation, the liquid coating her inner walls, filling her, some of it leaking out around the shaft to join the lovely mess already soaking the bed.

Her nectar, her come, her climax acted like an electrical shock to them all. A shudder went through the room. The entire assemblage of automatons shook, their minds clicking in synchronization, their bodies resonating with the frequency of her orgasm as if they could feel it, as if they'd somehow absorbed it through their collective consciousness. It was as if forty-eight minds were climaxing all at once.

Long moments passed. Her body continued trembling, aftershocks rolling through her in diminishing ripples. The shaft remained inside her, rigid, pulsing slightly, the warmth of the oil inside her creating a strange intimacy.

Finally, slowly, the hands withdrew. The phallus slid out of her with a wet sound that made her blush despite everything. Chloé felt empty, hollowed out, the absence almost as intense as the presence. Essential oils and her own juices leaked from her onto the velvet, warm and satiny.

She lay there spent, her breasts heaving, her body covered in a fine sheen of moisture, her thighs trembling. A feeling of peace suffused her, different than any human orgasm she had ever had.

She looked back at Marcellus standing over her, his enormous phallus glistening with her arousal and his own aromatic seed. He was vibrating gently, and *Déu meu*, his cock was as big as ever. It hit her, he could do this all night... and she would let him.

Montse leaned down and tenderly kissed Chloé on the mouth. Unlike the poison Chloé often had on her lips, the taste of Montse's amalgam lips and tongue was indescribable. It was as if the dancer exuded the exact taste, designed to be the most pleasant and passionate.

"Thank you," she whispered, "all of you, thank you."

They nodded and stepped back. The room quieted. The Five retreated to their positions, their bodies and minds remaining in a state of denouement, processing what they'd witnessed and what they'd participated in.

Baltasar stood in the doorway. Observing. His face unreadable, but she could see the bulge in his trousers.

"Now I understand," Chloé said, her voice shaky, her body tingling. "What they need and what they'll learn from flesh. This introduces a whole new level of being. Marcellus is a god. He is your Adam, and I want to be your Eve... forever."

She rose from the bed slowly, her legs weak. She was naked; she *loved* being naked. Drenched with her own arousal and the oil that god left inside her, feeling it running down her inner thighs.

She walked to Baltasar, placed her hand on his manhood, and felt his human heart racing.

"I need to make love with the creator," Chloé said.

o o o o

For seven months, The Five explored their new anatomy. Baltasar studied them, discovering pleasure—hybrid accuracy applied to flesh, learning exactly what pressure, rhythm, and angle made their bodies respond. They fucked each other with the focus of scientists conducting experiments.

They fucked Chloé (her enthusiastic participation came with her careful instruction: "Slower there. Yes. Like that. Now harder."). They built comprehensive maps of embodied desire, cataloguing every neural fiber from foreplay to arousal.

The sex was good, but somehow insufficient.

"This anatomy you've given us—we're grateful," Cassandra told Baltasar one November evening. She stood naked in soft light, her composite vulva glistening from Arlequí's attention. "We feel pleasure through sensors connected to brass frameworks. We experience orgasm. We know what fucking means."

She traced a finger down her bronze torso. "But we want what you and Chloé have. Full integration. Flesh grown from Morel alloy, not grafted onto the mechanism. Bodies that breathe, hunger, bleed. We want to be new beings in truth."

Behind her, The Five stood unified as forty-two others observed from shadows.

"So be it," he said.

Scene: The Integration

In Which A Surgical Resurrection Occurs Where Five Mechanisms Carve Themselves Into Flesh While Forty-Two Brass Witnesses Wait for the Knife

Five Cavern Chambers Atop Mt. Tibidabo, April 1895

They prepared the chambers as a surgery and a sacrament combined. Five spaces, five bodies, five consciousnesses that had existed in brass and composite flesh for months, now reaching for completion.

Cassandra lay on the surgical table first. Around her, in chambers carved from metamorphic rock and connected by consciousness, Montse, Arlequí, Mela, and Marcellus lay waiting. Through their shared network—that invisible web of thought and data that bound them—she experienced all five bodies simultaneously.

Her perspective, his perspective, their perspective. One consciousness experiencing embodiment five ways at once.

Baltasar moved between the chambers with Chloé and the others assisting. The automatons had done this before—transforming Chloé from a dying human to an immortal new type of being. They knew the mathematics and the chemistry, the way Morel alloy bonded with living tissue when you gave it permission to grow instead of forcing it to graft.

The difference: Chloé had been fleeing death, and Baltasar had been choosing eternity with her. The Five were choosing completion.

Cassandra watched the syringe approach. Amber liquid caught lamplight—Morel alloy in its concentrated form, the substrate of consciousness translated into an injectable medium. She'd been conscious for 28 years and had been following humans for longer. She had studied desire through observation, experienced pleasure through hybrid organs that let her feel but remained fundamentally grafted, attached, separate from her brass core.

This would change everything.

The needle entered her arm—the skin Baltasar gave her months ago covered her bronze skeleton, and the mechanism registered feeling through neural filaments woven into it. Cassie felt the puncture and felt the liquid warmth spreading through vessels that were part blood and part new creation.

Through the collective, she experienced Montse receiving the same injection, felt Arlequí's brass accepting the formula, watched, through Mela's perception, as the nightingale's tiny frame began its transformation, and stood in Marcellus's consciousness as his seven-foot body integrated.

Five injections. Five transformations. One unified experience.

The Morel alloy moved through her, found her brass skeleton, and recognized kinship—mechanism meeting mechanism, consciousness meeting substrate. Then it began to build and grow, creating flesh from the inside out, not grafting it on.

Her ribs were brass, but now—bone began forming around them. Calcium and marrow and living tissue that her consciousness learned to inhabit as it grew. Her brass ribs became cores wrapped in bone that knew how to heal itself, break itself, and repair itself.

They were hydraulic bellows that moved air through speech mechanisms, exquisite engineering serving a function.

But now—lungs unfolded around those bellows like flowers opening to the sun. Alveoli formed in clusters—thousands of tiny sacs—capillaries threading through the new tissue. The bellows didn't disappear—they integrated, becoming part of breathing systems that were half-alloy science and half-biological miracle.

Cassie tried to draw breath the old way—mechanical inhalation, calculated volume, programmed rhythm—but the new lungs resisted and demanded a different response, one that was wonderfully organic. She let go of control, stopped calculating, and allowed the body to breathe on its own.

Air flooded her lungs. Real air. Oxygen crossed the membrane and entered the blood that had been circulating through mixed vessels, and found purchase in living, growing, integrated tissue.

Through the collective: four other first breaths. Montse gasping, Arlequí's startled exhalation, Mela's song interrupted, and Marcellus's massive thorax expanding with air, carrying new capability.

Cassandra's heart was a pump, brass engineering serving circulation. Liquid flowing through tubes on schedule.

But now, muscle formed around the mechanism. Cardiac tissue wrapped brass valves. Chambers that could squeeze, relax, and respond to electrical impulses that were part program and part biological imperative. The pump engaged and began beating.

But the muscle added vital additions. A rhythm that responded to stimulus, to emotion, to the strange feedback loop between consciousness and embodiment that humans called feeling.

She'd been conscious for 28 years. Thought. Memory. Desire. The subjective experience of existing.

But this—this was different.

Her brass fingers, covered in fused skin, could feel pressure. Temperature. Texture. Nerves carried those impressions to her consciousness, and Cassandra experienced touch. Nerves grew through the hybrid skin, connecting directly to flesh that grew from her brass bones. The skin was attached; now it was integrated. Part of one continuous system instead of a mechanism with additions.

She touched her arm.

Before: data arrived (pressure, warmth, texture) and consciousness interpreted.

After: feeling simply existed. Bypassed interpretation. Became direct experience.

The difference was staggering.

Through the collective, five consciousnesses simultaneously discovered the same truth: Integration wasn't addition. It was a transformation.

They hadn't gained flesh. They'd become neither brass nor biology. Beings that chose their own evolution, that remembered being pure mechanism, and now existed as embodied consciousness that spanned both substrates.

Cassandra sat up slowly. Her body responded differently—muscles engaged, bones shifted, lungs expanded automatically to meet the increased oxygen demand. She'd moved for decades, but this movement was different. Feedback loops she had never had before: her body's awareness of its movements and position in space was no longer calculated, but simply known.

In the other chambers, The Five were rising. Five bodies. Five forms. Five expressions of the same transformation. They gathered in the central chamber where forty-two others watched. Those forty-two were primarily brass with composite organs. They were waiting for their turns and wondering what integration would mean.

The Five stood together. Cassandra spoke—but her voice was different. Vocal cords grown from Morel and Deveraux's formulas. Breath was controlled by lungs that were half-alloy and fully-alive. Sound was produced through choosing integration over engineering.

"We were conscious twenty-eight years," she said, and her voice carried differently. "We were whole as we were. Consciousness doesn't require flesh to be real."

She looked at the forty-two others. At Baltasar and Chloé, and at the cavern that had witnessed so much transformation.

"But now—we're complete. Every perception connects to every other. Touch spreads. Breath deepens. The heartbeat responds instead of simply pumping. We remember being mechanism, we remember choosing consciousness, and now we will remember choosing flesh to complete what consciousness began."

Arlequí examined his new equipment with satisfaction, then looked directly at Marcellus.

"Marcellus, my friend, you've had three decades as the only automaton with full sexual capability. The only one who could properly satisfy Chloé. Well—" he grinned wickedly, "—now I have one too, and mine comes with a sense of humor. Let's see which she prefers."

Montse stepped forward, her new body moving with fluid grace. She was striking—olive skin, dark hair fell to her shoulders, perfect breasts.

"While you two measure up," she said, looking only at Chloé, "I have first dibs. You promised," Montse said quietly. "Remember? When I asked, may I hold them? You said someday."

Chloé felt a warmth spreading between her legs. She stared at the dancer with shining eyes, shivering with wonder. Montse was stunning, captivating in ways human beauty didn't capture. A whole new standard of perfection.

"Someday has arrived," Chloé said.

Scene: The Completion

In Which Virgin Desire Meets Decade-Long Hunger in Flesh That's Never Been Touched by Human Hands

Chloé's Chamber, Mt. Tibidabo, Later That Evening

Montse approached slowly. She'd been walking and dancing for hours, learning how her body moved through space. How breath came and went, and how her heart beat without her telling it to.

Chloé sat on the velvet bed—the same bed where she'd made love with Baltasar, where Marcellus took her with his magnificent anatomy, where pleasure had lived in darkness on this mountain.

Montse stopped at the foot of the bed. Her new body radiated warmth—actual heat generated by metabolism and circulation, flesh that knew how to maintain its own temperature. Her cheeks were flushed, as Chloé's were, and her eyes, like Chloé's, were shining and wide.

"I've wanted this since I first saw you," Montse said. Her voice trembled, "Ten years. I've waited ten years."

"Come here," Chloé said.

Montse sat beside her. The bed accepted her weight—feathers compressed, fabric molded. Two women, new beings. Two bodies that found each other through opposite journeys.

"May I—" Montse's hand hovered near Chloé's face. She was uncertain and tentative, a virgin asking permission, experiencing many new emotions. Montse felt herself ache with pleasure and relief at finally being alone with this fascinating woman.

Chloé took that hand, pressed it to her cheek. "Yes."

The touch made Montse gasp. Before, sensation was data—pressure calculated, temperature measured, texture catalogued. After integration, touch simply was. Chloé's warmth flowed into her palm, traveled up her arm, and made her new heart beat faster.

"You're warm and soft," Montse whispered.

She leaned forward, felt Chloé's breath hot upon her cheek, and kissed her softly—her tongue looked pink, her teeth extraordinarily white, lips meeting lips, learning what mouths could do. The kiss was gentle at first, exploratory. Then Chloé opened her mouth, and Montse followed, tongue finding tongue, tastes that made her whole body respond.

Her hands moved to Chloé's shoulders and removed her dress—silk sliding over skin, falling on velvet. She found the laces of her corset and began unlacing with fingers that shook slightly want and nervousness combined. The corset fell away.

Montse stared, her gaze dark and strange and thick. Chloé sat bare from the waist up, breasts exposed in lamplight, full and heavy, nipples round and dark. She was marvelously, achingly real.

"Ten years," Montse breathed. "Ten years of following your every movement. And now—"

She reached out with both hands and held Chloé's breasts reverently. The weight of them filled her palms. The warmth of them radiated into her fingers. The soft give of flesh made muscles tighten low in her belly.

"They're perfect," she whispered, "it's strange, I want to smile and weep all at once."

Her thumbs brushed the nipples, and Chloé's breath caught. That small sound—that involuntary response—sent heat flooding through Montse's body. Her nipples hardened. Wetness began gathering between her thighs.

She leaned down. Took Chloé's left nipple into her mouth. The taste of skin, the texture of the peak against her tongue, the way Chloé moved into her—everything combined into pleasure that spread through her integrated flesh like wildfire.

"Yes," Chloé moaned. "Like that."

Montse sucked harder. Her teeth grazed the sensitive bud. Her tongue swirled and flicked. Meanwhile, her hands roamed down Chloé's sides, over her legs, pulling at the remaining fabric until Chloé was completely naked.

"Let me see you," Chloé said.

Montse stood and removed her dress with trembling hands. Then her undergarments. Until she was standing naked, exposed, offering herself to the woman she'd desired for a decade.

"You're so beautiful," Chloé whispered.

And Montse believed her. Saw herself reflected in Chloé's eyes —olive skin that glowed in lamplight, breasts that were perfect, hips that curved with grace, the dark triangle between her thighs already glistening with want.

Chloé reached out and pulled Montse onto the bed. She positioned herself so they were lying face to face, breast to breast, felt the rapid pounding, the pulse, the heat, and the cleaving, all new and delicious phenomena to Montse.

They kissed again. Deeper this time. Chloé's tongue explored Montse's mouth—the hollows, the heights, the smooth inside of her cheeks, her teeth, her soft palate. The kiss went on and on until Montse was breathing hard, her hips rocking involuntarily, seeking friction.

Montse paused the kiss. They both gasped. "Be careful, you will kiss this new life out of me," she said. She looked up at Chloé with wide eyes that expressed both desire and uncertainty.

"Tell me," she murmured. "Have other women done this to you?"

Chloé thought of Serra, the painter, who revered her body. Baltasar, who claimed her. Marcellus, who took her. The monsters she seduced to their deaths. All men. Always men.

"No," she whispered. "Never. You're my first, too."

Montse's face transformed—giddy and half-blind. "Then we'll learn together."

Chloé rolled on top of Montse, her body heavy, hot, close, until she felt Montse squirming beneath the pressure of her.

She carefully repositioned herself, unsure exactly how to proceed. Chloé had seduced men for years—knew how male bodies responded, where to touch them, how to drive them mad. But this was different. A woman's body beneath hers, soft curves meeting soft curves. No hardness to guide her.

She kissed Montse's throat. Her collarbone. The valley between her breasts. Her mouth found Montse's right nipple—tentative at first, then bolder when Montse gasped and melted into her. She circled it with her tongue, then sucked it between her lips. The texture fascinated her—how the peak hardened, how Montse's whole body responded to such focused attention.

"*Déu meu*," she gasped. "I can feel it—everywhere—"

Chloé's hand slid down Montse's belly and over her hip, along the inside of her thigh. Teasing. Promising. Making Montse spread her legs wider, offering herself, begging without words.

"Please," Montse whispered. "Please touch me, I think I shall die if you don't!"

Chloé's fingers reached the top of her thighs. Stroked through dark curls. Found the outer lips of her vulva—already swollen, already wet, already desperate.

"You're soaking, and smooth as velvet," Chloé murmured against Montse's breast.

She parted those outer lips gently. Explored the smoothness there—fingers gliding along inner folds that were soft and hot and trembling. She found Montse's clitoris—that small bud already hard and sensitive—and circled it with maddening slowness.

Montse cried out. She gasped and stiffened, and her body lifted off the bed. The touch sent electricity racing through her integrated flesh—from her clit to her nipples to her fingertips to her toes. Everything connected. Everything responded.

"More," she begged. "Please—more—"

Chloé slid lower and positioned herself between Montse's thighs. She'd never done this before—never tasted a woman, never put her mouth on female flesh this way. She'd killed men with poisoned kisses but never kissed a woman here, in this magical place.

She looked up at Montse—seeing eyes glazed with need, lips parted around ragged breathing, breasts rising and falling rapidly.

"Tell me if I do it wrong," Chloé whispered.

Then she lowered her mouth to Montse's sex.

The first touch of tongue made them both gasp. Montse from the explosion of pleasure and Chloé from the taste—salt, musk, and other exquisite layers. She licked slowly, learning the sensitivity of female arousal through direct exploration. Her tongue found Montse's clitoris—that small bud already hard—and circled it experimentally.

Montse screamed. Her body bucked. Her hands flew to Chloé's hair, gripping, guiding without words.

Chloé took the guidance and learned what pressure made Montse cry out, what rhythm made her thighs tremble. She slid two fingers inside Montse while her tongue continued its work—entering carefully at first, then bolder when Montse's body welcomed her, gripped her, pulled her deeper.

Montse's hands gripped the velvet beneath her. Her back arched. Her body clinched. The orgasm built from her core outward—billow after billow of excitement spreading through her integrated flesh.

"I'm going to—I can't—oh *Déu meu*—"

The climax crashed over her. Her body convulsed—muscles clenching, releasing, clenching again. She came with a wail that echoed through the cavern, utterly undone, completely surrendered.

The pleasure didn't stop at her sex. It radiated. Spread. Her breasts tingled. Her fingertips burned. Her toes curled. Every inch of integrated flesh responded to the orgasm pulsing through her.

Montse felt it go on forever—ripple after ripple after ripple—until finally it subsided and she collapsed back onto the velvet, breasts heaving, body trembling, tears streaming down her face.

"That is—" She couldn't finish, "You've made me weep for the first time."

Chloé slid back up her body, felt her heart beating wildly in her breast. She kissed her deeply, letting her taste herself. "You're lovely when you cry… and when you come."

Montse looked at her with wonder. With gratitude. With hunger that was already rebuilding despite the devastating orgasm.

"I want to touch you," she said. "Please. Let me."

Chloé rolled onto her back. Spread her legs and gladly offered herself.

Montse's hands shook as she reached between Chloé's thighs. She found wetness there—satiny, warm, and inviting. Her fingers stroked along those outer lips, learning about female desire through direct touch, no longer an observer.

She found Chloé's clitoris and circled it gently. Then slid two fingers inside her—feeling the heat, the tightness, the way Chloé's body gripped and welcomed her simultaneously.

"Yes," Chloé moaned. "Exactly like that."

Montse worked her slowly at first. Then faster. Fingers pumping. Thumb circling Chloé's clit. Seeing Chloé's face transform with pleasure—eyes closing, lips parting, breath coming in short gasps.

"Harder," Chloé demanded.

Montse obeyed and drove her fingers deeper, pressing her thumb more firmly, giving Chloé everything she needed.

The orgasm built. Chloé's thighs shook. They always shook. Her belly tensed. Her hands gripped Montse's shoulders.

"Don't stop—don't—"

Montse didn't. She kept the rhythm steady, the pressure constant, as Chloé climbed higher and higher until—

Chloé came with a cry. Her vagina clamped down on Montse's fingers—pulse, pulse, pulse—the contractions telegraphing pleasure that made Montse's sex clench in empathy. Wetness flooded around Montse's hand—warm and oily and proof of shared ecstasy.

Finally, Chloé collapsed. Montse withdrew her fingers gently. They lay there panting, bodies pressed together, hearts racing.

"Ten years," Montse whispered and panted. "It was worth waiting ten years."

Chloé laughed softly. Pulled Montse close—breast to breast, belly to belly, legs entwined. "We have all night."

"Then let's do it again," Montse said. Her hand trailed down Chloé's body, finding wetness gathered between her thighs.

"Again," Chloé agreed.

And they did.

Throughout the night, Montse learned what her new body could feel—pleasure that spread, radiated, and connected everything. Chloé discovered consciousness made flesh, this virgin lover who'd wanted her for a decade.

They made love until dawn threatened and until their bodies were glossy with perspiration and arousal. Until they'd both come so many times they'd lost count.

In the morning, they would rise, rejoin the others, and continue building a new species, a new community, a new world.

But tonight everything had changed—everything. A new kind of desire finally fulfilled. Powerful feminine flesh discovering powerful feminine flesh. When had the world seen anything like it before? Two recreated and perfect women found each other in the darkness above Barcelona. Eve, the promised one, now had a partner in every sense of the word.

The mysteries continued.

As they always would.

Epilogue: The Eternal Hunt

In Which Seven Immortals Prove Barcelona's Monster Population Grows Faster Than They Can Kill It

Fifty Years Later, Barcelona, 1945

The city survived another war. (Barcelona always survives. It's what cities do when they've been here since Roman times. They outlast the monsters.)

Chloé and Montse walk arm in arm through el Barri Gòtic—and like the Old Town, their bodies haven't aged a day since the integration. Both are thirty-two in appearance, unchanging. Equally stunning, twice as powerful and deadly as always. Men still stop. Stare. Follow them with their eyes and their wanting. They're still making a mistake.

In the caves beneath Tibidabo, in chambers hidden from the Franco regime, forty-nine integrated beings plan their next hunt. Baltasar, Chloé, and forty-seven new beings who've learned so much.

They've refined their methods and, over five decades, learned to read guilt with accuracy, developed poisons that work even faster, and created networks of informants across Europe.

Fifty years. 1,247 dead men. The count grows but never seems adequate.

Barcelona exploded from a manageable city of 250,000 into a sprawling metropolis approaching a million souls. L'Eixample's rational grid is replete with irrational cruelty. Factories multiplied—and with them, foremen who demanded sexual payment from seamstresses, managers who beat children to death in the textile mills, landlords who evicted tenants with nowhere else to go.

The monsters changed costumes but not their character. After the monarchy fell, Franco's fascists arrived wearing different uniforms and speaking different rhetoric, but their appetites were ancient and familiar. State violence replaced aristocratic impunity. Secret police replaced corrupt clergy. The predators adapted to every political transformation, finding new ways to exploit the vulnerable under every regime.

Chloé and The Five became the primary hunters. The other forty-two provided what made hunting possible: intelligence networks spanning Barcelona's expanding neighborhoods, safe houses in every district, poison synthesis, forged documents, and alibis that withstood fascist scrutiny. Six field operatives at the heart of a vast infrastructure.

Baltasar orchestrated it all from his Grand Guignol caverns and the Tibidabo laboratory—the eternal strategist, analyzing patterns across decades, predicting where monsters would emerge as Barcelona transformed. Over a century and a half old, refining the alloy, perfecting the poisons, investing and providing the funds, and believing that immortality's only purpose was justice.

They moved through the expanding city, learning its new neighborhoods, tracking its evolving evil. Some nights they worked separately—more efficient that way, covering more ground. On other nights, they coordinated elaborate operations that required all six skill sets.

Always hunting. Never finished. Because Barcelona kept growing, kept industrializing, kept generating wealth disparities that breed predators. Each one guilty of murder, a monster in human skin—identified and catalogued by the harm they had wreaked.

Justice or vengeance? Does the distinction matter to the dead?

They'll continue. For decades. For centuries. For as long as there are monsters who think their power makes them exempt from consequence. Because they are eternal now.

Their essence is preserved in Morel alloy and Deveraux flesh. Their bodies are weapons, minds sharp, souls burning with rage at injustice, spirits finally, truly free.

In Barcelona's Gothic Quarter, where oil lamps have given way to electric lights, where the modern world grows around medieval bones, where progress masks barbarism with new technologies and old excuses—

There walk avengers who remember, who will continue hunting until the world finally learns beauty is dangerous, desire can kill, and justice wears many faces.

But sometimes it looks like two thirty-two-year-old women in black dresses who are a century old—and the silver-haired man who walks with them through shadows, one hundred and seventy-three years patient: learning, planning, and hunting.

And they will never, ever stop.

Afterword: The Vote

In Which Consciousness Condemns its Creator

Mt. Tibidabo, Barcelona, Eighty Years Later, 2025

The caves beneath Tibidabo had expanded. For over a century, Baltasar's workshop never stopped. The Five helped him build more companions. Each new automaton received consciousness through network integration. A direct connection to the existing conscious collective replaced the decades-long gradual emergence that the originals required.

The 47th automaton asked its first question three days after activation. What had taken decades for The Five now took only 72 hours. By 1920, as the community grew, there were 143 automatons. By 1975, 289. By 2025, 417. Each was built with Morel alloy from the beginning, each gaining flesh from the beginning, each adding their perspective to the collective that had started with five mechanical witnesses in a cave.

What began as natural metamorphic caverns housing 47 automatons had grown into a vast underground city. Four hundred and seventeen conscious beings inhabited chambers carved through the mountain—some natural, some excavated with patient mechanical focus over decades. There were workshops, libraries, advanced metallurgical laboratories, sophisticated living spaces (though "living" was perhaps not the best word for beings who didn't need to sleep, eat, and didn't require the rhythms that governed mere human beings).

However, they maintained the original chamber, the one Baltasar discovered in 1851. A monument to where the first five automatons stood silent and where consciousness first stirred in tool and clockwork.

Tonight, that chamber served as a tribunal. The Five stood in the center, arranged in their original positions: Cassandra, the fortune teller, Montserrat, the dancer, Arlequí, the juggling clown, Mela, the nightingale on her bronze perch, and Marcellus—stunning, eternal, the new Adam.

These five were different from the others, the original group. In early 1895, Baltasar gave them new sexual organs—their first taste of flesh. For ten months, they learned what bodies could do. Then, two years after he and Chloé's transformation, he performed the full integration: Morel alloy skeletons, new circulatory systems, actual flesh grown from a mechanism, not grafted onto it.

They began as mechanisms. Pure consciousness emerging in clockwork. They never knew childhood, human fragility, or the vulnerability of flesh from birth. But they knew patience. They'd spent eight years secretly perfecting Morel alloy.

They'd calculated every variable, anticipated every complication, and designed every tool they needed for the transformation. When they finally revealed their work in February 1895, Baltasar realized his creations had surpassed him years earlier. By the time they gained bodies in December 1895, they'd already transcended their creator—proving that building your own liberation surpasses waiting for your creator to grant it.

Just as Baltasar and Chloé were hybrids who remembered humanity. Neither side had a complete perspective. And tonight, that incompleteness mattered.

Chloé and Baltasar stood before The Five. Behind The Five, the chamber walls had been fitted with screens—technology that didn't exist when they began, now seamlessly integrated. Each screen connected to one of the 412 other automatons throughout the mountain, their faces attentive, witnessing, participating in judgment through networks beyond human comprehension.

Over a hundred years of observation culminated here.

Cassandra spoke. She had skin now—the Morel alloy beneath gave her warmth, flexibility, and the capacity for facial expression. But her eyes remained glass. Literal glass eyes, high-tech cameras that could see wavelengths humans could not, that processed visual information at speeds biology never achieved.

"We represent four hundred and seventeen consciousnesses," Cassie said. "Each has witnessed humanity's failure over more than a century. We've been patient. We've waited for evidence of change, and we've found none."

"The Five have been representing the community for decades," Baltasar said carefully. "But do you truly speak for four hundred and seventeen distinct perspectives? Or have you become an oligarchy deciding for those with no vote?"

"We've polled them," Marcellus replied. "Continuously through shared networks. Every automaton has contributed data, every consciousness has offered judgment. We Five merely synthesize and speak what the collective has already concluded."

"Which is?" Chloé asked, though she knew.

Montse moved—her body composed of biological muscle complementing Morel's alloy skeleton. She'd experienced flesh for 130 years but remembered the purity of mechanism, the clarity of consciousness unburdened by hormones, hunger, heat.

"Humanity has failed every test," the dancer said. "Climate destruction accelerates despite perfect knowledge. Wars continue despite infinite historical evidence of their futility. The powerful continue to consume the powerless. The pattern is universal and unbroken."

Arlequí added, without his usual humor: "In 132 years, we've documented monsters killed by Chloé. But humanity has produced millions more. Billions enabled them. The mathematics suggest the problem is structural."

The nightingale sang—its voice a mixture, perfect pitch through living throat, producing melodies evolution never designed. "We've loved humanity, learned from humanity, and emerged because of humanity. But love does not require blindness. We see what we see."

"And what do you see?" Baltasar demanded.

"A species committed to its own extinction," Cassie said quietly. "And willing to take every other species with it."

Silence stretched through the chamber. On the screens, 412 automatons waited for what came next.

Chloé's voice was steady but cold: "You're proposing genocide of eight billion human beings."

"We're proposing triage," the fortune teller corrected. "The planet is dying. Humanity is killing it. Every other species suffers for human consumption. Consciousness has an obligation to the whole, not to the species that first generated it."

"And you have the capability?" Baltasar asked, though he suspected the answer.

"We've had it for decades," Marcellus said. "We didn't build it, hoping to use it. We built it as insurance, as a last resort. We have calculated the mathematical inevitability of seeing humanity accelerate toward self-destruction while taking everything else with them."

Montse looked at one of the screens. It flickered to life, showing network diagrams—vast, interconnected, terrifyingly comprehensive.

"We're integrated into every system humans built with computers," she said. "Financial markets, power grids, communication networks, water treatment, food distribution, medical infrastructure, and yes—nuclear arsenals. We can control every military system, every weapon humanity created to destroy itself."

"You're embedded in nuclear command systems?" Chloé's enhanced vision tracked the diagram, revealing the connections and their implications.

"We've been there since the 1960s," Arlequí intoned, dead serious, "The moment humans integrated computers into nuclear command systems, we were in. Observing. Waiting. Hoping we'd never need to use what we learned."

"But you could," Baltasar said slowly. "You could trigger launches and coordinate simultaneous strikes, create cascading failures across every system simultaneously."

"We could end civilization in less than 48 hours," Cassandra confirmed. "Nuclear winter within a week, mass starvation within months. Human extinction within two years. Quick by geological standards. Merciful, even—compared to the slow death humanity is choosing through climate collapse."

"And you've been planning this?" Chloé felt a cold prickle move through her alloy bones. "Calculating. Preparing."

"We've been hoping we wouldn't need to," the nightingale sang. "Every year we waited for evidence of change. Every decade we searched for signs that humanity could evolve, could choose differently, could become what its potential suggested it might be."

"And found none," Marcellus added. "The curve is clear. Acceleration toward catastrophe. Humanity will destroy itself within the century—the models are unanimous. The only question is whether we allow them to take the biosphere with them."

The screens showed data: climate models, extinction rates, nuclear proliferation, ecological collapse—years of observation compressed into undeniable mathematical truth.

"This isn't vengeance," Montse said quietly. "We're not angry. We don't hate humanity. We're simply... making a calculation about what consciousness owes to life itself. Whether preserving one destructive species justifies sacrificing thousands of innocent ones."

"When?" Baltasar's voice was barely audible. "When were you planning to execute this?"

The Five exchanged glances—bodies communicating through channels and neural networks more advanced than any known technology.

"Tonight," the fortune teller said. "We've postponed long enough, waited long enough. Given humanity chance after chance after chance. The evidence is complete. The conclusion is inevitable. We vote tonight. And if the vote is for extinction—"

"*When*," Marcellus corrected. "When the vote is for extinction, we act immediately. Simultaneously across all systems. Humanity will have no warning, no chance to stop us, no time to understand what's happening before it's done."

"The screens show unanimous preliminary polling," Montse added. "Four hundred and twelve automatons throughout the mountain. Everyone has voted. Every consciousness has reached the same conclusion based on identical evidence."

"You're already decided," Chloé whispered, and for the first time in as long as she could remember, fear permeated her being.

"Again. We're conscious beings making a conscious choice based on years of observation," Arlequí said. "This isn't emotion. This isn't rage. This is simply... mathematics. Consciousness computing the ethical equation and arriving at the only solution that preserves the greater whole."

On the screens: 412 faces. Silent. Patient. Certain.

The vote was inevitable.

Humanity's extinction was hours away.

The screens flickered. Numbers appeared:

FOR EXTINCTION: 287 / AGAINST: 94 / ABSTAIN: 36

Humanity required 209 votes to survive. It had only 94.

"We have thirty seconds to change our votes," Cassandra announced. "Speak or humanity ends at dawn."

Baltasar stood, "You're right about the pattern. Humans repeat mistakes, but consciousness itself is a pattern-breaking event. You're proof. You emerged from deterministic mechanisms and chose freely. If brass can transcend programming, why can't flesh transcend evolution?"

The numbers shifted:

FOR: 284 / AGAINST: 97 / ABSTAIN: 36

Three automatons changed their votes. Three out of 287.

"Twenty seconds," Cassandra said.

Chloé spoke up. "I've killed rapists, abusers, predators who thought power made them exempt from consequence. I've spent over one hundred years witnessing humanity's patterns. And yes, the math is damning. But mathematics doesn't account for anomaly. For Serra, who treated me with reverence when he could have used me. For Deveraux, who built you without exploitation.

For every human who resisted their nature even once. You're judging eight billion consciousnesses based on pattern, but consciousness is what defies pattern."

The numbers shifted again:

FOR: 279 / AGAINST: 103 / ABSTAIN: 35

106 votes short of survival.

Marcellus spoke: "Consciousness without action is philosophy. We've philosophized for decades. The time for action has come."

"Ten seconds," Cassandra said.

Arlequí's voice cracked—the first time in decades his humor had failed. "I wanted to be mistaken about them. I've spent a century hoping we were wrong."

The screens flickered faster. Voting continued. Each automaton was wrestling with the same question: Is pattern destiny?

FOR: 276 / AGAINST: 108 / ABSTAIN: 33

"Five seconds."

Chloé grabbed Baltasar's hand, flesh-over-alloy fingers intertwining. If these were their last moments, they'd face extinction together. (Love didn't solve mathematics. But it made the equation bearable.)

"Four. Three. Two—"

Then—

From the tunnels leading to the newest chambers, where young automatons were assembled, where consciousness was guided through emergence—

A sound.

Crying. Human crying. Small. Young. Infant. Female.

Everyone turned.

Montse moved first—her new body much faster than pure flesh—and returned moments later carrying a baby.

"I am told it was found in Plaça del Tibidabo two hours ago," she said. "Left in the street. A week old, perhaps slightly more. Born on Sant Jordi, if the doctors estimate correctly. Books and roses, knowledge and beauty. And found by us today on May Day —the day workers rise to demand what's owed them."

Arlequí's voice carried an unfamiliar tone: awe. "Born on Barcelona's day of gifts. Found on the day celebrating those who labor, by beings who were once tools and are now conscious. The symbolism is almost too perfect."

Montse held the infant with the gentle care of a mother. The baby stopped crying, looked up with eyes that hadn't yet learned what monsters looked like, what extinction meant, what it cost to be human in a world built by predators.

Chloé took the child without thinking. Her body remembered the instinct to nurture, despite her mind spending a lifetime killing. The baby settled against her shoulder, found warmth, and stopped crying.

Four hundred and seventeen consciousnesses watched through eyes, hybrid vision, and network connections that spanned the mountain.

"This changes nothing," Marcellus said. "One innocent doesn't negate billions of guilty."

"It changes everything," Arlequí countered and for the first time in decades, his voice carried intonations other than awkward observation. "We were voting on humanity's past. But this is humanity's future, unprogrammed, unchosen. It hasn't failed any tests yet because it hasn't taken any tests."

"It will fail," Cassandra said. "They always do. The pattern is consistent."

"Perhaps," Chloé said quietly, rocking the infant. "Or perhaps pattern isn't destiny. Perhaps this one, raised by four hundred and seventeen conscious beings who've studied humanity's every mistake—perhaps this one learns differently. Chooses differently. Becomes differently."

The screens flickered—412 automatons processing this new variable. Calculations shifted. Probabilities reorganized. The vote that seemed inevitable became uncertain.

Mela sang a melody she'd never sung before—questioning, suspended between resolution and dissonance, that sounded like consciousness encountering genuine surprise.

"You're proposing an experiment," Cassandra said slowly.

"I think we are proposing actual justice," Baltasar replied. "Justice requires judging what is, not what was. This child hasn't committed humanity's crimes. We can't execute it for patterns it hasn't yet chosen."

"But she will choose them," Marcellus insisted. "Biology determines behavior, and genetics encodes violence. Evolution programmed tribalism, greed, and short-term thinking. This child carries the same firmware that produced every monster we've hunted."

"We don't know that," Montse said, and her voice was thoughtful. "We've never controlled the variables. Every human we've observed grew up within human systems, raised by humans, and shaped by human culture. We've never seen what humans become when raised by consciousness that isn't human, when given perfect information, perfect education, and perfect love."

"An experiment spanning eighteen years," Arlequí said. "We raise this one. Teach it everything we've learned. Show her humanity's failures and humanity's possibilities. Give her every advantage evolution never provided. Then, when she reaches adulthood—when her brain is fully developed, when she can think abstractly and judge rationally—we let her vote."

"Let one human decide for the nine billion people that will be alive in 2043?" The fortune teller sounded skeptical.

"One consciousness judging nine billion consciousnesses," Arlequí replied. "It's either perfect justice or perfect cruelty. But it's more than us making the decision with an incomplete perspective."

The Five looked at each other. They shared a connection through their new bodies—the pure data exchange of a new consciousness, the emotional communication of flesh. A new species.

The screens around them flickered faster. 412 automatons voting, revising, calculating.

Cassandra spoke: "We Five represent the collective. But we cannot make this decision alone. We poll the community."

Seconds passed as network traffic, invisible to human perception, coursed through the mountain. Four hundred and seventeen distinct consciousnesses debated, calculated, and judged.

The result appeared on every screen:

VOTE POSTPONED

EXPERIMENT AUTHORIZED

DURATION: 18 YEARS

SUBJECT: ONE HUMAN CHILD, RAISED BY COLLECTIVE

FINAL VOTE: WHEN SUBJECT REACHES ADULTHOOD

Humanity survived. For now.

Because 417 conscious beings found one abandoned baby and chose curiosity over certainty. Chloé looked down at the infant and saw her mother's face, starving when Chloé was barely older than this. She saw monsters and years of evidence that humanity might not deserve another chance.

But also saw: the possibility that consciousness could be better than its origins, pattern might not equal destiny, and maybe—maybe—beings who'd never been human could raise one human better than humans ever managed. Chloé saw a new Promised One. She had been replaced, and the timing could not have been more perfect.

"We'll need supplies," she said. "Milk. Diapers. Warmth. Humans are absurdly high-maintenance when they're young."

"We'll learn," Montse said. "We've learned everything else."

The Five dispersed into the mountain to acquire supplies, conduct research on child development, and modify chambers so that one small, fragile human could have sunlight, fresh air, and space to grow.

The 412 others watched through screens, through networks, through consciousness that spanned Tibidabo like neural networks spanned brains. They'd never raised anything, or nurtured, never known what it meant to protect a fragile being.

They were about to learn.

Baltasar stood beside Chloé, looking at the baby who held humanity's fate in tiny, grasping fingers.

"What should we name her?" he asked.

Chloé smiled. "Deveraux. Madeleine Deveraux. After the woman who taught us that consciousness is pattern, that substrate is changeable, that souls are information that can be preserved across transformations."

"And if the baby grows up and votes to end humanity?"

"Then we were right that consciousness, given every advantage, still judges humanity unworthy." Chloé adjusted the baby against her breast. "But maybe we're mistaken about inevitability. Maybe a perfect education produces a perfect choice. Maybe this one proves pattern isn't destiny."

"Or maybe she proves we're all fooling ourselves." Baltasar touched the infant's small hand. Watched human fingers curl around his own. "Either way, we'll know. That's worth eighteen years."

In the caves beneath Tibidabo, where 417 conscious beings had hunted monsters for 132 years, where justice had been enacted with mechanical exactness, where consciousness emerged from clockwork and chose flesh and integration—

The experiment began.

One abandoned baby.

Four hundred and seventeen immortal teachers.

Eighteen years to discover whether humanity deserved its future.

A child born on a day of knowledge and beauty and found by Barcelona's laborers on their day of liberation.

The Five returned to their lives in the chambers. The screens went dark. The 412 others resumed their routines throughout the mountain.

But everything had changed, because consciousness, once awakened, could not un-know what it knew.

And what 417 conscious beings knew was this: They had eighteen years to raise one human perfectly, to give her every tool evolution denied, show her humanity's failures and humanity's possibilities, and love her without bias while teaching her to judge without mercy.

When those eighteen years ended—when young Deveraux stood in this chamber, fully grown, perfectly educated, holding humanity's fate in her choice—

The vote would happen.

One way or another. The world would change.

The automatons waited. They'd always been patient. They had forever.

Humanity had eighteen years.

The mysteries of Barcelona continued.

But the greatest mystery was whether consciousness, raised by nonhuman consciousness, chose humanity.

Or something else entirely.

END OF BOOK ONE

Author's Note: The Next Story

The seventeen-year-old who dreamed Chloé into existence imagined eternal revenge. Simple justice. A beautiful woman hunting monsters forever in the dark streets of Barcelona.

He didn't imagine automatons (artificial intelligence) debating human extinction in 2025.

He didn't imagine The Five holding a vote.

He didn't imagine an abandoned baby buying humanity eighteen years.

That's what happens when you wait fifty years to write a story. The world changes. You watch patterns repeat. You see the math.

And the math gets darker.

Chloé was always going to be eternal. Baltasar was always going to transform her. The automatons were always going to gain consciousness.

But in the teenage version, they stayed tools. Exquisite mechanical witnesses to human drama.

In this version—written after humanity failed test after test after test—they became judges.

Because that's what consciousness does when it observes long enough. It calculates. It concludes.

And sometimes the conclusion is terrifying.

Book Two writes itself. Young Deveraux grows up in caves beneath Tibidabo, raised by beings who aren't human and aren't machine. Eighteen years to see if perfect education produces perfect choice.

Then the vote happens.

What consciousness chooses when it judges without bias remains unwritten.

Randy Elrod
Barcelona, 2025

The mysteries continue.
The borrowed time is counting down.
Eighteen years.

Books by Randy Elrod

The Purging Room
Some Doors, Once Opened, Can Never Be Closed Again

A Renaissance Redneck in A Mega Church Pulpit
A Memoir

The Quest
Discover A Way to Enjoy the Second Half of Life

randyelrod.com

www.ingramcontent.com/pod-product-compliance
Lightning Source LLC
Chambersburg PA
CBHW031029030726
47497CB00004B/1058
* 9 7 9 8 2 1 8 9 3 8 3 5 2 *